MASTERING THE SUN

MASTERING THE SUN

V R Thornhill

V R Thornhill
Visit my website at valeriethornhill.co.uk

First printing: Jime 2020

ISBN 978-0-9550335-3-7

This book is published during the COVID-19 epidemic and is dedicated to the doctors, nurses and to all NHS staff in appreciation of their unstinting work and sheer dedication in the time of COVID-19.

"This intriguing and original book takes a different slant on our fears for the future of the planet, as energy resources melt away. The hero is Nicholas, a young scientist who with his small team of researchers has discovered a formula to 'harness the sun'. But he is a romantic young man as well as an outstanding scientist: he falls in love (but is she the right one?) and then finds himself being wooed by a predatory entrepreneur who wishes to make another fortune with Nicholas's formula. This seemingly amiable figure wields frightening power in the new Global Council of all nations. Will the stolen formula be saved in time? Can Nicholas find true love again and save all our futures, free from exploitation and a horrifying new 'global capitalism? Read on!"

MASTERING THE SUN

1

Winter

Nicholas *i-witnessNIC227.futurepast.com*

It is true! Peace everywhere!

People will think what I'm creating is equally impossible: clean, cheap, unlimited energy. They call me crazy if I explain what I'm doing, and even laugh. Will Magnus laugh too?

When I'm nervous my mind clicks into calculations, just like here in the woods behind the Institute. I love crushing the frosty grass and leaves underfoot and cracking the ice in puddles. Over the trees comes the evening swarm of airpods. Dom Ross Mackenzie of Global Enterprises GWP will be returning. He assumes he can touch down at the Institute and drop in on me just because his parking slot happens to be under my lab window. He wants only to *find out how I'm getting on*, in his patronising way! That's precisely why I have to see Magnus. Will Magnus understand what I need? Or is he, like most people, risk-averse?

The designers of this new estate anticipated warmer summers and milder winters, so oleanders and olive trees are shivering along the avenues. I must keep calm. Pause. Gather thoughts. His doorknocker looks like a geometrical afterthought, two trapezoids, one cut out of the other. My first knock is tentative. My second rattles the door in its frame. I'm apprehensive, standing here and thinking all this into my wordfree monitor for the *i-witnessfuturepast.com* project. It's hanging on a chain round my neck, small and shiny like my mother's old-fashioned locket, but records everything within earshot. Knock even harder. The door opens, leaving a narrow gap for me to slip in before it clicks shut. A tall, seasoned man stands surveying me.

'You must be Nicholas. Why didn't you voice me?' Caution, I suppose... uncertainty?

'I was afraid you'd refuse to see me.'

His eyes are hidden below a strong forehead and heavy brows - a handsome, leathery face, lined by experience. He seems diffident. Or arrogant? There's no entrance hall to pause in, just space with four square benches. The white ceiling curves imperceptibly into gleaming wallscreens. News flashes below people moving along a familiar street to aisles in a supermarket. Sound is merely a muttering backdrop.

'People shy away from the unfamiliar.' I like his gravelly voice. 'Local streets and supermarkets like these are unchallenging. They're only a kilometre away.'

My mum Eliza talks about tragedy sculpting people's faces into hollows under eyes and cheekbones. *There's a sober majesty*, she says, *in ageing.* She first heard about Magnus when he became rich and famous through his dance and mime videosequences and somehow imagines he could help me.

I can't help staring at a striking young woman in a supermarket aisle. She has thick auburn hair, and, well... an attractive figure.

'She's known locally as a fashion stylist,' Magnus says, and raises his hand towards the figures so his wordfree - a tiny internet-linked computer inset in his wrist - summons more intelligible sounds. Now I can hear her extolling the jacket she has plucked off a rail. 'Every room here is i-linked to local and global matters.' He's matter of fact: I'm concerned. 'Even the bathroom,' he adds, 'in case something crucial is lost'.

I thought my lab had the absolute latest technology, but these people walking and talking out of wallscreens make me uneasy. I remain stranded as he stands still surveying me. Life strolls through here as people from the screen walls laugh, utter convivial banalities, select stores, walk along the streets, greeting, waving, scowling, pleading, organising and looking at us unseeingly, in near and distant motion. He hasn't taken my winter jacket. I deposit it on a bench and wait, awkwardly clutching my T-reader and wordfree monitor close enough to register my thoughts.

'I don't think I can... talk to you here.'

'Well, this house is my workplace, my living area and my world space. I don't go out if I can help it.' Magnus raises his wrist as if blessing the fashion stylist on the wallscreen as she discourses on yet another outfit. She disappears into an opening. It's a sort of hidden door like one behind wallpaper in an ancient country house. I follow Magnus into a space with an actual window, so no screen at least on that wall! Outside a garden dissolves into the evening shadows beneath the flashing blue lights and faint throbbing of the airpods overhead.

'There should be less pollution now with fewer landborne vehicles and a decreasing world population,' Magnus remarks in a monotone. He sighs as he sits down on a sofa and points to an armchair facing him. The material looks shiny, almost as if wet. This room's airless. I need a drink, water or something stronger to give me courage. He sits looking at me in silence, his eyes so deep that I can't fathom any colour, sparkle or expression, his arms along the back of the sofa and his head on one side. I doubt I'll ever have his thick brindled hair in my old age. Nor those bristling eyebrows, the high forehead, or the air of a seasoned warrior. Yet he seems uneasy, haunted. I regret coming here now. We should have met on neutral ground.

'So?' He's waiting for me to start. I open up my T-reader, which everyone has now instead of the old laptop computer, to show the crucial calculations I still have to test. There's just enough information to indicate where they are leading, but not too much. I desperately need independent funding. Can I trust him? I stare out of the window to avoid screens that might be registering my thoughts as well as my image. African scenes are now rippling over the continuous wallpaper above the word-flow of breaking news.

'So?' He's observing me. Outside the window I glimpse a strip of grass, random trees and a fence separating us from the next house. The last airpods have landed and a squadron of geese flies into the fading sunset.

'Have you... been to Africa recently?' I break the silence, addressing the window away from the screens before looking back at him.

'Not exactly.' Magnus isn't given to lengthy answers. 'I don't travel if I can help it. It's better left to field workers.'

African wildlife ambles round the room. If only these creatures could tell me how to approach him. I'll start by asking general questions about world developments to combat injustice and secure sustainable environments. He mentions that birth-rates have fallen. When did the Goodwill World Parliament legislate for all tiny adult wrist wordfrees to contain a contraceptive, reversible for couples who opt for parenthood? Or should I discuss how effectively crops are cultivated, harvested and distributed where needed or ask how spare food is stored in World Food Banks, and if woodlands are being replanted? Or...

Pause.

'Is it too hot or cold in here?' Another pause. 'I'm afraid I can't spend too long with you. There are a number of urgent ecalls for me to deal with and vlogs to go through.'

I'll make a snap announcement.

'I think I've discovered a way to produce vast amounts of clean and inexpensive energy.' I hesitate. 'I just have to carry out a final series of tests.' There's no response. 'Perhaps you could help me?'

'Perhaps I could.'

'The trouble is…' How much should I tell Magnus? That Dom Ross Mackenzie's engineers are planning a worldwide network of dual-purpose receptor dishes? That his engineers can't yet transform a concentrated solar beam into electricity? Butterflies use solar energy to fly. That's what I'm doing – my 'infinenergy' invention. Dom Ross Mackenzie has every reason to fund my final tests. I just don't trust him. I imagine Magnus is thinking, *I've known young people like Nicholas. They think they have their equivalent of the philosopher's stone, that they and they alone can put the world to rights. If only...youthful impatience...* and so on.

'You're being harassed?' How does Magnus know, or has he guessed? 'Would you like a drink?' He raises his wrist before getting up from the sofa. A section of the wall moves again like a door.

'Don't you have a wrist wordfree?' he asks. I can't tell from his tone whether he is surprised I don't have one, genuinely curious or disapproving.

'No. Not with all the equipment in my lab.' That's my pat explanation if asked why I have a separate wordfree monitor. He nods as if he has known all along. I'm not sure whether I should follow him through the door, but I do. He's placing bottles and glasses on a tray. This sort of sleek, hi-tech kitchen is the latest trend: all metal sheen and no wood, but cleaned at a wordfree command. You have to leave the kitchen quickly, my sister Martha informs me. A strong draught blows the dust away, then scalding water laced with disfectfoam sprays all surfaces before they're rinsed shiny. Two huge dishwashers cleanse cutlery, dishes and everything removable. More interesting is a board on a wall in the eating recess. On it, behind glassite, are numerous sketches of streets and houses. They must be his own drawings, so minutely accurate that one can imagine oneself a fly buzzing round inside, or a miniature mouse creeping into every crevice. Not a detail missed. But no dust, dirt, smells – just pure unpolluted space in this miniature version of our city here in a corner of Magnus's kitchen.

'Don't look at that…' Unguarded moments reveal most. 'I don't like people coming in here.' He moves to take my elbow, his face disturbed, but I'm already slipping back through the door to pick up my T-reader from the table in front of the sofa. He's more at ease now, surrounded by African scenes and drinking a cocktail of his invention. It has a strange, yellowy tang.

'The amazing regeneration of the former Sub-Saharan war zone is at a turning point,' he remarks, 'with African villages growing into townships and organisations becoming ever more complex'. Yes. Fine, but I'm wondering whether he heard my request, so I try to reintroduce it.

'There's... a tidal barrier in the estuary. Offshore wind farms generate some, not enough, of our energy here.' I'm not getting anywhere. 'Nuclear fusion may, or should, soon produce more.' I state the obvious. 'But I don't think any of them can ... can provide the clean, reliable, unlimited, inexpensive energy I propose.' I pause. 'No need for raw materials. No noxious waste. No...' At last he takes my T-reader to scrutinise the calculations and, I hope, concise explanations. I'm waiting what seems a long, long time, then he looks up.

'What do you need for these tests?'

'A sparsely populated area and an unpolluted atmosphere. Near the equator. A lab capsule and equipment that can be sent by air... if I have the means to cover their cost, transport and installation.'

'It's hard enough,' Magnus comments, 'to co-ordinate initiatives involving indigenous populations, let alone a scientific one like yours. I dislike organisations or individuals who take over and profit from them,' adding, 'but it's difficult to devise a way to avoid this'. He refers to cautionary experiments with Communism in the past, and I immediately think of China's influence in Africa, but neither of us mentions it. 'Nor does the democratic process necessarily select the best person for the job.' He falls silent and continues scrolling through the T-reader.

Mum met him at a dance festival held in the main square years ago. She thinks he is part of an organisation formed to tap the energy of everyone wishing to change the world, bypassing governments and big business. A new route requiring a new economic structure. I still hear Dom Ross Mackenzie's condescending laughter from an unavoidable exchange on my lab staircase: *those who think there is an ideal way...we've been there before...look at history, the dictators, benevolent or otherwise, one-party states...Communism or Fascism or any other isms you care to conjure up. All succumb to some form of corruption because everyone's greedy - if there's the opportunity. Nobody ever has enough. Like it or not, rivalry, discontent and envy are in our genes.*

Should I say something? I'm hoping Magnus will comment on my T-reader material. Instead he raises his wrist to open the door to the entrance hall. Dismissed. Then -

'I'll voice you when I've set up the conference to decide whether we have the will and the means to underwrite your tests.'

I walk back through the wood, flicking the torch on my wordfree monitor to see the way. The lights are still on in my lab, but I'm not going in. One of my collaborators, probably Raphael, might be working late. Dom Ross Mackenzie may have dropped in and even now be waiting to pester me with more probing questions and invitations - his silver-grey limousine is parked in its designated slot.

Better to move away from the lab block towards the only old building on the site. I'm still upset by the ugly wound the code lock has made on the main door. It's the same on the oak door to my rooms. Shoes and pullover lie on the chair where I chucked them on top of the novel I'm reading. It's a luxury item, because nobody prints books anymore. People just sit back, enlarge the electronic text on a big screen or use their wrist wordfrees to read while eating. As I eat, I watch the latest news on my solitary wall-mounted screen. This evening it's all speculation about the future Chinese leader and the current US president. There must surely be other worthwhile stories somewhere in the world right now?

Reading in bed, with no screens around me - bliss! What would Magnus's bedroom be like? He told me every room was 'i-linked', so the bedroom too would have screen wallpaper: a landscape, or better, a cloudscape? Perhaps just blue sky. This Institute supports blue sky research. It's independent, though attached to the University, and funded by revenue from start-ups using inventions patented by its scientists. This isn't enough. That's how Xiang Lu, founder of the World Potential Company, became involved. Maybe Dom Ross Mackenzie as well? He pillaged my online publications and encouraged his scientists to develop my urban energy control-save-recycle invention, going on to patent and commercialise it – no mention of me or of the Institute. I found out, but didn't have the time or courage to protest. Anyway, by then it was too late.

These tiny wordfree insets inside people's wrists have been obligatory for some time now. They're pulse-charged. At first wordfrees just registered speech directed at them, then whispers, and now they are so sensitive that they pick up thoughts unless they are directed into the encoded section of the wordfree, a sort of personal thought-edit bank, open for perusal through a personal code. When I was a child, mum refused to have a wrist inset wordfree for her and for me before it became obligatory to ensure everyone is safe. A pity. It would probably be wiser to store my thoughts and ideas inside my wrist, but I never remove my wordfree from the chain round my neck. It's always on, as requested by the Goodwill World Parliament, and linked to the *i-witnessNIC227.futurepast.com* project. It is encrypted for fifty years, so I can feel free to think what I like.

As I turn off the light, half asleep, the after-image of Magnus's strange entrance hall looms into the darkness: the shopping mall and the young auburn-haired woman with the elegant figure. Her face comes closer as she whispers,

'This is right for you. It's the solution to your problems. Take this ...' and she holds out something too close for me to see, but I look into her eyes, believe her and fall asleep over my book.

BREAKING NEWS

(scrolled at the bottom of all screens worldwide)

PRESS RELEASE FROM A RECENT MEETING OF THE COMMITTEE OF WORLD CITIZENS PAST, PRESENT AND FUTURE

The Committee of World Citizens' Past, Present and Future unanimously agrees to the following four proposals:

Firstly, a Peruvian delegate has proposed the launch of a website to serve as a blog platform. Its aim is to record everyday life in its rich variety as well as hukind's crucial discoveries affecting future generations. The website will be encrypted for fifty years so that contributors may blog or vlog about anything or anyone without fear of complaint, challenge or legal action. A young German delegate proposed that, since many people are living well beyond a century, a further twenty-five years might afford website contributors more protection. After some debate it was agreed that individuals could opt for an additional twenty-five years and that passwords would provide an adequate safeguard.

The website name ***i-witnessfuturepast.com*** was approved by the Committee and is now officially in operation.

Secondly, it was agreed that the international news outlet ***worldaroundyounews.com*** should not receive a Goodwill World Parliament subsidy but remain a commercial entity enabling all world citizens to be heard. ***Worldaroundyounews.com*** will be responsible for the continuous local and global news scrolled below all screens worldwide together with the means to translate it into any language.

Thirdly, it was agreed that internationally significant companies and voluntary organisations supporting the Goodwill World Parliament's promotion of peace and population control, may be registered and put the letters **GWP** after their name.

Fourthly, in response to requests from Australia, India and Africa, it was confirmed that the Goodwill World Parliament should award an honorific title to world citizens who have performed exceptional public service for the benefit of hukind. The title **'Dom'**, from 'dominus' meaning 'master', was agreed because it is internationally recognisable, non-hereditary and gender neutral. It recalls the historic title 'Master of the Arts' awarded to those with exceptional gifts, skills and wisdom.

All the above proposals agreed by the World Citizens' Past, Present and Future Committee have been ratified by the Goodwill World Parliament.

worldaroundyounews.com

[The following is repeated after newsflashes or bulletins on w*orldaroundyounews.com.*]

- SPEAK **highlighted words** for more information or -
  - deaf and/or dumb world citizens touch highlighted words on screen
  - blind citizens say VOICE, NEXT, STOP and MORE to screen as appropriate
  - immobile citizens say VOICE to one of the above options

    - mentally challenged citizens say SLOW, REPEAT or AGAIN after any of the above options

- CHOOSE language by speaking it until a response in the same language is obtained. All languages still spoken available
    - If none of the above works, just bear with the system and wait for a virtual operator. The accompanying tune may be chosen from one of the 200 visually and audibly matched options

- ONLY TOUCH THE SCREENS IF DEAF AND/OR DUMB using a gentle fingertouch – do NOT use nail, knuckle, toe, heel (with or without shoe), head or any other part of the body. Do not use any instrument (sharp or blunt), as the surface crystals may take some time to heal. BE WARNED. The screen is not covered by any guarantee.
    - For emergencies call SCREEN CRISIS CENTRE on your wordfree inset or any other appliance incorporated into the worldwide web.
    - Say REPEAT if required, otherwise there is no repeat.
    - Thank you, danke, merci, gracias, grazie…
    - Say STOP to cease sound and return to the screen-saving wall design option you have chosen.

2

Winter

Magnus *i-witnessMAG931.futurepast .com*

Knocking - and a young scientist appears at my door! I never open it except once a month to receive my heat-sealed orange mart package from the delivery robot. It flashes a quivering green delivery notice across the screens until I tell it (or shout at it, to be honest) that yes, I've registered its arrival. Then comes a smiling red mouth and a robotic version of 'have a nice day!' Few utter words nowadays. Instead purple sense-sound pulses of positive feelings are projected onto the screens around me backed by poppies, sunflowers or whatever floating on blue-grey waves of soothing electronic sounds.

The young man pausing leaning on my doorframe is dark blue, all angles as he holds out his hand at 45 degrees, a luminous blue quarter circle saying, 'I'm Nicholas Middlethorpe'. His words brush over my face gently. He strides past, his nervous smile showing four regular teeth. A mobile mouth; six teeth, now eight teeth as he talks. He's wearing a soft-blue check shirt, more shapes and numbers. They layer themselves up into a picture of him settling into my space. He already suggests movement: I might try out a dance to represent him. Maybe, but I'm all aging angles and increasing numbers weigh me down. Nicholas is talking, his words in waves of grey.

I shouldn't have let him into my kitchen. These sketches are just for myself. Not sketches really, but meticulous drawings. I lose myself in the kitchen ones - a record of the streets and buildings where I grew up. Here I can adjust my space, keep the angles and proportions as I want. Mostly. I sometimes try to close the whole i-linked system and use candles, but it'll only dim down. If I try to turn my wrist wordfree off with everything else, to be alone, really alone and safe, it just goes on standby. The Goodwill World Parliament stresses wrist insets ensure everyone's safety. There could be another meteorstrophe or some unknown humade disaster.

There might be fewer calamities if we redistribute wealth and abolish poverty, which is what Reaching Out is supposed to be doing. But the rich are predictably resilient. They hang on. I could do without assertive politicians, diplomats, spymasters, footballers, pop stars and cult idols who inflame the public's red-mouthed hunger for secrets and salacious confessions. Reaching Out suits me. It operates quietly behind the scenes. Too quietly, perhaps, to help a scientist like Nicholas with potential to change the world. Low profile people like me are part of the decision-making process when our cells are activated. I may be dealing with oil wells in Africa and interfaith schools in Syria for the Peace Enterprise Zones, but I'm just Magnus in a home studio that could be anywhere in the world.

Convening a Reaching Out conference to discuss Nicholas's project takes nearly a week. With the problem of time zones, it's hard to summon a quorum of at least twenty-five representatives to debate any issue. Sleeping hours somewhere, waking hours elsewhere. We now take it in turns to have day or night sessions. Accept a fair share of inconvenience or don't become a representative.

Nicholas is disconcerting. He appears to confide in me, then veers away, almost in a panic. Too intelligent, people might say. Worse, too intellectual, implying a degree of arrogance. His face is so clearly cut in light and shadow that every emotion is clearly shaped, every thought hidden. A fine-boned face and spare body, strangely angled, always alert as if something is about to happen.

*****

I'm waiting for Nicholas in the living room and can just see the road to the right and the sky-blue helousine, its rotating blades spinning yellow. Every time Nicholas comes it appears at the same spot, just before he voices my wordfree to say he's arrived.

He is early. We are waiting for the conference in a cube of soft golden light. He asks how I came to dance.

'I was always, my mother said, "fidgeting to music" as a child. She warned me there was no money in dance and mime. She was right. It wasn't easy to pay one's way. A friend suggested I might donate blood as she did, or sperm, which she couldn't. So I did both.'

'And then?' I'd said enough, but he wanted to hear more. It seems to stop him fretting about the helousine and the conference delay. He wants me to explain my ideas about dance and numbers. With his brilliant mathematical mind, he'll probably find it odd.

'Numbers aren't only rhythms. Some have colour potential, like primary colours, and others have shades. Red is dominant for 3. So 3 times 1 equals 3, with the red enhanced three times over by the colours latent in 1 and so on. It gets more complicated. This is not a scientific explanation, but just as true. It's personal and, I suppose, emotionally charged, but none the less real for that.' Well, I have tried.

'Strange!' he says, distracted. He's sharply angled, waiting. So am I.

'You asked what I meant,' I say calmly, 'so I told you. It doesn't harm you or anyone else even if you think it's crazy, and it doesn't change what I think, or rather, feel'. Rationalisation tags on behind experience. There's smell and taste in numbers as inextricably blended as in food. Texture too. Numbers have these powers. Dance, rhythm and music recreate them.

'What about Reaching Out?'

'Those were the best years of my life. We helped to create a grass-roots revolution to promote peace and aid people in need of food, medicine, shelter, water, energy, tools - everything. Reaching Out gave us a voice. It was a cacophony for a while, and we all had to take our turn. Mine is now.'

Still waiting, silently now in a cube of grey light.

Often, like now, I'm amazed how rapidly everything changed. The world was in shock after the assassination of Pope Matthew and the peace and human rights activist Sheik Abdul el Khali on the steps of Saint Peter's in Rome. Miracles can happen. The Goodwill World Parliament was founded to oversee universal disarmament. Reaching Out became involved in the arms checks following the amnesty. Almost unbelievably GWP legislation outlawing all weapons was ratified by every national and zone government. It seemed the world was pausing with every colour saturated, as if imbued with hope. Is Nicholas too young to remember all this? Amazingly dictators, oil-rich sheiks vied to become peacemakers. Former warmongers doubted the GWP could enforce disarmament. Well, it has so far. Peace spread faster than doomsters predicted. After all, wordfree messages unite us physically through the throb of our pulses. People of my age are still amazed that we live in a peaceful world.

I look at Nicholas. He smiles. We sit in silence. Only the green purr of the network reminds us that our world of shimmering colours is in touch, if we direct thoughts towards it. I'm mid-term in my committee service and involved in a former war zone in sub-Saharan Africa. The Goodwill World Parliament warns that we need alternative sources of non-polluting energy to maintain world peace. Should Reaching Out support Nicholas?

Still waiting. The edges of the cube deepen into blue.

At last the Reaching Out icon is flashing. I'm about to convene the obligatory quorum of representatives for policy decisions and he's like a tightly strung, highly tuned Stradivarius.

'Please, Magnus, don't ask me too many questions!'

'I'll have to, Nicholas. First there must be a majority in favour of your proposal. Then, if it's passed, the test site has to be chosen. I'd prefer it to go to one in sub-Saharan Africa, but I've only one vote. I'll do my best. Let's get it through the first stage. They all have your outline proposal. You and your collaborators, Raphael and Esther, can create infinenergy with a satellite solar panel that concentrates a beam above cloud level and projects it on to a receptor. A trial infinenergy panel is already in orbit on a Goodwill World Parliament satellite. All you need now is funding for you to calculate and test the precise angle the infinenergy beam hits the receptor to avoid collateral damage. Let's hear their reactions.'

It's the Northern Hemisphere's turn to sit in darkness while the Southern Hemisphere meets in daylight. Screens are throbbing grey, yellow and blue throughout my capsule but I'm stationing myself in the living room while Nicholas walks out into the entrance area and back again.

'How long will it take?'

'Not long. We're waiting for Carlos and Ana from South America - Venezuela and Chile respectively. Africa and Australia are ready, but Asia is lagging. Some delegates are in transit and need to settle for the line to clear. Canada is just coming in with Tom from Calgary and the USA is waiting for Beth and some others. China and India have problems with local issues, but they'll come on soon. Be patient!'

Difficult, if your life's purpose, if all your dreams are bundled into a single, tight, blue-grey, minutely stitched project, so compressed that it could be smashed out of court in seconds. Scary, if you have invested your hopes and maximum brainpower in an ambitious scheme now to be judged by many who don't fully understand it. One face, then more faces pop up on the screens, all speaking out. As convenor, I click on each to be silent while Isabel from Puerto Rico is speaking and her face automatically enlarges. Reaching Out uses the old national identities to designate areas even if they have been tidied into new groupings.

'Does this infinenergy project override other sources? We have conventional solar power here and are developing tidal energy in a big way.' She's actually speaking Spanish, but we listen to the instantaneous English translation requested. It's mechanically accurate.

'That's right!' echoes Shilpa from Jaipur. 'India is combining solar power and biomass – algae actually - would we have to stop?'

'We still have reserves of coal,' Cheng-fu from somewhere in North China observes ponderously.

'Stop using it! You're polluting,' Jake from Alberta, Canada, almost yells.

'We too have coal to spare,' insists Alabu from Uganda, 'but if this revolutionary method works with costs as low as the inventor claims, then we should try it, just in case'.

'It's made out to be revolutionary,' Holly from Mississippi pipes up anxiously. 'Who will beam the laser or whatever to start the generating and where from? In lay person's terms, please.'

'Just so,' a shrill voice from Australia - Jane this time - 'we don't really understand how it works. The brain behind the whole fantastic or crazy or dangerous scheme, this Nicholas Middlethorpe, must explain it all, in every minute detail!'

'That's precisely what this conference is about,' I intervene. Why don't delegates read what they are sent? Like most people in this cyber universe, they never have time and will only have skimmed Nicholas's complex proposal minutes before the meeting. All delegates are volunteers and do as much or as little as they feel they should, for no personal gain. 'Does Reaching Out agree to support Dr. Middlethorpe's final tests?'

'Where?' Ramon from Peru.

'First,' I say, 'let's vote on whether we'll fund these tests and with what conditions. I know of at least two other major initiatives striving to solve the energy crisis. If we don't support this invention, it might be exploited by some huge conglomerate in global power politics and become too expensive for the world's poor.' I hope this doesn't sound like a threat and anxiously begin to summarise Nicholas's invention (such as I understand it) before leaving them to decide. He remains silent. More lights are flashing under some delegates' images to request a talk slot.

'Whatever we do, it must promote democracy,' says Lorna from Scotland.

'And peace.' That is Zuami from South Africa. He's the only delegate I've actually met.

After more deliberation, the delegates finally vote to support Nicholas's tests. Faces bob back and forth over the wall screens in bursts of vociferous discussion about proposed sites for the tests, with me stuck chairing the whole crucial process. An obscure village in North China appears to be the favourite, though two places in Africa gain support after the ones in South and Central America are discarded as too remote. Reaching Out Central Bank can only allocate a limited sum for scientific experiments and voices argue about the mountains surrounding the Chinese location and various sites' proximity or otherwise to internet, air, rail and road access. A message flashes over our screens: an anonymous donor has given a sum for a sub-Saharan site in a Goodwill World Parliament peace settlement zone, and that turns the vote in its favour. No one queries where the money comes from or why it targets the African site. As convenor, maybe I should do so, but that would mean postponing the vote, and then reconvening with a number of delegates who haven't been able to join in this time. There would have to be another session retracing the same arguments and Nicholas is, rightly, anxious to start tests and register internationally his intellectual property. Serendipity. It so happens that the site agreed on is where I was caught in the meteorstrophe.

I've turned the system off, that is, to the obligatory standby. Our white then grey cube of space is gradually suffused with the pearl tone of dawn. It's too late to sleep, too early to start the day's business. Nicholas has slumped, speechless, on to the sofa.

'Are you pleased at the outcome?'

He shrugs his shoulders. 'I need to test my calculations, far away, somewhere near the equator where people aren't watching. Just to make sure they work.' I feel he is dark blue and see his shape as 9x5=45, and 4+5=9, 3 squared. Nothing could be easier for him than to slip away to a remote part of sub-Saharan Africa. Or could it? Assumptions can be dangerous. Nicholas insists on leaving by the emergency exit in the kitchen to avoid the helousine. He glances at my drawings in the dining-area but doesn't say anything. When I return to look out of the living room window, the sky-blue helousine is whirling over my house towards the woods between here and the Institute.

If I had not volunteered to join Reaching Out, I might not have chosen to go to the Peace Enterprise Zone in Africa. I might not have met Gaia. I might have gone down another path into my future. Instead I am here without her.

Holding her rose-coloured stone in my hand while thinking this blog into my wordfree is a way of ordering my ideas and leaving something of mine out there in the future - a last will and testament to the purpose of my life. Those jagged brown and grey images of the meteorstrophe and Gaia's death made my fortune and created my nightmare. I must obliterate flashbacks to Africa. What could I have done? I re-live the nightmare of her eyes, of her hands outstretched, of other faces, of screams as homes tip into the chasm, bodies tumbling or whirling in corkscrew winds. No need for words; the wordfree images say it all. I was at the edge of a landslide, my arm raised. A mayhem of booms, cracks, screeches, acrid stench, vermilion gashes of light, people fleeing, gasping, whilst I stood apart recording a devastating meteorstrophe - and for whom? Posterity.

All I have left of Gaia is this stone in my hand.

Those images created my fortune and my nightmare.

BREAKING NEWS

LATEST REPORTS FROM GOODWILL WORLD PARLIAMENT PEACE SETTLEMENT AREAS

The current **Goodwill World Parliament speaker, Ramiro Palmerio of Argentina**, today issued a statement:

'The Goodwill World Parliament has debated the current situation in **northern Syria**. This peace zone is now fully self-sufficient in food production and has begun to export produce to neighbouring zones. Irrigation control has significantly increased the water level in the Tigris and Euphrates. The Jordan River has maintained its water level as has the Lake of Galilee, but much more still needs to be done in water conservation. Goats have been transferred from a **peace settlement in sub-Saharan Africa** to isolated **mountain communities where two more schools have been**

built and women's small businesses have grown in number and economic activity. Men from different faith communities, under the auspices of the **Order of the Dove of Peace**, have rebuilt torched churches in **Raqqa**, formerly headquarters of the discredited fighters who fought, tortured and murdered in a failed attempt to form a **caliphate** in the area. The **democratic government of Syria** consists of elected members strictly in proportion to the size of each ethnic community. It is monitored by **GWP settlement officers**. This government is to be congratulated on what it has achieved, but must develop **sport for both men and women at local, zone, national and international levels** to channel the population's energy into peaceful pursuits. The GWP will allocate resources when appropriate applications are submitted.'

The next GWP session in two weeks' time will review the **peace zone in sub-Saharan Africa.**

U S President Anya Lo Yin seeks a world platform to share diminishing energy resources. To ensure there is no conflict over their management, her message is: **Peace equals prosperity**. Repeat it to all your real or virtual friends. Make it your mantra for this year: peace equals prosperity, and say it with a smile.

Speak out highlighted word for more about it or - (as below **1**)

worldaroundyounews.com

3

Winter

Nicholas *i-witnessNIC227.futurepast.com*

I woke this morning imagining clouds gently floating across the blue sky of Magnus's bedroom walls. Mine look like faded parchment. The old radiators are stirring into warmth and the sun's shining through dusty panes. Friday. End of week. Time for coffee and toast and to co-ordinate everything we've been doing in the lab.

A breeze strokes the grass on the lawns between the Institute building and the lab block. There are snowdrops under the oak and a spring in my step as I approach the lab. Raphael's already there. I always feel his smile before registering what he's doing.

'A good week,' he says as I open the door. 'Lots of ideas. Can we talk?' I'm careful not to say too much. The conference Magnus set up for me isn't in his area of our energy project. I choose just two collaborators at a time - not enough space for more in the lab or my mind. Raphael's joint projects with Israel, Jordan and Palestine together with neighbouring states will, he predicts, become the engine of the Middle East Alliance. He's modest about himself, but ambitious in his aims and determined to achieve them, come what may. He calls me over-cautious. Esther agrees.

'You're so wary of everything,' she chides in the tone she might use towards her orphaned brothers and sisters. I suspect that Magnus and Reaching Out promoted the scheme that linked her village with two others to become a successful township in the Sub-Saharan Peace Zone.

We settle down. Every day I have to skim through ecalls from all over the world. Vmails like vlogs take too much time so I discourage them. We discuss what we're doing in the mid-morning coffee break. It was during one of these that Esther told me how terrorists had set fire to her village and destroyed the crops. Her parents were stabbed to death after weapons were handed in during the worldwide amnesty. Knives can't be abolished. My stomach tightens when I see her and remember her whispered account of what had happened. Her sponsorship here assumes that she will take our relevant discoveries back home. I'm relieved to see she hasn't arrived as early as usual, so I've no twinge of guilt. Her morning smile invariably accompanies a battery of questions. The more she wants to know, the less energy I have to explain, and that's unkind. My early morning glow fades under such uncharitable thoughts.

Esther has promised to stay on in the lab today. Now I come to think of it, her region in Sub-Saharan Africa would be perfect for my crucial tests: plenty of sunshine, close to the equator and sparsely populated, just in case something goes wrong. But Magnus needs time to co-ordinate funding and logistics.

I mustn't be distracted while entering the passwords for my latest calculations. Should I tell the Texan energy research team what I'm testing here on my lab model, or might they snatch my potential breakthrough? I stare at the master screen in my lab and whisper my passwords, then shout silently at everything I'm scrolling through: the calculations HAVE to be right. My discovery is priceless because it is low-cost and limitless. It just has to work.

*****

'You know I have complete confidence in you.' Dom Ross Mackenzie stops me on the stairs as I'm leaving the lab. I smile weakly and invite him into the staff room. He is one of the global entrepreneurs behind the University's transfer to this new campus on the edge of the city, but I don't want him in my lab.

'Would you like tea or coffee?'

'No thank you.' A pause. 'I am concerned, Dr. Middlethorpe, about your financial support in the future…' He goes on about how he can provide whatever I need. I half listen, studiously avoiding his face to look instead at his waistcoat. 'My scientists can check your core theory... solve the energy distribution... world network of receptors... free you to...' Waistcoats are now the rage. I start silently playing syncopated rhythms on his drum-like buttons, while he adopts a confidential tone in case the other scientists overhear him. 'Do let me know when you can dine with me and remember, there's always a spare bed. Here's my card.' Again? I must have half a dozen already.

For his age he's slim. No paunch really, just a sleek, well-toned figure which he likes others to notice. He moves away, upright and distinctive. A certain distance in his manner keeps one guessing his motives.

*****

After a day stretching my mind beyond its limits till chronic fatigue and listlessness set in, I look forward to a solitary meal and time to think into my wordfree monitor. My sister Martha calls my rooms *drab and depressing*, but they cocoon me. I can lean back and survey the screen in the kitchen as I eat. Events near or far are streamed on to it - the local beer club's activities, the endless virtual shelves of our local supermarkets, Sister Julian outside St. Thomas's pleading for help for her refugees, reports of the far-off vote count and first predictions of the Chinese presidential election. The last US election saw a close victory for the Democrat Anya Lo Yin, daughter of destitute Chinese immigrants, who epitomises the American Dream.

Oh dear! I've forgotten it's my birthday weekend and I always go home. *We're expecting you!* My mothers create a special meal and decorate the table as a surprise for Martha and me though today, at the close of the week, I feel like drifting. I'll only go home for a night so I hardly need to take anything, not even my wordfree monitor. I think I will, though, in case inspiration catches me unawares. It's on a chain under my shirt though I hardly notice it's there. Anyway, we're supposed, as Martha keeps repeating, to be traceable everywhere.

*****

St. Thomas's church is just outside the old city walls. I pass it on my way to the City Terminus, but have never really taken it in before. I only notice individual objects and features: a flower, a bird perched on a branch, a strange doorway, a pleasing shop display, the aroma of coffee, the glow of a lamp or the shape of a building. Nothing like the detailed cityscapes Magnus draws. Was I taken to St. Thomas's as a child? I can't remember. It's built in that pointed style called Gothic and is ages old. I'm curious. There's time to have a quick look inside.

'Nicholas!' I start when Esther taps my shoulder, 'follow me'. We leave the flickering lights and smell of burning wax to go under an arch. A face poking out of a voluminous red cape appears in a doorway. Why does a round face suggest a placid nature and dull mind?

'Sister Julian, this is Nicholas Middlethorpe.' Her face absorbed in others' woes smiles at me distractedly.

'Come in.' Sister Julian turns into a room lined with wide benches and chests. Above them a large window transmits the chill outside. Bundles lie neatly on benches near a large table. She slides them along to make space for us to sit.

'Tea? Soup?' she asks. I shake my head.

'These bundles are all our refugees have,' she continues. 'There's little heating in the church, one outside toilet, no showers and no proper kitchen. We can manage hot drinks and soup, but it's all rather rudimentary. Worshippers have taken some of the refugees out to buy their basic needs. They're confused by our shop robots. Fortunately, we still have the open market – until it's dismantled to build new housing in the historic centre.'

She stands up and Esther beckons me to follow them back into the aisle where Sister Julian pauses by a side chapel. Seven candles illuminate a book. Two women sit, each holding a candle. Sister Julian pauses, bends her head, then whispers,

'Abraham is our common spiritual ancestor. We're all members of the same body. Mohammed too was a holy man. For him, Jesus was a prophet, another holy man of peace,' and she leaves with Esther through a door opening on to a courtyard.

I sit in the nave and think about what she said and what Raphael has told me. Peace seemed impossible when he was a child. Some countries in the Middle East were, it was thought, building nuclear arsenals. Now the Universal Legal System, backed by the Goodwill World Parliament, bans all weapons. Gun ownership is tightly controlled. Global pressure has turned Jerusalem into an international city.

A young woman carrying two large bags passes me just as Esther returns with Sister Julian. 'Wonderful!' she calls out, 'just leave them in the sacristy,' and hurries into the shadows. Esther sits down by me. Sister Julian, she explains, belongs to the Order of the Dove of Peace. They only have to make one vow – to spread peace and goodwill by helping others, especially the ill and homeless. She's called 'Julian' after a female saint of that name. I ask her why there was no mention of these refugees on *worldaroundyounews*. Apparently mining companies don't want the world to know that harvests have been ruined and water supplies contaminated and populations displaced as a result of their activities. Sister Julian needs support to set up a village-barter initiative for them here in this town. She's eying the old university buildings threatened with demolition. Esther's standing up to leave. I'm surprised by what my fellow scientist says and does. African solutions here? If not mad, distinctly odd.

I hear footsteps and see the young woman returning without the bags. She's unbelievably beautiful, almost radiant in the candlelight caught in her hair. I recognise her and stand up.

'We met, though you don't know it, in a friend's house.' I hope she's curious.

'Was I presenting the new spring styles? People everywhere buy the same tech fashions now. My job is to suggest personalised variations on current fashion. That's fun. Helping women create their own style.' She laughs, 'I give Sister Julian my cast-off clothes for her refugees.'

No precise time was fixed for my birthday meal. Shall I ask her to have coffee or a glass of wine in one of the new café-hubs that have taken over part of my old university? Yes. She agrees. She's called Helen. I hold her arm gently not to lose her in the evening crowds hurrying home.

I can't avoid the people I know, so I take Helen over to introduce her to them. Someone tells her I'm at the University Science Research Institute, which doesn't seem to register one way or another. At some point she smiles and murmurs that she doesn't understand science. I shouldn't tell people what I'm doing anyway, so by making it highly scientific, I find they rapidly lose interest. Helen is no exception. I'm surprised when she asks if I have some free time next week.

BREAKING NEWS

DISCOVERY OF PRICELESS MASTERPIECE, LOST FOR CENTURIES

A lost canvas by the Italian Renaissance artist **Leonardo da Vinci** has been found by a refugee among vestments in **St. Thomas's Church**. If proved authentic, it could raise a huge sum of money for the finder – Sister Julian of the **Order of the Dove of Peace** – who looks after the many refugees and displaced persons passing through her church. 'It is a Godsend!' she declared today. 'Now I can really help those with nothing to make a new life for themselves and their families.'

The painting represents a princess, **Leda**, who fell in love with a swan, the disguise of **Zeus, King of the Gods on Mount Olympus**. Famous in its time, the painting mysteriously vanished – until now! Sister Julian interprets the picture as representing the springtime of birth, and hence of Christ, and sees it as a symbol of hope for our world.

worldaroundyounews.com

4

Winter

Eliza's Journal

Mothering does not fade away even if you want it to. The shadows gather as I write this. I am alone sitting in the bay window with Foxy, my terrier, on my lap, waiting for Nicholas. Martha is always considerate. We know she will arrive on the 6.20 monopod and make her own way here. It will be dark then, and Nicholas dislikes twilight. He hardly admits it, but I suspect dark evenings and hurtling underground at huge speeds, however environmentally efficient, depress him. I expect him to arrive in daylight and am waiting. He has probably forgotten his house keys.

At least when he comes it is at a weekend. I can soon retire at the earlier pension age, though I quite enjoy working as a full-time enabler managing a network of haven homes for women. Not so many with drug problems these days, or victims of domestic violence (they move out rapidly at the first signs of aggression - how wise women have become!), but internet loners. They can only communicate through screen chat clubs or the plethora of games and alternative worlds on offer - which for them are the 'real' ones – and suffer from all the physical and psychological symptoms of internet alienation. Many rely on the so-called 'stressless pill'.

I am not entirely convinced that these pills, together with our new-fangled capsule haven homes, provide a solution. The capsules can be inserted into historic houses with large enough rooms, though they block out anything of beauty that might remain - mouldings, fireplaces, that sort of thing. Nothing is actually destroyed, though it cannot, in current usage, be enjoyed. New haven homes are built in shiny, rain-washed, time-resistant blistone blocks, never more than four floors high and clustered round a courtyard garden like the old stone Institute building where Nicholas lives. These capsules have everything comfort demands: maximised use of space, state-of-the-art wrapped-round screens in every room, digitally directed cooking facilities, refrigeration, plumbing and plenty of storage space, if used carefully. An amazing design, if you think about it. The trouble is that they are all the same, to reduce costs. Perfect symmetry and no variety. The occupants are supposed, Martha says, to stamp personality on to their capsules. Guestrooms are provided elsewhere in the building for a small charge, as well as a spa, sports complex and heated pool in the roof area to economise land-use - everything residents could wish for. Designed happiness in sharply defined terms of comfort and facilities. People 'rent to buy', as the expression goes, so they don't lose any money. Everything is decided in common, which is part of the anti-alienation therapy. That is where I come in as an eternally optimistic arbitrator. Karen loves the capsules. They have no atmosphere, are imaginatively sterile, but are deemed perfect for the people who live in them.

I am wearing the dark green trouser suit that I used to keep for special occasions - I do not buy clothes anymore. Former best clothes are now everyday wear. As I wait with Foxy on my lap, nose on paws, looking out of a window down a street of small front gardens, I think back to how I met Karen on an excursion to Petra in Jordan. It was during a break in the old conflict between Israel and Palestine, the year we lived, touched and smelled history. A tall, rather leggy blond was holding a stone and staring at temple fronts carved out of pink rocks.

'Where did you get that stone from?' was my way of starting a conversation. From then on, we were inseparable. The pink stone is still here on the mantelpiece where she put it the day we moved in. Ten years after we met and before she developed her wine business in China, Karen decided it was time for us to have a family. We joined her surname with part of mine to make Middlethorpe and chose a young, tall, intelligent, fair-haired, athletic and healthy donor, or so the description went. Memories fall like leaves to fade into the past. 'Now' seems lost between 'then' and what is to come.

That's him. Dark straight hair like me, except mine is now dyed back to how it once was. His father was supposed to be the athletic type, which I assumed would mean a more muscled build. Nicholas is certainly not as I pictured he would be. His eyes are greenish brown, like mine, I think, but I'm built more assertively. Broader shoulders, more rounded. Tending to put on weight. He probably finds me podgy. He is angular and so pale.

Foxy is yapping at the front door.

*****

'Hello, mum!' He had not forgotten the key. 'Is Martha coming?' He must have known she would. Like Nicholas, I do not have the latest gadgets that never turn off and throb for attention through wrist implants. I may be old-fashioned, but I do not want anything inserted into me. They started using implants for dogs when I was a child, later tagging troublemakers on probation. Now wrist wordfree insets are not even a fashion accessory but a necessity. Our Goodwill World Parliament prescribes them, all part of connectivity and population control. So they are supposed to be a force for good.

Nicholas always goes to inspect the dining room where, each year, Karen prepares a birthday welcome for him and another for Martha. Foxy pads after him in slavish admiration. Snowdrops are this year's theme, grouped round beeswax candles that sharpen the whiteness of the flowers. The dark green sprigs of yew seem rather out of tune, I think, but avoid saying. Yew in churchyards. Yew with poisonous berries. Still, it was Karen's idea for the table centrepiece and I had to keep quiet. She rarely listens to me. Martha swept in exactly when she said she would, chirpy as ever and bearing gifts wrapped in gold paper. Nicholas hugged her. He adores his half-sister, and who would not? She has bright blue eyes and honey-coloured hair, and is as lively as Karen was when I first met her.

'This house is to be demolished,' she announced. 'I did warn you.' She sat down at the table, cheerfully dismantling her childhood home and my secret place to paint - the loft. 'All who have already installed a capsule with sensor screens and world-wide links into their existing homes will have it inserted into the blistone newbuild free of charge. The ones lagging behind like you two' - was there a touch of condescension in the way she smiled at us? - 'will have loans'. She shrugged her shoulders at the inevitable, adding, 'meanwhile there'll be alternative housing for you both and loads of free storage'.

We are to become part of a modern residential zone, our 150-year-old house not deemed interesting enough to save. Martha gave us a brief lecture on how streets of half-timbered semis in mock-Tudor style were often built on the edge of golf courses - as if Karen and I didn't know! They have apparently had their time, and are now to be crushed into the foundations of a whole new suburb, to everyone's advantage, or so we are told by our zone government. Martha is already our zone member. She intends to be our zone's candidate in the coming elections to the Goodwill World Parliament.

'Capsule houses are designed to last over one hundred years,' Martha continued. Even she will be unable to test all she asserts as female life expectancy is only 98 years and she will probably have died before her company's new homes become eligible for replacement. I toyed with the first course, feeling as if I were about to be crushed into compost for the future. Karen was in the kitchen putting the last touches to the main course while our children sat discussing what was about to happen to their childhood home.

'The design does incorporate your urban control-save-recycle invention,' Martha reassured Nicholas, not noticing how unhappy he looked. She must have forgotten about Ross Mackenzie, that entrepreneur who stole it. She seems to have settled neatly into her job of fitting the latest energy-saving devices outside historic houses and capsules inside them. She expounded:

'We need capsules of all kinds to suit everyone.' Except me, I thought. 'People,' she added, 'like to take some part of their old interior with them when they move back into the rebuild.' Our space remade new. Martha also helps people experience a smooth changeover, a tender dismantling instead of a systematic destruction of all associations. We shall relocate to a new home devoid of memories, squeaky clean, waiting to be sullied by our physical and emotional clutter. Designs are decided with the greatest care and attention to what others are convinced you want. Karen, now serving her goulash concoction, would understand me. Or am I unwise to assume she would? She might agree with Martha.

I refuse even to consider our coming eviction, whatever the assurances that our new house will be incomparably better. Martha's brisk enthusiasm jarred. Nicholas was quiet, out on his usual limb though it was his birthday celebration, the last one he will have here in his birthplace. He smiled and fidgeted less than he used to, but his mind was far off, probably deep into his latest calculations.

'Try this wine.' Karen sat down with us at last. 'It's the first serious one from China. Their red vintage has greatly improved and was quite highly rated at the wine fair last week. Xiang Lu – who is funding your Institute, Nicholas - will export 80% of the wine produced in China.'

She has always been adventurous, and that is why she has become a wine connoisseur with one of the most visited websites.

'It's fine,' I lied, 'here's to Nicholas!' and we toasted his 27th birthday. The conversation continued with Karen expounding on how China is about to choose its next president, now the mourning period is over. A woman perhaps, especially if with the US President Anya Lo Yin's support.

'Let's get this right,' Karen insisted, 'after centuries of injustice we should celebrate that women are now leading the world'.

'There should be many more women at the top.' Martha said, pursing her lips. 'Let's see what happens in China with its surplus of males!'

Karen laughed. 'Serves them right for forcing every couple to have one child only. It was some time before they changed this law. Most preferred to have a male child, of course; ways were found to deal with the unwanted females.'

'Horrible. Don't even think of it.' Martha tends to draw curtains over any window into a world she does not wish to contemplate. It is all history, she reminds us, as world population is now under control. True, but less freedom, some might think. Freedom to make mistakes. Everything Martha says seems to come from a politician's standpoint.

'So with more men than women,' Karen continued, 'there was fierce competition among Chinese males. Some wanted there to be "special houses", but sharing women leads to obvious paternity confusion, hence brisk business in DNA tests.' Karen irritates me when she expounds on Chinese matters just because she goes there so often on business. 'I like the way Chinese women have bonded. No sex unless we say when, where and how. Minority power.' She laughed.

Nicholas sat silently, probably not listening. He was like that as a child. Politely present, but abstracted from what was said or happening. Round him swirled comments on women in China and the usual condemnation of sexual prejudices and past injustices. He had heard it all too often to listen. I was engraving the scene on to my memory. Moments passed as I observed them from the edge of an unknown future: Nicholas with his presents piled on our Art Deco table and our faces around him, gentle in the candlelight. Contemplating us from the mantelpiece, in front of the stone from Petra and Karen's fussy figurines from China, are framed photos of

Nicholas and Martha playing together, and another over a decade later when they graduated. As I write, this room and the four of us round the table are shrinking into the suitcase of memories that I see myself carrying into the house of our future.

I am shivering, though it is not cold inside here, still hearing the two of them playing years ago, hiding and jumping all over the sofa in the sitting-room, chanting,

'You're the Middle, I'm the Thorpe, together now we're Middlethorpe!' That was when they were seven, around the time of our marriage. We had a lot to celebrate. Everything had gone to plan. We had a family, a name, and now after so many years, Karen and I are amazingly still together, though we have been arguing on and off for some time. She is often away on one of her business ventures and I am about to hand the haven homes over to a new manager.

Karen coped with Martha's tantrums over what to wear, buy or eat. The head teacher in their school asked to see us when Nicholas kept on outstripping his class in maths and science subjects, but we didn't want them to push him up two classes above Martha. Karen found her a place in another school but she refused to move. She might have a brilliant brother her age, but she was the one who was admired for her looks. Then Nicholas was chosen for the new International Academy for Gifted Children where he met Ezra, the brilliant pianist and Lizzy the artist. Ezra often comes to stay and we play piano duets. He has Nicholas's build and they are even alike in temperament. Martha says he may be coming soon to be the soloist in a concert here. I hope so.

Karen hurried in protecting the twenty-seven candles with her hand. The ribbon I gave her with HAPPY BIRTHDAY NICHOLAS wasn't round the cake as I wanted but messed up with the yew and snowdrop arrangement. Martha started 'happy birthday…' I watched Nicholas opening the parcels as if already in the past: the designer pullover Martha chose for him (he doesn't care for shopping); from me, a fine reproduction of a Rembrandt self-portrait he particularly admired and an old book (he, too, still reads) and from Karen a pellet of music she likes which he can insert into the computer synthesiser in his Institute rooms. He still looks needy but I didn't know what else to give him. Maybe the music I used to play to calm him to sleep? It's one of the most beautiful arias Mozart wrote, a song lost in one of this house's many technological makeovers since then. Perhaps he has asked Ezra to play it for him? It is Zaïde, a slave girl's love-song, a lullaby so beautiful that it hurts - a still moment of ecstasy in the frenetic dance of time. A present without past or future.

My joy in us all being here together was fractured by Nicholas jerking to his feet,

wordfree monitor to his ear.

'No.' Pause. 'Sorry,' teeth gritted, 'No, I can't. Really,' making for the door with a scowl that I had never seen on his face before, 'I can't. Please believe me. I'm not free tomorrow, or next week, or…'

He came back, apologised, asked for coffee and started clearing the table as if nothing had happened. If he does not want to tell us, he will not. While the rest of us returned to what we were saying, I could see he was bruised inside. Before he went to bed, I held his shoulders and looked up at him saying,

'Don't attempt the impossible, Nicholas.'

'Why not?' He looked slightly hurt as he went upstairs to his room.

5

Spring

Martha *i-witnessMAR754.futurepast.com*

Foxy can't settle into my parents' temporary home. He sniffs and licks and scratches all he can reach. We all wince, but mum doesn't seem to care.

'Must we get his claws clipped?' She's in tears of course. 'He hasn't left any marks. These doors and room surrounds below the wraparound screens are so dense and shiny that nothing can graze, scrape or cut them!' She's right. They're created to be tough, durable and to outlast one's lifetime. But it's pointless trying to reassure her. She's inconsolable. She's missing the 'lines of feeling' that Foxy inscribed on every wooden door at 11 Acacia Avenue, in spite of her 'No, Foxy, no, no, no!' and smart taps on the animal's back.

Every time I look I see mum huddled in one of the two comfortable chairs we've brought here from 11 Acacia Avenue. One by one the old houses are being demolished. They'll be rebuilt over underground storerooms and shelters, all spaces webconnected for future innovations.

'You'll be offered a temporary house,' I assured them on Nicholas's birthday. Soon afterwards, mum told me, the digger bared its teeth outside their front door. Number 11 began tilting into number 13's cavity already gouged out for storeroom and shelter. They had to leave. There was no space for them in Nicholas's rooms at the Institute or in my capsule, so now they are crammed into one of her haven homes, their belongings piled into a storage unit.

'Why don't they build capsules for households in transit?' she wanted to know.

'Too much bother,' I explained patiently. 'You can put household goods into any sealed, lockable space; furniture, ornaments and pictures don't complain and create easy profits.' I'm only echoing what zone governments and entrepreneurs say.

An air of doom pervaded their temporary home on the day 11 Acacia Avenue was destroyed. For the first time I noticed mum's shoulders curving forward and her movements slowing down. Until then I had admired the spring in her step and her waves of enthusiasm, now destroyed by the move.

Was I shocked - is that the right word? - by mum's strange paintings? I knew she had converted the loft in 11 Acacia Avenue while mother was away in China. She needed space for her books, I assumed, and a room to herself. She never mentioned her paintings.

Mother has always been our more enterprising parent. She started sous-chef, soon becoming wine waiter and then an importer of wine - from China of all places! Mum is miserable here literally in the midst of her work, surrounded by the people she's caring for. Like them, she's cast adrift by a society in renewal.

'Why does our house have to be crushed into dust?' she repeats.

'It's obsolete.'

'But if we like it as it is?'

'Others don't. They want here-and-now technology.'

'I don't.'

'Most do.'

Mum wanted our old home to remain a historic eyesore in Acacia Avenue, stranded among sleek and shiny techno-dwellings with unlimited virtual space and unsullied surfaces. She's too involved with past associations; her sense of ownership and money is outdated. What a relief mother is moving with the times!

'Who's paying for all these houses to be built?' Mum is worried in spite of my patient explanations.

'It's the "Put-Back" system. You voted for it in the elections nearly five years ago.'

She obviously doesn't remember and that makes her vulnerable. Voting is obligatory, but you can effectively not vote just by clicking the presence box. That's what she probably did.

'Mum, the Asset Redistribution Law gives us our freehold as part of the zone's future. The wealthy feel they're enabling others and improving society at the same time. It promotes the feel-good factor. They donate money to the Put-Back Fund that has, by law, to be spent on improving local building stock. It's people's second nature to thirst after money and influence, and also to help others.'

'I can't bear being patronised.' She hunches still further back into her chair with Foxy snuggling into her lap like a baby.

'Just ignore it. You'll have a place without draughts and with far better sound insulation - no more jolts and judders from airjuggernauts.'

I wish mum wouldn't be so mournful. She used to be quite cheerful. There's an acrid smell of fear about her now. She objects to condescension. There was a fair amount of that towards mother from mum's prosperous and sniffy family. Mother keeps on reminding her that she comes from a tougher background. 'My lot either sink or swim.'

I'm trying to stop them quarrelling without taking sides, but mum has just leapt up, dropping Foxy and glares at me.

'You too, Martha, like Karen, you always wave your wrist wordfrees around like, like everyone else, giving orders for everything to happen in this world of total connectivity…'

'At least -' my hands on mum's shoulders stop her lurching at mother, who's trying to speak, and flinging any object that snatches her fury... 'Mother can use her wordfree here, mum, to see what's happening in the world and…'

'So you were frustrated at number 11 Acacia Avenue, were you, Karen?' Mum is quivering in anger – what can I do? 'I might have known Martha had persuaded you. Long ago, I imagine. Were both of you setting up this move behind my back?'

I feel exhausted at the idea.

'Calm it, mum! How else could we have kick-started the redevelopment of this zone? It's inevitable. The Put-Back Fund has to be spent. It's illegal for it just to remain unused and increase by doing nothing.'

'Martha, you have contacts all over the place, mostly political.' Mum's tone is deliberate, slow and painful. 'Look how well you're doing out of it all!'

That's unfair, but I don't react.

Change can be exhilarating, but mum is distraught at seeing her paintings publicly stacked and stored alongside mother's ethereal Chinese landscapes with craggy mountains and twigs sprouting blossom. She turned away with a sob when her piano was pushed into storage, probably remembering the times when she played duets with Nicholas's schoolfriend Ezra, now a world-famous pianist. They were inseparable at school, even looked alike.

Mum has always tried to create an atmosphere just by being there, talking, asking about the people she knows. Mother instead needs a core to build around, like an event, a celebration or an outing. Take Nicholas's birthday celebration. Contrary currents must be ignored, always with a masking smile – I learnt that fast in politics. Nicholas was silent most of the time. Even as a child he took time out in company. Mum used to read to us at bedtime, sing or play on her piano while we fell asleep. She would often key her favourite aria – a slave girl Zaide's song - into the landing sound sensor and tiptoe down the stairs as it played.

No piano now. She frets that the sound board will crack while it's in store. She just has to wait until they move back to their new home. Their Petra stone is here with the framed photos and now the yellow brick. They aren't on a mantelpiece because there isn't one, but on top of mum's bookshelf next to the Chinese figurines. She couldn't be without her favourite authors. All her other books are in store. She seems to miss them, even the ones she never reads and paperbacks that people used to give to charity or throw away. Books have a rarity value now, what with everything being recycled into something entirely different. Nobody reads anymore.

Two days ago mum vanished. I found her in Acacia Avenue watching the demolition of their – our - past. She was sitting on the low wall of the front garden, lost in the rumble of the digger and its rhythm: dip, crunch, swing up and sideways to dump bricks, slates, plaster and dust between each future dwelling. Crunch, swing, dump; burnt smell of crushed brick powdered into nostrils and eyes. 'Get out, lady!' They yelled at her and I flinched as she darted in to snatch a brick before the monster teeth gripped the rubble. It's that yellow one on the bookcase by their stone from Petra.

When we turned away to leave, I noticed a silver-grey limousine on the other side of Acacia Avenue. As we moved away it followed us. In the twilight I couldn't make out whether there was a driver or not.

BREAKING NEWS

COMING ELECTIONS

Preparations will soon start for the election of zone delegates for the Goodwill World Parliament.

Meanwhile in China **Chang Lin**, graduate of Beijing, Cambridge and Harvard Universities, has changed history. Male dominated Chinese society has surprised the world by electing her the first female Chinese president in a country where women remain a minority. This is the result of the long-discontinued policy of one child per family to curb population growth, formerly resulting in illegal antenatal sex discrimination by aborting female foetuses. Commentators have noted that this may have been behind the significant advances that China has made in **genetics and stem cell research**.

Think **Chinese presidential election** for more information.

worldaroundyounews.com

6

Spring

Helen *i-witnessHEL527.futurepast.com*

Guess what! Apparently Nick's a brilliant inventor! I've found some online chat about him. It's not that I was lying in wait for him that cold afternoon in St. Thomas's. As if! But if that's how people see me, that's fine. I see myself now completely naked in a full-length mirror. I have firm breasts and a narrow waist with curved hips just right for tight-waisted skirts, trousers, shorts or whatever. Men get excited and try to guess the colour of one's pubic triangle by stroking my hair and looking at the parting. There are no surprises with me. What you see is what you get. Some fool suggested I should insure my legs. Why not the whole body? Can one insure body without brain? That's how I feel next to Nick. He should do the opposite.

Here I am happily thinking into my wrist wordfree blog. What about silver grey underwear for a spring day? I always match underwear with what I wear on top. A colour sensitive man might notice - not many of them around!

Nick followed me after I had dropped a couple of bags of clothes for the refugees in the church. I was also testing my light-reflective yellow top, brown skirt and crimson scarf in a dark place. St. Thomas's is perfect. Fashion ideas come from all over. I want to launch a new colour range. Of course it's all been done before, but unless we sprout another leg or arm or whatever, there aren't that many shapes and lengths to explore. Suppose hourglass curves come into fashion again. You tweak here and there, so granny can't just bring out her old clothes and be back in with the swim!

I must have lost weight. These shorts should show off my waist but they're resting on my bum and reveal the tattoo I'm trying to remove. Perhaps I shouldn't. Midriff display has been so long out of fashion it may return any time now. I can't have people laughing at a descending crotch. Better to wiggle into my colour-changeable rainbow skirt and top it with a tight blouse to feature one of its colours. Red today.

Martha persuaded me to move here. It's an old stone house built ages ago. She has preserved the old exterior by inserting these new-living capsules. They're just right for now and save energy.

I suppose I was a spoilt child. Everyone looked at me. It didn't take long for me to realise why and play up to it. Auburn hair is unusual with my skin, which looks tanned. Here in my mirror alcove I can see my face and hair from all angles, even from behind. The shelves are crammed with tubes and snappy compacts, markers and long thin containers with all sorts of make-up. Eyes. Everyone thinks about eyes. In the best of all worlds, mine could be rounder with more of a surprised look. I make do with lots of eyeliner, and the lashes are long enough to curl upwards. What should I emphasise? Today strong eye colour, lush mascara and lipstick to match my red top.

My Powerdress fashion partner, Cara, and my girl friends wonder what I see in Nick. Was it risky to pair up with a brainy person –a genius no less? Ages ago I watched a docudrama about Arthur Miller, that American playwright who fell for the film star every man lusted after: Marilyn Monroe of the breezy skirt. An old, old story, but lots viewed in. It had Screen Appeal. I'm not Marilyn – if only! But Nick dreams of making a great discovery to solve some universal problem. I don't understand it all, though he rattles on about it. He invented something a year or so ago. Then a global company grabbed it for 'a fraction of its worth' – my mother Karen's words. Our zone government was 'supine' – his word – so it missed what was happening under its very nose, literally, as it funds his Institute. Inadequately, it seems, so other donors step in. He mentioned Global Enterprises GWP, the company with the patent that was his. It's now tempting him with offers of research money but with too many strings attached. So he refuses to get entangled. I'd take it and run. He thinks he's on to something better. I might try to wangle more for him through my contacts. Nothing's without its price.

Wouldn't we all like to change the world for the better as he thinks he's doing? Leave our imprint, and not always for the best, I suppose. I don't understand much of what he says. Take this: 'Fame and notoriety are twins.' Odd.

He looks intelligent. A sort of sensitive face, handsome some would say, but not to everyone's taste. A bit too long, with a thin nose. Too many lines on his forehead for his age – he thinks too much! I do like slender and light-footed people. Too many plod around the world to mark their presence. His fingers are so long that I'm afraid they might snap. They're a pianist's fingers, he says, and that's probably what he'd like to be - if he had another life. Like his rather boring friend Ezra. They were inseparable at school, he says. They do look alike. Some even think they're twins!

He likes to walk in the woods near his Institute or along the river, not talking of anything in particular. He worries about the future and his invention. I live for the moment. I'm happy as I'm young and having fun - and then who knows? I don't buy into all that anxiety insurance for illness, pensions and the rest. Better to plunge into what's on now, and not bother about what may happen. We're staying young longer with healthy-living lessons, exercises and sport at school and beyond, plus all the stem cell products thrust at us. Here I'm surrounded by free samples of creams and lotions for every possible blemish.

That's that. Bit more powder on an irritating spot and an extra line on eyebrows. So. Right. I'm off.

To lunch first in a café spa. To meet there for the monthly work-through with Cara and others from our Powerdress business. It's our chance to chat while being manicured and pedicured or in some sort of hair treatment. Often we get together to twiddle ideas around on our website. A design to be desirable in some new-tech shade or pattern, say, to plant into customers' minds. Then it's my task to nurture it on as many internet outlets as possible. To make everyone feel not fully themselves until wearing our clothes to bring out the best in them, whatever that may be. Actually this may not be the case, but as long as the garment pleases their inner eye, mission accomplished! Then our outfit - identical cut, pattern and fabric but with personalised features of choice - turns up on every street and avatar in some interactive online game to prove we've really hit the public's inner eye.

However, now is a lean time; too late for a spring launch and too early for a summer one, so we'll just spa out. Back home later to hyperdress for the evening. Nick is fetching me to go to dinner in a hill resort or something.

My aim is the same as everyone else's: to go on the Moonshuttle. That's why the waiting time is more than three years. It's the same for the caves at Lascaux and the Cro-Magnon skull in a museum in Africa. They're all bundled together in the once-in-a-life-space-and-time experience at a sky-high price. Carbon emissions are rationed, so if one goes a distance, it has to be on a sky-shattering airjuggernaut. Instead I'll persuade Nick to take me again to our nearest Experience Dreamland. There you can select journeys to the past or the future through virtual flights. You can sample the latest in fun ground fantastic, with the ultimate digital operas of future sounds, sights and simulations. All depends on what sort of swings, swoops, churners or flingers you select for stomach-turning thrills. It beats those bankrupt Disney worlds. For quieter moments you can wander around Venice, New York, Barcelona, London, Rome, Rio de Janeiro or anywhere in the world that's interesting, getting better time value than actually going places. On offer right now are virtual journeys sneaking into private palaces and other buildings normally closed to the public. Everyone nowadays has been virtually everywhere interesting starting early and continuing later in life, without actually leaving their own zone. All this started long ago at Las Vegas. That's now almost a holiday slum. When I told Eliza what Nicholas and I had been doing, she said it reminded her of a book she had read a long time ago by some writer called Huxley. No idea what she meant.

I don't want to sound like an advertisement, but it's amazing how Experience Dreamland combines skating rinks, rock climbing, skiing and all sorts of snow activities in all seasons including grit-free snowball fights on every hour. Afterwards snowballers queue at healthy doughfruit and hot cocachoc drink stalls as part of the event. Lists are boring, but anything anyone wants to do or see, eat or drink is there. This includes comfortable rooms to hire by the hour for tired families or others who need rest and refreshing sessions. The temperature is moderated by control-speak to the left of the door. I selected pink and blue mood cushions from the alternative cupboard inviting you to create your own atmosphere. Nicholas still has to learn, but we had fun.

People-watching is fantastic in these Dreamlands. Lots come seeking adventure dressed like their avatar in some internet game or whatever virtual life they're into. It's far more amusing than any street scene in our town centre, except when Cara and I are displaying our new styles there.

Nick and I once went to a strange property not far from here. It had lots of pictures and carpets and objects on elegant tables, very different from houses now. There's an organisation that protects such places. He's bothered, Eliza too, that people aren't interested in the past. The massive over 75-year old population is into all types of wraparound screen activity and keeps fit in a sportsdrome. Eliza complains that we're 'dished up plenty of sport but a meagre ration of history'. She would. Karen is more future-free.

When I've a bit of spare time, I hold my wrist wordfree close and think as many memories as I can into it for future retelling. Years of them. Anyone interested can access them here on my website. Now to my screen diary to see what's on tomorrow. Did I promise to help Eliza and Karen move?

BREAKING NEWS

CRISIS TALKS ON WORLD'S ENERGY NEEDS!

Russian president **Igor Durgenev** yesterday welcomed an energy delegation from **Jerusalem.** This special meeting was arranged symbolically in a remote **Siberian oil prospecting site.** Bear hugs were exchanged in icy surroundings appropriate for the long-awaited world conference. **The European president, the Neapolitan Ambrogio Palumbo**, left early with frostbite. A statement will be issued later today.

worldaroundyounews.com

7

Spring

Nicholas i-witnessNIC227.futurepast.com

I knew I was being watched. It comes with the territory - branded a 'producer' or brainworker and having to attract money. As a so-called 'child genius', I was protected at first. Money flowed in for 'gifted children', for education and, in my case, for experiments in high-tech laboratories with all the latest computers and test modelling apparatus any scientist could wish for. My happiest school years were when, aged eleven, I became a boarder at the International Academy for the Gifted. There I found my best friend, Ezra, a brilliant musician. We went around a lot together. People thought we looked alike, except he's chubbier and I'm a bit taller. Also Lizzy, who buzzed cheerfully in and out of others' rooms. She's a landscape artist creating her own version in the Middle East of the mysterious Nazca Lines in South America - they can only be deciphered from high above. We were chosen for our special gifts. Mine lay in maths and physics and all sorts of hypotheses about the universe.

So why am I being watched? Because what I'm doing could change the world materially? I often think of Ezra and Liz. They create beauty: I solve problems.

Of Helen there is too much to think about, and I can't explain it to myself. I've even tried compressing all she means to me into an equation, but it doesn't work and I can't show how she affects me that way. Why should someone so striking fall for me? I don't look exciting or romantic and I certainly don't turn heads as she does.

I did realise from occasional news flashes that there is a youth culture I'm not part of. Helen is initiating me into the all night drongs, literally 'drown songs', which resonate round the city ballrooms in winter and the squares in summer.

'A drong shakes everything out of your head,' she smiled, holding her arms out to draw me into the body of laughter, heat and beat, tangled scent and sweat. 'It's mindless. Don't bother about anything, just be!' Go with the flow. Beat in the heat. Hum the drong. Live your dreams.

I would never have ventured there without Helen. I chose to stay on the edge of it all, wondering, rarely joining in. The idea didn't appeal. I don't like losing control over whoever I am. But Helen is changing all that. She brings back music pellets of the latest Stormpower rave. *It's only a rehash of the heavy metal I was into ages ago,* Magnus tells me. It throbs so loudly that Helen and I can only smile at each other, not talk, as we prepare meals, dance or listen from bed.

Martha. What a relief Helen isn't the slightest like my sister. Helen is so patient with our parents, while Martha organises them, whether they want it or not.

'Martha almost always agrees with her mother, Karen,' Helen once commented, 'because she's a doer like Karen. Martha's our local government member, isn't she?' True. But Martha can be tiring. We're half brother and sister with the same father, though we're not alike in looks or character.

When Helen announced that she had accepted Dom Ross Mackenzie's invitation to lunch on behalf of us both, I was horrified.

'You can't be serious?' I was vehement. 'How do you know him?'

'What's wrong?'

'How do you know him?' I didn't want to tell her what I thought of Dom Ross Mackenzie. Too complicated to explain with all its ramifications about the Institute losing the patent of my first invention to him. The Rector was displeased but let it go, probably to avoid offending a benefactor.

'Oh, he is sponsoring my Powerdress label and helping me promote it.'

'Clothes? Isn't he into commodities, minerals, mining, petroleum, alternative fuels - all that?' Helen nodded.

'Of course, but people like Dom Ross Mackenzie have charitable foundations as well.'

'You can't pretend that promoting a fashion house is a charitable exercise! Come on, Helen; don't try to sell me that!' She pouted a little.

'I can. Powerdress now donates to one of Dom Ross's good causes - I've forgotten which.'

Magnus has pointed out how conglomerates are supporting good causes in order to camouflage more dubious activities in what they think are forgotten parts of the world. That's where Reaching Out is trying to encourage local initiatives, especially in the Sub-Saharan and Middle East Peace Settlement zones. Helen seemed genuinely surprised by my attitude.

'I think it's wonderful,' she insisted, 'what global companies are doing to help others. Dom Ross Mackenzie's Global Enterprises sponsors our local festivals. He makes stacks of money and gives some back to others. If only I could do the same! Our tiny business isn't doing badly, but we're a minnow, not a whale.'

'Don't try to be different,' I said. She stared back, mystified.

'I think Magnus has influenced you, Nicholas, hasn't he? Dom Ross told me he asked Magnus to support some of his chosen charities, but he refused.'

If only I too had been quick enough to refuse the invitation! I had to accompany Helen but deliberately took off the chain with my wordfree monitor and left it in my bedroom. I'm recording this for the i-witness project back there.

Where do I begin? Our host sent his driver in a silver-grey limousine to fetch us. Helen was disappointed it wasn't the helousine. I wanted it to be driverless so I could refuse to start it. I assumed speedways would serve grand houses, not winding lanes with rough stone walls smelling of moss and fern and age. Tall trees branched over us. Then an unexpected break into upland, with discreet country estates widely spaced, dwellings enclosed behind walls and clumps of highland pines.

The car approached a grand pair of gates. Our driver tapped the dashboard, and they swept open into a long drive that led to a large house with outbuildings round a wide courtyard. It commanded a view over the city to the woods and meadows and the estuary beyond. It was a fresh spring evening with an air of excitement and expectation.

'This building is the largest existing version of Palladio's Villa Emo,' Dom Ross Mackenzie announced when he received us in the library.

'Palladio's Venetian patrons only used their mainland villas as summer retreats and at harvest time. Their principal residences were in Venice; mine is here.'

Helen murmured appreciation. That was only polite, I suppose.

'I have many properties worldwide, but this is where I prefer to be.'

He insisted on concocting his version of the classical martini. Trophies from the world's great auction houses jostled on every surface, inviting touch and admiration. Helen followed Dom Ross, fascinated. While he was extolling the magnificence of his collections, I noticed security blinks neatly disguised behind carefully copied 16th-century mouldings. Picking up an exquisitely inlaid casket, I heard some strange buzzing and felt stabs in my fingers.

'No problem,' said our host, raising his wrist, 'please examine its extraordinary craftsmanship'. The sensations ceased. 'A most rare Florentine work in *pietre dure* - semi-precious stones - and this is one of the earliest and most valuable exemplars. Look - ' he leant towards me to take it and point out to Helen the intricacies of the leaf and flower patterns round the sides. On the lid there was what seemed to be a Florentine *palazzo*. Back in his red leather chair, Ross Mackenzie continued determinedly,

'Are you aware there is similar inlay on the Taj Mahal? I go there in the full moon, at sunrise or sunset. My residence nearby has a traditional Mogul design, a *nauchgahr* where women once danced – and still do - as well as courtyard gardens with many fountains, more than there are around the Taj. I love the place, now that we've conquered the pollution problem and are relaying the drains in Agra.'

I wondered who the 'we' referred to.

'Are these your family?' Helen was looking at the large wall portraits in the spacious sitting room.

'My ancestors. Scottish aristocracy, I suppose one might say, like Robert the Bruce, though, regrettably, the portraits do not go back as far. I alerted my agents in the auction houses years ago, but few of my more distant ancestors had their portraits painted.'

Helen was clearly impressed as she gazed at the dresses. She would not have approved of my secret laughter at the absurdities of our host. Dom Ross seemed to assume that, as a typical scientist, I would be visually ignorant. If mum had been with us I'd have worried. She would have been unable to control her expression of disbelief at the tell-tale smooth texture of the canvases and the subtle sheen on the family job-lot, clearly reproductions off-loaded on to Dom Ross Mackenzie at the best available at any price.

More recent generations stared mournfully from the dining room walls, a pinched Victorian bunch. I wondered whether he had bought his stained glass coat of arms in the staircase window along with the portraits. There were no family photos on the desk in the library or the grand piano in the music room.

'It’s a rare luxury to have one's guests to oneself,' Dom Ross remarked, settling himself at the head of the long dining table and nodding at the butler to pour Châteauneuf du Pape. 'Boardroom lunches are infrequent, now that business is conducted through internet conferencing. I've introduced a more informal atmosphere in these conferences by offering coffee breaks with light refreshments wherever they are in the world. We not only share the friendly chink of coffee cups but also that distinct aroma transmitted though the sensometers we have installed.' Helen was wide-eyed and I smiled in what I hope was a friendly way. I soon found that nothing disturbed our host. I could have yawned for all the effect it would have had on him. He continued, 'I believe that it improves results if we provide breaks and light conversation with the appropriate sensory accompaniments'.

I recalled the clatter down in the common room under my lab where Esther, Raphael and I, over mugs of Honest Reward coffee, bounce ideas and solutions off one another. I couldn't stop myself speaking out when our host paused.

'Is there something wrong in our world, Dom Ross, when matters affecting us all are distorted by companies making ginormous profits while wages remain so low? And this continues despite generations of protests flooding the internet.'

'Dr. Middlethorpe - or may I call you Nicholas? 'I nodded, though I hadn't heard him asking Helen if he could use her first name...' the collapse of communism in the twentieth century taught us that people want to make money and that it can only be done through the profit motive, which involves building up capital and working with complex market mechanisms that become more intricate by the second. People are not naturally compassionate - until their greed is satisfied'.

Silence. Helen looked mystified. We sipped the Châteauneuf du Pape. The face of the mantelpiece clock stared down from the carved marble fireplace at the three of us crowding one end of a long table. Tick tock. Take stock. Don't rock the…

'There's a natural balance in all this,' our host pronounced. Plover's eggs, on a fresh bed of organic green salad with seedless tomatoes from his walled kitchen garden, were placed before us. Ross tackled the eggs. Helen followed his example. I navigated round them, thinking they looked like gouged eyeballs.

'Vegan, Nicholas?'

'No, just…' I was confused. Helen glanced at me, eyes narrowed. Ross turned towards the butler who removed my plate.

'Self-interest is the strongest motivation of all,' he said, looking at me.

Lobster soup and warm rolls arrived with an accompanying pat of butter from his pedigree dairy herd.

'I started off in the usual way,' Ross went on between mouthfuls, 'studying internet science and economics at the best business schools. Then fast forward up the rungs of management to the top. Christ taught everyone to treat others as you wish them to treat yourself. Fine. Achievers pursue their own interests, and others reciprocate to their advantage. All balances out for the best'. He sat back contentedly.

Tick tock, mantelpiece clock. Move your hands faster. The plates were replaced by large ones for the main course.

'Hukind is untidy,' he went on. 'Look at the messy way democracy creaks along with endless debates across our screens and in blogs or vlogs - you name it! And so little concluded. The old problems persist. I avoid dealing with actual people as much as possible. Far easier to run enterprises with machines and robots that don't answer back. Where it can't be avoided we do employ line managers and a small workforce, all paid, I must stress, above the GWP minimum wage. They are the vital links in our worldwide network.'

Unpolluted vegetables accompanied sirloin steaks from our host's upland herd. The ease of it all, summoned by raising his wrist!

'Your friend, Magnus, is heavily involved in some world project, isn't he, Nicholas? It sounds interesting. I hoped he would join us today, but it seems he is otherwise engaged.' Pause. Recognising this as an invitation to describe Magnus's activities, I sat silent.

'Yes, I think you're right,' Helen broke the silence. 'He's in some sort of world organisation. I don't know how it works, but it's to do with the grass roots, enabling ordinary people, all that sort of thing...' She faltered, sensing my disapproval.

'Yes, I understand,' our host nodded. 'I was wondering about your laboratory, Nicholas.' At last the point of my being here. I mustn't foolishly put my head into the noose I'd avoided before. Hold back. Leave the Châteauneuf in your glass. Just toy with it and smile. Keep your defences up. 'How are things going?'

'Well, thanks.' Silence surged between us. Helen breathed in and opened her mouth to speak, but -

'I'm well versed in physics and a fair amount of chemistry,' our host continued, 'fascinated, in fact, by what you're pitting yourself against. The race. The challenge of all the others in the energy game '. I didn't see myself 'against' anything. Mostly 'for', I should think, and certainly not in a game. I was uncertain exactly what he was hinting at, though I did know he was trying to dig something out of my mind, prospecting for the nugget he was convinced lay hidden deep inside. Minerals. Extractions - the main thrust of his company, Global Enterprises GWP?

'Yes. Well, I'm making progress.'

'Your assistants - Raphael from Israel, is he good? And the girl from Africa? Surely you need more help? I would be only too happy to sponsor more lab space.'

He was trying again to offer me funding. The same rigmarole. This was just the moment for Helen to slip in one of her fashion anecdotes. Instead she was wide-eyed but silent, leaving me to struggle alone.

'My present arrangements suit me. I can't think with a lot of people around.'

'Ah, silence is golden, eh?' Ross leaned back laughing as if at a shared insight. 'Searching for some base metal that turns into gold, the universal elixir – that recurring day-dream we all indulge in.' Tick tock.

'More sirloin? Vegetables?' Helen declared that, although she was on a perpetual diet, she couldn't refuse such delicious food in so beautiful a setting. Concern throttled my appetite.

'When was your last paper published?' A host's privileges extend to wearing out a guest with studied politeness and generosity whilst interrogating him.

'A few months ago. On the World Science site. You must have seen it.'

'Of course. I thought there were others.'

'No. That's where I am currently.' Why tell the truth to a gold-digger?

'Still?'

'Yes.'

Sharp, seedless raspberries followed, *just ripe from the hothouse canes that I'm experimenting with by binding in a blackcurrant gene,* snug in a meringue nest topped with whipped cream, also, of course, from the pedigree herd.

'Untwist and retwist DNA,' Ross was attempting vaguely inaccurate popular science speak,' and you can wander into infinite combinations. Where do the infinite possible combinations lead in your field?'

Tick tock, mantelpiece clock.

I looked at Helen in desperation. She glanced with a glint of comprehension and seized the first idea available.

'To cheer up people's lives,' she said brightly. 'Give them a chance to colour their personality. Clothes and accessories make life much more interesting.' At last she was actually veering the conversation away from my work. I was deeply relieved.

The instant we stepped out of the front door into the drizzly dusk, lights leapt to attention in the vast forecourt and the wings embracing it. Relentlessly, Ross gave us a tour of *the mightiest cyberpower centre in private ownership* - a throbbing, sleepless heart of world communications. Always a step ahead of anyone else, on constant alert, a new strategy every day. Fired on adrenalin, our host sped ahead of us through his armoury of cyberpower.

'You need to check your theory, don't you? Try out this new program that my scientists have just developed. It tests and corrects any sort of calculation, and saves so much time. Give me your wrist inset code and I'll send it to you.'

I hesitated. Should I tell him I don't have one? All my personal details, medical profile, research papers and my latest theory, everything normally stored on a wrist wordfree inset, are in my wordfree monitor usually on a chain round my neck, and I left it in my rooms.

'You may perhaps still prefer the old datadrive?' I didn't reply. He looked at me, and then went over to a scientist on the night shift, returning to continue our tour of the laboratories.

Outside, just as the limousine glided into the forecourt, the scientist came running towards us.

'Here it is.' Dom Ross held out a tiny datadrive. 'Take it. Call me next week. We could set up your research laboratory here. No cost. Here's my card.' Another to add to my store.

Twisting lanes prevented a swift getaway. Helousines could doubtlessly airlift him and his powerbase if need be. We descended the mountainside in our host's now driverless silver-grey limousine.

'What a place!' Helen exclaimed, 'and what a life!'

'On a perpetual high, borne aloft on the best of everything,' I said ungenerously. 'Self-maintenance as a perpetual superlative requires constant vigilance. It flows in his blood, a sort of scheming gene.'

'No, Nick, he's kind. Really generous, though you'd say that's easy enough for him with all that wealth.'

'Please don't call me Nick.'

'Sorry, don't let's spoil the evening.'

'I'm so relieved I didn't tell Ross Mackenzie I am going to Africa. He thinks I'll call him next week, but I won't be here!'

I spent most of the night calming Helen. She was angry and distressed I hadn't told her I was leaving for Sub-Saharan Africa. I didn't want anyone to know except Magnus.

'Alone?' she eventually asked, 'or with Esther?'

'I'm not sure. She may leave later. Magnus has someone meeting me.'

'Who'll look after the lab? Raphael?'

'No, he's going to Israel for some conference. I'll leave the lab on stand-by. No harm doing that.'

'No,' she said, in a strangely subdued voice. 'When exactly are you leaving, so I can see you off?' I said I wasn't sure and would let her know.

I'd have liked to call Ezra and tell him about the dinner at Ross Mackenzie's country estate, or laugh over it with Martha, but Helen reacted differently - she didn't even giggle. She seems in awe of him. No time to spare. I must leave. No need now to phone Ross Mackenzie this week or ever to talk to him again – if the tests succeed!

BREAKING NEWS

MAGNATE SPEAKS OUT AGAINST POLITICAL HEGEMONY

The normally reticent **executive chairman of Worldwide Enterprises GWP, a** mining and energy conglomerate, warns of the dangers of Russian and Chinese indiscriminate exploitation of Africa's vast potential.

'Political hegemony can only lead to a Sino-Russian dictatorship of the planet,' **Dom Ross Mackenzie** asserts after his meeting with **President Igor Durgenev.**

worldaroundyounews.com

8

Spring

Martha *i-witnessMAR754.futurepast.com*

I've just thought through my wordfree diary to find out what I shall be doing before the elections. My agent doesn't seem to be keeping it up to date. Normally I work out my activities hour by hour, but moving my parents to their new house has taken more than its allocated time. Mother has settled in fine, but mum has been a pain. It's either 'Martha, can you please…' or she mopes. Look at her now, moving listlessly round her sparkling new home, incapable of any glimmer of enthusiasm. I have to deal with people like her every day in my campaign, whinging on about losing their houses in the massive redevelopment plans.

Suffice it to say that the hour I can now devote to just the three of us is also the time for me to relax and blog away, freezeframing what I've accomplished since my last entry. It helps to pace the hours ahead. Mother is tuned into the problems I'm facing. Most of the viral attacks I have to counter online are personal and predictably vile. Luckily, as I'm a newcomer on the political scene, I don't get as many as more seasoned candidates like Roland. He has to wade through daily waves of fan mail, some obscene. I admit I have some too, from all sorts, but Jan's policy – she's my agent - is to invite them to become 'friends'!

Chang Lin won't have such problems. Chinese peasants are still clamouring for their hovels to be replaced by whatever is the Asian notion of a house for the future, such as this one.

Hovel. I'm only repeating the word mum used in, 'treating our Acacia Avenue home like a hovel to be ground underfoot'. Hardly. We're inevitably sandwiched in the present between our baggage from the past and trying to pack our lives as best we can in preparation for an unknown future. Politicians should help people do this. So here my parents are in this brand-new capsule house. I'm already in mine and loving it.

I kept silent, knowing that the real reason behind the new design was to stuff all the hi-tech connections into the cavity between the shared walls. They link everything and everyone to the crucial worldwide network. Energy is provided by solar panels, wind turbines and recycling systems. Nothing is wasted in this house, even from the WC!

It's amazing how people still get in your way even when they know you are at crisis point. Here I am running for election, and Helen turns up with some trivial matter to discuss. I like her well enough, with her cheerful smile and even temper, except when she comes into my election headquarters to pester me about Nicholas.

'Why doesn't he ever leave the lab nowadays?' she complained.

'He has a lot to do.' That was only half the reason. I didn't tell her he was going to Africa, why should I? It's for Nicholas to decide whether to confide in her or his sister. She persisted,

'He told me the theoretical stuff is done. Ready for the tests.'

'Right.'

'Martha, don't keep it from me. There must be something else.' There was. I kept silent.

On and on. Then she changed tack and told me about her new range of fashion promoted by the usual patter of 'build on, play with, flatter your best points…' Though I was frantically shuffling on screen forecasts and focus group results and interview analyses, she prattled away oblivious.

'Look, Helen, can you help me with my election manifesto? Redesign it?'

'I assumed you had others to do it. From your Party.' She paused, adding, 'they're far more experienced. I'm only in fashion. Something has happened to Nicholas and I want him to tell me what it is.' My first impulse was to repeat, 'Just ask him,' but I thought better of it. I knew he didn't want to be disturbed before he left. It was too risky. Some of his calculations had not turned out as expected. He was in a panic and refused to see anyone. I respect that. So I fiddled around on the screens and waited for her to be bored and leave.

Nicholas is informing people that he'll go earlier than he actually plans to, so he can have time when people think he's not around. He'll be undisturbed while sorting out the lab to make sure he doesn't forget anything, especially all the technical stuff for the lab capsule to transfer to Africa. He asked Magnus whether he knew who would meet him in the sub-Saharan zone as Esther won't be there. It'll be someone he's never met. An aid worker for Reaching Out called Celia. Raphael is abroad on a project and Esther is busy preparing her return to Africa, so he has the lab to himself. Ideal.

He told me about the knock on his lab door. Did he have to open it? Insistent knocking, then a pause. He was using all the lab screens, cross-checking and testing everything one last time. Or so he thought. He opened the door, just a crack. What he saw made him want to fall on it with his full weight to push it shut, but he was wrong-footed by Dom Ross Mackenzie.

'Nicholas, you must use the program I gave you when you came to lunch. Do you still have it?' He insinuated himself round the door and cast a rapid glance over the screens. 'It will save so much time, eliminate all mathematical errors and attack any viruses that might be homing in on your key calculations. It's crucial. The ultimate defence against hackers.'

Whatever happened in the lab, it upset Nicholas so much that he came to see me here at the election office. He says that since the importance of his work has been recognised, rivals in the energy game are trying to wheedle the core of the theory out of him. Most are way off what he's doing, judging from their publications in the usual areas: cleaner nuclear fission, or better, nuclear fusion, not to mention hydro, wave or tidal power, solar panels of all kinds and a variety of biofuels. But he feels watched.

Dom Ross, it seems, left after promising more of the help that Nicholas mistrusts, financial or otherwise. He is worried about his preparations for Africa. He was upset, wanting to talk to me while I was in the midst of a life-changing campaign.

'Come and stay with me. The divan in the sitting-room can be turned into a bed. You can help me in the campaign.'

'No. I must go away. I can't face having to explain why I'm not already in Africa. I can't let down the organisation financing my tests.'

There wasn't much I could say to help him.

I should have been preparing election e-shots, snippets for the influential local online newscasts, researching the reality programmes that might host me, or not, and all the infinite electronic methods of promotion. Instead Nicholas haunted me as he often did when we were young. Almost twins with the same father, almost fully understanding each other, he would slip off, though physically present, almost as if he were swimming away from me into the unfathomable sea of the future. Then I became frightened and cried for my mothers to comfort and cuddle me. I would sit still, silent, as I do now, afraid of when he might next disappear.

* * * * *

Mum was predictably edgy about Nicholas's planned departure. She fidgeted with familiar objects, shifting their stone from Petra and her brick from the Acacia Avenue house, fingering mother's Chinese statues and nudging the piles of books on the floor with her foot, intoning mournfully 'never enough shelves...' and 'nowhere to paint...', all of which was untrue. I expected her to paint in the empty bedroom with the wide north-facing window, or the high-ceilinged room on the ground floor. Mother says she is eating compulsively, hiding chocolate bars, putting on weight and furiously redirecting her frustration on to me.

'Look at what your lot's done! Torn out the heart of this ancient city and rebuilt an incredibly ugly imitation just so you can cram in all of today's super-integrated technology. Houses used to be built using stones dug out of the ground beneath them.' Mum is showing her age.

'Now all you people want is to eradicate the dust and dirt of time to create a perfect living space,' she declaimed. 'Your capsules are insipid. They have lost the touch of hewn stones and carved wood, the smells of quarries and woodland, the reassuring feel of time passed on to us.'

Insipid, no; recreated, yes. I was furious as well.

'You have the arrogance to wish people back to the hovels you find - God knows why - romantic! To the discomfort and misery that our forebears struggled to escape from and not, emphatically not, to bequeath to us. Like them, we too want to improve things for everyone, not just for the next generation. For you as well. And there's beauty too, here in the pure, dustless design around you, in your home, the end-product of countless centuries to release hukind from physical labour, and you're insensitive enough to dismiss it, just like that - ' I clicked my fingers, not very effectively' - no, worse. You're betraying what our ancestors have passed on to us - an ever-improving quality of life'.

Mum turned away muttering, 'It's useless, she doesn't understand a thing, contradicting herself… What can you do with these politicians?' and so on. It's happening worldwide, the great awakening of the masses, more than even Marx and Engels could have imagined. Whole slum areas are being cleared. 'It depends on what you call a slum area,' she says, citing the so-called historic buildings in our city centre. China is showing the world how to build up-to-date tourist attractions around, say, an authentic pharmacy, recreating genuine old streets with shops selling traditional remedies and crafts in hygienically safe surroundings. The workers in those areas pass through security checks and are tagged. All mum can add is that they are tearing down what is unique to that place, honed over centuries, to rebuild it in historical costume. It might work as a theatre of the past, she says, but what does that actually mean?

She is distinctly out of sorts with these times, and can't find any group to identify with. That's her problem. The women's groups she joined when she was young were changing then. Thanks to them, I reminded her, women like us can make a career when and how we like, have children when and where we wish. She resents the way no political movement represents her convictions about what she calls 'raping the soul of a place'. She is glancing at me now, aware that I'm thinking her into my blog, though she can't read it. This is encrypted. My political one is open to all and sundry - in particular to sundry's numerous postings on it. Jan deals with most of them. She advised me early on in the campaign to contact Magnus, probably because he has some connection with the Reaching Out movement. I had started to sleuth for ideas and thought he might help, so I went to see him.

I expected him to exist in a pared-down way, somehow. I didn't realise he lived in Newborough, a neighbourhood recently built on green fields now only separated by a narrow belt of meadow and woodland from the University. I bleeped my wordfree and found the door ajar.

Magnus has more in his capsule than I do. I like his virtual office in the entrance space, but he walked too quickly through it to the main room for me to make out what was happening. He sat down on a sofa without saying a word, almost grudging my presence. For a man of his age, at least twenty years older than me, he is attractive in a sturdy sort of way. Tall and muscular. I turned my back on the wallpaper of African wildlife to look through the window on to a strip of lawn and the street.

'You wanted to see me?' I was glad he broke the silence though I was surprised he didn't ask about Nicholas, seeing that I'm his sister. I suspect Nicholas now confides in him more than me. Man to man. Well, we both have more important things to think about now. I began,

'I wonder if what you are doing, Magnus, is connected with President Lo Yin's Worldwide Energy Pact, or WEP?'

'No.' Perhaps he wanted to keep out of the latest US initiative to control Chinese expansionist policies. With the election of female presidents in the two powers already challenged by the European, Central Asian and South American trading groups, there had been a surge of hope amongst smaller unaffiliated nations. But things habitually turn nasty over the control of energy. The US now says it will remove tariffs from Chinese imports in exchange for no interference in its African oil exploration. Was it called exploitation? And was it oil or some rare metal – lithium or something – used in nuclear fusion?

'Local people,' Magnus said after a long silence. Was he referring to Lo Yin's Worldwide Energy Pact, other initiatives or to Nicholas's tests?

'The WEP is about to involve them, insofar as the technology is available on the ground.' I was deliberately vague as I don't know much about the WEP or Nicholas's tests.

'If they are allowed to use it.' He was quietly terse.

'They will be.'

'Sooner or later, I suppose you mean. Now is when they need it.'

So he is involved in Africa, or at least interested. That must be why Nicholas wants to test his invention there. Or it could be Esther's influence.

'You represent Reaching Out, don't you?'

'Yes.'

'Tell me about it.'

'It's a long story. Would you like a drink? Tea? Coffee?'

'No thanks. Just the story.'

A long pause. 'Everyone knows it's about enabling people, wherever. Using their own resources and so on.' He trailed off and looked out of the window. His face matched his frame: wide, strong with darker skin under his eyes. They were sinking into his head and his thoughts with them.

'How about schools? Clinics?'

'Yes?'

'My Serendipity Party could focus on them in its overseas budget.'

'Yes, I know,' and not even a glimmer of interest. There was no resonance, nothing. When I stood up, he repeated, almost petulantly,

'Won't you have a drink? I can make coffee for both of us.'

I was mildly curious to see the kitchen behind the zebras now grazing over the walls, but he slipped through the door that opened behind some wind-fraught trees next to them and closed it firmly behind him.

'There are things to be done in a particular way,' he said, returning with two mugs on a tray. I wasn't sure whether he was referring to himself, Reaching Out or the Serendipity Party. 'A lot still has to be worked out, and…' He trailed off again.

'Such as?' I tasted the coffee. 'This is good. African beans?' I was beginning not to care.

'Yes.' He looked sad, as if searching vainly for sunlight in his thoughts. 'I believed...'

'Yes?'

'... that things might happen as a result of ...' he fell silent again. Not long afterwards he raised his wrist inset to open the door to the entrance hall and held the other hand out to me. I didn't expect this gesture and shook it more vigorously than I should have done, but he didn't seem to notice.

'How is Nicholas?'

'Getting ready...' (how ridiculous to tell him what he must know already) '... to leave for Africa.' He nodded. The door clicked shut leaving me alone in the neat avenue of olives and oleanders. Mother would like the regularity of it all, as I do, but mum yearns for each plant in its season: wisteria, climbing roses, the scent of white jasmine flowers set against deep green leaves. Her words. Spring running riot into summer. She's waiting impatiently for that to happen.

I walked back to the town centre bewildered by Magnus's intelligent evasion, and passed a rather ugly stone church. It has become the focus for demonstrations led by an irritatingly calm nun from some obscure order devoted to good deeds. She's one of those people who smile sweetly as they listen and carry on as before, your argument running over their impermeable skin of belief. Her church has a considerable open area around it that is needed for town housing, to draw people back into the centre. Particularly the older community. I went in, not to find Sister Julian as no one can persuade her to relocate, but one of her acolytes. Esther is a different matter.

She happened to be in the church talking to a woman with three young children. She hugged me, saying,

'I should return to Africa. I have more to do there.'

Does one choose one's friends to satisfy some unconscious need? I first met Esther in the Institute common room with Nicholas, and then noted she was next to Sister Julian on the march protesting about the zone's proposed demolition of this church and again in the town centre with some of the refugees that are setting up this strange self-regulating community in our midst. I have contributed to it but don't really know how it works. In fact, I would like to talk to Esther about this project, her research with Nicholas and her family back in Africa, but there never seems to be time. She tends to be non-committal about most things. Just her way.

When Sister Julian emerged from a side chapel, Esther and I were immediately gathered into her enthusiasm for the refugees and how they were forming by themselves a 'creative community of self-sufficiency', though I'm not sure exactly what she meant. She spoke admiringly of the prisoners-on-parole who were tidying up the churchyard and another team clearing the undergrowth in the woodlands near the Institute.

'They'll be taught the ancient art of coppicing,' Sister Julian added cheerfully. 'I love looking through woodlands, don't you? Flickering light from above on carpets of woodland flowers - snowdrops, wild garlic, cowslips, primroses, bluebells and foxgloves. They need light and space, just like us –' and the elderly people, I thought, that the Serendipity Party wants to house here, on this prime site of spiritual space.

'I couldn't bear to see all those dead trees crashing on to other ones,' Sister Julian continued, 'crushing life beneath them and left to rot. We have permission from the owners to cut some of them and sell the logs. They said it was unprofitable to do it themselves, but the prisoners-on-parole are keen to take it on if they can keep any money made out of it. Which they can. We only take a small amount for their keep. With God's will, it all works out,' she spoke in breathless enthusiasm, heedless of any comments around her. I drew my breath many times to try and force entry into a pause to tell her what my party was doing and get her support for the elections - everyone has to vote - but she neatly side-stepped with, 'Martha, we do things in our own way. Just love your neighbour. Turn the other cheek if snubbed and carry on regardless. Take what's offered with thanks. Rejoice. Encourage people to love others - ' she raised her arms and laughed. 'I almost forgot to show you the latest miracle! Come!' and she reached out for my hand, 'come and see what we've found'.

We crossed the nave borne on the wings of her joy to the vestry and there, hanging high on the wall was a painting of a naked woman and a huge swan, with four babies. It looked as if they had just appeared from two cracked eggs. Esther gasped, whispering that it wasn't here before and is totally unsuitable for this building.

'One of our refugees found it at the bottom of an old chest with rarely used clerical vestments!' Sister Julian smiled at us. 'It was possibly stored there for safety on the way to somewhere else, then forgotten and vestments piled on top of it… I only came across it when we were fighting the campaign. The threat to pull this church down for housing, all that. And those zone officials didn't even look at what we are doing for homeless refugees and old people. Nor even ask. That's what politicians and planners are like nowadays. They wander all over the internet, grazing on data selected as relevant to what they have decided to do in the first place! You might call it a waste of time. Where we now stand is close to the city centre, therefore a prime site for some good social scheme. So they clap demolition orders on our church and surrounding buildings, declare them ugly and useless, and offer to swap them for modern premises on a site they don't need! It's not on the main road, so people won't drop in as you have done. Community death by slow asphyxiation.'

She looked up at the painting. 'In the process we discover this lovely painting. Serendipity, some say. I know it is an act of God. I've called the director of our museum and he'll arrive at any moment. It may be a lost work by Leonardo da Vinci - how's that for a real miracle?' and Sister Julian breezed off without realising I'm one of those zone government members trying to relocate her church and demolish this building! Frankly I am relieved that the whole question has been shelved until after the election.

BREAKING NEWS

A MASTERPIECE OR NOT?

A leading art expert is astounded that a reputed **Leonardo da Vinci** lost masterpiece has been found in a church. He asserts that the subject matter - the classical myth of **Leda,** a princess who fell in love with **Zeus**, the King of the gods on **Mount Olympus -** is an unsuitable subject for a church painting. However, this may be another copy of the lost but documented early 16th-century original oil painting.
Worldaroundyounews.com

9

Spring

Eliza's Journal

You have always had your own way, Martha, of flying kites kept airborne with your mother Karen's help. You resented me saying there were good and bad winds, squalls, all sorts of unforeseen tempests, and tossed your head of curls, lobbing back at me a succession of 'whys' and 'don'ts' and 'spoilsports.' I retreated and instead wandered up the chalk slopes of Quarry Hill to the ridge, before Dom Ross Mackenzie and his like built their pseudo sixteenth-century country houses. There I could in my imagination soar with eagles over fields and forests, streams and canals to the city and beyond it, the ocean, or over dales and moorland up to the mountains. Infinite possibilities.

Martha and I have always had totally different ways of coping with the future. She could be described as manipulating it - perhaps too harsh?

'I want to create opportunities,' she is always saying. 'That's what the Serendipity Party is all about.' I asked what opportunities were generated by uprooting quietly contented communities and she just stared at me, amazed that I was unable to see what is obvious to her.

'You must realise that people are marginalised when they are condemned to live in centuries old slums. They tend to cling to what they already know - that's human nature, isn't it? But it's everyone's right to live in an environment that nurtures-' (her favourite word nowadays) '- individual talent, and that's what our party, if elected, will do'.

It depends on what you call a slum. A church? A college refectory? A medieval timber framed cottage, if any remain, or a genuine 18th-century Palladian house?

True, she did all she could to settle Karen and me back in our space, but it is not Acacia Avenue in name or atmosphere. Modern streamlined living, fit for the rest of our century. That is what she wants. She nurtured our needs. Our Petra stone, the brick from 11 Acacia Avenue and Karen's knobbly Chinese statues lie on top of my bookcase, adrift in a house with no mantelpiece or chimney, just contorted aerials and a clutter of dishes, windmills and solar panels.

Until after the elections Martha can only come to see us at a prescribed time. Karen provides supper and, after the last spoonful of dessert, Martha gracefully moves to one of the living-room internet points to update her blog – her own, not the political one - using a personalised screen. She carefully avoids it spreading all over the wraparound ones, especially if she is writing about stubborn old Eliza who refuses to settle down in her ultra-modern new-in-old home in Beech Drive, not side-by-side but back-to-back with her former neighbours. They are still in Acacia Avenue and used to cook in what is now our living space. Smells hang around like uninvited memories. Everything in our new dwelling has been thought of in terms of space, not atmosphere. Space flows indifferently through it. I need an area to myself. I'm not happy, never have been, with open spaces: kitchen into dining area into living room into a recreation space ending in a conservatory that, weather permitting, opens on to the garden zone, paved or grassed according to taste.

To cut costs, designers (in cahoots with planners who are beholden to politicians) create three sizes to fit all (unless you have Dom Ross Mackenzie's wealth) - large, average or small. Of course we are average. However, as Martha repeats, we are free to impress our individuality on our bare capsule home; it provides opportunities for maximum personal fulfilment. Does that make sense? For me, it does not. The elements of choice come far down the line. I cannot choose to have a fireplace and mantelpiece because no fires are allowed - environmentally unfriendly - so there is no focus in the plain open area wrapped round with endless screens. I must make my focus, choose the electronic wallpaper I want from too many options, and select the screen sections to display news, films, history documentaries (not many now; unpopular), or sites like *intoit.com, ourlives.com, disgusted.com, twinnies.com* or whatever you choose from more offerings than one could ever dream up. And then there is Karen to think about, though we have our earphones and do not need to view together. All the rooms have screen walls, including the two Martha designates for me to choose from for a studio. One of them has to suit me. Neither do. I try to explain that I cannot hang pictures on the screen walls and both rooms are too public, but she only screws up her eyes, shakes her head and says, with a tinge of exasperation,

'They're not open plan areas, Eliza, they've got doors. I was careful about that. And locks. Here's the key to the downstairs room. There's plenty of space for you. I can get you all the easels you need for your paintings.' Plenty of noise too, I think, when Karen asks Martha to play her favourite drong pellets in panoramic mode enveloping the living, dining and kitchen areas where they sway and dance and sing, even yell when joined by her political friends, all mesmerised remembering some latter-day version of historic Glastonbury. Karen used to go to similar events, if she could get a ticket, while I looked after the children. Fine. We took it in fair turns then. What I cannot bear now, more than the noise, are the vrooms - the incessant beat and reverberation that set my canvases jittering.

They are now piled in the ground floor studio as it is difficult to find someone to hoist them through the window of the less noisy room above. My hesitation allowed it to become Karen's office. Her steps ring down on me below her as she paces over the new hard and resistant floor with a 100 year guarantee.

Yesterday I sat in my armchair from Acacia Avenue for what seemed like hours staring at the paintings stacked against the walls. Here in the room designated to be my studio, I cannot hang them on the screen walls for others to enjoy their colours and shapes and stories, creating links between paintings and people. They can only be perched on easels as if still unfinished. I tried to find the energy to fuse mental, emotional and physical strength into some sort of creative arrangement. Instead I found myself fixating on trivia: a scratch on a picture; the sag in a canvas; the hem of my new trousers unravelling and leaf mould on a rose bush outside the studio window. I hadn't forgotten to take my stressless pill. The weekly one is, on medical advice, sufficient. They are free and issued to all and sundry. Most people probably take them. It is something one doesn't talk about. I wish there was a similar one for Foxy, who either snuggles up to me or walks round the house sniffing, tail between his legs.

Now during the run-up to the elections Martha and company often congregate here. There is nowhere to escape the hubbub. Her capsule is small, so our living space suits her better. Back in our new home, temporarily roosting, she is taking us over. Or my invisible share of the place. Karen is helping Jan, Martha's agent, run the campaign. Roland often turns up. Even though he was elected to a safe seat in the last elections, he should not spend so much time distracting her. And partying. He has read my thoughts.

'I can still run my campaign from anywhere through my virtual office,' which he frequently accesses on our screens. 'Don't worry, Eliza,' he adds with an internet star's frank smile, 'everything's galloping along on my turf, ready for the last spurt'. He tips his sleek head back in an open-throated laugh, rather like my neighbours' daughters. I object to an unsolicited view of others' tonsils but suspect my averted glance is misinterpreted. Of course I approve of him and the advice he is giving Martha for her first campaign, but his mannered courtesies make me grit my teeth, especially as Karen finds he is 'just perfect'.

'It's part of the Roland Wrightson package,' she informs me, 'and if it suits Martha, it's fine for us, isn't it?' He is certainly prepossessing in the way people are judged now, as he has the sort of physique that leaps out at you from the screens - lithe, tall enough to balance Martha without dwarfing her. Each massages the other's image. They have devised an excellent double act for the internet campaign to improve her chances from average to likely.

Slender males like Nicholas don't conform to current taste as defined by advertising and fashion. Perhaps Helen is attracted by the difference. His intelligent face doesn't actually put people off, but disturbs them. Martha included. She assumed she knew her childhood playmate and half twin, and was annoyed more than hurt when he didn't offer to help her.

'I can't help with your campaign,' he told Martha when busy moving us here. 'It all happens on the internet - hustings, interviews, debates, policy bullets. No leaflets to deliver, no doorstep contact or constituency tours. It's all done by crunching voters into numbers; the only human contact is with internet helpers in your election office.'

'Then why can't you help us find the internet disfranchised voters for me to contact?' she countered. Apparently they are the Big Question of these elections. With wrist wordfrees almost universal, is anyone still unconnected to the internet? Shopping malls all have free big-screen internet outlets catering for travellers away from home as do cafés and restaurants. For some years now zone governments have been handing grants out to people who can't afford internet links, windmills, solar panels and all the other updating paraphernalia. I overheard Martha telling Karen that she tried to involve Sister Julian. Martha promised to find out whether her refugees could vote, as residents in church property. The proviso was that Sister Julian must be free to respect the refugees' right not to tell her if they hadn't voted, even if it meant that they were breaking the law. Nicholas said he could hardly canvas colleagues in the lab building's Common Room or Helen's friends. It would border on the insulting. Soon after that he stopped dropping in. I caught sight of him recently while exercising Foxy. He was walking slower than usual, as if he was puzzled or upset. When I almost caught up I realised he was trailing a man talking to a child as they moved, side by side, down the street, and watching the father occasionally touching his son's shoulder, ruffling his hair and bending towards the upturned face. Odd.

* * * *

The noise in this house before the elections prevents me sleeping. Nor can I stop myself replaying Nicholas, the father and son in the street. Does a mother's love for an adult child really depend on shared interests? What do I share with Nicholas? Or Martha? Do we have anything to talk about? Karen does. With Martha. But what about me and them? These questions churn around in my mind and I cannot find a way to stop them.

Perhaps I lack clarity about what their lives mean now, in the future, and about the flux and flow of their time, anchored as I am by the past. I would like to talk to Nicholas about this, with his command of mind over matter, and the sheer beauty of those expressions, equations and formulae: symbols of creation even when you can't figure them out. Patterns describing existence. His words.

I have digressed. Martha would say my mind is wandering, probably the first signs of senility. She knows exactly where she wants to go: beyond our zone government to the Goodwill World Parliament. No lack of ambition! Let us hope for all of us that she succeeds so this house – capsule calms down and she becomes busy elsewhere.

Nicholas wanted to know how I heard of Magnus. I knew him as I knew stars and starlets. He was once an important part of my imaginative world way back when Nicholas and Martha were young. Like millions of others I was intrigued by his medley of music, dance, history and drama in videosequences that could be streamed and linked to later additions to create a sort of cumulative masterpiece. It nourished my eyes and ears and inspired me. Nothing was too old or too new for him to attempt. It recalled collective experiences from the Ancient Greeks onwards, maybe even before them, back somewhere in India or China down to our times. His videosequences were posted online and then went viral. There was also something about one and three, then multiples and additions. All this was mimed and danced on a bare set with lights and colours brilliantly modulated; there was nothing garish, nothing forgettable. Then he stopped. Just like that. End of story. Now one cannot buy his videosequences, not even on the *intermart.com.* No one since him has been able to capture the genius of past time and mould it into visual creations that become your future memories.

Nicholas said he would take me to meet Magnus, but I refused. I do not want to talk in a halting, incomplete way, to a younger person who has inspired me. It would sound too embarrassingly trite, especially now that he is older and past it. The dancing at any rate. No.

Somehow I must leave. Get out. Away. I could take my electroVespavan and head north into the wilds without anyone noticing. Why not?

10

Spring

Martha *i-witnessMAR754.futurepast.com*

Six-thirty on election morning! A day when my dream becomes everyday reality or my hopes are shattered - to piece together as best I can. Without leaving bed, I direct my thoughts to pulse screens into life around me. The first people in the streets are being interviewed; most are a bit dazed at being asked so early how they have voted. Others just smile or say they will vote after work.

I slept badly. So did mother. She is up early. Lips pursed, T-reader beside her, she is watching the first commentary on the screen section she has programmed into the Goodwill World Parliament election channel. Another section shows my office, where volunteers on the night shift are about to leave. The first calculations reveal that 48% of the early voters had ticked the box by NONE OF THE ABOVE CANDIDATES. Consternation round the election office, but it isn't long after sunrise and few have voted.

'55% of the electorate must vote for someone,' she reminds me, 'otherwise the election is invalid. 43% blanks in this constituency so far, and you're just ahead. Only just.'

'Too early to be sure of anything.' I try to think positively.

'I'll get you some breakfast. The usual?' I nod and she mutters something about obligatory voting being supposed to ensure 'a good turnout'. Voting now couldn't be easier. Just access and fill in the online ballot form, synchronized worldwide, using the individual voting code issued to everyone over 16. There has been a protest about prisoners voting, so prison computers are being temporarily disabled today.

Mother says she has always been a dreamer, projecting scenarios into the future, morphing herself into a famous chef or the first female butler to preside over state banquets. Then I was born. From the very first she always thought I'd stand out in some role, though she didn't imagine it'd be politics. My dream may be coming true now.

When I started campaigning, she was the one to suggest I should tap into people's discontent and channel their frustrated energy into support for policies that pleased them. I doubted it would be possible. Jan, my election agent, doesn't access sites like *moanersandgroaners.com*. She has her time cut out to sift through the obvious ones, however fatuous, indecent or ridiculous - the barometers, she says, of future preoccupations. All provide useful fodder for her to chew over. I am aware of international policy projections, though she encourages me to focus on local issues to increase my chances in the zone I hope to represent. The Goodwill World Parliament election is far harder than the local zone one, but nothing ventured, nothing gained.

Jan has gleaned most from *disgusted.com*. I expected more males than females on that site. Not so. Indignant females rage at time-worn issues like being sold seedless tangerines with seeds, or at inaccurate labelling and so on. Others on *amazing.com* are suspicious of being cheated by the shift in their clothes size. Online providers have been sending them their usual size but the garments inexplicably float around them as if they had lost weight. Helen tells me that it empowers women and makes them feel, as they try them on, that they are a size smaller, so more attractive and in control of their bodies. They protest in surprise, though secretly flattered when returning the garment to purchase a smaller size.

'And if they haven't really lost weight?' mum butted in rather unimaginatively.

'Does that matter?' Helen smiled with a professional assurance that rather grated. 'Sow an idea, and if it bears fruit and makes people happy, so much the better! If not, too bad!'

Mother shrugged her shoulders as if to say, 'Your line, not mine.'

*****

Eight o'clock. We're in the election office. A section of one wall screen is permanently tuned to the Town Hall, our mayor and his election officials. They are wandering aimlessly in and out. The other walls are covered in tilecasts, the size of small book covers, from election offices in our zone's constituencies. They have candidates' names with the number of votes already cast below them. Roland's tilecast enlarges from time to time, with him smiling out at us in close-up or turning to shake a hand, pat a shoulder or kiss an admiring female. Mother likes him. He's my latest admirer. No more than five minutes' full screen exposure is allowed to any one candidate before the tilecast diminishes back to the size of all the others. Candidates seem to find little to say that is new - except for me, though I may flag as the day wears on.

*****

Ten o'clock. The voting is slow. Ballot papers came online a minute after midnight, but Goodwill World Parliament voters outside our time zone

- in Australia, say - can vote long before us. I chose to stay with mother last night as Roland was in his constituency and I didn't want to fret on my own. Nor did she, as it happened.

Mum did a flit yesterday while mother and I were in the election office winding up my campaign. What an unkind time to choose, when she knew we couldn't do anything about it on Election Day. 'I'm leaving for a break in the countryside.' Just a brief note left on a sheet of kitchen roll. That's all. Not even her name. It upset mother and infuriated me.

Wherever mum is, she can vote through her wordfree, assuming she has taken it. We have tried to contact her, but she isn't answering. It's a problem with people like her and Nicholas who choose not to have a wrist inset. So inconsiderate. Mum knows that we're anxious about her, and she takes herself off just before the most important day in my life. I would have reminded her to vote. She can't have forgotten, but one never knows with her. I sometimes wonder about her mental state. She wasn't really upset or angry about their new home in Beech Drive, just disgruntled. She finds it difficult to adapt to innovation. Anything aimed at improving her quality of life seems to depress her. Mother and I keep on trying to help, but it's not easy. Nicholas is as wrapped up in his work as mum is in her art and music, though she hasn't held a brush or touched the piano keys since the move.

I can't afford any more time thinking about her. I'm supposed to be planning the post- election party, but it depends on the results. They will come soon after ten in the evening when the unused ballot forms are withdrawn, and fines issued to those who haven't voted. There may be additional problems like virus vengeance, when rivals or lunatics try to destroy votes for a particular candidate. We shall see. My office is small but mother will help me cram it full of faces as celebrated as possible, as well as international guests. There will be an intercast immediately the results are known, with the mayor coordinating the images from the Town Hall, and then the party begins. Or not, as the case may be.

Worrying about mum keeps nudging the election out of my mind, on this of all days when I need my wits about me. Mum was never open about what she wanted to do, hiding with her canvases in the attic at Acacia Avenue while mother ran the house. She has no right to be moaning around in my head on this day, of all days.

* * * * *

Midday, and nothing much is changing. I'm closing my eyes to take a break from the restless election specials on the screens to imagine my fate at 10 this evening, only ten hours away. A new life could be starting for me as a key player on the international stage. A new role too for mother. I imagine her smiling as a vast crowd of supporters look at me, slimly elegant as I step into a monopod, bound for our city hall on the first rung of my new career: politician in both our zone government and the Goodwill World Parliament! My eyes are open now and I'm cautioning myself: don't run ahead of your hopes, Martha! I can't stop twisting a lock of hair just like when I was a child. Mother's worried I look tired already. She says my voice, normally soft, now has grit in it.

'They have the chance to vote without leaving home, so why aren't people doing it?'

'They are,' she says, being logical.

'If you call a vote for nobody a vote.'

'Well, strictly speaking, it's a choice.'

'Not a democratic one.' I'm irritated.

'Only 32% blank votes cast up to now in your constituency.'

'That means 32 out of every hundred voters in this constituency aren't voting for me.'

'Or for Sebastian Hollaway and the Freedom Party.' My main rival, known here as Sobaway, is a local businessman, successful, dapper and given to compassionate statements that his listeners take more literally than he does. His is a patient ear, a kindly expression, his hands less 'on' than expected. His credibility has worn thin while I have been playing on the local need for change. I'm lively, practical, a doer. My work underlines this. My aim is to bring not just better but the very best housing for all. Capsules are the answer and, being manufactured locally, they provide more employment than my rival's business interests outsourced to Afghanistan. We get on well enough, but our appearances together on neighbourhoodcasts, mother says, contrast my neat outfit, clear colours, and firm but not permanent smile when answering questions, with Sobaway's worn-out pleasantries and studied casualness. He is just that bit too plump to sport the latest nantung cloth of strengthened fibres that has consigned denim to history. His hair is thinning and, in spite of the message that his heart is in the right place, Sobaway, at 45, is already yesterday's man.

At the last election over a third of the members of the Goodwill World Parliament were women. Men no longer have a built-in advantage, but even so, I am running my first campaign for the GWP. Affable, accommodating, ineffectual Sebastian Hollaway at this point, is just ahead of me, but only just, at the halfway mark. Most vote after work. I am trying not to look at his tilecast, but I do. Sobaway is acting confidently playing his 'you know me' card reassuringly as his aides glance casually at other tilecasts. Jan is cheerfully straightening up my election office. Her helpers are looking at projections and trends in other constituencies. The day is sagging and the future is still to be won.

* * * * *

Fourteen hours. I prefer arranging events well in advance so I can sit back and enjoy them, but today it's impossible. Mother is ready with all the e-messages to send to her secret contacts. She's trying so carefully to avoid sounding uncertain or negative.

* * * * *

Sixteen hours. I've been out jogging, hood over head so I'm not recognised, leaving Jan and mother to manage the office. Back, I'm less fidgety.

'How's Roland doing?' I ask them - a tactless question perhaps.

'Can't you see? His tilecast is twentieth on the right of the third row down. He's the sitting member and that's an advantage. In addition he's male, good-looking, popular and in the lead. His rivals lack charisma, and that counts a lot.'

Jan is calling me. My tilecast turn has just come round, earlier than expected, and I'm in the bathroom. Mother goes on screen with Jan, who has more energy than presence. It's irritating to come out and see mother mouthing strangely, emphasising words too much, rounding her lips and blinking more than normal. I'm not happy about it, but my tilecast time has ended. I'll have another chance later on.

*****

Seventeen-thirty hours. Just what I hoped would happen. People are back from work, turning on their computers and hearing the latest on the voting. That reminds them to mark their ballot paper waiting to be downloaded when they type in their voting code. The evening surge is starting. I try to smile brightly. My total votes have just topped Sobaway's!

'Martha Middlethorpe is now leading in her constituency,' mother murmurs excitedly. I swiftly move in for a screen close-up on my tilecast, hoping I'll soon have my turn. Here it comes!

'Thank you, thank you for your vote, and for the support I hope you will give me if you have yet to vote.' That's the cue for the last spurt. My tilecast diminishes and in zooms Sebastian Hollaway enlarged on his. Jan is screwing up her eyes and gritting her teeth over her personalised screen section as she summons up the last-stage program. It's primed to calculate how many have yet to vote, to flash out reminders and messages over their ballot papers and beat off possible virus attacks from Sobaway's lot or just simple spoilers. His office might have found a better program than Jan's, but not one, I hope, to mess up the x's by my name, maybe even shift them. Updates happen by the minute. Jan's ballot messages are honest. We have agreed that fair is fair, and all they will flash over the unsent ballot forms is a reminder to undecided voters that I am young, active and the voice of the future, while a non-vote – that is an X by NONE OF THE ABOVE

CANDIDATES - would be a nail in the coffin of democracy. To be fair, we don't mention Sobaway.

* * * * *

Twenty hours. Two hours to go before the result. The screens seem to be closing in on me, my heart thumps, and everyone blurs into grey shadows swirling, detaching, amorphous. I'm ahead: I'll win! I shut my eyes. An intense shudder of joy mingled with fear. Mother is there on the tilecast behind me. I wonder if she and mum ever feel like this about Nicholas? Their son, my brother, a glum genius hiding the theory that might solve the world's energy problems deep inside his wordfree monitor. He is the only one with the key. How can his family dream him into the future if we can't comprehend what his work is all about?

An unprecedented number of viral spoiler videos have vitiated the campaign. Nothing can be found to block them. An anonymous internet army has run a dirty campaign against my Serendipity Party. Political sites have mushroomed to counter the contagion, but there's confusion on the web with candidates showcasing their own policy messages through tangled channels of communication. A medium without morals sending out mixed messages.

* * * * *

Twenty-thirty hours. I have been saving the remaining messages for my tilecast appearances, two in the last hour. Everything was prepared beforehand, but I've exhausted my material too quickly. The experienced Jan has been sandwiching my appearances with pre-recorded interviews, just in case. Helen was persuaded to help with an interview and here is Sister Julian talking to me about the refugees and their plans for a self-sustaining settlement in this zone. I hoped to have a clip with Magnus and took some images with my wrist inset when he wasn't looking, but I ditched them in the end. Your time together with someone else belongs to both of you, the Party's legal expert advised me.

*****

Twenty forty-five. More votes are trickling in and I'm still ahead. Not by much. Jan has finally run out of pre-recorded interviews and ideas, so she's walking round the office asking for ours. Journalists on the neighbourhoodcasts, like the international political sites, are grabbing interviews where they can: in the streets, outside gastrohubs all over the constituency, with an occasional flash of what is happening in the Town Hall. Nothing much. All the candidates are expected to be there, but I shall only go if Sobaway does. Jan is undecided. They have a huge screen in the Hall and can easily conference on it, so why should I, or Sobaway for that matter, move away from our respective power bases and party venues? The returning officer can announce results below the candidates' tilecasts and on the political websites.

Too many tilecasts and political sites are confusing the voting public. Too much choice - is it heresy to say this? Jan's assistants have been sifting through them all day, downloading key issues revealed by public response and not identified by the candidates. What use is all this if I lose? My lead is still wafer thin; the ballots are registered electronically and allow for no margin of error as in antiquated vote-counting methods.

My team has decided to concentrate on the most watched site, the public one without advertisements so, allegedly, there is no bias. It is deceptively simple. Brief soundbites and lots of vacuous election entertainment, usually anecdotes about funny things that have happened to candidates while electioneering. They seem designed to take people's minds off the serious matters in hand. It's the most popular website for precisely that reason. The results in this constituency are reflecting the situation elsewhere: The Serendipity Party is just ahead, but the Freedom Party may hold on to power with the help of smaller parties. Not a pleasant prospect.

*****

Twenty-one hours. Time drags. The polls close in one hour's time and all the screens do is to burble on about what will happen to the 2% who haven't registered their electronic ballot forms. Even the homeless have been issued with these forms, their temporary addresses being the nearest gastrohub where they can use the computer to vote. What more can be done to mobilise the voting public? By now we have an unprecedented 98% turnout and roughly 38% have voted for no candidate. They will be criticised, mostly by the Union of World Citizens, for their fickleness, ineptitude, social cussedness or just laziness, though it is a valid option. Was mum one of them? I'm postponing all thought of her until tomorrow.

*****

Twenty-two hours. The election is over and I'm elected to the Goodwill World Parliament! By how much we'll know in a few minutes' time.

We're all hugging and almost weeping with relief, but I can't be caught off guard. The intercasting eye is still on me while I thank everyone in the office and out there on the web. I'm undecided about whether to go to the Town Hall. Everything will be on my intercast anyway. Is Sobaway going? Does it matter? Will it be interpreted as a snub if I don't go? I keep on changing my mind. Knocks are echoing up from the street door. Knock, knock. Here's Helen and a trail of colleagues and friends. Knock, knock, and a burst of noisy Serendipity party workers. Knock, and Dom Ross Mackenzie enters alone. Why is he here? I assumed he supported Sobaway. His Freedom Party is financed by international business. Knock, knock and a steady stream of all sorts of people flows in. A helper goes down to deal with the door and another one web-orders more champagne and party packs.

Hustle and bustle: exhilaration and exhaustion. We're celebrating, cast on to screens worldwide by the tele-imaging eye.

* * * * *

Twenty-two thirty. With absolutely all the registered votes now calculated, we are beamed into the Town Hall where my victory will be formally announced, unless there is a challenge. Sebastian Hollaway is glumly walking up the steps to the Town Hall.

Should I go too? I've already changed into the dress Helen has picked out for me, all flame-patterned flounces. It's just what I need to celebrate, now it's all over and I've won!

'No, no, no, don't go!' shouts the assembling company, invited or not, 'it's your chance to celebrate with us here!'

'All of you quickly face the tele-imager,' I tell them. The fairweatherers look embarrassed, Dom Ross included, and quickly try to present their profiles only, assiduously turning to talk to a neighbour. Now the tilecast is being maximised and our office background vaporised to merge into the fine mouldings and panelling of the grandiose 19th-century Town Hall. We virtually enter it.

We're now gazing at ourselves crowding the dais end of the great chamber, a motley contrast to the staid burghers weighed down by chains of office in portraits on the wall above us. The Mayor, the Returning Officer and their respective teams, have quickly moved in front of our enlarged tilecast, the Mayor motioning the candidates present to join him. I'm skilfully cut forward to their level and placed in virtual proximity to Sebastian Hollaway. Silence. The total number of votes cast is announced; each candidate's name is called out in turn, head nodding impassively at the number of votes cast, then finally,

'Martha Middlethorpe, already our member for the zone government, is therefore elected deputy for this constituency to the Goodwill World Parliament.' An outburst of noisy euphoria in our election office is visually recorded for posterity, the sound thinly conveyed to the chamber. It's the moment I've dreamed of for so long! The Mayor and the Returning Officer turn to shake my hand and exchange a few words while usefully standing in front of my image and blocking the tele-imager's slight mismatching of the virtual handshakes. All the banal utterances are clearly recorded.

After a few seconds the Town Hall weblink is discontinued before anyone might realise there are scarcely more than a dozen people in the vast chamber. Such are the marvels of modern image making that one can outwit most people who, in any case, don't really care. What matters are the votes, who's in, who's out, and life whirls on in our rave-up backing all the screen messages now tumbling into my website. We had hopefully booked a 'fair-weather-foul inflatable add-on street venue' for a party. It's already screenlinked to the election office for all to see the reactions, were I to win.

It's thrilling. Verbal congratulations are insufficient nowadays. Videopods are rapidly alighting onscreen while my election technician, Mustafa, frantically downloads and pastes the most important ones on my tilecast. We maximise them on the largest screenspace, obliterating a whole wall of telecasts from other constituencies. Too bad.

'Here's Roland's tilecast!' I shout out in the hubbub. 'He's back in and congratulating me.' I don't mention his reduced majority. Local dignitaries are screened forward towards us but go largely unnoticed in the excitement of everyone writhing and stamping here in my election office and out in the street to the latest drong hits from Helen's numerous pellets. I note they are interspersed with concoctions from the emerging group, Sighlady, crooning songs laced with sentimentality. Most like a bit of fun if they can get it, except for Ross Mackenzie. He stands, tall, aloof and alone. Why has he come and why does he stay?

'At last!' Here comes the videopod mother is expecting.

'Good evening, Martha!' and a familiar figure is rapidly enlarged to my size so I am now standing beside Anya Lo Yin. The US President can only join our party for one minute, so I introduce Jan, Mustafa, my helpers and Karen, while Dom Ross Mackenzie neatly inserts himself on the other side of the President hoping for a virtual handshake and verbal exchange.

'Congratulations, Martha. You have come from nowhere, just like me, and won on your merits.'

'President -'

'Anya, please.'

'Anya, I pledge my support for your Worldwide Energy Pact and your World Peace Consolidation Plan - food and water and technological aid in exchange for a total enforcement of the arms amnesty and free and fair elections for incorrupt leaders.'

'Women can peacefully change the world,' Anya continues.

'And nurture it…' I enhance Anya's theme with the president's favourite word. Anya is waving goodbye with airborne kisses to my faithful, a forest of waving arms.

Mother arranged this. She last saw Anya over 15 years ago when she was showcasing Chinatown in San Francisco and buying Californian wines. Anya gave her the figurines that mum dislikes so much. She would ... but where on earth is mum? Mother has masterminded my campaign almost more than Jan and Mustafa, and has another star appearance arranged for me. I'm waiting for it now, standing beside Mustafa, our brilliant technician.

'Let up, Karen,' he grumbles, tired I suppose, and irritated at not being able to join in the fun around him. 'Haven't we enough going on to Martha's tilecast? I need time to debrief the genuine verbal and visual communications, not to mention weeding out the virus jokes and webclogging. Look at all of it here.'

I am looking, at the videopods in particular, and here it is!

'Here, Mustafa, quick. Access it!' The image is fuzzy at first, then Chang Lin advances smiling, hand extended, the sensometer transmitting her warmth, vibrancy and the tang of perfume or the scented candles flickering behind her in some sort of shrine. China has certainly veered away from the political strictures her parents grew up with.

I'm speeding across the office to share the screen with President Chang Lin.

'Martha Middlethorpe. I congratulate you on winning your place in the Goodwill World Parliament as well as your Zone Government. I know your Serendipity Party shares our values.'

'Of peace,' I add before the President can continue, aware of this statement's impact on whoever might be viewing her tilecast, especially the other successful Serendipity Party candidates.

'And of happiness and good fortune.'

'Yes, and above all peace,' I repeat, smiling back half looking at President Chang Lin in the way public figures do so that at least their three-quarter face can be seen by the viewers instead of a profile or the side of a head.

'And prosperity-'

'Indeed,' I smile on,' and – '

'- and longevity.' All Lin says is what Chinese philosophers have written on their prayer scrolls and repeated for centuries. I pause at the longevity. More than 50% of the world's population is over 60, and many of those will live to be centenarians. I continue. 'Yes, but for all you wish to come true, there must be peace – and population control - are as important as having air to breathe, food to eat.' The Chinese president smiles even more and agrees.

'My farewell to you and to your party. May we all strengthen peace in the world.' Some of the election party try to smile and wave while mother moves in closer to shake Chang Lin's hand before she fades away. They first met twenty years ago when Lin stayed with a neighbour. She had come to study English and business at our university and they have kept in touch.

*****

One thirty. We are partying into the small hours. I snatch a moment to sit down and voice Roland.

'He's not coming tonight,' I whisper to mother.

'Difficult. He must be at a similar party.' I'm concerned about all the adoring females he's handling - all as part of the job, of course.

'Men let you down,' mother warns me, 'look at your brother Nicholas. He could have waited for this and left later for Africa.' She knows I miss him, and resent him not being here for my greatest test, and now my triumph. Yet mum too has deserted mother and me. That snag in my heart again.

Shut them out, slam the door to your heart – mum and Nicholas with all the males that rock your universe. The presidents of the two most powerful political blocks in the world are female and they both virtually came to my victory celebration. Shut the windows too while all is well; keep your mind closed, uncluttered, unfettered and unworried for this charmed night at least. Dive deep into the heart of time and stop it beating. Relish the present before it escapes. Grasp the instant between past and future and revel in it.

Tomorrow who knows? Forget for a while the 2% or so who have broken the law and not voted - probably including mum and Nicholas. They're tomorrow's problem. Wrench yourself away from the so-called blank returns, the 38% who have legally participated by making no choice. An ill omen?

NONE OF THE ABOVE CANDIDATES X

Why bother about them? Dive into the body heat shimmering around the whooping, cavorting, drinking, chattering, nibbling, all-embracing crush of my supporters.

'Martha, here's your champagne.'

'To Martha! All shout together, Martha! TO YOUR SUCCESS.' Now and forever. If only.

Or...

BREAKING NEWS

DIFFERENCES OVER DISPOSAL OF NUCLEAR WEAPONS RESOLVED

Concern over effective means to verify that all remaining stockpiles of nuclear weapons have been disabled has persisted long after the **worldwide agreement to destroy them** and the formation of a **Goodwill World Parliament peace-keeping inspectorate.** It has been monitoring the total extermination of all nuclear or chemical weapons of war after the arms amnesty, so that no research or manufacturing capacity remains. The GWP is convening nuclear scientists to report whether dismantled nuclear weapons can be recycled and to ensure any relevant manufacturing capacity still in existence is being converted to peaceful use.

worldaroundyounews.com

11

Spring

Nicholas *i-witnessNIC227.futurepast.com*

Everything undulates as thermal currents ruffle the haze over this endless plain. Too much heat here to waste; excessive cold elsewhere in this unbalanced world. I'm on the veranda of a wooden bungalow, dazed by the heat I should be harnessing. After dark the light flickers. The aging solar tiles can barely provide enough energy. They're unreliable. Flawed technology. My wordfree monitor needs recharging. If I had a wordfree inserted into my wrist like everyone else, my pulse would charge it. Instead this slim wordfree monitor, a little smaller than the old mobile phones, has to be charged. Energy is required to create energy. Sun, photosynthesis: vegetation bursts into life. Sun drunk on earth's moisture: drought. The land is dying in front of me and there's nothing I can do without the energy I came to create. Two years ago a meteor struck this plain and buried a village in its crater. The survivors fled, hit by flying fragments and fireballs. Hell on earth, they call it. Susannah, one of the few inhabitants left, looks after my bungalow. She stayed to be close to her family, alive or dead.

If what I am doing has any sense, it's here I should start experimenting. My lab hasn't arrived. I'm stripped mentally naked, idle here and simmering mindlessly in the untapped, desiccating, powerless energy of the sun. Without it, we and all forms of life would die. I must create some sense from all this.

If Esther had been sent out with me I would have been happier. I should have insisted. Instead Celia came to meet me. Unless she is communicating information or finding out something for you, she isn't a person who impresses herself on your memory. She's like a negative to Helen's positive, the shadowy pre-print stage of the old photos mum showed me of her dreamlike childhood.

Celia is easily lost in the crowd, though less so here in Africa. I followed her pale blue blouse through the colourful jostling at the only railway station for miles around. People here like her, probably because she is unassertive, undemanding, un-everything. She's even smaller than most of them. That's odd. She can never have been undernourished. They look at her mousy hair, plain face, drab clothes and trust her. She's Chief Walanka's key advisor.

'When will the lab arrive?' I asked her this morning.

'When it will,' she answered, calmly irritating. 'It's been delayed for final checks at the airport. It will soon come to Mybeki by rail.' It is the nearest town with some semblance of a working electricity network, ten kilometres away as the crow flies, but almost twice as far by the road curving over this meteor-scarred moonscape.

* * * * *

More days spent sitting in another space and time, my mind as barren as the landscape. I'm slightly restless, not unhappy. I thought I would be miserable. I ought to be. No Helen, no Martha, no parents, no Magnus. This is the bungalow where he lived. It's the only suitable building in the area. Celia brought me here as the obvious place to stay. Magnus supported the

Mybeki area as the preferred site: remote, unpopulated and not known for its natural beauty, though some might find a meteor-ravaged landscape has its own desperate allure. It should have attracted geologists and astrophysicists. They came for a few years afterwards, Celia tells me, but now prefer to go on moonshots. So much the better. I mentally ticked off my requests to Magnus: isolated place; plenty of sun all year round; nobody to offend so no protesters; water. That's missing. I've no one to ask except Celia and Susannah, who uses an artesian well sunk with money from the meteorstrophe appeal.

Is it wise of me to trust Magnus and his Reaching Out network with the whole trial? Others, not just Dom Ross Mackenzie, are pursuing me. I could pick and choose. I believe it will all turn out right when I wake up on a fresh morning, that is, until the rising heat makes me throb and stream with sweat. Then Susannah calls me in from the verandah to lie in a hammock, damp, dozy and despairing. When the power fails, she pulls the strings of two fans like the predatory wings of a giant eagle. Afternoon slumbers into evening, when coolness breathes over the boulders and crazed earth while the sun sinks blood red behind dark hills. Something must come out of all this.

'There are sacred seams of water,' Celia tells me, '"the sacred river, ran through caverns measureless to man" -

'"- down to a sunless sea" - '*Kubla Khan* was one of the poems mum read to me before I went to sleep. Celia smiles.

' "So twice five miles of fertile ground

With walls and towers were girded round." '

Not quite the same here, unfortunately.

‘Once all this - ' she opens her arms, mouth wide - ' was covered by forests. The Zueto and other tribes cleared it for grazing. Their savannah, before the meteorstrophe.'

Yesterday I asked Susannah whether her village was near a spring.

'No.' Susannah's eyes say so much more than she can express. 'I to water. I return water in pitcher.' She tapped the crown of her head, 'and demon come.’ Her language has, Celia says, an untranslatable word that is used here for a meteor, literally a spirit in an evil star. ‘There,’ we were on the veranda, Susannah pointing into the distance, ‘the land cut, make hole’.

'Why did your chief and his tribe settle there?'

'Our spirits there. This our place.' She looked as if about to weep. 'Now away!' and she waved her arms, 'men and little boys and girls'. She held up her hands, ten fingers with three curled to leave seven, her family I imagine. Five more curled down to leave two. They would be Susannah and her daughter Anna. Some of the younger women survived because they had left to fill their pitchers at the spring. Old women, watching the small children and menfolk, herding cattle, were swept into the crater.

My lab still hasn’t arrived. A pattern is shaping my idleness. I walk over the land taking my forked stick to ward off snakes, tapping it from side to side as Susannah had showed me, like a blind man tentatively marking out his path into the future.

* * * * *

Two days ago I think it was - days are all so similar that I only blog occasionally - Susannah took me to the edge of the abyss where her village had been. She came for me just as the sun was rising and we walked towards it together. It was about the same time of day that the meteor had struck. This time she wasn't balancing a pitcher on her head.

'Rain,' she said, 'no today. Rain good. Savannah green, cows happy. I walk heart up.' She stretched her arms above her head, smiled and danced a few steps. All had been well with her world just before the meteorstrophe when she was carrying water. She seems to live in a string of present moments shining bright in her mind, not set in a past or a future; just there, being.

'That's their language,' Celia says. 'It's embedded in now. Past and future are lived in the present. Not a bad philosophy, at least for some parts of one's existence.' It explains Susannah's strange way of intertwining joy and grief when she ran towards the edge of a chasm that was her village. The pity of it all, I thought, staring down a jagged slope to the dust and rocks that covered whatever remained of her home. Susannah raised her arms above the rubble and began a chant that rose into a song ending in triumphant notes hurled across the crater to ricochet from hill to hill, ulululuting as I had never heard before.

'They answer,' she said. 'I hear my man, my babes, my people. The spirits hear. They speak. My man tell me of song story. Houarh, houarh, houarh! Song man no good. Houarh, houarh, houarh!' I had no idea what she meant, but stayed silent beside her, aware of the rising sun warming my back as we returned to the bungalow.

* * * * *

Yesterday morning, or maybe earlier, I took my forked stick and tapped my way further along the rim of the crater to stop at stones piled up to form a cairn with a sealed photo of a woman in its base. A circle of stones and another incomplete one surrounded it. There were some cactus flowers in an empty jam jar. I stooped to look at her. A smile, a generous face fading fast. No name or date. I added a stone to the incomplete circle and stood motionless for a while until the sun glared at me and I retreated to the bungalow.

I've asked Susannah to take me to the new village, but nothing has happened. So, while waiting, I think into my wordfree, working out calculations, trying other ways of looking at the coming tests, turning them over and over again in my mind when a new angle arises or a different possibility nudges into my conscious thoughts. Or I play patience until the sun sets. Why upset the natural order of things? Rise with the sun and… well, even in the hot season, no one would want to go to bed at sunset. What do the villagers do? *Make love*, would be Helen's reply - I can imagine her looking at me laughing and longing for night. She has her wordfree contraceptive – do they here as well? *Make babies*, would be Celia's answer. No fuss. Just as it is, and on to the next matter on her agenda. Does she have any fun?

I'm sitting inside the mosquito net I've rigged up with poles on the verandah? Here I can watch the sun, a huge red ball often with a flame-coloured halo, sinking behind the distant hills. I could have a whole cage constructed for me to sit inside and avoid stings and bites, watched from outside by a battalion of buzzers and flutterers from mosquitoes to moths the size of small birds. I hope I'm not here long enough to need one. Susannah is inside cooking my supper on Prometheus's gift – fire.

The sun has set and I feel acutely alone.

*****

This morning I went to Mybeki. Still no lab. Celia asked me where I'd like to set it up. I'd prefer to be quite isolated, not to be disturbed. I must check the receptor is sited as far as possible from any living creatures. I don't say so, but if my calculations are even slightly inaccurate, the concentrated energy in the beam could cause grievous harm.

*****

Celia is driving me to Susannah's new village.

'What did Susannah's husband do?'

'He was a shaman and recounted the story of their people. He healed bodies and souls, as shamans are supposed to do. The narrative is connected with the healing process. People outside see them as witch doctors casting spells. They are not without their uses.'

The village has been rebuilt about a kilometre from the bungalow, the same distance roughly from its former site, now inside the crater. Mud huts with straw and twig thatch are cool and dark inside, not airless like my bungalow. Susannah invites us into her spotless home, a minimalist's dream: beaten earth floor vigorously brushed; pots hanging from a beam; quilts and thick blue plastic sheets folded over another beam and her clothes on a metal clothes-stand, like the ones found outside shops in Mybeki; broom, dustpan and dusters hung outside under the eaves. Every space is carefully thought out.

A tall girl with a steady unsmiling expression is standing facing the door, the only source of light. She would have been old enough to carry a pitcher on her head when it happened. That had saved her.

'Anna is studying in Mybeki,' Celia says. 'She hopes to become a teacher.' Anna nods slightly, and then continues staring. Perhaps, unlike her mother, she feels their tragic past is unredeemable, a dead weight lying on the present. As I expected, Celia has come to see Chief Walanka about inserting more pulse-charged wrist wordfrees and setting up a community bus service to take the children to school. There are not enough teachers, and classes need to be smaller. She also wants his approval for the receptor and his suggestion for a site.

I'm not sure exactly what is happening to my project. Celia must be in contact with the relevant agencies in this zone, but Reaching Out tries to avoid official channels where funds and valuable hard and software might still slip into the hands of corrupt leaders.

'I'm surprised they don't build in stone,' I say looking at the cluster of huts, 'there are plenty of boulders'.

'Stones are used for cattle wind and sun breaks. The tribes around here were nomads until recently. Didn't you feel how well ventilated Susannah's house is? It's never really hot or cold. When it rains the eaves are wide and the thatch expands to keep everything dry.'

On our way to the Chief I asked Celia about Susannah's husband, the shaman.

'The storyteller's wife helps him dramatise tales of adventure' Celia said, 'fighting demons and wild beasts and other tribes who try to steal their cattle, and of terrible disasters, all overcome with the help of the spirits that protect them. They are summoned through these tales. All the shaman needs are a few props, simple objects like carved sticks, gourds, feathers and flowers - and his wife, of course! You must have seen it all on one of those internet clips.' Yes, all but the spirits.

Susannah had to dance the spiritual transfer, as Celia put it, from her deceased husband through her to the new shaman storyteller.

'Tell me how Susannah did it.'

Celia is no storyteller. You have to prise what happened out of her, unlike Helen who brims over with things to say. She can even chatter too much. I miss her!

'Not now. I have to see the shaman before meeting Chief Walanka.'

The shaman is in a hut that serves as an emergency hospital. There are camp beds with thin mattresses and a basin of hot water on the fire outside. Celia slips inside without asking me to follow. I can see her talking to a man of about forty, thickset and with a rather stubborn face. Not charismatic enough for the spirits to enter him, surely, nor lithe enough to dramatise the stories he should be telling? Celia moves with him to examine the patients, one by one, occasionally thinking notes into her wrist wordfree.

'Time to see the Chief,' she says, leaving the shaman in the village infirmary.

Chief Walanka has a more aquiline face than is usual in this part of Africa. He moves with the assurance of a leader, without any need for a chain of office. Deep lines cross his brow and curve under his cheekbones to plunge into his neatly combed beard. He could be a sober businessman, except that he wears a rough cotton toga-like garment and no shoes - his tough desert sandals lie neatly outside the door, where I sense mine should be. Pans are ranged along a shelf below another with sculpted figures. It's a larger hut than Susannah's; light from the open door illuminates him in the only chair. A polished horn hangs from the rafters above it. Celia and I sit on cushions side by side. Mats cover the floor, the only luxury allowed to the chief of the Zueto tribe. Life pared down to essentials.

Not understanding the Chief's words, nor Celia's responses, I watch and wonder uneasily. He talks with many gestures, his face unmoving and eyes swinging from her to me, then over our heads as if to survey his people through the door behind us. Laughter is more of their language than smiles; laughter and tears. Celia turns to me.

'You're invited to witness an initiation ceremony. How the spirits are transferred to a shaman.'

'Didn't it happen after Susannah's husband died?'

'Yes, but the Chief doesn't like the present one. He lacks spirituality. I agree.'

I'm surprised to hear Celia pronouncing on the efficacy of a tribal witchdoctor. Then I remember the hospital hut.

'He was helping the sick, wasn't he?'

'Hardly,' she says. I frown at her. Isn't she expecting too much? 'Even after the training I've given him, he's still hopeless. This is partly because he's lost respect. He's not seen as having the gifts of a storyteller and healer. No charisma, we'd say. It's a tricky business. He won't go easily.' Demotion is an issue everywhere.

'Yes, I see. But what's it got to do with you?'

'I visit tribes, listen to the leader, try to gain his confidence and gather his views. He always has someone he favours, usually a member of his family and not necessarily the tribal storyteller and keeper of the oral tradition. I need to find the person most trusted as a healer to train in first aid. They learn basic treatments, how to recognise symptoms, sterilise instruments, particularly syringes, which pills to prescribe and which disinfectants to use.' So Celia is creating a network of paramedics. She must have had some sort of medical training. The more I learn about her, the more enigmatic she becomes.

*****

I'm breaking my unwritten rule and working after dark when it's cooler. Communications first. Martha has been elected - just! My vote may have helped. She's sent me lots of videopods but I'm not opening them as they might clobber the system here. I'll keep to words. Less energy used. A pity, but there it is. I wonder how she's getting on with Roland the Fox. Helen's brief message says she wants to see me and misses my blog. She intends to come but has so many celebrity appearances now on worldwide sites that she may not find the time. Maybe for one or two days. She doesn't mention Martha.

Nothing from mum. Mother writes at length about Martha's election, elated and repetitive. Still no mention of mum. Helen's message says she walked out on Election Day and isn't forgiven. Another cause for useless worrying. I repeat to myself that mum is resilient, capable and resourceful. She refused to have a wrist inset because they weren't obligatory then. Martha did buy her a wordfree monitor, though she rarely uses it. She may have left it behind at Beech Drive.

It's hard in the faltering light to read the messages and to think the replies back. They all want to know what it's like here. People talk about a non-place, and Mybeki is just that. I'm spending more time there now my lab is arriving in bits and pieces. The station is the hub of the town. Market stalls cling to the old tracks of communication. People come and go, but all buy something from candles to clothes or cattle. The market is all day every day, all similar merchandise together. My favourite part is the animal section, with cows and goats and much that is less familiar, like the rainbow-plumed birds. Elsewhere are endless arrays of vegetables, fruit, and heaps of spices amid the potent mix of scents and open sewers. Everywhere workmen swing along with buckets of muddy water, planks, straw, and breeze blocks because houses are being repaired, added to, or pulled down and rebuilt - constant demolition, addition and reconstruction. I find it all a stimulus for ideas, opening up, reviving, even extending theories I've been worrying about, aiming to try out so many applications that I may have to modify the lab before it is even assembled! It's a strange sensation, thinking through the senses. I must have done it before, but never with such results. I need my lab, but am amazed at my patience. I can hardly recognise myself!

A man is sitting under a rare awning, not squatting like people here, and watching. He's wearing a loose beige shirt and trousers, collar buttoned down, clothes creased into a pattern of wrinkles that continues over hands and face; soft fair hair greying and gimlet blue eyes. The only place in the shade is by this spare figure. At first I see my seated companion as middle-aged, about sixty perhaps. Mum's generation. He arrived here after the tragic civil war when a rampaging group of fighters kidnapped young girls from their school and tortured people from other communities. This reign of terror ended just before the worldwide arms amnesty. Mybeki is one of the key areas chosen by the GWP for peaceful resettlement.

'Have you seen the shrine on the edge of the crater?' I ask him. 'A woman's photo is placed under a cairn and circled by stones? Who was she?' I can't hide my curiosity.

'A miracle maker. That's how they remember her before the meteorstrophe. She was working for an organisation that came to help traumatised communities after the peace settlement.' His voice is deep, accented - not a native English speaker. Why am I curious about two mysterious people, one beside me, the other depicted on a cairn?

'Did you see a man there, when it happened? The meteorstrophe, I mean?'

A pause to think back.

'I remember a man running towards the crater holding his arm up like a prophet.'

'Yes. Tell me what happened next,' I ask greedily.

'The meteor demolished the village of the Zueto and so their creation myth came true. Outside time, their shaman chants, their ancestral spirits guide the Zueto people to where they must stay. There they build shelters for themselves and their livestock and an altar of stones for their forbears. When these spirits shift the stones and the shaman hears them crying, he chants their story and the Zueto people move on to their next settlement. The men sing and dance before they leave, placing stones in circles round the altar, one after the other. Thus they can go in peace and their spirits are safe. That is, until the reckoning, when the ultimate spirit, the great sigh of the universe, comes for them at the end of time. It is some unnamed disaster from the skies. That is their legend, their world picture.' My companion appeared to come out of a trance, leaving the Zueto in their eternal present to tell me about the meteorstrophe.

'It had been a good year. The rains had come. Cattle prospered in the land of the Zueto. Around the settlement, fields were green with crops and the wild fruit trees in the foothills were laden. Here in their Promised Land, their shaman spoke of a sacred river running abundant underground; they had found a spring which never ran dry. That in itself was a bountiful sign. The day dawned still, as if suspended out of time. No twitter or croak or howl. The women and girls, pitchers on heads and hands on hips, the oldest first, walked in a line to the spring, leaving the men to herd the cattle and the aged to care for the children. All was well with the awakening world. Then just a flutter in the air, a fitful breeze stirring the stillness.

'The white woman didn't leave with the others to fetch water. She was inside a hut caring for the ill when it was swept away. I saw a man, his arm raised, running towards the woman at the door of the hut. Then a sound came like a wind howling or a moan issuing from the earth – buildings, people, huts and cattle slid into the crater the meteor made.

'As foretold by the ancients, so it came to pass. The Zueto had heard it sung so often that they knew what was happening. A Zueto myth come true.'

BREAKING NEWS

DANGEROUS STORE OF CHEMICALS FOUND

Goodwill World Parliament inspectors may have found a **store of chemicals** that could be used to fabricate bombs in the **north of Argentina**. The owner of the laboratory, who cannot be named for legal reasons, has denied any such intention. He is well-known locally and internationally for his philanthropy.
This incident highlights the almost impossible task for the inspectors to determine whether such chemical stockpiles are for peaceful or aggressive use.

worldaroundyounews.com

12

Early summer

Helen *showspot.com*

When the day starts with putting a garment on back to front, then things are going to get worse! Today, during a football match in our local stadium, I'm presenting our casualwear personisations – the Powerdress base range has taken off dazzlingly worldwide. Our company now does drong fashion sprinkled with classic offcuts for the mid-range population. The teams flexing their muscles provide a useful backdrop. Their glances track me as I strut and pout in the interval, my image replicated all round the huge banner screens while smaller versions of me are snipped from the local internet to transmit any and everywhere.

Martha goes on at me about all shapes and sizes having the same old formula: head, arms, hands, body, legs and feet, identical form and function, just different dimensions. She would. All our elected member thinks about are her housing capsules and the Centre for Genetic Wellbeing - the star enterprise of her Zone Government. Even Esther has become involved in the Genetic Centre. She's been working for the remainder of her research grant on something top secret. I've promised to meet her before she too leaves for Africa.

Since Nick - I call him that in his absence - left for Africa I have drifted away from his world. I'm lucky and find easy company, especially in the sports arena. He still haunts me. Silly, isn't it? My female business partners and other girlfriends just don't understand. Instead of all the muscled bodies I can enjoy at will, I long for his lean one. A sort of soft firmness. Difficult to describe because it's so privately delicious. Just the little things - nothing spectacular. I've not found that before. 'Those countless small courtesies' - that's what Eliza would say. Where is she?

* * * * *

Nick introduced me to his lab colleague Esther and we meet up sometimes for lunch in the old uni snack bar. Esther was all over the place yesterday, waving her arm in friendly recognition towards the refugees helping the regular servers behind the counter. We both are, I realise, fine specimens of our respective races, almost an internet advertisement! People, especially men, glanced at our table. Esther was blissfully unaware, absorbed as she usually is in her own lifestream.

'Listen,' she said, 'I shouldn't be telling you this -' (should I then be recording it on my wordfree?) '- but while Nicholas is away I'm doing something else outside his area. He won't notice.' She looked gleefully around her. 'This is a secret,' almost laughing, wide-eyed, 'but my people have a genetic resistance to HIV, or so it seems. Imagine! And no one has noticed it yet. It was an unexpected by-product of the samples I brought back from Africa. The Centre for Genetic Wellbeing called me in soon after Nicholas left. "Can you come this afternoon?" one of the managers voiced me. I must work out a programme urgently. All shrouded in secrecy, you see. So don't, please, let on about all this. Big profits may be made, but not without some community payback. I'll insist on that.'

I can see her now as I record this into my wordfree, sitting upright in her favourite colours, blue and red. Not very subtle, I've told her, but she doesn't care. Her boyfriend back home seems to like it, and that's good enough for her.

Esther has planted the Africa idea in my mind. There's always a gap in fashion after launching the summer styles in spring, so why not visit Nick? I'll surprise him - more fun that way. I could add it to my expense account: to Africa to find new colours and textures - beads and baskets and bandannas! And whatever else they have. I wonder how he's getting on, which is more than Esther seems to do. She might want him to stay out there as long as possible so she can get her new brainchild off to a good start here at the Centre for Genetic Wellbeing.

*****

I couldn't secretly think into my wordfree when I was with Dom Ross Mackenzie. He obviously liked me the first time we met for dinner at his mansion. I could feel him running his eyes all over me when he dropped in on Martha's election celebrations. He smiled as he left, whispering, 'I'll be in touch'. And he was, saying he's interested in my fashion activities.

I was tipping my backease chair, gazing at my capsule's screens and wondering whether I might sign up for a virtual singsong competition when, just as I stretched my legs out to zip on dance boots, my wordfree throbbed. Left wrist to my ear and right hand zipping -

'Yes, Dom Ross. Tomorrow evening. Yes, I'm free -' still tugging away, furious that evidently one of my calves is fatter than the other! My wordfree reference will have given him my house code.

It was the same silver-grey limousine as before with Nick, but instead of welcoming me into the mansion, he glided down the steps, a black

Labrador on one side and a golden one on the other. Taking my arm in a trying-to-look-young way, he pointed towards the buildings on the left. He isn't the sort to embrace one.

So there we were in his shining high-tech paradise with the night shift in white overalls. I couldn't help redesigning them as rysol lab coats bound in the colours of his coat of arms. It could become the brand on lapels and cuffs fastened with sealon.

I happened to be wearing my latest creation in rysol. It's the most fantastic material ever invented, and that includes denim. It's a natural golden rye colour, doesn't crease and dirt bounces off it. It's soft like silk, synthetic with a touch of rye in the weave to give it the natural look, you see. No ironing, quick drying and tough. It's a more relaxing colour than white, not drab like beige and totally without associations - except for the ones I'm trying to give it.

'How's Nicholas getting on?' Dom Ross was steering me back across the gravel area to the wide open front door.

'Well, thank you.' He expected me to continue. 'Nicholas seems to be waiting around in Africa for things to happen. I may fly out to see him.'

'When?'

'Soon, I think.'

'Has he downloaded the program on the datadrive I gave him when you both came here?' I was puzzled. To be honest, I'd forgotten all about it. 'The program would help him check the calculations, and save hours of time better spent on thinking and inventing.' Nothing to get fussed about, but a kind thought just the same. 'Could you bring it back when you return from seeing him – you said you would be going to Africa? My scientists need it.'

'Yes, Dom Ross. I'll ask him if he found it helpful. I don't really understand what he's doing.'

'Call me Ross, please.'

We were now in the dining-room. He opened a bottle of champagne, filled two glasses and handed me one while whispering into his wordfree. I must have looked surprised.

'I've a few more things to check with the chief technician. There's one for each shift, all answering to me.'

While waiting for the first course, Ross asked me how business was going. Here was chance handed to me on a dish! I suggested that we might freshen up his technical staff, having checked his coat of arms in the staircase window when we passed it to the dining-room.

'Good idea,' he said. After the meal and back in the library, he thought images of his cargo ships and planes up on to the wallscreens. He explained how he maximised profits with minimum manpower. It's easier, he says, to deal with objects because they don't squeal, snap or answer back. All evening his black and golden guard dogs sat on either side, yelped when he trod on a paw or nudged them away, to return, muzzles uplifted, eyes adoring him.

The evening passed quickly. I haven't exactly forgotten it, but can't recall much before or after the limousine brought me back home, except that he's the first man who has kept his hands off me when I'm alone with him. Strange.

*****

I sent Nick a voicemessage to let him know I was coming. He hasn't replied. His wordfree doesn't seem to be functioning. His blog is encrypted, so that's secret. I should be annoyed, but I'm not. I'll take the first place available on the airjuggernaut to Mybeki. It flies only twice weekly to cut down on Co2 emissions. Planes leave when full, crammed with over 500 passengers. The likes of Ross fly in their own bio-fuelled executive fleet. No private jets are allowed any more. He goes with the flow in all this. I haven't heard him complain, now I come to think of it.

I didn't expect Esther on this flight.

'I've finished most of the work on Nicholas's project,' she said, 'and - don't tell him this - I need to see my family and decide what I'm going to do. The next step is probably the genetic venture.' Nice to have choices.

Our allocated seats aren't near each other. A pity. She may be worried that Nick will be at the airport to meet me. I still haven't managed to speak to him, but someone called Celia answered the voicenet code he gave me for the zone. She said she or Nick would meet me at Mybeki airport. I hope so. This is a long boring flight. Passengers are nodding off on either side of me. I'm wondering how on earth I shall recognise Celia. She could be like Esther, an African speaking perfect English, or from any ethnic group. Here goes! We're landing.

*****

'How did you recognise me?' I was curious.

'Nicholas described you with superlatives.' Celia is small and so insignificant that even as a non-native person here in Mybeki she doesn't stand out. Lucky her! I've been jostled from airport to train and now in the main street, with people running out of alleys, toppling street sellers' carts and treading on granny and child vendors squatting along the roadside. They smile and jabber and touch my clothes. I'm glad that I've packed away my solar jacket - it would have been pulled off my back. Celia is no bodyguard, but she is pacing a clear path ahead of me to her office in what seems to be the business zone. A huge board in front of a vacant building site proclaims

NEW CENTRE FOR GENETIC WELLBEING.

That reminds me: not even a glimpse of Esther after we took our separate plane seats.

Celia has voiced a driver to take me to Nicholas.

'Why isn't Nicholas's lab here in Mybeki, near the station? Like the Centre? - ' I indicated the board. 'Actually, its headquarters are near where I live.'

'Really?' Celia said. 'Nicholas needs clear air and you can see how polluted it is here. The Centre has to be close to the particular tribal group it has come here to research.'

She is matter-of-fact, with a pointed chin, slightly pouting mouth and mousy hair that could do with an interesting colour rinse. Her nondescript trousers and shirt need sharpening up. She's practical and gets things done. Like calling up the dilapidated car and its ancient driver.

* * * * *

Well, here I am in Nicholas's bungalow, the only decent building around here, safe after many bumpy kilometres that seemed like a hundred. The old man drove me across unending sand sending dust all over the car and his old fashioned safari suit with knobbly buttons on all those pockets. It just floated off my rysol outfit, just as it should. I ought not to be whispering into my wordfree about this skeletal creature but about Nicholas. Celia voiced him that I had arrived, so it wasn't a surprise as I hoped it would be. His face lit up when I walked in, though not as much as I expected. We kissed, but he didn't hug me tightly. And I had come all this way to see him!

'There's a lot on, Helen, now the lab is assembled. It's hardly what you'd expect, but I'll show it to you. Perhaps you should rest first?' Yes. No. I wanted to be with him, but it was sweltering and he looked tired. Not the best of times perhaps. He wasn't even curious about what was happening back home. 'Tell me later,' was all he said. We lay on his bed under a mosquito net like two effigies, and I dozed off. When I woke up I was alone. I'm now thinking into my wordfree and trying to find energy for a shower. I don't feel like getting up. The building is buzzing with insects and creaking. He's deserted me in a strange country - some cheek! This bungalow is a male set-up. Just bare essentials.

I've tried the shower and it works, just, but I can't find a way to heat water for tea. The fridge isn't even cool and there's no ice. I don't feel like beer.

Susannah has just turned up, a large person with not much English but a lot of common sense. A mug of tea appears as I sit here at the rough wood table he uses as a desk. Papers everywhere. A print of what seems like a pile of stones. Then a close-up of the stones and a photo framed by them. A woman with large eyes. Not beautiful but, well, haunting.

'Susannah, who is she?'

'A lady Gaia.' She has already turned away from me. She might be crying.

'Who is she?' No answer. 'What was she doing here?'

'Good lady. Good.' She's busy preparing the evening meal, trying not to let me see her face. I show her the photo of the stones.

'Where is this heap of stones?' She points at the open door.

'Out –'she looks through it at the setting sun.

* * * * *

Nicholas still hasn't returned. The sun will soon sink behind the mountains. I'm walking towards it with the woman's photo to show to people on the way. I'm not prepared for strange sounds and keep on looking down hearing what I think is a snake. Plenty of them around, Celia says. Nothing. I'm not usually afraid, but here every movement or sound makes me jump. Over sand past rocks and scrub. No trees. Celia said they had all been cut down for firewood. There's no path. Sand covers everything in this wilderness that goes on and on into the mountains. It'll soon be dark. No twilight at all.

The land falls away. It must be the side of a valley. I shouldn't have set out just before sunset.

I'm tense with fear. And thrilled. Above me are millions of stars like pinpricks. No moon.

I must stay calm. My pulse charges my wordfree so I can voice Nicholas. No response. He's forgotten his wordfree. Or it isn't charged. Oh Nick, that's the whole point of having one! Nobody nowadays can ever be lost, as I am now, because we are always in wordfree contact, asleep or awake. I bleep for help.

'I'm just going out, Helen!' I didn't mean to disturb Cara, one of my fashion partners, the one I like most. 'What do you want?'

'I've lost my way.'

'I'm not surprised, Helen, the way you carry on. Where are you? Can't you call the night wardens?'

'No. I'm in Africa.'

'Where?'

'Africa. South, I think, of Mybeki.'

'You've lost me.'

'No, I'm lost!'

'Helen, are you all right?' Cara sounds anxious, as she should. 'You have an automatic code for the night wardens on your wordfree. We all do…'

Useless. What night wardens are there here in Africa? This miserable part of it anyway. Who can I call? Celia? She hasn't given me her code. I didn't think I'd need it; I thought I'd be with Nick. Send an SOS to World Watch? It's supposed to locate people as accurately as buildings on the geomap. Set up to detect criminals and displaced people, not silly ones who've lost their way. Try Esther?

It's not cold but I'm shivering. Gusts of air, not breezes, from the valley behind me. I'm trying the SOS and my wordfree lights up with the geomap rapidly zooming onto Africa and then to roughly where I am. Crackling voices - Mybeki I can hear mentioned repeatedly - then silence. No cover. The map fades off screen.

Must I sit and wait for dawn? Or try all the codes I've stored on my wordfree. Wake everyone up at this hour? How could they help?

If nature was decent it would go to sleep after sunset and stop making all these noises. If I continue talking into my wordfree there's my noise to add to Africa's night-time chatter so I don't leave myself space to panic. Throbbing in my wrist.

'Helen, did you try to contact me? It's Esther! Where are you?'

'Esther I'm so relieved. Please help. I'm lost.'

'Where? What on earth have you been doing?'

'Nicholas left me sleeping and went back to his lab so I woke up and decided to go out. There's nothing to do here. Then it went dark so suddenly that I can't see where I am.'

'Don't you know there's no twilight here? Helen, you must check places on the internet before you travel.' This wasn't like the Esther I thought I knew, happy-go-lucky, the last person to go on like this.

'But I'm here and lost and Nick can't have charged his wordfree. What can I do?'

'Shout.'

'There's nobody here!'

'I doubt it.' She sounds impatient. 'I'm about ten kilometres away with my family. I'll call the police in Mybeki, but they'll take hours, if they agree to go, and probably won't arrive before sunrise. You wouldn't need them then. You could retrace your footsteps using your wordfree light while shouting from time to time. Or wait till dawn. At least it's not cold. I must go. It'll work out, Helen. Don't worry.' I could hear children crying, probably part of her extended family.

Sit on a rock and wait for dawn? Not like me. I'm swinging my wrist over the way I came. The wordfree light does pick out my shoe prints. I'm trying to follow the way the heels point, easier to see when on sand but not on hard ground. I yell, but the sound doesn't carry. I'm scanning the ground closely but, help! I've fallen on to a pile of rocks. My shin's badly grazed and my trousers are sticking to the blood. Ugh! It's throbbing. Stabs of pain. Those may be lights bobbing in the distance and people calling me. I must shout, I must…

*****

I'm in bed and it's probably midday, it's so hot. My leg is aching and I'm hungry. I did have something, I think, when I woke earlier but I can't remember much. Nicholas is sitting on the bed beside me.

'How are you feeling?'

'Fine.' I'm lying.

'How did you get to the stone monument?'

'I followed Susannah's directions.'

'But why did you go out?'

'To see the sunset. Get fresh air. Do something. You weren't around.'

'Why did you take the photo with you?' All these questions.

'Because Susannah pointed to where the cairn is. I had nothing to do here.'

'Only that?'

'Yes.' He doesn't understand feminine curiosity.

'Who is Gaia?' My moment to ask questions.

'I don't know. She helped people here. Celia says she is revered by the Zueto people. They built the shrine with her photo and hold some sort of ceremony there from time to time, mainly on the anniversary of the meteorstrophe. She was swept into the crater then, with many others. You were lucky not to stumble into it.' Then, after more fussing around me,

'Would you like to see my lab after lunch?'

'If it's not too hot.'

'A little later then. After a rest.'

I almost forgot.

'Nick – Nicholas, your Mum is with people who live near the mountains. She left on election day – did you know?'

'No. I wondered why she wasn't answering my messages.'

'Martha found her when on some visit representing our zone. I don't know why.'

'At least she's safe. What a relief.'

I dozed off.

* * * * *

The wound is quite deep but I can walk. His lab is between this bungalow and the mountains where, he said, the energy receptor is set up for his tests. It had to be as close as possible to the equator – something about the angle of the sun's rays – and as far from settlements as possible. I might have known the lab would be a Martha-type capsule full of satellite links. All the latest machines and gadgets are fitted into hardly enough space for the two of us. He doesn't seem to need any more. Bright eyes peer in through the door.

'Come on!' Nicholas smiles at the child.

'This is Joe, my messenger.' Nicholas's adoring helper? He pats the child's head.

'Shouldn't he be at school?'

'He is. But he hangs around here a lot, wanting to help. He was found abandoned beside the railway line after the meteorstrophe.' By now Joe is inside, arm round Nicholas's waist, gazing at me.

'You'll be a scientist when you grow up, won't you Joe?' Nicholas can't stop hugging him. 'He's learning English so quickly that he's interpreting for me.' I've not seen Nick so affectionate before. It annoys me.

Before we leave the lab he hands me a datadrive marked with his serial number.

'This is for Raphael. Please leave it in the lab for him. I'll give you the door code'

'What about the other datadrive, the one Ross Mackenzie gave you? Have you tried out his program?'

'Helen, stop probing. I may have done... I think I did. When I was frustrated. Things weren't going as I hoped. It did seem to help check the figures... difficult to explain.' He didn't want to talk about his work.

Why doesn't he send Raphael the calculations via the internet instead of bothering me? He knows how forgetful I am. He's so fearful of hackers and what he calls 'that tribe of internet hooligans'. I'm amused and I shouldn't be. He's out here testing his infinenergy theory and says something about not getting enough reliable energy to do it! Here my wordfree is fully charged from my pulse backed up, if need be, by my solar jacket.

Strange Esther hasn't been in touch again to find out if I'm safe.

I put the datadrive carefully into my pocket. Celia is waiting outside the lab.

'I'll take you back to the bungalow while Nicholas works,' she says, as if prearranged. Celia doesn't seem keen to take me to the Zueto settlement as I hoped. That would be more interesting. She has to ask the Chief something, and he's away or unavailable.

'What does he do? There's not much to hunt or gather round here, is there? No trees. Few berries.' Celia doesn't answer so I ask,

'Who is Gaia?' She stops and looks at me. 'Why do you ask?'

'Because I've seen her photo.'

'Oh,' Celia pauses. 'I came here to help her, learn from her, but she was already dead, swept into the crater. So I had to take over everything. I'm working in her shadow. She was almost a legend even before the meteorstrophe.'

* * * * *

I'm wordfreeing this on the plane back home. Celia invited me to stay with her and showed me round Mybeki, not that there was much to see beyond endless street markets where everyone is selling or buying or standing or sitting and staring at me. It was like being on a catwalk in the wrong surroundings. Nicholas was worried, working from dawn till the heat was unbearable, and then in the evening until late at night. Not much of a love life in these circumstances. And there was no double-size mosquito net. I don't even want to think about it. He wasn't communicative, just needy with bouts of hugging and kissing and conventional love-making. He was worried about some calculations, especially after the daily downloading of all sorts of messages, many of them getting stuck on the way and crashing the system.

I've almost forgotten to say that they have started to build the Mybeki Centre for Genetic Wellbeing. No shortage of money there. Nicholas's lab is a midget in comparison. I didn't meet Esther again - everyone was so busy except me - but talked to her on my wordfree. She seems undecided whether to stay in Mybeki or return to work in Nick's lab.

Just before Celia came to collect me, I was looking round the bungalow to make sure I hadn't forgotten anything, when I noticed a datadrive left on an old bookcase. It had Ross Mackenzie's code on it. Nick was so preoccupied that he must have forgotten to ask me to return it to him. Ross told me his scientists needed it, so I put it with the one to take to Raphael.

*****

I'm the first to complain about wind and showers, but was I glad to step out into fresh air, a cool breeze on my face. Only an hour or so ago I returned home, opened my door and what do you know? There on the screens was a flashing message:

'Come to Nicholas's lab with the datadrive he gave you for me, urgently, please. If I'm not there, leave it in an envelope with my name on it. Thanks, Raphael.'

BREAKING NEWS

LIBERALISATION OF DATA PROTECTION URGED BY FREEDOM PARTY

The **Freedom Party** is flexing its muscles now that it has a working majority in the **Goodwill World Parliament.** It promises a **liberalisation of data protection regulations** to enable more scientific co-operation worldwide. This is strongly opposed by the deputies from the **Serendipity Party** and the **other smaller groups**. **Stock exchanges** the world over have reacted positively to the results of the worldwide elections.

The **communications sub-committee of the Goodwill World Parliament** is concerned about fluctuating energy supplies in some parts of the world resulting in wordfree crashes. For citizens' safety, and to **ensure Wi-Fi feed to the soon-to-be-obligatory wordfree wrist insets**, energy must be shared and used carefully. The sub-committee urges citizens to be conscientious and reduce wordfree usage until resources are added to supply more energy for the existing network or a new source of energy is found.

worldaroundyounews.com

13

Summer

Nicholas *i-witnessNIC227.futurepast.com*

I've done it! Helen's arrival spurred me on. I made another effort to find the ultimate key - the calculations that direct each beam with 100% accuracy on to the Reaching Out energy receptor. The one they installed far from any habitation – just as I asked.

Before Helen came I thought I might at long, long, last have reached my goal. I hadn't then used the program Dom Ross gave me to check the maths. I never intended to use it but just accepted the program to please him. Then Helen went on at me with, y*ou never know, it might save time and find an error*, or, *you invent- you ought to try everything out. Dom Ross only wants to help*. So I did use it. She said Ross Mackenzie asked her to return it, but I made excuses and didn't give it back to her. Now I can't find it anywhere. Did I drop it on my return from the lab to the bungalow? I'm sure I gave her the then up-to-date datadrive for Raphael. It had the stuff hackers want to steal. I'll never transmit crucial data, even encrypted, over the internet. And certainly not now I have the very latest accurate calculations in the encrypted, ultra-safe section of my wordfree monitor. I always have it hanging round my neck on the gold chain Helen gave me.

I can't bear to see much of Helen – she distracts me. I didn't ask her to come to Africa, but I couldn't stop thinking of her. Her delight in teasing. The way she finds fun in everything. The way people like to be with her. Is she my muse? Before she came I was testing my theory over and over again.

It seemed to be working! My mind sparked in all directions. But close to me, Helen invades my thoughts. She left as unexpectedly as she arrived, just before the final break-through. Sad I couldn't celebrate with her. She lingers in my mind, here, or wherever I find myself...

After Helen left, I decided to try out once again the calculations I'd checked with Dom Ross's program. I hadn't estimated precisely enough the energy beam's angle from the GWP satellite payload towards the trial receptor out in the savannah between my lab and the mountains. Raphael's Energy Research Centre near Jerusalem manufactures the compressed solar energy panels to our specifications and also, crucially, provides the finance for the satellite payload. The result was a perfect hit, right on the receptor's core – it's hard to explain in words – and the solar energy was renewed again and again, all to plan. It behaved just as I thought it should. The perfect solution! The relief felt like when steady rain follows a storm: refreshing, unthreatening, renewing.

*****

Celia doesn't often come either to the lab or the bungalow. She says she didn't want to disturb me, and is probably right. She was kind to Helen. Gradually I'm learning how wise she is - not a quality usually found in young people. She's unexciting but wise. Boring but wise. Plain but wise. She said she realised I was on the brink of 'balancing the crucial equation' as she quaintly put it. She recognised the symptoms: walking with the forked stick into the wilderness of boulders and scrub, especially at sunset; restlessness at the thought of moving lab; doodling over recycled paper brimming out of waste bins and infinite hours spent sighing from one internet calculation to another, increasingly morose.

'Your face is rarely smooth and settled,' Celia observed, 'but now it's creased, with narrowed eyes darting all over the place.' So I must have looked unappealing. I didn't want to meet anyone except her, because she is my route to lab supplies and to Susannah, who deals with food and lighting and ventilation problems at the bungalow. All these calculations, so near in mind and far in space, invade my thoughts, even like now while I think this into to my wordfree monitor.

When Celia invited me to witness the initiation of the new Zueto shaman, I didn't want to go, but she insisted I should take time out from my calculations.

'What has happened to the shaman I saw with you? The one who followed Susannah's husband after his death in the meteorstrophe?'

'You saw he was hopeless.' She could be infuriatingly matter-of-fact.

'Yes, but what happened to him?'

'He lost spirit. That's what they say. He sort of melted into the background.'

'How?' She wasn't irritated by my insistence.

'Usually they walk into the scrubland and forage on their own. If they return, it's always after the new shaman is well established so it's easier to slip in almost imperceptibly. Or so I'm told.'

Celia seemed calm, but she must have been concerned at the part she played in demoting that healer. At having to ease the new shaman into being her medical assistant and starting all over again to weave a modern strand into the pattern of his traditional duties.

'Susannah can't just invite us to go with her. Initiations are for the Zueto tribe only. I've asked Chief Walanka and he says you can come with me as an observer.'

*****

Celia arrived that evening, just as the bats began swooping in front of the bungalow. I love sitting on the verandah at sunset when nature's daylight cacophony dies away and the sun sinks into the horizon before the night-time crescendo. No twilight, only a sudden awareness that all light has fled.

'Why do they hold the initiation after dark?'

'They say it's because the spirits are free then. Light locks them inside matter, whether animal, vegetable or mineral. Flames help. You'll see!'

I like watching Celia when she pauses to think. Her eyes tighten a little, her eyelashes flicker and she tilts her head so slightly you hardly notice it. Her mouth - one side goes up as if in a quizzical smile while the other half opens to answer. It may sound odd, but it's different and very personal. It makes her expressions, not her face, so memorable.

'Also,' she continued, ' the men are out with the herds or hunting in daytime. You must have noticed how the days are equally divided between light and darkness, hardly changing from one month to the next.' Silence, then as the night chorus of croaks, snuffles and peeps started, she stood up.

'We can go now. The fire will be lit in the village compound.'

It was. We were to sit on the matting beside Chief Walanka's chair.

'Do you have any say in the person they choose?' I whispered. 'After all, you'll need to work with him.' I remembered that she had tried to teach the rejected shaman basic first aid. The new one would have to run the clinic when she wasn't there, linking it effectively with the health unit in Mybeki.

'Only if they ask me. I can hint at the sort of person I'd prefer, that's all. I don't know many of the prominent men in the community. Susannah does. All are curious about the Mybeki Centre for Genetic Wellbeing. They believe they are special, favoured by the spirits - nothing new in that - but they don't understand why they are singled out by the Centre. They haven't heard of AIDS because no one has it - precisely why the new Centre is located in Mybeki and not near the original one in our city.'

Here in the airjuggernaut everything I think into my wordfree is remembered as if so long ago, seen through the wrong end of binoculars, but also here and now. The dancing figures. The old man I'd met in Mybeki appearing out of nowhere to stand behind Chief Walanka. The men leaping round the fire to fall back and leave one, the new shaman, their instinctive choice, nearest the flames. Then the test. Throaty cheers as Walanka raises his arm. A crouching woman, Susannah, jumps out of the darkness whirling her arms, then runs towards the dark figure hunched by the fire - his umbilical cord to the molten heart of the world. All hands reach up flailing against the light cast by the flames; words are hurled at the stars.

'What's this all about?'

'The spirits,' Celia murmurs. 'Don't you recognise Susannah? She's chanting the stories she told with her husband.'

'And the meteorstrophe that killed him?'

'It's already part of their legend.'

Then the procession. Women start humming to syncopated handclaps, feet drumming the bare earth. Children, confused, follow their mothers to the Chief, who touches their heads. Then on to the shaman to place food by him - knobs of bread or little round cakes made from the groundnuts they harvest here. Afterwards the women and children turn towards the men on their haunches at the edge of the open ground. As if choreographed, each leaps to catch a woman's waist and hoist her into the air with a yell. I try to see who takes Susannah, and glimpse that she has an eye painted on her forehead. I can't make out who chooses Anna, her daughter. The flames shoot distorted shadows of elongated skulls, knobbly fingers and taut skeletal bodies with legs flailing and feet pounding. The chanting soars above the hum and regular clapping and stamping of the women, laced with ululating yells that echo into the night to welcome the spirits. Celia crouches beside me whispering that it is happening. That the shaman will work as the soul of the community - she can't find a better expression for the 'hoaaah' they say, which has entered him. Everyone knows it is happening, because everyone wills it must.

As he drove us back, the old man talked intermittently of the other initiation ceremonies with dancing and primeval sounds that he had witnessed over the years. As in the shaman ceremony, there was a communal release of pent-up emotions and deep-set anxieties. There's no interface for the Zueto people between past and future. Their myths pick up the pieces where reason can't cope with them. The future is sensed before it arrives. People around here may be ignorant, though only the old ones are illiterate, but their legends have a certain erudition. Stronger than any reasonable explanation is their apprehension of time. A massive disaster is a new signal. The oral tradition bends, and gathers it into itself. Joe, my faithful little errand boy, is part of all that.

‘He was found abandoned by the rail track, a child from nowhere,’ the old man told me when I asked. ‘It is said in the Zueto tribe that his father was a snake and that his mother bore him under a blue star after she drank tea made from cactus flowers. Spirits are thought to dance in the flowers. His mother disappeared after he was born. She probably knew she was dying.’

'I have many fathers and mothers,' Joe told me after he started coming to the lab. ‘First ma Susannah. Then after a father eaten by meteorstrophe, Chief Walanka another father.’ He is a child from nowhere, a different, light shade of brown with smaller, sharper features and hazel eyes shot with green. Here in the airjuggernaut, I look around at figures bending in isolation before screens, tapping away at computers and feel the urge to shout something silly...but I don't, because Joe is grasping my thoughts. He wanted to leave with me. I could have bought him a ticket but disappointed him with, 'no, not yet.' Where could he go to school? Could he live with me? I don't know whether that's allowed in my Institute lodgings. I miss him already. That chain of cartwheels when he sees me coming. The circles he runs round me when I reach him. His keen, laughing eyes, sensitive face and his whole body quivering to know, help, find out. Such rare, total intelligence. No wonder he's the tribe's mascot. I too need him.

I must concentrate on patenting my discovery and find people who will back it financially. Convince them. The initial cost may be considerable, but infinenergy will be cheap, very cheap in the long run. Solar power is inexhaustible and, in this form, constant.

Why do I shudder when I sit here flying high above Africa, and remember how I went into the scrubland with my forked stick? I caught a snake just behind the head, as Joe said I should, but I couldn't kill it, though it might have finished me off. I watched it slither under a rock and imagined it coiled back observing me, tongue flicking. Or is it because of fear that the hum of the plane engines might stop? That would be the end of me with my invention in the datadrive hanging round my neck – both lost forever.

No, it's only the air conditioning that‘s making me shiver.

BREAKING NEWS

ABANDONED UNIVERSITY BUILDINGS ON FIRE. ARSON SUSPECTED

The handsome buildings of a renowned university founded centuries ago have stood silent and deserted for nearly a decade since its academic core moved north of the city to the specially-designed modern **Greystone University,** funded by the generosity of Xiang Lu of the World Potential Company.

Proposals and counter proposals have been made for the reuse of these magnificent stone structures lined with priceless panelling and carving of great delicacy, challenged by others who clamour for the demolition of existing structures and redevelopment to fit contemporary needs.

'These ancient buildings are too costly to run and maintain,' the zone government member, **Martha Middlethorpe**, reiterated in an online statement to all residents in her constituency. 'All suggestions for alternative uses may be sent to my office - click on my icon or voice "**Martha at Town Hall** "'.

She has been overwhelmed by suggestions and protests, both for and against demolition. She has postponed her response until more assessments have been made.

No one knows when the electricity supply was cut off and the alarm system dismantled, or why such unoccupied buildings did not have the water tanks drained. The water pipes burst and some of the buildings were flooded during the recent harsh winter. Dry rot soon penetrated the edifice, making it unsafe to enter.

The fire started in a room next to the monumental carved staircase leading up to the main hall. Flames were only noticed after the fire burst out of the roof. Initially only two fire engines were called. Unable to cope, the remaining ones crammed into the main quad.

Crowds thronged the streets making it even more difficult for the firemen to tackle the blaze. Sparks and cinders covered a vast area. Rumour spread that it was arson. Figures were seen darting in and out of the smoke and spray, removing old tables and chairs, cutting down valuable chandeliers, prising out panelling and carved over-mantels. **Sister Julian**, the nun who discovered a lost work by **Leonardo da Vinci**, was glimpsed in the swirling smoke and confusion directing a cohort of helpers, her robe billowing around her. It caught fire. Undaunted, she stripped it open tugging at the adhesive fasteners, pulled a handkerchief from an inside pocket, tied it round her mouth, and plunged back into the building to come out clutching a carved lamp stand, badly singed.

Two firemen, who also required treatment, took her to the nearby infirmary.

worldaroundyounews.com

14

Autumn

Nicholas *i-witnessNIC227.futurepast.com*

The return home. For generations it's been just like this, hovering over the earth waiting for your turn to land on a tiny slice of it. The clouds are heavier now, weeping over the land, anchoring roots. Slowly down over the historic city centre, shrunk still further since I left; more demolition of old buildings and more new ones replacing them.

Martha voiced me that mum is still away, spared its destruction in the name of progress, modernity or improving the human condition. I must see her. She's somewhere. Where? Her wordfree isn't responding. I couldn't contact her while in Africa. Martha, yes, and mother. Magnus quite a bit, and Helen - a lot. When I wasn't working, I automatically imagined her like an intense point of light, far off, that approaches and bursts into this startling woman, beautifully groomed and as fragrant as, as - jasmine. Curvaceous, yes, but slender as well. She dresses with flair in the latest tech fabrics she loves. She says it's a hard look to carry off, and I believe her.

Like Martha, Helen is an achiever. Focused. Clear goals. It's the only way to leave a mark on the world, so one's whole existence doesn't just become another statistic. Landed. The quick trail out. All baggage is sensometered for any dangerous element and dispatched directly to one's legal residence. People are waiting behind the glass walls. Helen will be there.

Out into the glare of the vast concourse. Where is she? I'm stranded ridiculously. A tired individual holding a T-reader with all the crucial calculations but without the ultimate key. That's in the datadrive on the chain round my neck. I couldn't risk sending it online to my lab or directly to Raphael. I'm a prime target online. Welcomers have already moved off; other people walk purposefully in different directions. Perhaps she's mistaken the time? Or the day, though I've sent her wordfree messages. She didn't answer when I tried to voice her – and she blames me for not having a wrist wordfree! *Just like Eliza*, she insists on reminding me, *you are deliberately elusive,* because I forget to recharge it.

How long should I stand here without calling her? All delays are posted on the web, so she would know that the airjuggernaut from sub-Saharan Africa has arrived. I'm voicing her wordfree and can hear it buzzing. No answer. I'll think my message into her wordfree memory and try not to feel angry.

It was easier when Esther or Raphael came to meet me, but she's still in Africa, involved in the new Mybeki Centre for Genetic Wellbeing, and Raphael is busy at the Jerusalem Energy Research Centre in the Middle East Alliance. Will he be checking the payload on the GWP satellite that I've been using? We are ready now for the next step: an energy-generating satellite. Perfect!

Action is the answer. Why doesn't she respond to her wrist wordfree now I'm thinking into it?

Monopods leave every ten minutes. Mine runs along the track behind Magnus's garden, skirting the meadows not yet part of the Newborough housing belt constricting the historic city. It hurtles into a woodland of rust-leafed oaks, golden beeches and yellow lime trees, the full scale of autumn colour in the midst of evergreens like shadows. Relief - not yet felled. Tightness in my guts. A spasm of apprehension. A faint but distinct churning in the stomach. My stop for the Institute.

Whispers. Imagined? Should I walk towards the Institute lab or my lodgings first? Lab. I have to check whether the T-reader's back data – minus the ultimate key - has been automatically locked into the Institute datasafe as well as the Goodwill World Parliament cyberstore. I sometimes have the stupid urge to swallow the crucial datadrive for its own safety, instead of carrying it round my neck! No sign of Dom Ross Mackenzie's silver-grey plaything parked outside. Relief. I think in the code for the laboratory block and pause to glance through the glass door of the Common Room - empty at lunch time - before going up to my lab. Another code to think my way into another space. Mine. Raphael's term here has ended and my grant for research assistants has to be renewed, so no one will be there. The code number sequence is etched on my memory, but the indicator below the handle isn't clicking to register it. No blinking light indicating Security has reset it. I'll check my wordfree. No automatic notification of the new code. Try again. Ahh – I'm leaning against the door to rest a moment and find myself falling into my lab. Who has left the door open? My heart's beating in my head. The computer system is encrypted. It must be safe. I touch a screen and it quivers into pale shapes and vague icons then a flash warning: virus infected - do not proceed. Other screens don't react. They're dead, hard drives extracted. Empty carcasses.

Stunned. A pillage of my mental territory. I'm quivering in fury and frustration. Here. Powerless. Standing shivering - alone in the debris of my life's work. The walls are swaying. I feel sick. I'm leaning over the lab sink shivering. Can't think. Must do something. Can't. Alone. Head between hands I'm sitting on a lab stool.

Who could have done this? Only Raphael and Esther have the code. All the cleaning is done from outside by the dust suction and flushing method - that's why all surfaces must be left clear after each day's work. *An inside job*, as they used to say, *is impossible.*

At the security lodge the head officer's mouth opens wide in amazement.

'It can't...'

'But it has. While I was in Africa.'

'...because the security program has just checked all the laboratory lock codes. It happens in rotation for different parts of the Institute buildings. We can unlock specific security devices but I have to authorise this. And I haven't. Not for the last six years at least. Why did nobody report it?'

'Because nobody is there. My two assistants left about the same time as me.'

The lab was empty, though no one knew it was. Should I have told him this? The officer is looking around fearfully. As I feel like doing.

'Dr. Middlethorpe, I'm so… I didn't know... I forgot you were going… faulty intelligence…' He's flailing around for words. If I report him, then he's finished. No wonder he's trembling. 'Was the door to the lab block damaged?' I shake my head. Someone may have slipped in behind another who had the code to open it.

'You're in charge of security and you don't even know that my lab has been broken into?'

He hangs his head and fusses over papers on his desk. So much for our paper-free world.

'Tomorrow there'll be a full report. Please leave everything as it is. W-would you like your luggage to be carried to your rooms, sir?'

'No thanks. Has it arrived from the airport? I'll take it myself.'

I'm trying to stop shaking.

I need to be alone to confront the possible violation of the last space I may call my own - home. Others have their cases taken straight to their rooms by a security officer with the electronic mastercode, so they can just walk in and unpack. I'm never happy with that. No one, but no one can have the security code for my rooms – except the security people, in case of fire. And Helen, of course. Nowadays objects aren't stolen; only electronic money and personal data are worth taking, and people have them stored inside their wrist wordfree.

Outside now, I'm trying to calm down. Trees are shedding a rusty pattern of leaves on the immaculate lawns. A soft breeze carries the damp freshness of mowed grass and the last of the roses. Anxious, tired, I'm slower than usual up the worn steps - to a gaping door…? No. The code works this time. My rooms are as I left them - I think. Dusty, but this is an old building.

I should slump, relax, and recharge before leaping on to the next stage of my professional and emotional existence - instead I'm battling waves of nausea and trying not to panic. I'm voiced to return urgently to the porters' lodge. I'll leave my wordfree monitor in my rooms. Deliberately. It records everything. What can I tell them? Nothing useful. Raphael must have returned from Jerusalem to collect his datadrive – the one I sent with Helen – before the break-in happened. She was to leave it in my lab for him... Of course, I forgot I gave her the code to do this. I'll have to tell the security people, the local police squad and the Zone law enforcement officers – the lot. My brain's like a shrivelled kernel rattling around in an empty skull.

Now, what to do about my lab?

* * * * *

After more questions from the security and the university's head administrator, I want to get away. To wander aimlessly along familiar streets, checking fearfully my crucial datadrive is hanging under my shirt. I must get everything on it to Raphael. Safely – how?

Even in the few months I've been in Africa, many old houses and shop fronts have been straightened into sleek variations of Martha's capsule. Magnus's drawings will be the only visual record of our town. No one bothers to digitalise such relics of an environmentally unfriendly past. St. Thomas's still stands here to defy the path of progress. I turn right through the open arched doorway. As if on cue, Sister Julian is there talking to some of her refugees. She calls out,

'Nicholas, back among us!' half in surprise while smiling a welcome. 'How was your bit of Africa?' I'm not sure where to begin and whether I even want to.

'Anywhere near Esther?' she continues. 'And how is she?'

'Fine, I think,' but I'm not sure. Esther is now busy with the new Mybeki Centre for Genetic Wellbeing. That's probably why she didn't offer to help me. She did say something about following the conditions of her assistantship with me: to return to help her community with her new knowledge and skills. I accepted that - how could I not?

Sister Julian is staring at me.

'Have you eaten? You look starved.' I am. Of love too. I hesitated.

'No, but -'

'Come with me.' Oh no, I don't want to cope with the badly phrased and well-intentioned chatter of her refugees, but she's off to the refectory without waiting for an answer.

'This is homemade soup from their allotment,' she says as she sits down on the other side of the table. 'And our bread too, though not our flour,' she adds, laughing at the gap in their self-sufficiency. Small groups are twittering outside the door. I ought to leave. Cheese, bread rolls and fruit are carried in by the smallest and darkest of the refugees. She has been watching us from the shadows at the far end of the room. I can't refuse. I eat: Sister Julian talks.

'Have you heard about our Leda? And the swan, of course!' I nod. 'Ah, I forgot. You could see *worldaroundyounews.* Wherever you are, it reaches you. Not as miraculous as when Nina –' Sister Julian turns to smile at the refugee in the shadows, '- asked if she could air all our vestments. That huge chest probably hadn't been cleared for a century or more!'

I concentrate on peeling an apple, instinctively not wanting to become involved. My hands have never trembled like this. I'm emotionally battered – but not destroyed.

'Experts still come, but I send them to the museum. We need peace and quiet here while we work, sing and pray together.'

'Museum?' I'm surprised. 'Isn't it the original work? A lost painting by Leonardo da Vinci?'

'Yes, so the experts say. Probably, they think, hidden in the chest about the time this church was restored, nearly 150 years ago.'

'What about the World Heritage Decree that all masterpieces must be preserved inside the Repository of the Originals in the Art Cavern, wherever that is?'

'Not if I can help it. The Art Cavern trustees tried to force me to give it to them, saying I couldn't prove ownership. Does this church own it? Or finders keepers? Then it would be Nina's. They assert it should be preserved in the air-conditioned cavern. No, I reply, it should be experienced by all, as the artist would have wished. No one, as far as we know, has contemplated the original for five centuries or more, so now is the time. There are long queues, just like when the Mona Lisa was on show. An art historian, Vasari or someone wrote, so I'm told, that all Florence crowded the courtyard of the Convent of San Marco to see it a long time ago. In the early 1500s. Now the same is happening here!'

'Can I see it?' That might dislodge the vision spinning round and round my mind of my raided lab.

'Yes. Come with me. You're tired and don't want to spend hours standing in the queue.'

I don't. The clouds are undecided, but thinking of rain. I prefer looking at art on my own, or with Helen. No, better with Mum; she knows more about it. Sister Julian will have to do.

Autumn draws the evenings in too quickly, brushing leaves along streets and huddling passers-by inside jackets. My steps strike dumb notes from the paving stones while Sister Julian patters along lightly beside me. Dazed, I've come from the Zueto trodden earth paths to slabs and hollow sounds in hardly more than a day. Following the murmurs, we catch the tail end of the queue. People of all ages are sitting on stools or rugs or leaning against walls talking, drinking, laughing, just being there and waiting for as long as it takes to see an original work of art. Extraordinary. Nothing like it in my lifetime. In mum's perhaps. And mother's, though she wouldn't then have bothered to go out to look at art.

Sister Julian guides me past them to the museum entrance. The vestibule bristles with indicators to all the galleries with brightly lit digitally exact exhibits that visitors can touch, turn, caress or just peruse, eyeball to object. All are exact copies of original works of art without market value or alarms. Security guards are having difficulty handling a crowd round the booking counter; one hurries over, inclines his head towards Sister Julian and slides a pass card over the turnstile. Only fifty people are normally allowed into the main gallery at a time to stand behind a semi-circle barrier, all equidistant from the dimly illuminated display case.

'Turn the lights up!' Sister Julian almost shouts. 'How dare you shroud a masterpiece in darkness? What did I tell you to do?'

'It isn't yours to decide,' announces a man with a bow tie who must have followed us out of the entrance hall.

'Why not? You may be the museum director but it was found in my church.'

'It belongs to all hukind,' intones the director.

'Yes. So why can't everyone contemplate it in clear light? As I stipulated, you remember?'

'I do...' and he lowers his voice as the semi-circle of onlookers stops peering at the priceless work to gape at the director and Sister Julian while I shrink into the group to spy what I can of Leda. She is a bit like Helen, undressed.

'I do remember, but I am responsible for this rare masterpiece which must be preserved forever.'

'For no one ever to see it?' Sister Julian is striding towards the climate and light control panel. Even under her red robe I think I see her bottom shift up and down determinedly just as Helen's does when she prowls towards her goal. Mother's too. Female body language. I feel slightly sorry for the director half running in tiny anxious steps after her.

'You mustn't touch it,' he whispers.

'We agreed on the level of lighting at the opening. Why did you change it?'

'Legally I had to -'

'You didn't say so at the time.'

'I couldn't because -' his voice peters into silence.

'Because?' Sister Julian stops abruptly, turning to meet him nose to nose. 'Because you have gone back on your word. Because you think that this work of art - it may belong to hukind but it was found in my church - should be incarcerated in the Caverns of Oblivion!'

'In the Repository of the Originals in the Art Cavern, the world centre for the safety, security and sustainability of all masterworks, past, present and future,' states the director with bureaucratic finality just as the picture is unexpectedly lit up.

Fifty-one people draw their breath in unison, gasps of sheer delight. I'm the fifty-first, and not the least or last to marvel at the work revealed, though it made me feel strangely uneasy. The director is fussing and perspiring behind Sister Julian who had changed the controls.

'I'm breaking the law, risking my position. What will others waiting say when this lot leave exulting and racing to tell everyone else out there that they've seen the masterpiece in full light? I've created a precedent because of you -' he raises his arm angrily as if to hit Sister Julian '- and will have to pay the price.'

'There's more at stake than you know,' she replies just before the bell rings and our fifteen minutes are up. 'You'll keep your job. I'll see to that when the bargaining begins.'

My way back passes St. Thomas's, so I'll accompany Sister Julian. Being with her takes my mind off the break-in. At least I have the key calculations safe in the datadrive here round my neck – I can't stop tugging the chain to check it's still there. So I accompany her, hurrying past the long tail of people waiting.

'What's at stake?'

'It's to be decided next week,' she says. 'That is, my idea of trading Leda for the historic university buildings by the canal. They are being deliberately neglected so that they'll become unsafe and can be scheduled for demolition, to be replaced by up-to-date buildings.' Martha could be behind that.

'It would tear out the little that still remains of the city's heart.'

'True. It seems they can't be refurbished to modern requirements. But they suit mine. We can do a swap. The policy makers take Leda if they let me have those buildings for my refugees.'

'To do what?'

'Form a sustainable community. As Reaching Out is doing. A hospital too. It's part of the worldwide peace plan. You must have seen this when you were in Africa.'

'I did.'

'We already have secured unwanted land on peppercorn rents,' she's almost out of breath, speaking enthusiastically, in short bursts as she patters along, 'mainly abandoned woodland for prisoners-on-parole. They're making a business out of old-time coppicing. Using every bit of the land. Wood for building and fuel and charcoal and fencing. Sunrays now reach the woodland floor – it's so beautiful to look at! Flowers poke up all over it. Last spring they started to sell violets, daffodils, primroses, bluebells and even cowslips. Now, I hadn't seen those since I was a child. Think of all the beauty lying under those trees! This is only their second season. They tell me they'll sell plants and seeds too.' As she pushes the church door open she adds, 'they're spreading a message about nature, and they're proud of it,' and disappears inside.

There's a shiver in the twilight and a delicate beauty in the dark leaves dangling on the trees along the street and crackling under my shoes. Instead of taking the shortest route back home, I follow a father and child Joe's age for a few streets, not really going out of my way. Joe, how I miss him! That's the chill I felt in my homecoming. Not just no Helen, but no Joe as well. No grin as he runs towards me; no cartwheels, one hand hardly touching the ground before a foot bounces him upright in front of me with,

'Yessir!' and a funny attempt at a salute.

I can see him as if here, hair tousled so I could stroke it back, eyes glinting with hope like a child by a wishing well. Oh, Joe!

No Joe. No Helen, and now the lab disaster!

My bags are still where I dumped them. I slump on to the sofa. What next? More calls from Security? From the Institute's Research Protection Centre? I could microwave a frozen pizza from the fridge, unpack, activate the sensor so the room heating comes on and the screen too. There's a strange fragrance in this room, not the dank smell of cold stone walls.

I'll relax on the sofa. Try to forget the rape of my lab. Close my eyes to relive the good moments. I'm home. I can relax - the datadrive with all the crucial calculations is safe on a chain round my neck - and try not to think of what has been rifled from my lab's hard drive. At least no one has burrowed into the technology here.

I've never realised quite how much floorboards creak in old buildings. Dust usually smells musty, but there's a distinct scent of roses.

There's a presence - I can feel it! I stiffen on the sofa. Something moves - I open my eyes and turn - there, framed in the doorway to the bedroom, hair ruffled, arms out towards me,

'Nicholas!'

'Why didn't you come to meet me?'

'Don't ask. Just come.'

Where has she been?

'I've waited so long for you -'

'Oh, Nick!'

Lying back she's drawing me to her, slowly lifting the datadrive on the gold chain she gave me over my head,

'It tickles,' she said, letting it slide down the side of the bed.

BREAKING NEWS

TRAGIC STORY OF IMMIGRANTS FROM AFRICA

In the long history of would-be immigrants leaving their place of birth and nurture to escape poverty or seek a fortune, few have suffered so many setbacks as the two who are now on the 'lost persons' list.
A group of Africans from different tribes turned their entire savings over to traffickers who crowded them on to a 50-year-old ferryboat. It capsized in a

crocodile-infested river. Two young boys swam to the shore unharmed. They followed tracks leading to a nearby settlement, later moving on northwest along a trail towards the nearest seaport. They stowed away on an old-fashioned steamer still chugging along the Atlantic seaboard to provide an authentic experience for off-the-beaten-track enthusiasts, one of whom was startled see a blood-streaked foot protruding from under a tarpaulin. The tourists insisted that the cold and hungry boy was given a free passage in exchange for some job. He ended up scrubbing the decks when not indulged by everyone except the ship's crew. As soon as the boat docked he disappeared, slipping away unnoticed into the crowd. He has been put on the worldwide missing persons' index. Click here for a description and artist's impression of the African youth.

worldaroundyounews.com

15

Autumn

Eliza's Journal

I compile this old-fashioned journal sporadically between tending my animals and vegetable plot in whatever light the sun stores up for me. I have procured a couple of solar panels and a water tub. There is also a pool filled from an unpolluted mountain stream. It is clear and cool and tastes of rocks and blue skies. The goats and sheep have their own troughs and the ducks their pond. I meet the other outwebbers once a week for matters of common interest at the terminus of the North Moorland Divergence Route. There is no social life to speak of, but that is one of the reasons why I came here. And the others too, I suspect. As well as issues arising from the basic desire to survive – eat, sleep and so on - we all need physical space. No children, no schools. A clinic? We have keys to the first aid unit in the station. It is internet-connected only for calls to the city emergency services. We are not entirely abandoned.

I have started painting again, eking out the pigments and brushes I brought with me, and am working on an earth art project. There is so much space here to be articulated: rocks of all hues, sandy soil, and also areas of chalk and clay. Some streams are clear and others red with iron ore. In places there is even gold, just glistening specks of it. I have started to collect stones and trowel up plants to stuff into the holes and crevices of the dry stone wall I am building. It should keep the hens and goats away from my cottage and vegetable garden, and stop Foxy chasing them. I change the stone pattern every day as I look and think about it.

Those of us living here represent 98% of the book of hukind's history before the internet era. We are not even part of the chapter of industrialised society, still less the paragraph of everyone out there entangled in the world-wide web.

I have just returned from the city. I have mislaid my wordfree monitor and it has the electronic codes on it for Nicholas, Martha, Karen, Sister Julian, Magnus and many others. Martha is 'out of office', Karen is abroad and not responding and Sister Julian is busily engaged. The porters at Greystone University said they did not know where he was if he was not in his lab or rooms. His colleagues, Esther and Raphael, were not there either, so who else could I ask? Nicholas seems to be close to Magnus so I could leave a letter at the Main Square info-hub for him. We have never met, though I know who he is. Nicholas is always talking about him and sees him a lot. I need his help to find Nicholas.

In the squares and down by the canal everyone was talking about Leonardo da Vinci. About seeing an original work by a genius! After delivering my message to the info-hub, I queued and queued outside the museum, but it was worth it. The handout said the painting needed little restoration as it was in a miraculously pristine state. In it Martha, our local member for the zone government, is quoted as saying, 'this is because it has been hidden from light and kept in a steady temperature for all those centuries. No handling, no bumpy journeys...' What rubbish! I should not say that about my daughter. Leonardo never came to our city. In his time there were only carts and saddlebags. The people I left to live here assume monopods, hoverpods, airjuggernauts and the worldwide web have existed forever! They do not probe the past. It's irrelevant to them.

Why then, are there lines of people to see the painting by Leonardo? Who can resist the touch of genius? Literally he, the great artist, touched, carried, and above all created this work. He stroked those warm colours across Leda’s body and mingled blues and greys in the misty landscape behind her and the swan. The shape of her body is soft and warm but as strange to Leonardo as it is lovingly familiar to me. More me than Karen. Leda is rounded but firm. Growing old she would have put on weight but never become taut, wrinkled and nervously alert like Karen.

Martha came here not long ago. She too only has an electronic address for Nicholas.

'I need to go to the mountains,’ she said. ‘That's why I'm here. Except of course, I want to see you.'

I do want to see her, and Karen, but not yet. I am not ready for the high charge they always emit - do this, buy that, go here, try there, and so on. Action, no time to let one’s imagination soar. Still, it was good, I suppose, to see Martha.

'Karen couldn’t find you on the Geomap. I asked for you when I arrived at the Terminus and everyone knew your cottage.'

'The Geomap? What's that?' Being an outwebber, I am ignorant of the hottest inventions off the netgeniuses' minds and, in theory, don't want to. However, curiosity won.

'Don't you know?' Martha was genuinely surprised. At least I think she was, though she did laugh in her nonchalant way. 'The genetic sensors can search the Geomap, so all one has to do is to supply the person's DNA code. It's quicker if one can also indicate approximately the relevant zone on the world map.'

Is this spying? I thought.

'It's a break-through above all for medicine,' she added.

'How?' I was still startled by the fact that I am now unable to move out of my cottage to potter in the garden or vegetable patch without being eyed from a satellite, albeit benignly in the case of Karen. Satellites are supposed to be amoral and impersonal. All depends on who wants to know the whereabouts of any live person whose DNA is recorded - and that now means almost everyone in the world. To access medical care, police protection or any sort of education, we must register our DNA. Outwebbers were supposed to escape all this.

'By anticipating and plotting the possible spread of epidemics,' Martha continued, 'and there are more recent examples I won't bore you with.'

'Can you contact Nicholas?' I asked anxiously, 'through his wordfree monitor?'

'Occasionally. He doesn't always remember to charge it. He told me that he would return soon and come to see you.'

I have no idea where he is in Africa. I imagine they were not allowed to tell me at the Institute, though I went there to ask them, insisting I was his mother. I need to picture people in their surroundings to feel comfortable about them. I have heard nothing since he left.

Martha refused to tell me why her visit here is 'confidential', but she has returned, the second time with Roland Wrightson.

'It's all top secret,' she insists, but not, I note, for other members of our zone government, like Roland. It would be easy then for one of them to confide in some investigative hack, but I do not want to get involved. It must be something to do with the causeway from the rail terminus to the mountains. There is a huge entrance to something that outwebbers say must be a network of caves.

As deputies for the Goodwill World Parliament, Martha and Roland did tell me they are on the same policy committee to do with original works of art. I would like to know more, but they seemed reluctant to explain what it is all about. I think they are 'an item' as we used to say. If I ask her, she laughs in a loud, open-mouthed way, and then smiles to stifle any verbal response, hers or mine. Affable or irritating? It can be both together. Their life, their affair.

I live beyond the North Moorland Divergence Route terminus on the edge of open moorland. From the kitchen window and the bench by the front door, I can trace the shape of the foothills and peaks already white after the first autumn snowfall. All this gives me another perspective. I have learnt how working with the terrain through the seasons can sustain me physically and mentally. I brought all I need in my electroVespavan. It is easy to charge and I lend it to other outwebbers. They give me practical help in return. I have a library of books that others have abandoned, and my piano came here straight from the storage capsule. In daytime I read or play it, even tune it after a fashion, and sing now that no one can hear me.

Luxuries? The word implies you do not need them. True. Comforts? More difficult. Now I am older, I am more susceptible to draughts, dampness and the like. But instead of putting woollies on in summer in the mortuary chill spread by inbuilt air conditioning, I wear light clothes in warm weather, and now it is cooler, thick jumpers with my old worsted skirts and various trousers. The caves in the foothills serve as natural larders - a word excavated from the times of our grandparents. One learns to respect other forms of life, to understand and live with them. We outwebbers share our caves and protect our stores from a number of harmless mammals. All creatures here are harmless unless hungry, afraid or attacked. But there are wolves eyeing the poultry. Their descendants, like Foxy, bark when the predators are on the prowl, so other outwebbers helped me build my henhouse. There are beavers too, chewing away in the forests that line the foothills.

This is what it is like to recolonise the 98% of our communal book when hukind lived in pre-industrial times. It is not Arcadia or the promised Land of Milk and Honey. I am trying to balance my time in the house, garden and vegetable patch with reading and music and thinking. Not a work-or-play division, exactly, though I do prefer some activities. Who really enjoys dusting, for example? But if the sun panels have generated enough electricity, I can play my antiquated collection of compact discs. At other times I work on my earth art project. I have almost finished the wall and have started a cairn made from the different rocks, varying the patterns and colours.

Not everything goes so smoothly. Sometimes there is friction. We barter, mostly in the twice-weekly markets, or use coins, still our small change. Most of us have our Goodwill World Parliament pensions to spend electronically only. More often than not solutions are found helping each other follow the grain of events or nature's seasons, whatever they happen to be. Useless to oppose what one cannot change.

Common sense, part of the oil that enables people to co-exist, is dying back there in the city. Lawsuits have long instilled a culture of fear and entitlement and the refusal to tolerate risk. The presumption is that one can insure and commercialise the future and muffle fear of the unknown. None of that here. We know we cannot control all outcomes and are much the calmer for it. There are meetings from time to time to resolve the few issues that arise. We keep to our own space, and there is enough of it around here.

However, we have nothing like the internet freedom to create all those virtual reality sites that keen webbers inhabit with their own avatars. Here we deal with what actually happens. No invention of perpetual sunshine without drought. Here we have weather to deal with in a constant dialogue for survival. It is not always easy, but as satisfying, I imagine, as creating your own fantasy world online. Here there is no illusion about anything or anybody! I do not need the stressless pills that were common in the haven homes, though I remember taking them in the Beech Drive capsule.

Rain and wind permitting, I write this journal on the bench by the front door. It is where I sit and look at the stone patterns in the wall and the late Michaelmas daisies, waiting for sunset. I've started planting a south-facing winter garden at the side of the house. Years ago I walked up Quarry

Hill on a bright, frosty afternoon, too cold for Karen to come. I took a short cut to the plain above the hanging woods and found myself - I don't know how - in a green oasis with the sunrays bouncing off holly leaves and rippling over the smaller tufts of yew and conifer spikes - all a symphony of evergreen foliage with baubles of red berries. A haven of winter stillness to warm body and soul. I returned in springtime with Karen and the children but could not locate it. They thought I had dreamt it. Nor could I find it on later attempts. So I am recreating it close by me. The holly will have berries for Christmas; the laurel hedge is growing slowly - one learns patience here – like the yew that I shall train into a hedge to shelter a south-facing bench. I hope to sit there and think in winter sunshine. It will all take time. In the early morning this summer I sat on the east side and watched the sun rising behind the peaks, touching the highland and gradually descending the foothills and over the moorland to find my cottage. The front of the house looks south towards the distant city and the sea, often shrouded in mist. On my left, about half a mile away, is the train station. Someone has just come out of the last hoverpod and is starting up the grit road. It's a man.

Nicholas?

16

Autumn morning

Nicholas *i-witnessNic227.futurepast.com*

'Dr. Middlethorpe, who knows your lab code?' The College security officer was drumming his fingers on his desk. 'The Institute inspector, our zone police and the GWP legal teams have been and gone, but they still lack basic information! Who has access to your lab?'

Who indeed? I hesitated and that irritated him, visibly thinking *why on earth does a scientist take so long to answer such a simple question?* Do I have to mention Helen?

'My assistants. And a friend.'

'I need their wordfree codes immediately,'

I thought them up on my wordfree monitor and transferred them to his wrist wordfree while he grunted on about having to question them. Easy, all done with a refined version of the old conferencing system. Face to face procedure is rare nowadays. We communicate through screens, a step outside reality.

'The Institute rules insist that you change your lab code every three months. Did you do it?'

'I – I think I did. I was away.' Luckily the security officer's mind was elsewhere too as, with one finger he jingled a large ring with useless, antiquated keys hanging from it, while poking the keyboard with the other. I rarely remembered to change the lab code even when here, still less when in Africa. I could have, but forgot. Or rather, I couldn't be bothered, and now the worst has happened. As an extra precaution, the Institute security officer sometimes changes the code and notifies the relevant users by wordfree. I wasn't notified of anything.

I suffer from the Procrastination Syndrome that psychotherapists go on about nowadays, undecided whether it's caused by the tyranny of digital gadgetry, or it's just day-dreaming. They don't deal in imagination it seems.

'Can I return to my lab?' It has been sealed off since I discovered the break-in. It would happen just at the moment I've proved my theory, testing over and over again the crucial calculations for the angle of the beam. Now I need to consolidate what I found out in Africa. I'm powerless. Downcast. The Institute will want me to patent my discovery. And then, I hope, confirm that Raphael's Energy Research Centre in Jerusalem will develop it.

'Yes. We have completed the investigation. The damaged hardware has been replaced and technicians have transferred all data back from the Institute database, checked with the Goodwill World Parliament cyberstore. You can access it all now.' He sighed and shook the keys that no one needs, fingering them admiringly. 'Just let us know what they were after and what they've taken.' He yawned.

*****

I'm slumped on a bench in the sunshine contemplating the fading flowers and trying not to panic. Silence is scratched by a falling leaf or rent by an air juggernaut.

The database isn't on the chain round my neck. It's on the gold chain Helen gave me. I've looked everywhere in my rooms and can't find it. It was round my neck in the airport, and I don't remember taking it off. All I know is that, when the security officer voiced me this morning I checked my neck – and it wasn't there! I stripped the bed, brushed the floorboards, looked under and on every piece of furniture in every one of the four rooms. It should be easy to find with a shiny gold chain. It wasn't there!

I might as well give up! What's the point of it all? My lab ransacked, my crucial database lost, my research assistants gone. What can I do? Fill in numerous forms to find suitable replacements? Re-run the final calculations in Africa? With whose money? Ross Mackenzie's? Worse than soul-destroying. It's as if your life is flowing away like a stream down a mountainside in front of you. My mind moves as if trudging aimlessly through sludge. Leaden, I open the door to the lab block. Dully, I climb the staircase past the Common Room, turning my head away from the glass door not to be noticed by its inmates in relax-and-chat mode. Numb with apprehension, I stab the new combination into my lab door. An incomer would not detect that it had been broken into as I do. Immediately.

The screens remain scratched but the hard drives are back. I go from one to another, noting the gashes in all of them. Not one spared. The model in the centre of the lab has been repaired, clumsily.

I have always been wary of the Institute's datasafe as well as the GWP's cyberstore, both automatically backed up in the early morning. Like the twin towers of financial power, the cyberstore and database would be easy targets. Too publicly known. Never violated but that is no assurance it will never happen. Someone else now has all my calculations right up to the last trials in Africa. So I always keep the crucial final calculations on a datadrive hanging round my neck and the password locked in my mind. Now the database is lost, I am too.

Oh Raphael, come back! Esther, where are you? Their voices. I can hear them as if they were beside me. Grit, that's what I need, Karen would say. Think positively, Eliza would add. Think ideas into the wordfree monitor. A kick-start. It's more comforting than filling online forms for grants, assistants and so on. But I don't know what to do without the datadrive. It can't have left my rooms. It's there. It must be there.

I'm laughing bitterly into my monitor. Here I am in my lab trying to jolt myself into action. Sit by the counter in front of the one small window; imagine breathing in fresh air and inspiration. Around me creep whispers, whiffs of hot busy bodies, the scraping of tools as they prise out my invention - the breath of violation. Enough! I'm shrieking silently. I had my life's work round my neck. My datadrive on the gold chain Helen gave me. Check. No, no, no. It isn't there. Then it must, just must be in my rooms. Quick. Back there now. It can't be anywhere else.

*****

I'm still trembling, back in my rooms. When was it I last worked out my thoughts calmly in lab or home? I've just left the lab to find refuge here. It was impossible to avoid the helousine in the parking lot on my way back. Two figures stood beside it. I couldn't see who they were. The sun was behind them.

'Nick!' A female voice.

'Nicholas!' A male one.

Both pronounced with emphasis, and in unison they continued.

'So glad to see you!'

I felt like a nut being cracked.

'Can we talk?' Just the male voice this time.

'Sorry.' My voice wavered. 'I have to go.' Flee. To my rooms. To find that datadrive.

I wondered whether it really was them.

'Can we take you?' The figures moved out of the sunlight closer to me in the shade. Helen had a sharp look about her, though her eyes were tender. She would be thinking, *things happen to forgetful people who don't have a wrist implant*, her usual reproach. It was hardly the moment to ask if she'd given my lab code to him – or anyone else. I glanced round. No silver-grey limousine. The helousine couldn't land where I wanted to go.

'Don't worry,' she said. 'We can take you anywhere.'

I must have seemed like a trapped animal, eyes swinging from left to right to avoid looking at them. As Dom Ross Mackenzie closed in I tried to edge away. I could run across the lawn in the quadrangle to the short cut into town.

'I can refinance your lab, re-equip it and pay for any number of assistants. Do you need to return to your testing area in Africa? Just let me know... come to my place…dinner…in peace and quiet…'

He seemed far-away, only the odd word snagging my attention. 'It will…I…can…'

I felt faint. Does he know about the lab break-in? Or is he finding another way to offer me help? Is he behind it? *We want hard evidence*, the security officer had insisted. *No suppositions or suspicions.*

'Has Helen anything to do with your offer?' An incautious question to ask. She looked startled and displeased.

'Why shouldn't I help you?' she said, a touch petulantly, shaking her shoulders. She was improbably lovely. I needed to clasp her and bury my head in her warmth, but her suit looked like defensive armour.

'Thanks. Tomorrow. Sometime.'

'Tomorrow evening. Dinner. I'll send my car. 7.30?' I noticed how strangely plump and smooth his hand was. Not a handshake to inspire confidence.

'No... No, I'm not free,' and I turned away to avoid looking at either of them.

* * * * *

Are they together? I'm only thinking it now, into my monitor. Not when I almost ran across the lawn to my rooms; searched them not once, but over and over again. No datadrive. Despair! I have to get out. Go somewhere else. Think. Decide. To get away I took the longer route to town along the canal to avoid passing St. Thomas's.

The canal is the calm waterway that bypasses the turbulent Greystone River. Our favourite expedition as children was to the mountains where the river poured over a wide ledge into the plain below. Mother told us that for centuries, before films and the internet, the Middle Sister Falls were a romantic place to visit and frequently recorded by artists and poets. The Greystone River irrigates some of the richest agricultural land anywhere, fought over in history and now intensively farmed by rival international conglomerates.

The canal leads you into the ancient part of the town, past warehouses and old town dwellings. I dawdle by the abandoned university buildings where I studied for my degree. I turn through open gates into a courtyard of buildings that housed students for centuries. There are muffled sounds. Hardly workmen. It's after hours. I kick some stones and broken glass and glance up at the great hall where I graduated - three years early, my mothers would repeat too often, as if expecting still more from me. Slates slipping off the steep roof; windows and stones charred by recent arson; panes gaping here and there. I shiver, hear running feet and turn - nothing. Laughter from the gable windows above the courtyard? A flickering light? No, a ray teasing the panes still unbroken in the high windows. Walk faster. Leave through the gates by the canal with its freight of discarded bottles and cartons floating by.

If only Ezra were walking across the cobbles towards me, smiling. Same height, similar build – almost twins other students used to say, though he's a pianist and I'm a scientist. I took it for granted he would always be around. Instead I stayed while he has become so famous that he is always on tour somewhere else. Martha assures me he will return here to give at least one concert. She plans to promote it.

Bright lights and voices. Hungry, I stumble into a supermarket, unsure what I want to eat. Picking items off the shelves, I'm mesmerised by the glare and noise.

'No good being too intelligent,' remarks the girl at the checkout, for no good reason.

'Why not?'

'That sort asks too many questions.'

'Isn't that good? It's the way to learn.'

'What?' She's cramming the groceries into one bag, splitting it in the process. 'That sort gets up to bother.' She pushes it towards me, smiling. 'We need p and q, that's all!'

Peace and quiet. No bother.

Gathering shadows cross stones worn by centuries of hurrying feet. The patter of memories. Straggling couples of varying ages, men and women, women and women, men and men, a father and son. They turn left along a cobble lane, still talking, and then out into the busy square where the first of the canopy heaters warm the chatter round tables. Lives united in a buzz of contentment. He and his son sit looking at each other, then at the waiter and at others around them. Bonded. Belonging.

I take the table next to them but can't think of an excuse to join them. I'll just observe. I imagine a father and son sharing time and hopes. That particular texture of male lives. Mothers and daughters: Karen and Martha. Fathers and sons.

NEWS BULLETIN

LATEST NEWS FROM CHINA

President Chang Lin has been inspecting the centres known as Queen Bee Huhives in the industrialised north-east province of China. Partially inspired by the defunct **Kibbutz** movement many decades ago in **Israel**, now the engine of the throbbing **Middle East Alliance**, these centres in China provide luxurious self-contained capsules for women and their main partners, while their other male admirers are lodged in single ones. Women used to have open houses for what was then called their 'harem', but fighting among male visitors led to these dwellings being turned into individual cell nests, each with a double bed, internet access and twenty choices of sleep sound.

The President praised the amenities that have been provided around each cluster of **Queen Bee Huhives**: excellent medical services and schools for everyone in these communities and, if capacity allows, for people living outside the clusters. However she declined to comment on the recently passed **stricter laws prohibiting female infanticide.**

A prominent Sinologist, Karen Middlethorpe, visiting professor at the new Sino-World University of Shanghai, has found a little-known **ancient legend of a swan giving birth to hukind children** during her research in the remote north-west of China.

'It will be posted in due course on an archaeological website, with accompanying publicity,' she promised.

worldaroundyounews.com

17

Eliza's Journal

Autumn is indecisive. I still try to sit by my front door facing west as now, to write my journal. Oh, the sheer pleasure of pressing ink on to paper through a soft nib! Before I left, I bought all the writing material I could find from a shop in the city that was closing down. It should last me out, as long as I do not write too much. Two days ago it must have been - repetitive calm makes it hard to recall precise times - there was a strong breeze from the north, so I sat for the first time inside my new winter garden, facing south and the sun, such as it was. Outside my green cocoon the wind carried the thunder of the Middle Sister Falls, a boom beyond my evergreen tranquillity. The wind dropped unexpectedly. I returned to my usual watch in front of the house. The green smell of water floats down on the northeast winds from the waterfalls, following the Greystone River that flows through, it is said, the world's most productive orchards and vineyards into the sea.

That is, unless the snows from the saw-edged heights melt into the Falls and the estuary floods. It has never happened but is predicted in the 'Every Eventuality' scenario. We have all rehearsed our roles. Up here we outwebbers would be the first to test the safety measures.

The wind has swung the tumult back east behind me and the sunset is shedding a golden sheen across the agricultural paradise. The last hoverpod of the day has emerged from the tunnel to stop at the terminus before looping back the way it has come.

Two days ago I watched a man leaving the station. He did not follow the path to the outwebbers' renovated shepherds' huts, but turned up the hill towards my cottage.

Nicholas - at last! Martha said she would trace him on the Geomap if she had time. Nothing was mentioned when she came here. It was obvious her mind and emotions were too fully engaged with whatever she and Roland Wrightson had to bother about at the end of the causeway.

He walked like an older man. Oh Nicholas, what has happened to you in Africa? So aged in those few months?

No. It was Magnus.

*****

Magnus paused when he saw me outside the cottage, observing him. He must have found the message I had asked an outwebber to voice him from our Moorland Station hub. He was not unexpected. I invited him inside. Humming, almost childlike, he wanted to help by placing logs geometrically in the large fireplace. I eat, read, paint and play the piano in the kitchen - my living space.

After sunset, at supper, Magnus told me why Nicholas was not with him. Just back from Africa, he had found his lab broken into. Quite a lot of damage which was being repaired. So sad. He was too busy – probably depressed – to come.

'Can I do anything for Nicholas?'

'The Institute is repairing the lab. All his material is safely stored in the Institute Database backed up by the GWP Cyberstore. He hasn't lost his invention.'

'What about the final tests? The ones in Africa?'

'He may have stored them elsewhere. I hope so. If he doesn't tell me, I don't ask.'

'But you helped him with the crucial research in Africa, didn't you?'

'Eliza, he's told me the project was successful. That's all.'

Unlike most people, entranced by the flames bobbing, curling and licking the air under the chimney hood, he leant back in the only other armchair to contemplate the rafters instead, one hand beating out a rhythm.

'I thought that ants,' he said quietly after a long silence, 'ate onions, peppers or sweet corn strung from beams'.

'No, they don't. People have stored produce like this since -' I was going to say since agriculture began after the hunting-and-gathering chapter of human existence, but it sounded obvious or silly, '- until refrigeration'.

'Yes,' and he continued humming and jiggling a foot to the beat of his fingers as he looked into the darkness above my recent harvest. I couldn't see the dust up there and wanted to ignore it.

'In the city everyone's talking about the Great Fire.'

'What fire?'

He stared at me. It seems hard for those entangled in the web to understand us outsiders. How can we bear to live in ignorance? Well, we can.

'The one in the old university. Fire fighters were injured, but no loss of life.'

'What happened?'

'It started in the main quadrangle of the old university buildings - the disputed ones. I don't know the ins and outs. Your daughter Martha, even before she was elected to our zone government, wanted them to be gutted and renovated. Some building consortium has proposed demolition and redevelopment into a zone of state-of-the-art mixed business and housing units. It's a prime site. Just by the canal.'

'And an historic one.' I thought of the centuries of people living, studying, loving, shaping their future there, all gutted. The past burnt away. 'Was the old university quarter burnt to the ground?'

'No. Not so starkly tragic as that. Nobody knows how it began. While arguments raged over the future of the so-called 'obsolete historic buildings', they were neglected and the electricity cut off. So no alarm system. Nobody thought of draining the water tanks. During that harsh winter two years ago they froze and burst, flooding the lower floors. Dry rot spread unchecked.'

'Deliberate neglect?' I hate myself for always finding the worst motives, especially if Martha might be involved.

'Some say so. Even a group formed to save the historic centre began to whisper that, given the dangerous and decrepit state of the structure, demolition might be inevitable.'

The flames had died down leaving glowing embers in the fireplace and dread in the cold spreading from the space behind us. He warmed his hands before adding more logs, criss-crossing them carefully.

'People only realised it was on fire when the flames hit the roof. All the local fire engines were called and she arrived with – '

'Who?'

'Sister Julian with her refugees.' I frowned. How odd.

'Not surprising,' Magnus continued, 'since she had made the offer to exchange Leonardo's Leda and the Swan for the abandoned university quarter.'

'Was it accepted?'

'Yes.'

'So the painting has left the museum?'

'Just.'

'Where?' Why was I asking this and not more about the Great Fire? So I added, 'how much has burnt down?'

'Only one corner of the Great Quad. It could have been far worse. Sister Julian's cohort of refugees saved much from inside, but she disobeyed the firemen, went too close and her robes caught fire. She was taken protesting to the central infirmary with some of the firemen.' He paused. 'They have all been discharged. There is a lot of wood in those old buildings.'

* * * * *

Magnus has stayed on here. I do not know why, but it was not to scrounge. His knap sack was full of pressure-sealed beef, chicken, vitamised seaweed, bars of Reaching Out chocolate and dried fruit. He asks me to play tunes he can dance to, goes on long walks in our valley, and talks of exploring the Middle Sister Falls, but I am trying to dissuade him, especially now night falls earlier each evening. The higher you go the more likely you are to encounter a sudden blizzard, even in autumn.

Maybe he needs open spaces and solitude like me.

I am amazed at how much I want to hear about what is going on, gossip, anything, though dismayed that he does not seem to know much, or want to tell me - apart from the Great Fire. Some people - perhaps most of us - have a huge narrative inside struggling to be freed. The tittle-tattle of everyday events that most of us cling to crowds it out.

'We're bombarded with unfiltered local, regional and world news,' he explained. 'It becomes like a minestrone of happenings - nothing singularly impresses you -' he paused, '- unless it is haunting and tragic or so immense that it stifles all that onslaught of visual chatter'.

'Martha told me a bit about Karen,' I said, 'but I couldn't figure out whether her involvement with President Chang means she is actually or virtually in China'.

Magnus laughed. He seemed more relaxed. 'I think one can only dabble in archaeology through the internet, even though literally everything above, on or beneath the earth's surface seems to be visually and verbally available in detailed online libraries.'

'She studies ancient Chinese legends, so I suppose she could do it all from Beech Drive and through virtual conferences with experts in China,' I thought out loud, wondering how affectionate internet contacts might be.

'She was on *worldaroundyounews* recently,' he said. 'Something about researching for an internet book on Chinese cuisine and inspecting the Queen Bee Huhives – as the new-style harems have been renamed. Difficult to do that from a distance.' Magnus smiled and poked the fire. He has taken over the task of clearing the ashes and laying it, always bringing more wood back from his walks and arranging it in meticulous piles near the hearth. He has also tuned my piano!

His words came out of the darkness around us in the kitchen, his face and hands picked out by the dying flames. They haunt me. Do I miss Karen or is it envy that she enjoys a high profile existence without needing me - probably not even thinking of me? She is now, he says, a 'visiting professor' at the new Sino-World University in Shanghai. Her right. I was the one who left. No regrets.

'You wanted to know about Nicholas,' he said. That was, indeed, the whole point of my contacting him. 'Well, I forgot to tell you of a strange coincidence. He has been living in Africa where I was. The same bungalow. I was there before the meteorstrophe.'

'Oh?'

'And, in a message about how the tests were going, he mentioned that he'd found a photo of a woman. That would have been Gaia,'

'Who is she?'

Then he began painfully walking back into his past.

'I was rich then, and famous and lost. What was then called "a celebrity". I couldn't go out into the street without people mobbing me. It was a prickly sensation - eyes poking at me; people stopping and expecting me to do an impromptu dance - particularly my pattern of three turns. Nosing their way under my skin - more concentrated even than a stage spotlight - they realised that was my favourite dance, my symbolic core.' To my amazement he got up, driven by inner impetus or the cold around us, and whirled, beating a rhythm out on the earthen floor. Now, as when I first saw him online, I realised why people couldn't turn away and how, moving with feline fluidity, he hypnotised you.

Then he stopped.

'Age tells. I'm nothing like what I was when I gave money to the fledgling Reaching Out organisation and went to see what was happening to it in Africa. There I met Gaia.'

A log burst into flame. Sparks shot up and out at us.

'She was the one that mattered. So different. She had become part of the social landscape in the savannah where Mybeki was the end of the rail, air and internet links with the world. Wild open spaces where the local people, the Zueto nomads, had recently settled. She was sent by Reaching Out to help them develop as part of a Goodwill World Parliament agrarian and industrial peace settlement in a former war zone.'

I had somehow heard about this almost secret organisation and how it helped supervise the arms amnesty and transform weapon manufacture into peaceful enterprises.

'My emotional skeleton developed from an early age, from before I can remember, always around number patterns and the rhythms and shapes and colours they created. Gaia helped make sense of it all.'

What could I say? It was late and only the shadows were dancing now, till they too died into the embers. We sat silently hunched by the fireside.

'Please ask Nicholas to come here. He can come any time.'

Yesterday when Magnus was about to leave, we saw a procession along the causeway to the mysterious portal on the lower slope of the mountains. It is remote and inaccessible except on foot. To deter any unwanted activity, the causeway is under electronic surveillance. It must have been programmed to allow this straggling group to reach the massive doorway. Two figures at the centre held a large box. I almost tripped over the threshold in the rush to find my binoculars. The first and last in the procession were carrying animal stun rifles.

We watched them transfixed. Then Magnus checked the throbbing in his inset and held his wrist to his ear.

'Martha apologises. She can't drop in, as she has to catch the last hoverpod back. An important meeting.'

'How does she know you're here?'

'The Geomap. They have my DNA with everyone else's.'

Not Nicholas's or mine.

'Come back!' I called as he walked down the path to the station, 'any time you feel like it.'

He half turned and waved with,

'Yes, I shall.'

18

Late autumn

Martha *i-witnessMAR754.futurepast.com*

I'm assaulted by stressful situations:

The fire in the old university buildings.

Nicholas's DNA not being registered in the world genetic archives - how could he have escaped? And how many others have too, one wonders? Like mum. That upsets the world's safety system. Terrible, when you come to think of it. How many have not been DNA registered in school or hospital? There can't be many of them, surely?

What one doesn't know one doesn't care about. Anyone in public office like me knows too much. To add to my stress list there's Sister Julian and her crazy idea to lodge her refugees in the old university buildings. I won't add her prisoners-on-parole to my list as they seem well settled in their woodland activities. Some say they'll never want to leave their forest prison!

I should nudge my PR about this. 'Prisoners-on-parole are bringing abandoned woodlands back into production by creating an eco-viable business. Modelling themselves on ancient woodland self-sustaining industries of long ago...' I could rumble on. Why hasn't Jan picked up on all this? She has lain fallow since masterminding my election campaign.

Jan is another stress point. Add Roland Wrightson, member of the Zone Government and delegate to the GWP like me. This list might never end. Above all, I'm worried about Nicholas and the lab break-in. Is enough being done about it? Why didn't I stick to my job designing stress-free living capsules for present and future generations? Why, I ask myself, did I stand in both world and local elections when I'm always complaining about the sheer volume of work, the weight of responsibility and the weird stew of niggling, peevish issues that boils over to submerge the crucial ones?

I'm trying not to swallow another stressless pill. Delegate lesser problems to people in my team? They juggle them, occasionally finding a solution but more often muddling matters.

Mum used to hum some sort of song about, 'The politician's life is not a happy one!' But it does give power and you're often elated. For the first time I'm wishing my wordfree wasn't implanted. I'm trying to take a day off in spite of the fire in the old university and the stack of constituency messages I should be sifting through.

I can't ignore the unrest here at the Centre for Genetic Wellbeing. They don't want their research focus removed to Mybeki. I've no idea what Esther will say to calm them down when she returns. Yet another stress point. If I mention those Chinese Queen Bee Huhives to Roland, he won't stop laughing, as if hilarity would solve world problems! This morning I propped myself up on my elbow to contemplate the celebrity politician prostrate beside me in the carefully filtered low-level lighting that I have assiduously orchestrated. Off guard, he revealed an incipient gut bulge, sagging lower lip and a hint of greying sideburns. He smelt of fresh sweat laced with Olympic aftershave, his youthful venture into such products after the last Olympics. But he isn't unaware of what's happening. Last night, after an elaborately exciting moment, he whispered, 'What are you doing to help your brother?' in my ear. It froze me, and he rolled away with a moan,

'Hasn't he told you? He's lost the key datadrive. The one with the final calculations for his invention.'

I can't remember whether I even answered, stunned because Nicholas hadn't told me – his message was probably lost in the cascade of all the wordfree messages I hadn't accessed. So here is another to 'chalk up' as mum would say, quaintly, on my lengthening list of stress points. Nicholas's lab raid and now his lost datadrive. He should have hidden the crucial calculations safely on a wrist inset, but he refused to have one inserted. Obstinate, just like mum.

'Datadrive?'

'Yes. Our office cleaner told me this morning. She also does Nicholas's rooms. He asked her to help him scour them for the missing datadrive. She said he was almost crying, he was so upset.'

Roland's bulging waistline disappeared as he stood up. 'Do something to help your brother,' he said as he pulled on his clothes. It happened yesterday and he's telling me now! Roland is neither imaginative nor practical, it seems. He always thinks he can sail by on his inexhaustible charm.

I must find Nicholas. He's not answering his voicemessages. I'll have to look for him dressed anonymously. What are all the Helen-led women wearing this autumn? Vlason is still the fabric in fashion, affordable for most women and you can choose the surface quality of any material you want it to ape. You name the traditional cloth and vlason can imitate it ready to dispatch in a few hours. Thus the marvels of modern photosynthetic 3-D garment printing. I love it.

I digress. Digressions are often more creative than the main narrative. I'm still trying Nicholas's wordfree monitor without success. I'll put on my green vlason trouser suit, and wind an olive and cream Nantung scarf round my hair so people won't recognise me, though they hardly turn to look now that nearly every woman is blond. I've gone off this shade of green, so it's downgraded to mundane activities when I don't want to be noticed, such as shopping or now.

The first stop is the obvious one: Nicholas's flat in the Institute… It is locked and silent… His lab is the same. Where next? As I pass the security office I hear,

'Deputy Middlethorpe!' My disguise isn't working. 'Please come in.' He's jiggling a ring with heavy old keys on it. 'A child of about twelve, olive-skinned – he said his name is Joe – is looking for someone he met in Africa. That could be your brother. He isn't in his rooms or lab. The child slipped away while we were trying to contact Dr. Middlethorpe.'

'Yes, yes, I'll find them.' That could be Joe, the child he befriended in Africa.

'Please inform Dr. Middlethorpe that his office in now fully as it was... as he would like it to be...'

'Yes, I will.'

I don't relish the city centre and the gastrohub he usually frequents. People stop me in the street mainly to mouth irritating protests or petty requests. Still, that's the place to start. The quickest route from the northern outskirts is past St. Thomas's, but I don't want to bump into Sister Julian. Her piercing grey eyes make me wince because the old university buildings haven't yet been officially transferred to her refugee commune, as agreed. The fire and much else have delayed the handover. Has she changed her mind? The development consortium is still interested. I'll take the monorail into town instead.

* * * * *

The terminus is in the main square with the old university. People are congregating to look at the fire damage and pronounce on it. I can hear them in my mind's ear and don't want to. More people, less likelihood they will recognise and hinder me. A crowd, so less chance of finding the child. The security office says he's about twelve and olive skinned. I could splash that description over all the plasma screens in this square - the huge outside ones that mum detests so much. She's quite illogical.

'You like opera on the big screen,' I used to remind her before she deserted us, to be rebuffed with, 'only in the right place, and not on an ugly screen hiding superb buildings in our city centre'. Then up comes her pet phrase, 'They've an historical statement to make,' and on she goes about all the lives that have stepped through this space and left part of their being. I don't take all that. Space is space to move in; buildings have specific functions, as well as protecting us from heat or cold. They exist because we want something practical from them, not all her sentimental history stuff.

I'll wander around, weave in and out of the labyrinth of streets outside the main square and the old university quarter along the canal. No sign of either of them yet, but then it's easy to miss someone down a side alley, in a dark corner or behind an old shop front - all the clutter that history brings with it. Thank goodness new towns have neat grid plans, streets at right angles and carefully slanted so they don't become wind tunnels. New buildings are faced in breeze-dusted, rain-washed multi-purpose Drastone Composite surfaces impregnated with any colour the owner chooses. It must be rather like the owners of the green, yellow, pink or even blue houses and towers in the paintings of Italian hill towns that mum showed us when we were small. They looked like fantastical cities of a child's building block towers, a sort of medieval New York.

I digress while thinking into my wordfree and searching for them in the city centre. It calms me down.

No sign of Nicholas. Would I recognise Joe? Nicholas did send pictures of the boy while he was in Mybeki, or Zueto, or wherever. I can't remember exactly what Nicholas said. Medium height, wasn't it? Tousled hair, tanned skin and fantastic eyes? Probably with heavy eyelashes that curl up at the tip. A slight eleven or twelve-year-old.

Back crossing the main square to head for the gastrohub Nicholas usually goes to - someone's coming up behind me -

'Martha!'

*****

I stopped thinking into my wordfree to deal with Helen. Alone now, at home in cleanlined comfort, I can gather my thoughts about our gastrohub conversation while I sat there hoping Nicholas would walk in with Joe.

'Nick? I've seen him since he returned from Africa.' She kept spreading out her hands to look at her fingernails. 'He's voiced me. Sounds frantic. He's lost his datadrive. He kept it on a gold chain, the one I gave him to hang his final calculations round his neck so he wouldn't lose them. Now he's done just that! I offered to help look for it, but he said he had already done so, and just broke off. Like that.' She clasped her hands and looked at me. 'So what could I do to help him? Now you say the African boy is looking for him at the Institute. I saw him in Africa, in Nick's lab. I must tell you...'

My mind was drifting. Helen's wasn't. She clearly needed someone to confide her tremendous luck. She was about to appear on *worldaroundyounews* channel for the first time ever.

'Though my promotion slots are based on the local high street, they are web-linked and transmitted all over. Other promotions try to block them, of course, but many internet programs take clips of them. I'm not well known beyond the local network, so this is my big break!' She was shimmering with excitement.

'So?' I wasn't concentrating. Where could I find Nicholas?

'I've been chosen to promote a world-shaking discovery. Something… I can't tell you, but it's so important that it will change everyone's life - for the better, of course.'

Beech Drive. That's it! Nicholas will have gone there hoping to see one or both of our parents.

I tried to stop thinking about Helen while sitting on the Eastwest monopod line. I've never thought her smug. She has probably always preened herself, but I haven't before seen her stretch her legs out from below a glossy pleated red skirt under a jacket cut to emphasise her breasts. Her shoulders were pulled just a fraction too far back. Brash was the word once used. And her whole marketing business is supposed to epitomise stylish individuality! Once gained, it's hard to maintain celebrity status in the commercial world.

Mine is more secure because it depends on a democratically chosen mandate, not a whim.

What a relief. I found Nicholas at Beech Dive, in the capsule I had installed specially for our parents. He hugged the breath out of me.

'Martha, I was so hoping to see you. D'you know about the lab break-in?' I nodded. 'Worse still, I've lost the datadrive hanging round my neck. The chain must have broken. Something has happened, and I can't find it. I've looked everywhere.' He slumped into mum's armchair, head in hands, sobbing.

'When did you last see it?'

'I'm, I'm not sure. I can only remember checking it when I stepped off the airjuggernaut. And again, when I was talking to the security officer at the Institute. After the break-in. Then – nothing.' He was running his fingers through his hair, almost tearing it out. 'I've looked everywhere, stripped my bed, and swept the floorboards – everything. It's not there. All my final calculations lost.'

I took his hands,

'Let's look again, together. Then come to my capsule and I'll make supper.'

I didn't want to complicate matters by saying that Joe has somehow found his way here from Africa and is looking for him. He seemed more cheerful telling me that Ezra, now an international pianist, is out of hospital after a terrible accident. Ezra wasn't allowed to tell him exactly what happened – something about it being a first time and to avoid copycat attacks. Anyway, he'll be giving a concert here in the New Year. Then, just as we were walking across the Main Square, a photomessage flashed across the plasma screens. It was a close-up of a child's quivering face, with beneath it in multiple languages,

'Does anyone know Joe?' Nicholas stopped, then cried out, 'I do!'

BREAKING NEWS

MERCY MESSAGE

A twelve-year-old child from Africa has been found wandering around the **Institute at Greystone University** asking for someone he met in Africa. He speaks little English but is determined to find the person he knows. Appeals have been made to find someone connected to the Institute who has recently visited Africa and met this child.

Meanwhile Joe has been taken to **St Thomas's Church** to join the refugee community about to move to the old university buildings. Though he has been welcomed, **Sister Julian** reminded us that the accommodation is too crowded.

'**Jesus** would never have refused shelter and food,' she affirmed, 'but the fire in the old university buildings has delayed our move to form a sharing community there. There is simply not enough room for all of us here in the church and adjacent buildings.'

Sister Julian was speaking to journalists and photographers and a small crowd outside St. Thomas's: 'I shall look after the child, but on condition there is no internet publicity,' she stressed. However, the authorities have decided to send out this Mercy Appeal on our newsscreens.

worldaroundyounews.com

19

Winter

Nicholas *i-witnessNIC227.futurepast.com*

23 December

Martha and I hurried across the square, almost running along the street to St. Thomas's. There he was, Joe squeezed between two grown-up refugees on the crowded refectory benches!

'It's merciful that you've come,' Sister Julian said as Joe clung to me, almost hurting in a desperate hug while uttering fragmented sentences in his own mix of English and Zueto - our way of communicating.' Even if God didn't exist, we'd have to invent him to carry the anguish of all these wandering souls.' She waved at her family of refugees. 'No keys yet for the old university from the local authorities. They have Leda, their part of the exchange, but the fire seems to have caused delays. I can help with the fire damage,' she surveyed all the willing hands in front of her and probably thought of others, 'but it's not easy with all these vulnerable refugees crowded in here'. Her eyes tightened slightly at the corners. 'There's space in those unloved and abandoned university buildings to care for many more of them. And to create a hospital area with new state-of-the-art surgery capsules.'

* * * * *

It's impossible to express my feelings of joy mingled with apprehension, unaware of how deeply I missed him. Or my amazement at how much I have to deal with: identification papers, registration permit with

DNA imprint, medical papers with DNA recognition again. Joe has a gutful of parasites and a nasty rash. How bright his eyes are, his smile so spontaneous and his hair so sprightly in spite of all that he had gone through! And he has never left the Zueto area before.

Some are born resilient, some learn to be, while others flounder. Like me? How could I so stupidly lose the crucial datadrive? I was sure it would be safe hanging round my neck on the gold chain Helen gave me. I must have taken it off without realising – but where did I put it? Gone. Just like that. Into thin air. I've searched for it everywhere, looking over and over again in my rooms. What else can I do? I've been wandering around listless. Go back to repeat the tests in Africa? Where's the funding? But now – here's Joe!

After registering him, I shall find him a school. Mum must see him. Mother too, but I'm not sure how to contact her. She's always travelling somewhere. Mum's easier. Her cottage is near the last station on the North Moorland Divergence Route.

* * * * *

Joe understands more than I realised. Once inside my rooms, he started searching over every strange surface repeating 'datadrive'. No luck, but he keeps on looking. How hyperactive children are and how tired they get! We had an early supper here with Martha, and he's sleeping now on my bed.

'Can't he have his own?' Helen is prickly. I might be too when she drops in at her pleasure. I shouldn't have given her the lab code, or the one to my rooms here. I was having fun with Joe pulling out cardboard boxes from under my bed to unpack the remains of my childhood, salvaged from the wreckage of 11 Acacia Avenue.

'He's taking you over all right!'

Is she being ironic or just vexed? I get up to hug her, but she remains immobile, unresponsive.

'We've eaten,' I say, 'have you?' We have an unwritten agreement that she can't expect any food here without voicing me beforehand. 'I can find something'.

'An omelette?' There's a slight sneer, I think, in her voice. 'That's all you could manage when we first met, and it's about all you can do now'.

I look at her. She has changed. I can't make out exactly how. Plumper perhaps. Yes. Larger. She often comes in the evening when her skin appears luminescent and her hair a deeper auburn.

'We could go out. Or to your capsule.' I shouldn't suggest that. She doesn't like me to go there, for unstated reasons.

'With Joe?' I was unexpectedly shaken by the hostile tone. Of course. I can't now eat or sleep or go anywhere without thinking of him. But he can also be an excuse for not doing things. Like dinner with Ross Mackenzie.

'Yes,' I say simply, and she leaves after a perfunctory kiss.

'Sleep well,' she says opening the front door, 'now that you have new company'.

* * * * *

I sleep well enough and wake to find Joe already in the kitchen tearing at what remains of a loaf.

'Ungry,' he says smiling. His appetite is insatiable. The gut parasites - I must get him to a doctor. Perhaps a pharmacist can help. A medical outlet has appeared close to Martha's constituency office in a fiercely new complex. It slots all health, hygiene, administrative and related commercial and social facilities into mutually advantageous proximity. Contemporary technolust has been satisfied. The pharmacist knows exactly which pills are needed. Why not see if Martha is in her office?

'He looks better already,' she says, holding out both hands to Joe. 'Welcome.' A pause. 'Does he understand English?'

'A little. More every day.' She hugs him, repeating how she had looked all over the city centre for both of us. She has been worrying about me since I returned from Africa and was baffled when she too couldn't find the datadrive.

'Are you sure, Nicholas, you didn't drop it somewhere outside your rooms? In the lab?' My memory is drifting. Butterflies are fluttering around in my head. I shook it, wishing she would stop feeding my despair. For now, I want to concentrate on Joe.

'Or in the airjuggernaut, Nicholas?' She goes on and on. I want to forget it all – at least for now.

'No, Martha, it was round my neck when I carried the luggage to my rooms.' Stop, just stop! She changes tack at last.

'I'll get him new clothes!' So off we go, crossing the main square to the dome outlet by the old university, where he can poke at images of the clothes he needs and have them brought to try on. We spend the rest of Saturday together in a commercial comfort zone - brother and sister with a young boy. Martha wants to talk, so we sit down in the gastrobar under the dome.

'We shouldn't have accepted Sister Julian's crazy idea for the exchange. 'She's on the defensive. 'Old and energy-wasteful buildings can no longer be preserved. They are not environmentally efficient. It's imperative to use natural and hukind resources with the utmost care. You are the one to understand me, Nicholas. I want you to carry on your work, perhaps with another team in the field of energy. I might be able to get you a contract from the Goodwill World Parliament. Your work involves the future. So does mine. We are both creating a better world,' she glances at Joe,' for the likes of him'.

Hukind has always imagined Paradise. Why not strive for it? She in her way and me in mine. And so she weaves in and out of my thoughts, ending, 'I'm for technophilia, not technolust. Don't forget that, Nicholas, and explain it to mum. And to Sister Julian. She won't listen to me when I explain. It's people like Sister Julian and our mum,' Martha insists, 'who get in the way of technological and social advances'. She will hand Sister Julian the keys to the old university when the written agreement is ready.

All the groundwork of my infinenergy theory, the solid base of my pyramid theory, is stored in the Institute datasafe backed by the Goodwill World Parliament cyberstore. All that is safe. It's the tip that is lost and without that – nothing. Panic at the thought of what I should be doing to retrieve those crucial calculations. What should I – can I – do? It hasn't even been patented. Everything now lost.

I voiced Magnus immediately I realised I'd lost the datadrive. *Has anyone helped you look for it?* Martha. My cleaner. *Good. Come and see me then.* From the way he looked at me, I felt he understood my despair. Head in hands, butterflies still fluttering, I crouched on his sofa avoiding his eyes, but from his voice I heard he understood my utter despair. *It would be hard – impossible even – to convince Reaching Out representatives to fund you again, even though it would only be for the last part of your experiments.* I was grateful he didn't suggest I should ask Ross Mackenzie for financial help. *What about teaming up with others in your field?* Why not, except I would lose my own creation to others. Raphael is my partner in all this, but his Energy Research Centre is fully stretched financing the high-charged solar panels we're using. He is now waiting for those final calculations. I couldn't bear his silence after I told him I had lost the crucial datadrive. It was both understanding and disapproving – and he was my assistant!

*****.

I'm enjoying the journey with Joe on the North Moorland Divergence Route. It allows time to think through what's has been happening. Martha's rare confidences, for example. Her office is bombarded by Sister Julian's unremitting requests for access to the old university buildings. She is vague about what has happened to the picture of Leda and the Swan. It's no longer on display in the city museum, amid protests. Her staff are trying to divert the nun's repeated requests to the zone government or ignore them, consequently increasing their frequency. Martha even seems to regret having to refuse a tempting offer to demolish the old university and transform it into one of the so-called 'areas of innovation'. It came after the agreement to exchange the buildings for the Leonardo painting.

I've sent Ezra messages but can't voice him while in the outwebber community. Joe can't stop looking out of the hoverpod windows at the motorcyclists racing alongside us. He's amazed by their antics. Just before sunset they meet at a gathering point where the old city gate used to be. There they adjust their much-vaunted vlason space-resilient gear and moon-tested helmets before racing alongside the last hoverpod.

'Where go?' he asks, eyes dilated with excitement when we boom into a tunnel.

'Nowhere,' I hope, but can't explain how the new multi-purpose bikes, with small but powerful heliwhirls, can leap over tracts of boulder-strewn hillside to land on smooth spaces and then take off for another hop. All very thrilling; they burn off testosterone-fuelled energies no doubt, but are unlikely to beat the hoverpod's smooth passage in and out of tunnels. He is even more confused when we shoot out the other side of the hill and enter the terminus.

'No drooomm, droooommms come?' Joe has picked up sounds for motorcycles and plurals. Mum will be pleased. She notes such things; most people don't. No sign of her at the station, but then I couldn't tell her I was coming, except by writing a letter and that takes longer than getting here. From January next year there will be no more letterpost. I must remember to warn her. Martha keeps reminding me that once one leaves the station hub there is no way for any outwebber to know what is happening in the world. I sometimes envy them.

We start climbing the hill, the last sunrays on our backs. Martha described how to find mum's stone cottage. I can see it, a small grey rectangle fast disappearing in the dusk. Space is flowing freely over us like water over rocks. All afternoon we had scuttled around in artificial light moving through the vast commercial complex with the pharmacy to the domed pivot of a shopping mall. There are plans to extend it right over my old university site. Sunlight had been banished from our day until now. Did Joe miss it as I did?

What if everything were done by machines, the ultimate aim of technophiles? Will people still be able to work to earn credits for, say, clothes like the ones I've just bought for Joe? We are already divided into four sorts of people: first, those who create and invent and, second, those who maintain the technology underpinning the whole world economy. They are the producers and maintainers who earn and buy. They turn the wheels of industry. Other hukind tasks remain for the enablers. Only one nurse – an enabler - and a robot now do the work that used to be carried out by four people in a hospital, so there is still a warm touch as well as major savings plus high efficiency. What does efficiency exactly 'save'? Money or jobs? Or both? The elderly end up in homes run like happy departure terminals. Every creature comfort is provided by robots and a few enablers. Some say suicide rates are rising to avoid travelling slowly to death. Others insist this is only because people are living so long. Science creates spare organs in laboratories, all stored ready for use when required.

What about the rest of hukind? The fourth category, the leisuretimers? Mum, and people like her, say there's a need for a helping hand – not an electronic one – to give care and companionship, and also to clear up the waste people leave in their trail. Efficiency savings, a world 2% sales tax and donations from the ultra-rich like Dom Ross Mackenzie, are now flowing into a Goodwill World Parliament fund to pay for pensions and for leisuretimers. They can choose to do voluntary work in all sorts of socially useful areas from sports centres to care homes or whatever else takes their fancy.

Lights are on in the cottage. Music. Framed in the window two figures are singing an aria from mum's favourite opera, Mozart's *Don Giovanni.* A baritone voice 'Là ci darem la mano…' They're dancing now, mum holding her hand out to someone. It's Magnus! Two souls singing, oblivious. Another two standing at the window looking in at them.

NEWS BULLETIN

WORLD-CHANGING DISCOVERY

The bronzed starlet of niche fashion, **Helen Runciman**, is to tell you about an earth-shaking discovery. She has been chosen by the reclusive inventor, entrepreneur and philanthropist, Dom Ross Mackenzie, to broadcast how his world-famous company **Global Enterprises GWP** will develop, in his ecologically friendly laboratories, the provision of unlimited energy, the goal that has eluded scientists and inventors for generations.

'It is the ultimate quest,' she informs us, adding, **'Dom Ross Mackenzi**e knows how important this is since he trained as a scientist before he founded his company to capitalise on such crucial inventions. Dealing initially in **eco-friendly petroleum substitutes**, his brilliant mind has latterly been exploring the most unique and outrageous theories as **Leonardo da**

Vinci once did, in his determination to find the philosopher's stone. Until now, as with Leonardo, numerous theories and experiments have remained inconclusive. Next year will see a world first: the production, storage and distribution of infinite, cheap energy from solar power. It will provide a unique, renewable and constant source of energy. This will be the twenty-first century's philosopher's stone!'

Helen Runciman also announces that this breath-taking invention, which has been discovered by a brilliant scientist who prefers to remain anonymous, is being patented and that no more information will be released or questions answered at the present time.

worldaroundyounews.com

20

Winter

Eliza's Journal

24 December

As the notes rose to '*la mano*' and Magnus took my hand on the rising 'o', Foxy began barking, the door opened and there he was. Nicholas at last! Behind him a slight, hungry-looking boy. Nicholas found him, an orphan, somewhere in Africa. Is this Tiny Tim? I thought, and is this a neo-Dickensian scenario, except there's no Scrooge and no Christmas. Just the rather dull-sounding Mid Winter Festival.

The child looks so wise for his years. Nicholas found him, an orphan, somewhere in Africa. Only eleven and already his mind grasps English words, leaping into action to anticipate our needs.

Wood for the fire. He is quicker than Magnus at gathering twigs and snapping them, at chopping branches and laying the hearth.

Vegetables. Joe entered my kitchen garden as if it was a wonderland. Together we are happily climbing an essential learning curve. Carrots, swedes, turnips, parsnips - he was not too sure when he tried his first forkful - and the 'green', as he says. Cabbage he knows, not the red sort. He carried the basket while I poked and cut. He stopped to think as I tugged at the weeds, then asked, pointing, 'Wot plse?' Three-syllabled potato is mastered with difficulty but, fascinated by colours and impatient to learn, beetroot has become 'red potato' and sprouts 'baby cabbage'.

Nicholas followed us, entranced, and I slip back into memories of him, different yet hauntingly similar: both alert, tense, almost quivering with those same enquiring eyes.

I meander happily into the past, humming nursery songs, swinging to the rhythm of 'Over the sea to Skye, Hail to the Lad born to be king…' or jolly with 'Goosey goosey gander,' which is hardly the way to teach someone English! Anyway, he's too old for these songs. After dark on an evening of faltering light we sang rounds like 'Brother Jack, Brother Jack, Are you sleeping?' and played memory games or tiddlywinks with the pieces I kept from my childhood. I've marked out hopscotch in the earth outside the front gate, and Joe is playing it with Nicholas. Magnus and I watched, tempted to join in.

I haven't felt lonely before, but I shall when they leave. I'm so worried about Nicholas. He did mention the lost datadrive with the calculations – the tip of the pyramid, he said, that he had been so painstakingly constructing with the data for his invention, 'infinenergy'. While I was showing Joe how to do a jigsaw puzzle, I overheard Magnus whispering to Nicholas that he should alert the director of his Institute, or even the Rector of Greystone University about Ross Mackenzie and the patent for his invention. I couldn't make out his reply. Nicholas seemed to be sinking into himself, eyes wide, despairing. I caught a few phrases: 'I must contact Raphael,' even, 'should I repeat the experiment in Africa?' They clearly did not want to upset me. All Nicholas told me was that he had to settle Joe into a school. Nothing else.

*****

When Martha dropped in two days ago after another of her mysterious expeditions along the causeway to the foothills, she mentioned something about coming for the Winter Festival. Is she yearning for Christmas? Where will everyone sleep? If Martha comes, then Karen follows, and probably Roland too. Helen? I don't think so. She does not seem the type to enjoy a cramped existence. Not one to 'rough it' as we used to say.

Nicholas and Joe sleep on a spare mattress Magnus found in the loft. Joe does not complain about the cold. A thatched roof provides good insulation and plenty of dust. I've just climbed the ladder to the loft to see how much space there is if everyone comes for Mid WInter. Two folding beds are stored there. We used them ages ago when we took the children camping.

Magnus has been coming and going as I encourage him to do. I did not realise that he draws as well as dances. He has laid boards on two trestles by a window that peeps out from under the thatch. I glimpsed a pencil drawing of two people before he closed the sketchbook and wonder whether he has looked at any of my canvases stacked in the loft on one side of the chimneybreast.

'I have just come up to see how much room there is for Martha and company, if they come.'

'Plenty,' he said, indicating the area in front of me. He has staked out his space behind the farthest beam from the trap door by hanging old curtains over it. He has to bend down to get underneath. I had forgotten them. Karen and I stuffed our things in grey storage bags when we left 11 Acacia Avenue for 12 Beech Drive. Most of them are still unpacked.

'Can I see your drawings?'

'They are only sketches,' he said, 'nothing much'. He opened a page to show minutely detailed drawings, shaped and shadowed by millions of fine lines sometimes parallel, more often criss-crossed. No colour. There were the Three Sister Peaks, the highest points of the distant range to the north, my small cottage, scenes of boulders and of the Greystone Estuary from some perch high up in the mountains. Or so I thought as he quickly turned them over. There were some of Nicholas and Joe, mostly asleep on the mattress. Then a lot of women - or the same one, I think. I strained to see if he had been sketching me, but I don't think so.

* * * * *

I found my Christmas tree in the meadow below the Middle Sister peak. There's a narrow valley there with a velvety carpet of moss under pine trees. It was only a seedling, and is still quite small here, in its tub. I plan to bring it indoors every year. Magnus has hooked a branch on a nail in the far corner of my kitchen living room and hung on it twigs of holly and mistletoe, and also strange leaves I haven't noticed before, green with silvery hairs that catch the firelight like long glow-worms. After Nicholas and Joe arrived, he took me with them to gather more leaves in as many colours as they could find to make a leaf chain to hang from the beams. Foxy was excited, barking at Joe who was the nimblest, leaping behind boulders to find leaves and grained pebbles and tipping up stones to marvel at bugs and worms and veins in the rocks that he had never seen before. A different sign of delight – a whistle, grin, indrawn breath, his hands held high or a whoop - accompanied each find, so we all became children again. My little tree bore the scratched baubles from my childhood and my children's too. Joe added his leaves and twigs.

Down by the station there are shop-huts where we can barter or pay with credits. Enterprising outwebbers share space in them to display their wares; we find Christmas pudding, mince pies and cake, sparklers and all we can carry back for Joe to try out. Strange to him, they are reminiscent for us of former times.

Nicholas has lost weight. He talks a lot to Magnus. They do not want me to hear, but I know they mentioned Raphael, also Africa. Dom Ross Mackenzie too. I so wish they would bring whatever it is out into the open. If Nicholas must rerun the final experiment, redo those crucial calculations, then so be it. The cost? Greystone University, the Institute, Magnus – someone will find the money. But for now, all must enjoy the festive season and forget everything else. Nicholas especially.

*****

24 December

It's brighter this morning, still cloudy with a brisk breeze. I can see my wind turbine is working and the solar panels registering. Good. Extra energy for tomorrow when Magnus's present for me is to dance his 3/9 sequence, and others; mine for him is to play songs from operas that we can sing and act together. He's tuned my piano again. I have been rustling through the piles of sheet music that I had forgotten in a corner of my studio. Oh, those tingling joys of anticipation!

Something has just happened to Magnus. He has opened the trap door and rattled down the ladder in such a hurry I feared he might fall, and he is agile all right. A handsome, balanced body for his age. He is gnarled, resilient, and light on his feet. He has hurtled out of the front door, sketchbook in hand, mumbling something I did not catch. I followed him to the door. He was half running up the path to the foothills and then veered towards the causeway. No procession this time, but four or five figures hurrying towards the massive doors - the entrance to what? Why today, when most people are on holiday or preparing for one?

Nicholas and Joe returned with more objects to decorate the main room, bursting to tell me what they had found. They did not mention the people on the causeway. Magnus came back after dusk. He said the entrance closed before he could reach it. He immediately started to help wash and sort the pebbles and flints for the new game that Nicholas and Joe are inventing together.

I have been sitting by the kitchen window. The last hoverpod has looped back into the tunnel leaving a knot of people under the lights outside the terminus. I watch it disentangle and, as I almost feared, two women and a man are leaving the others to climb up the path towards us. No, I thought, I won't have Karen sharing my bedroom. Not after she has been flying all over the world as if I did not exist. There is just about space for Roland and Martha in my studio next to the shower and toilet. Karen can sleep on the sofa in front of the fire. This is only a cottage on one floor with a large kitchen living area, two small rooms partitioned off it and a loft above. Strange the way people have always assumed I have space for them if and when they need it.

Perhaps they will miss the cottage in the twilight. It is only lit by firelight and one shared candle to save energy. Magnus and Nicholas have to take the friction lamps and wind them up if they go outside.

'Eliza, you could make up games for blackout sessions,' Magnus was saying and laughing. He talks more now and has started to tease me. Even so, he has not explained why he comes here, except for a vague need to escape the city.

I feel serenely distant from everything happening down in the city below us. Here is my space, my universe. It is reassuringly predictable: the sun rises and sets; the clouds gather or disperse above my scrap of the earth's surface; the heavens arch over me at night and, though not always, the sun shines in daytime. Stormy weather drives me inside giving me time to think, paint and play music. I've moved my dwelling place, and my perspective.

I am writing by candlelight. Magnus is looking at his recent sketches by firelight. We think or talk, draw or write. Joe and Nicholas are trying out the game they invented with the pebbles. I am looking forward to hearing tales of Africa from Nicholas, Joe and even Magnus. I long to imagine those spaces in their company.

Perhaps I am mistaken. Perhaps the two women were not Martha and Karen and the man was not Roland. I must have been turning the distant forms into the people I feared they might be. They have not loomed out of the darkness and might be lost along the track to the foothills.

Quiet. No sound of a gate clicking open or footfall on the path to the front door. Should I ask Magnus and Nicholas to go out with the friction lamps and search the area between the cottage and the station below and, if need be, between here and the foothills? Mad idea. It is ink dark outside and smoky warm in this room. It would be a shame to disturb them. The people by the station were strangers and they have gone elsewhere.

* * * * *

Just after I put my pen down and closed my journal I heard voices outside and a knock on the door. Magnus looked up. Nicholas and Joe turned towards me as I went to open it to the three of them stamping their feet and rubbing their hands.

'Can't you use proper lights?' Martha lacks tact. 'It's all very well, economising and all that eco stuff to save the planet, but first one has to see where one's going.'

'We couldn't find the cottage and went up the track for some way before we realised we'd gone too far.' Roland stood in the threshold behind the other woman - Karen? Her face was in shadows.

Martha removed her fur hat, elegant though inappropriate. Roland, voted I am told the most eligible member of the zone government, flaunted a black Cossack hat and fur collar (both suspiciously like real fur, rare nowadays). Exaggeratingly gallant towards the women, he forgot to close the door behind him.

'I've only just returned from China.' That was Karen's voice all right. She didn't move to embrace me. We had not met since I left Beech Drive and I was not sure what to expect.

'You must all be cold.' I moved behind Roland to shut out the night air already below freezing point, and turned the electricity off. My house, my decision.

Silence. Everyone was looking at someone else in the firelight.

'So this is where you live.' An innocent statement in a critical tone of voice. Karen's. 'Lovely blaze,' and she held out her hands towards it, not me.

'Roland is carrying the food for a Christmas feast,' Martha said to keep a flow of sound. 'We'll sleep on the divan in the studio and Karen can pitch in with you.'

No way. Karen's face looks different. Eyes narrower, nose smaller, a valley behind her chin. A sudden jerk in my mind. Her face's geography has been altered. It has wandered east to Asia and acquired a distinctly Chinese landscape.

She whispered to Martha something about Nicholas, glancing at him. I could only hear something like, 'they can't have been accessing *worldaroundyounews* here...don't let's tell him now. Later...'

BREAKING NEWS

INTERNATIONAL PIANIST ATTACKED IN FIRST-EVER WORDFREE THEFT

The Goodwill World Parliament has just issued the following bulletin:

'We regretfully announce than the gifted pianist Ezra Tenenbaum is the first person ever to have his wordfree stolen. When taking a shortcut to his rehearsal studio three months ago, he was attacked by two masked men. They pushed him to the ground and severed his left arm below the elbow. He was speedily taken to the nearest hospital where he has been recovering. Doctors report that he is already practising an adapted piano repertoire and may soon be able to leave hospital. This criminal attack, tantamount to stealing an individual's official identity, could not be reported at the time for security reasons. The Parliament is happy to report that there have been no further incidents of a similar nature. World citizens should therefore remain calm and go about their business as normal.'

worldaroundyounews.com

21

Mid-Summer - Argentina

24 December

Helen *showspotHEL22.com*

I am the news and I'm not sure I like it. People stopped me in the street before, when I did my impromptu fashion demonstrations and appeared on local internet promotions. Now the world is peering and babbling at me in vlogs and blogs. Like this one.

So what's it like being famous? For what?

Well, I've talent. Martha invited me to design her firm's capsule interiors for the maternity-and-leisure buildings under the Middle Sister Peak. That was before she was elected and got all uppity. Then Dom Ross decided I was the one to front his world-changing announcement of how he is realising Nicholas's great discovery. I'm so glad for him. We're protecting him by not mentioning his name. Dom Ross's scientists and engineers are brilliant. I don't know how they do it, but they are about to rush Nick's invention into production. I'm so glad for him. The patent was fast-tracked and I'm here in Argentina with Ross to publicise his engineers' energy-receptor network worldwide. He's helping Nick as I knew he would. Ross says his purpose in life is to develop great inventions and make the world a better place for all. He's starting in Argentina because here the receptors are widely spaced – something about it being safer for the direction of the beam in the clear mountain air. I think that's why he's brought me here.

This place is something to brag about. Vast spaces and rocks 'sculpted by wind' as he says, to look like giants or lions or those strange Egyptian animals that don't exist - sphinxes, aren't they? The 'wind theatre', as they call it here, is a space that you enter through a gash in the rocks to find a hollow shaped like an amphitheatre with creepy echoes. He whispered to me while on the far side and I could clearly hear him say,

'It's the greatest discovery for centuries.' And he wasn't referring to the natural theatre gouged out, he says, by wind and rain or 'atmospheric corrosion'. It's the discovery of infinite energy, or the modern 'philosopher's stone', as he strangely calls it. All about plentiful, cheap solar energy from his Global Enterprises GWP.

He told me all this here, in his latest mansion. No expense is spared to make this the most future-anticipating building imaginable. It's built out of pink rocks with window frames in green basalt. The granite is the colour of an elephant's skin, he says, though I've never seen one for real. When we drive through the canyons, the pink mountains come first, with the grey peaks further back, often merging into the evening mist. Then suddenly the road curves and you see the green basalt crags ahead of you with sunlight on the tips of still more rose-tinted ranges behind them. It's fabulous or 'awesome' as they used to say when I was little. Nick and I have already seen them in the landscape options at the Pleasure Dreamland. This is for real but looks unbelievable!

When I first saw Ross's mansion here, I thought it was a computer-designed mirage. It is set facing south overlooking a river that twists through a vast plain towards another range of pink floss mountains. It's smaller than it seems from the outside because, he says, he doesn't want the fuss of numerous helpers around him. There's a house manager though, and I don't trust him. He has a healthy tan like most Argentinians. It's becoming fashionable again. But his eyes are narrow and inscrutable. His only words are 'yes sir, yes madam,' even when they don't fit his expression. The floors are polished slabs of different mountain rocks; they look slippery shiny.

Dom Ross has bought me a new wordfree hot off the orderline from *newinventions.com.* There are so many online ordering companies now, but he uses the best. It's as easy to insert into the wrist as it is to pierce an earlobe. I'm speaking all this into my blog section on it. I don't like being overheard so this is only in a whisper. So many devices have probably been built into this mansion, like in the larger one with his laboratories on Quarry Hill. Here it's like being inside a welcoming bubble, and Ross is really good to me, though I still feel the shivers when I peep out of my comfort zone into the vast rooms of the central block, or look out at the river plain and distant mountains or just the empty spaces above and around me, inside and out.

We have dinner in the green dining room, supervised by the inscrutable house manager. He comes from the original inhabitants of this mountainous region. Perhaps the manager's strange look tells us that we're trespassing on their territory.

I feel odd inside all this wealth. A bit of me is yearning for Cara and the others in our fashion business, for the fun meetings we had, giggly and usually creative. But vlason goes on and on; nantung is still popular, so we have used up all the fashion permutations we can think of and are back at the beginning again. Dress fashion seems to be stuck in a repetitive rut, unlike music. Dong drong is out. Too many styles and rhythms and tone-or-beat experiments have evolved from it for us to keep up parallels in outfits, accessories and colours. We need to create an independent and exciting visual statement and all we can do is repeat themes from the past. To be fair, some like it that way. 'Reassuring,' says Nick's mum, boring old Eliza.

It's serendipity - the world's favourite word - that I'm here in Argentina and, it seems, set on a new career as a celebrity. One who announces the future. The Miss World of earth-shaking discoveries - and my brain must be pin sized! A thought - is Ross making fun of me? Where will all this lead when I'm well and truly outside this bubble existence?

Enjoy it while you can, Helen, I repeat and repeat and repeat.

I miss Nick too. More than I had expected because there's a lot of anger between him and me, though I don't think he realises it. I never thought he was the type to become besotted, if that's the right word. Well, I won't share him with anyone.

I'm not being exactly literal. Or maybe I am. But the moment that child turned up, I knew things would start going sour. Nick doesn't seem able to think of anyone else. Why does Joe have to come and upset everything? I see his face in every reflecting surface around me, and this whole place is like a huge marble mirror echoing what's on one's mind, whether one wants it there or not.

When I saw Nick in that news clip, he registered as a sensitive person hiding behind the label of 'a genius', which he definitely doesn't like. I admit my curiosity was whetted. Too many tanned, lithe, sporty types had been after me, and I yearned for a change. I thought he would be a passing fad, as we used to say at school. Just a brief shiver of pleasure - all that. But the longer Dom Ross wants me to stay isolated here, the more I need to see him. Though Dom Ross gives me everything he and I can think of, he doesn't interest me at all. Strange. He almost repels, though he's tall, well built with regular features some would find pleasing. But his eyes are cold even when he smiles. It's lucky he doesn't even try to touch me. He has no feelings.

I have to stay in South America because it's good for my celebrity status, Ross says. No outside factors must harm my screen image. He doesn't want his staff to know why I'm here. When sitting alone here between these columns in the portico, I'm not just contemplating the patterns of sun-baked earth where the lake has shrunk or trying not to notice the bird carcasses before someone rushes out to remove them - he's furious if they are left there. No, I'm not idle. I've been thinking out virus-spreads for him. Viruses are not negative as old people automatically think. Virus-spreads deal only in rumours. Internetters can take them or ignore them. It's not a question of truth. The effective ones only propagate if integrated into other sites. I learnt how to do them while publicising our Powerhouse fashions. My virus-spreads look like messages from ordinary people anywhere, just anxious to get their views known. Except that they hold the views Dom Ross Mackenzie wants them to hear and pass on.

Who you're with adds to your marketability. I knew this, but could never have imagined that Ross was lining me up when I went with Nick, the genius, to have dinner in his Quarry Hill mansion – the one with all the labs. Surprise, surprise. And now I'm a celebrity!

I hope Nick never sees my second interview. It was earlier today in Ross's studio here: floor of polished green slabs with walls of shiny, rose-coloured ones, like being in a huge candy box. I was to interview Ross spontaneously, though his PR person had carefully prearranged the questions from the Quarry Hill mansion site. Nowadays location doesn't matter and is hardly ever mentioned. Everyone travels virtually, it seems, except for us here in Argentina and people like Nick and Esther who go to Africa to test things out. Most others stay put. No, I forgot - 'the current travel slot is the moonshot' as the song goes. But the waiting list is long and the satisfaction level mixed. Ross is non-committal about his moon journey.

'Interesting. Yes, worthwhile, I suppose. Arid, rocky - what one expects. Air different, lighter. Odd sense of space. Worth the long wait? I suppose so…' except he didn't have to wait. Paying a heavy premium, people like him jump the queue.

Back to the interview rehearsal. I had to ask him what the impact of plentiful, inexpensive energy would be on the world.

'Incalculable. An amazing extension of human freedom, knowledge…' he didn't say 'power' but one felt it. I looked at the viewers – the autocue really – and continued.

'Hallelujah! Everyone will have access to electricity even in deserts, rainforests and the remotest regions. It will be stored in infinitely powerful receptors that are constantly recharged from a solar satellite above cloud level. The sun is always shining above the clouds! It's the elixir for our future.'

I had to look up 'elixir' afterwards, not a word one hears much, but I didn't want to do it in front of Ross. After the actual interview he was 'auto ignited' as the term is nowadays. I'd just say obviously self-satisfied. Thrilled maybe?

Later I thought elixir up on to the wall screen = an alchemical (what's that?) preparation supposed to be capable of prolonging life or of transmuting base metals into gold. This must be linked to the philosopher's stone that Ross goes on about. It can also be a medicine with syrup or something pleasant in it to smother the horrible taste. He can't be referring to that. Odd. The word comes from a Greek one meaning powder used for drying wounds.

'What a curious word-journey,' I was thinking when a shiver came over me and I looked up. He was actually standing behind me checking the wall screen with a smile on his face.

'Interesting word. Great potential.' Now if there had been a book dictionary lying around, I could have done it secretly, not in front of him. There are no bookcases or shelves to spoil the smooth expanse of polished stone walls and creamy screens.

I'm starting to worry. He's wandering from room to room. Nervous. Uneasy. Something must have gone wrong. He's spending hours conferencing his scientists at his Quarry Hill laboratories. I returned, as Ross asked, the datadrive he gave me for Nick to use in Africa to check his diagrams and calculations. The other one? That was for Raphael. I left it for him in Nick's lab. I told Ross that I had voiced Nick before I came here and that he said he had 'cracked the problem of the angle of the beam hitting the receptor', or something similar. Ross looked at me curiously. I suppose the calculations will be stored in the ultrasafe section of Nick's wordfree. The

GWP reminds everyone to do this to safekeep important information of any sort.

Ross has promised to help promote my fashion business through his contacts. He hasn't done much yet, except, I suppose, by putting me on *worldaroundyounews* to announce his plans to the world. That 'hallelujah' interview is creating internet waves - analysed, ridiculed or raved about all over the internet. I want to get away from it all and have been trying to find a book to read on the balcony to my room. Difficult. Ross only has internet reading machines. There are many versions but they all tire my wrists. They are supposed to be so companionable with nice people introducing each book and giving you options to chat about it in virtual reading groups or ask questions or whatever. Help or intrusion? I know what Nick would say.

Ross is interested in the datadrive that I told him Nick keeps hanging round his neck – I didn't add that it tickled me when we made love! That's probably the latest version, so what's gone wrong? Or was that another datadrive for Raphael? I don't really understand what's happening. Nick hasn't kept in touch. Too involved with Joe, I suppose. I'm the one who voices him. I know Ross was waiting for Nick to complete the tests in Africa and share the results. I just don't understand all those calculations and theories and mathematical expressions for what's hanging out there somewhere. Nick hasn't asked about the datadrive I returned to Ross, so he can't need it. Certainly not since the break-in. Whoever it was, he - or they - came too early. Unless there was something different on his lab computers. How should I know? A pity Nick didn't want to share his invention with Ross. Or me. I don't think he likes to see me sitting pretty and pretending and nodding my head to be nice and polite with Ross, smiling along. He hasn't the patience. It's all a shame, as Ross really wants to help him.

There are streams of online chatter about Ross. People find it strange that he has no family but lots of ancestors on the walls of his house on Quarry Hill. I'm not sure about my new role as I was plunged right into it. He doesn't want to give me an official position so that I'm seen as being independent. An interviewer. A celebrity interviewer. Everyone is curious about our relationship. I don't do intimacy in public, though I don't mind here on my blog, Ross confides up to a point, but then stops. I used to think that everything came so easily to him - wealth, ideas, organising, snapping his fingers and it all materialised. But behind what Nick calls his 'fashioned nonchalance', there's a hint of a tic in his left cheek, and I've even noticed him turning away, clenching his fists. More recently, that is. There's always a show of politeness, whatever happens.

Our new highly secret venture has started just as he said it would. It's like other implants – wrist wordfree or whatever. While it's happening you submit to the usual pleasant scenes, sounds and scents. He is honest. He said he had an idea that might interest me. It should be a way, he says, to help so many people and also be highly profitable. It's part of an experiment. But right now I would prefer to be with Cara and other friends actually in her kitchen, or have them over here to keep me company.

*****

Dom Ross has unexpectedly come into the library from his studio and is trying to relax in one of his special comfort chairs over there by the end pillar. It's hard to relax when your mind is making, protecting or giving away money. He's pretty inactive physically and emotionally. Difficult to get your act together when your mind is 'monetarily encumbered' – Nick's expression! That was difficult to think and also to say! Like describing Ross, so spare and neat in his 'retro' style, as it used to be marketed ages ago. He calls it his original sartorial style: tailored to fit, neat and deliberately unremarkable - his words.

Well, he's sitting there and says, quietly but firmly,

'I'm leasing a satellite.' Just like that. No exclamation or explanation. My jaw's dropping, but I don't think that is the reaction he wants.

I digress. This is what I'm always doing here. He's looking intensely at me now, uncrossing his legs and leaning forward. A tremor in my guts, deeper than ever.

'A Hallelujah interview will be on this evening.'

NEWS BULLETIN

ENVIRONMENTAL SOLUTION TO SCARCE ENERGY RESOURCES

Good morning, afternoon, evening or night, wherever you are! I'm Helen, known as the Hallelujah girl, and I'm back to tell you that, for the first time since the formation of the **Goodwill World Parliament**, the delegates have voted to lease one of their satellites to **a private individual**. They are convinced that it will enhance world peace and create prosperity for all.

Hallelujah! The good news is that the inventor, scientist and disseminator of **infinenergy, Dom Ross Mackenzie** is here in the studio.

'Dom Ross, please tell the world about your plans.'

'Thank you, Helen. My conglomerate is now preparing to distribute **energy receptors** as widely as possible over the earth's surface. Through them constant power can reach every hukind habitation. No appliance is too large or small for this extraordinary provision of infinite energy. In these exceptional circumstances, Goodwill World Parliament delegates, at a special session, have agreed to **lease a trial satellite for one year** to **Worldwide Enterprises GWP**, renewable if the project enhances the wellbeing of hukind.'

'This is amazing news, Dom Ross Mackenzie.'

'I wish to assure you all that my invention is what the world has been waiting for – unlimited, clean, low-cost solar energy. Without the sun, we all perish. With the sun, we have all the energy we need – and, I promise, more still.'

worldaroundyounews.com

22

25 December, Mid Winter

Magnus *i-witnessMAG931.futurepast.com*

As the outwebbers' winter festival has now reverted to the traditional Christmas Day, we can take Joe back into our childhood. Eliza is supervising the décor while Nicholas and Joe drape her pictures with sharp, green angles of holly and mistletoe and other evergreen leaves. I never thought I would need to rehearse my rainbow dances again and particularly Eliza's favourite - the 3/7/9 sequence. I waited until everyone was in bed and then tried out variations in the kitchen living area. Earth floors covered in old carpets absorb the footbeats. Hardly a sound, except for my humming waves of blue, and barely a thump from time to time, though Nicholas must have heard me. He came down to watch and ask about the number sequences and their colours. I like the way they fascinate him. He looks older, his face faintly lined. He's paternal in his response to Joe. Eliza is worried.

'There's no space for a child in his rooms. I asked him about Institute regulations and children, but he just shrugged his shoulders.'

'He's happy, Eliza. Don't worry.' But I did. Nicholas must have left to see his mother before Helen's announcement on *worldaroundyounews,* so he doesn't realise that Ross Mackenzie intends to commercialise his invention. Or has Nicholas given Dom Ross the calculations without telling me? I hope not. I won't ask him now because I don't want to spoil the festive mood. It began with omelettes, all yellow and brown, and fresh rolls. Eliza had prepared creamy dough yesterday while I was stoking the wood oven ready for her to use later. She slipped out to check the weathervane behind the cottage. It was moving lazily south-east in the slight morning breeze.

The outwebbers have, Eliza tells me, invited Sister Julian to their Mid Winter celebration. I was standing outside the station calculating the various angles of the building and what was left of the food from the morning market when she arrived. She had hitched a lift with one of the mountain motorcyclists, idle without hoverpods to race at the Mid Winter. Her scarlet cape billowing at 45 degrees behind the black robe must have slowed him down.

'Well, here I am!' she announced brightly as she dismounted. I wonder whether she too might have danced in her youth, she's light-footed enough. Eliza was at her cottage door watching me return. She held binoculars and must have been following the commotion down by the station hub.

'There's no room for Sister Julian at this inn,' she said.

* * * * *

We're watching outwebbers appear above us from the woodland and the lower slopes. Specks dotting the snow move down from the highland valleys; groups merge into others over the pale cropped grass in the green lower meadows to follow the mud track past this cottage down to the station. Spots grow legs and wave arms, some ringing shiny handbells called Vox Angelica, Claribel Flute or even Tuba Mirabilis after their different coloured notes. They gather at the station hub bearing knobbly brown firewood, small sharp green strands of holly, ivy and mistletoe. Joe and Nicholas have just joined Eliza and me to watch.

Nicholas starts down the path with Joe and Foxy running, brown and white, ahead of us. This is the usual celebration of the Mid Winter, of the evergreen holly and ivy and mistletoe; of winter life, of survival and the green man who grins with a sprig in his mouth at a right angle from the arch over the main door to St. Thomas's. Many are jostling outside the waiting room at the dark blue station hub, steamed windows obscuring the jolly buzz inside. The door bursts open and a familiar figure in a black robe under a scarlet cape appears holding a silver cross and a candle. Deep brown planks, piled horizontally, ready to build another kiosk in the outwebber market have been set on smooth grey rocks to form makeshift benches. Joe and Nicholas help divide the branches and twigs to throw on to the bonfire by the waiting crowd. Hands rub and feet stamp in warm conviviality while Sister Julian finds a way to prop the cross up on a rock and melt wax to fix a candle on a flat stone. A hush.

'Be joyful!' she begins. 'This is a festival of hope. Bleak midwinter, but with snowdrops already peeping out in the woods as harbingers of spring.' Someone has placed a jar of them on the stone. She smiles at a stocky man in a leather jacket and gaudy plaid trousers who hastily squeezes his accordion and plunges heartily into deep blue notes soon joined by Vox Angelica's high yellow pitch, Claribel Flute's throatier tone and by booming brass Tuba Mirabilis. 'In the bleak midwinter…' sing the onlookers in and out of tune from shrill soprano down the scale to join the accordion man's rasping notes. A pause to listen to Sister Julian.

'Be joyful,' is her theme, 'rejoice that here, in the mountains behind you, are the finest artworks that hukind has ever created, all praising the greatest work of all - this universe, this world'. Arms outstretched, head raised, she starts in a deep golden voice, 'Hark the herald angel sing…' with the accordion anxiously following her and everyone soon singing or humming along.

'Be joyful! Here we are singing and marvelling at our blessings from Jesus, born today, and at all we have done and can do. At what we mean to ourselves and to others. Hallelujah!'

That's a word I've heard recently, but can't remember where.

There's a murmur; people are looking at the pale orange sun bathing the plain and touching the snow on the upper slopes. As we sing 'Oh little town of Bethlehem,' I contemplate the Greystone River and the canal to our city, and wonder.

Hallelujah!

It's a day of radiance. Like manna, abundant food is scattered over tables brought out from the kiosks. We are creating a Breughel painting, bringing my onscreen copy to life.

* * * * *

In the deep midwinter…There is room at the inn this evening. I didn't hear Eliza ask her, thinking of the sofa in the kitchen perhaps, but Sister Julian came back with us in the twilight. Chris, the motorcyclist who gave her a lift, had left early to meet his girlfriend before she had finished talking to the outwebbers.

There'll be a sharp frost tonight.

Nicholas is silent, his arm around Joe when the child hasn't escaped to help Eliza at the oven. I'm raking the red embers ready to toast shiny chestnuts and turning over the potatoes already there. Sister Julian is peeling vegetables. Martha is busy talking policy with Roland on the other side of the room. A blessing about this basic sort of living is that winter brings us together in the only room with warmth, like monks in their warming house in ancient times. Karen, who looks different, is sorting out the wine and liqueurs she has brought back from China in new, sleek, wafer-thin glassite bottles. They resemble the old classical ones, labels and all, but the writing is in the cyber-compressed glyphics that pass for the new world language - Babel.

Eliza is calling for someone, Martha or Karen, to lay the table, for Nicholas to set out the chairs and Joe to wash mushrooms and slice the beetroot. A pot of soup is bubbling suspended over the fire. Thick with vegetables from her plot, only five strides away from us now, it’s redolent of flavours to come, a black shape against the glowing fire. I stir the pot occasionally and feed the fire and the oven beside it realising how rare all this is nowadays. No chimneys at all on new buildings, and they are even torn off old stock, being too expensive to repair and utterly redundant. The vertical thrust of chimneys, towers, steeples and pinnacles, has been lost to rows of horizontal buildings lying heavily on the land. Few seem to care what they look like. That's why I draw the old ones before they are demolished, then print and seal them for my kitchen wallpaper after keying the drawings into my blog record. Someone maybe sometime will see what our city used to be like many decades ago, if they ever access what I’m creating now.

While I'm ruminating at my fireside tasks, the table in the middle of the room has been transformed and the white linen cloth submerged beneath dishes laden with turkey and vegetables, and two old brass candlesticks circled with deep green holly, mistletoe and ivy. It's a good year for red berries. Outwebbers, Eliza tells us, have set up a collective poultry farm. Bears come down in the winter; wolves and foxes fight out their territory. All who have turkeys or chickens or guinea fowl have to take it in turns to feed and tend the birds in the protected yard and poultry houses. They are cleaned by each owner in turn. She has hinted that Foxy's barking does help, and that wild animals are not the only predators, but I haven't picked up the sequel.

We have finished the soup that tasted of breezes and clear water and of Eliza's outdoor world where she toils and dreams. Hot and welcome. I'm back stoking up the fire and oven while the wind fingers the stone walls and more heat is needed to banish shivers inside. I whisper all this into my wordfree while by the fire away from the chatter round the table.

I'm leaning back now to listen to Karen discoursing on the wine to accompany each dish. Eliza has procured some of that brightly coloured crinkly paper she used to have when she was a child, and yesterday she showed me how to make crackers and find little surprises to put into them. Joe wanted to help, so Nicholas did too. The child's eyes were wide open and so was his mouth when we pulled them - without a pop as we couldn't make that - and the gifts spilled out, two in each. That was my idea. No one wins. We used two of everything, like two small hardboiled eggs that Joe painted with spots and twirls - flies and worms, he said they were - two walnuts, two little chocolate balls which Nicholas had brought, two shells and two variegated pebbles found by the stream. Now paper, ribbons and contents are scattered with chatter around the table.

It must have been all that sugar, especially the sticky chocolate cake brought by Martha, that spurred Joe into action. He took a mistletoe sprig from the decorations and, holding it between his teeth, began to dance, stamping out rhythms on the earthen floor. Eliza moved to the piano to work the beat into a tune. I lit the piano candlesticks. Others picked up the brass ones on the table to move it and the chairs back, clearing more space for Joe's dance. His body curled and dipped. Gasps. Someone dropped a candlestick, sparks flying. Wonder. Rainbow movements entwining beat, body, fingers and toes.

Where does this child, found by a rail track in Africa, come from? Does it matter?

I too have been dancing. Something new I had only just thought about, working in hesitant movements, but they all clamoured for my famous sequence. The one that made my first fortune. Joe was watching it intently and started to dance following me. Now I'm back at the fireside throwing logs on the fire. Eliza is singing a forgotten song by Mozart - Zaïde. Nicholas's lips are following hers. Joe is staring at her, trying to shape the notes with his fingers.

Out for more logs. The sky has cleared. There's a touch of frost and the lights at the end of the causeway seem dimmed. I thought I heard voices, even shouts when I came out earlier for more logs. I probably imagined them, as it's too far away to hear. But the lights are dimmed. I'm sure of that. Inside Martha is talking animatedly.

'- a yearly changeover, done at Mid Winter when people are busy and won't notice...'

'What's she talking about?' I whisper to Sister Julian.

'A visit to the Art Cavern.'

'What? Where? When?' I must have shouted.

'Now.'

Everyone is pulling on coats, scarves, hats and boots. I'll follow them.

*****

No live person ever guards the Art Cavern. The cyber security system is turned off twice yearly to be checked and fine-tuned, so only the code and password for entry are needed.

'Martha says she has them,' Sister Julian murmurs as I follow her out. Eliza is closing the door, without locking it.

My wordfree hardly throws enough light to see my shoes. The sky is clouding over. Another snowstorm? It's frosty, but we're burning in expectation. Darkness grips us groping in single file after Martha along the causeway. It advances up the valley from the sea to the terminus and then over meadows to the dark foothills. She leads with Eliza's candlelit lantern and we follow along the narrow paved surface, anxious not to slip over the edge. I fear the dark. No shapes, colours or textures to mind-photograph and then draw, if I want to. Sister Julian's cape blows against me as the night wind rises. How steady is she? How steady am I, or anyone? I'm sliding the soles of my shoes along the middle, fearful of the rough edge and of tipping into space while aiming for the dim light at the cavern's entrance.

The massive doors reach high beyond the light remembered by the cells as they are rechannelled, reconstituted and recharged. We're present at the bi-annual crack in the cave's protective armour. Martha is holding her arm up, hailing the doors with palm and wrist facing them so the code thought into her wordfree and the spoken password can let us in. She isn't supposed to reveal that she has been initiated into the secret society of the Trustees of World Art. I overheard her telling Roland that it happened after she had brokered the exchange of Leonardo's Leda and the Swan for the old university buildings..

Martha's shaking her wrist and tries to hold it higher. Nothing happens. Roland whispers to her - what does he know about the secret combination? He's not a trustee – at least, I don't think so. The doors are foreboding, even in torchlight, studded and incised with whorled patterns as if they were the ancient portals of a sacred chamber deep in the mountainside. Martha hesitates, then holds her wrist against her shoulder, palm towards the portals as if greeting them. Maybe she's whispering the password?

A section of the doors slides back to leave a sliver of light for us to enter. Sister Julian has to turn sideways to squeeze in and I lower my head. We move from the end of the causeway into the Cavern. Glyphics about twenty centimetres high signpost the sections. Cabinets of all sizes in incorruptible glassite line the hewn walls. Martha is leading us silently past signposts to veins branching out for African, French, Italian, Indian art and so on. Holbein's Henry VIII stands out in a container hung with others on a tall pivot in the British section. Further on is another pivot with Eliza's favourite works by Turner, of mists and castles, rivers and mountains barely discernible against golden sunsets.

Across the main artery is a contemporary area, if I read the glyphics correctly. Martha is expounding:

'... Here's the most controversial part. It's difficult to judge who are the great living artists, so we have a temporary status section.'

'That's why living artists are so popular.' Sister Julian's voice quivers, a muted echo as she has lagged behind the rest of us. 'Their work is in cities out there on display. As art should be.' She is standing in the artery's widest area, arms outstretched, palms turned upwards. 'Appreciation is an act of creation too. We're all there, inside a great work of art.'

She often explains that they are the handiwork of God expressed only through hukind. Joe's dancing and mine, Eliza's music and painting, are all unique and practically useless. They inspire and speak to the soul.

Smaller veins spread out like capillaries reaching into the mountain, each with its glyphic signposts. Martha is pointing to a leg-shaped signpost - Italy. I think she wants to check that Leda is where she should be, with Jupiter disguised as her swan, because this is Leonardo's original work. Frankly I'm surprised to see all these originals visible behind glassite. I expected them to be hidden in dustless darkness, sliding behind one another as in the old museum stacks. Here they are poised on pivots that rotate and are graded according to size - the frame is included where it is part of the original work.

Oh dear. Joe has found out how the pivots rotate and he's pushing the one Martha wants to search. A whiskery, upright man in a velvet cap swings past.

'That's Castiglione, the one who wrote a book about how to behave. Raphael's painting. Once in the Louvre, Paris.' Eliza's whisper shushes dryly into the darkness along the Italian vein. Mona Lisa swiftly follows Castiglione and fast behind her - Martha grabs Joe's shoulder to stop him turning the pivot - the next picture swings into view. Leda's smile is more irritating than enigmatic, almost a smirk: 'I've got him, and he's not really a swan. Sod you!'

Sister Julian stops to look closely at the painting. Joe glances at Nicholas who reaches for his hand and they wander towards the signpost for the Africa vein, a black spot over an elephant horn. I follow. The Benin bronzes are in smaller glassite cases, dwarfed by the ceiling-high ones with totem poles of every size ranged like sentries opposite one another. Who comes here to see them? Martha must know. These painted faces are crying out at me and I must get away, find the others, leave here. The lights are stronger now. I can see Nicholas and Joe further down the African vein becoming smaller and smaller to disappear round a bend.

I'm back in the main artery, almost spotlit and a noise is rising and falling away like the distant thunder of waves on the shore. Veins radiate out in directions I hadn't noticed with still more capillaries branching off. The speck in the Chinese one must be Karen seeking the celadon vases that she treasures. Eliza is still with her landscapes, her Turners and Constables. Sister Julian has just branched off into a capillary in the Italian section, no doubt seeking Duccio and Giotto madonnas, while Roland and Martha are locked in discussion - or argument, these echoes distort - down by the great portal.

The wave sounds have become a boom with thuds in it, like the earth's heartbeat. Threaded through it is the moan of a siren, dying away to return louder but half a tone lower.

'Hurry!' Martha cries, 'the security system has re-geared.' I try calling the others but the words turn back on me and my voice echoes away. Who should I fetch? I run back to the African vein with the garish green, red, brown, yellow, orange masks madly grinning, calling, crying. Nicholas and Joe see me and I beckon them back. Joe's eyes are dilated. Karen is striding unflustered into the main artery in front of us and Eliza is already halfway to the doors with Sister Julian straining after her.

The lights are overpowering.

The boom and siren echo, moan, soar and vibrate.

Martha and Roland are gesticulating and mouthing shouts that swirl high round the cave. Eliza breaks into a run and I race after her, as fast as I can. Martha is raising her wrist towards a panel above her head. She tiptoes to whisper the password. The door opens and we escape into the darkness outside.

23

27 December

Martha *i-witnessMAR727.futurepast.com*

We left yesterday on the first hoverpod from the North Moorland Divergence Route Terminus. Magnus stayed behind to finish some sketches he had started. I was tense, wondering whether I should have let everyone into the Art Cavern when I didn't have a permit. The visit was an impulse. To give everyone a surprise. I knew mum so wanted to see it. I may have to call a Trustees' online conference and that could mean some sort of punishment. Perhaps demotion? I must get in touch with them. It can wait until I'm back in my capsule.

When we separated in the Main Square, Sister Julian went straight to the old university and Roland said he would get some constituency work done in his official apartment. Nicholas and Joe were to take the monopod from the Central Station to the Institute. When I turned just as mother and I left through the main entrance, I saw two policemen approach Nicholas. I started to go back to him but mother tugged at my arm. She was upset and needed to talk to me alone. I'll call him as soon as I've settled her back at Beech Drive.

'Martha, you designed this new capsule for both of us. Now Eliza's in her cottage; we're apart for the first time in, how many years? Twenty-seven. Or more.'

She is looking at me. What can I say?

'I don't like being in Beech Drive alone, Martha. Eliza's crazy to move out. But then she has always been attached to the past, like the stone from Petra, now in her cottage next to a brick from 11 Acacia Avenue. Plus all her bric-à-brac from our mantelpiece there. Fortunately there isn't one for all her clutter in in this house. No fireplace needed, so no mantelpiece or chimney.'

I go into the kitchen. She starts up again when I return with tea and biscuits.

'Those bluey green celadon bowls that I thought I really liked look duller, less attractive here on top of Eliza's bookcase below the window. They're probably copies, like the Chinese figurines I bought in San Francisco when I first met Anya Lo Yin – never in my wildest dreams did I imagine she'd become President of the USA! Eliza didn't approve of them. Since then I've been looking at genuine celadon on my visits to China and unforgettable five-panel screens with fantastic mountain landscapes - jagged rocks where herons perch and spiky pines rise above the neat pattern of rice fields. I thought they were an artist's fantasy until I saw them for real down south, by the river Lu.'

I pause before putting the tray down. 'I wish I knew China as well as you do, mother.'

Here in Beech Drive the Chinese blossom wallpaper is still on the wraparound screens. I suggest a static sunset for a change but she is already enlarging her Chang Lin business tile. I don't know how a President can find time to support mother's promotional site – albeit one championing Chinese wine - as Lin does. True friendship that is, though mother did help her with the recent agreement to send Leda to China on loan. Funny the way Sister Julian looked at the painting with the originals in the Art Cavern. President Chang is paying our Zone Government a huge amount for the loan thanks to mother and me. The Trustees of the Art Cavern agreed to the Chinese tour. Was Sister Julian concerned, even confused over the version of Leonardo's painting that turned up at an auction, and was snapped up by our government? The original found at St. Thomas's is in the Art Cavern and the other is travelling to China. Mother continued,

'Well, Eliza went on at me for leaving her alone for so long. I had to travel abroad for my work, but I always came back. Now she's done that to me. Permanently. She knows I couldn't live as an outwebber.'

'Just visit her then.'

I'm trying to get mother to confront mum. To work it out with her, not to let mum determine their relationship. She doesn't like the idea. She wants me to intervene, to bring them together. I'm silent. She reaches out to take another biscuit and slumps back into her chair. I must voice Nicholas. And there's so much zone and GWP business to deal with, not to mention local matters such as what's happening to our Centre for Genetic Wellbeing and Esther, but mother has started up again.

'Why isn't anyone confronting the Planet Supervisors?' Does she want a verbal battle? I remain silent. 'All right, they are chosen by local zone government members like you, Martha, from GWP deputies like Roland Wrightson. It's a secret ballot. We know their names and what they look like, so they aren't artificial beings. They have special powers to supervise world peace and ensure our safety, but are now lobbying for even greater scrutiny of citizens for their own security.'

'Challenge them!' I say, not wanting to become involved.

'For example, the wraparound screens here were on standby when I came in. Why can't I turn them off? For my security, I can hear you say. To keep a watch out for potential troublemakers. Didn't it all start with those terrorist outrages killing innocent people enjoying themselves at football matches and concerts? We can't exist unless we're safe. Goodwill satellites are out there to help us survive. That's why some call them peace satellites. And you could say, Martha, they have succeeded. Almost. But now any protest is zapped out as potentially leading to conflict…Eliza would say I am programmed to think like this. I could argue that she is programmed to paint those pictures of primeval chaos, or the dreamy evocations of places, in the style of Turner, she says. She goes on about how the paint is real and one can touch the surface, feel the colours, so canvases like hers clutter up our place on the planet. Objects that have no function. Mess or inspiration? Interesting clutter, beautiful clutter, she would argue, not really knowing what she means.'

I suppose mother has a point. The problem for people who paint and create is that there are more art works or objects than spaces for them. Museums are built to provide accommodation. Mum obstinately refuses to use competitions and self-publicity to get her works into them or other people's capsules – that is, if they still have any unscreened surface in them.

While she's talking I've been trying to contact Nicholas but he isn't answering. He must have put his wordfree on hold. If only he were more organised...

'I'm angry, Martha. I should get on with my activity as a maintainer. My wine business is going well, helped by the illustrious backers I have in China. Eliza mutters about the support being more significant than the wine.'

She's looking to see if I agree. I smile and keep silent. On she goes.

'Does my archaeology make me a producer instead of a maintainer? If I'm a producer I'll get a better pension, "scaled up for brainpower".'

'Do what interests you,' I say, worrying about Nicholas. 'Nothing prevents you from applying for producer status.'

'As a businesswoman or as an archaeologist? Are they both rated as producers?'

I'm not going to enter this argument.

'Eliza is still an enabler, Martha, because she couldn't be bothered to contact the zone's status office when she started running groups of haven homes – a maintainer position surely? Her pension is smaller as a consequence.'

Mother doesn't seem to notice that I've got up.

'In any case, Martha, I need to return to China and continue my exploration of the old library at Ciongu before it is transferred to the Book Cavern. There every existing written work on stone, bark, parchment, papyrus, animal skin or paper is conserved and preserved. Almost all are on the internet, so the world has only lost contact with primary sources. Does it really matter?' She takes the last biscuit.

I'll carry the tray out to the kitchen and check she has enough in the fridge before leaving Beech Drive. How can I contact Nicholas? Find out where he is?

*****

I'm back home after looking for Nicholas in his rooms and the lab, both deserted. The porters haven't seen him since the solstice. Perhaps he has gone somewhere with Joe. St. Thomas's? I didn't think of that. I'll voice Sister Julian.

Loud knocking at the door of my capsule. Nicholas? Whoever it is had better be careful as the sletic planks can splinter if banged too sharply. It's called an echo fracture. I didn't note my wordfree 'home visit' alert. I must do something about my pulse. My battery's low. Should I use a beat enhancer?

'Can we come in?' I was expecting Nicholas, not his research collaborators, Raphael and Esther. I'll get them some tea. They look cold and concerned. The tea should also strengthen my pulse and charge my wordfree battery.

'Where's Nicholas?' Esther's asking. 'I returned from Africa just after the solstice, went straight to the lab and then his rooms in the Institute. Nobody there. Security doesn't know where he is. Then to St. Thomas's. Joe's there but no Nicholas. Sister Julian tells us she last saw him at Central Station. His wordfree isn't responding. Do you know where he is?'

Raphael now. 'He messaged me before the solstice about sending the final accurate calculations. I need them urgently. He said something about mislaying the datadrive. I'm so worried. We're waiting for them.'

I can't really help.

Raphael is standing by the window. 'Something's happening,' he says. He seems smaller, as if tensing against an uncertainty. 'Someone's following me. I can feel it.'

'That's why I'm here with him,' Esther explains, joining him at the window. 'Raphael's getting threatening messages on his wordfree that can't be obliterated. Nothing clear. He needs to see Nicholas urgently to discuss the crucial next steps. The latest calculations. The accurate beam angle on the receptors, and much else. But he isn't answering our voice calls.'

I'm behind them at the window. I think a helousine has just whirled away at the end of the road. Or maybe not. It's grey and misty outside. Have I imagined it? They return to the sofa, talking in low tones, probably so my wordfree doesn't record what they're saying. Almost conspiratorial. I don't like it.

Esther and Raphael sense I'm agitated though I'm trying not to show it. Raphael is gaunt. His looks are deteriorating. I remember him wiry, the athletic type. He wears his light brown hair longer than most do. It's usually curly, not lank like now. I didn't think he'd return. He should be busy. He's now, Nicholas says, some sort of high-up scientific adviser for the Middle East Alliance.

'We should send messages to the Lost Persons Centre on the Goodwill World Safety satellite, Martha.'

'Do it from here.'

They hunch over my high potential microscreen. We register Nicholas as missing. His DNA wasn't recorded at his special school for the gifted – no idea why – so he can't be traced like the rest of us. He was born before it became obligatory to register at birth. He can only be checked through his wordfree, but isn't answering. Esther looks tired; taller , fuller, and less open-faced somehow. Like she has something to hide.

'Martha?' she asks. 'I need to talk to you soon about the Centre for Genetic Wellbeing and its offshoot in Mybeki.'

'Yes,' I said, 'but not now, please. I'm exhausted. Can we meet at the Centre? Voice me.'

Esther nods. Her eyes are that strange murky blue-grey mix of a new-born child. She must have come back in a hurry as she is still in her brightly-striped African robe with a jumper pulled over it. Before she used to fit in with the asexual uniform of vlason sweater top and slacks, all tech-shaped, patterned and dyed according to current fashion.

Raphael has opened the World Safety tile and enlarged it to accommodate Gem, the Planet Supervisor on duty. She - or he? - is dark-haired, Asian, a bit asexual but attractive. Gem is pointing at a slowly rotating globe while Raphael beckons me towards the sensor. I don't really know what to tell them.

'Dr. Nicholas Middlethorpe, my brother, was last seen at the Central Station yesterday with... He is now missing.' I pause to focus on Gem's tile image and minimise it. Gem looks perplexed when I start to fade out of her view and she out of mine.

'Would he be with Magnus?' Raphael asked me.

'No. Magnus stayed at Eliza's to finish some sketches he had started. We left without him.'

I must put space between me and the anger that Magnus provokes. Or is it just irritation? All his dancing and inscrutability. He thinks he's handsome. I suppose he is, in a gnarled way. I can't stand how he takes people over. First Nicholas, then Eliza. He'll soon be back in his home now, a semi recluse, but his tentacles reach out. Esther is inviting me to go with them to the local diner. They're restless and anxious. But I just want to… I don't know. See Roland. Above all, to find Nicholas. Wrists to ears, they don't hear me.

They've left. I'll contact Esther after I've located Nicholas.

I should enlarge the newstile. The blinking and bleeping are more insistent. That means we must participate - it used to be called an SOS. What a relief Helen isn't on it. Just an announcer who could be anyone from anywhere, another visual compromise in looks, but vaguely male in voice and physique.

BREAKING NEWS

WORLD-RENOWNED SCIENTIST ARRESTED.

The famous scientist **Nicholas Middlethorpe** has been arrested in Central Station. He is accused of child molesting in an anonymous note placed in the

Mouth of Truth mask on the south wall of the old university building. The person who wrote it was wearing DNA-denying gloves. It has come as a shock to all who knew this publicity-shy scientist whose research aimed to provide **unlimited low-cost and environmentally neutral energy.**

Financed to test his theory in the sun-drenched meteorstrophe area near Mybeki, Africa, he returned to his hometown with Joe, his young protégé, who was abandoned as a baby by the railway. Joe was fostered by the Zueto tribe and is now an intelligent boy of 11 whose parentage, though unknown, is clearly non-African.

The boy ran out of the station into the network of medieval alleys in the town centre to find his way back to St. Thomas's refugee centre.

worldaroundyounews.com

24

28 December

Magnus *i-witnessMAG931.futurepast.com*

I'm shaken, relieved to be back home. I stayed an extra day with Eliza to finish my sketches and help her clear up after Mid Winter. The outwebber community doesn't want cyberaccess except at the station hub.

What can I do? I should be tranquil here sitting surrounded by my moving wallpaper motif of winds sighing through autumn trees. Usually the colours calm me. Not now. They jab through me, scarlet and blue in cacophony. It's all over the news. A famous scientist has been arrested on a charge of child molesting! Words run down my spine in a cascade of colours. What can I do? How can I see him? No mention of Joe.

What am I looking for? All I see is shaded in purple. Oh, I remember. Those newstiles I've missed. To find out if Joe has been found and where Nicholas is jailed. I've voiced Martha, but she's on hold, involved in some meeting about the Goodwill World Parliament reserve currency crisis. No response from Karen. The prison authorities are legally obliged to tell the occupants' relatives. I'm surfing through items from 26 December onwards. The tiles are now dotted over a backdrop of yellow trees. Leonardo's painting of Leda is in China? I thought Sister Julian was looking at it in the Art Cavern – or mausoleum. That reminds me. I must find out what the museum director has done with my original sketches, black ink on cream paper, of our city's remaining historical buildings and of others before they were demolished. I'll keep the copies on the kitchen wall. At least the museum will have something, however modest, that's not a copy. Directly from the artist to the public. No one will want to preserve my sketches in the Art Cavern, so they'll be safe from the conservationists.

How can I see Nicholas?

I'll enlarge the newstiles, the ones I hope he hasn't seen. And now he's in prison. They're disturbing. I can't believe it! Helen announcing that Dom Ross Mackenzie is leasing a satellite from the Goodwill World Parliament – is that legal? Ross Mackenzie will be in control of the satellite with the high energy panels, of the flint so to speak, which produces the spark from beams of light in space to relay down here – Nicholas's miracle. I'm shivering ice-blue sparks of anxiety. How could Helen announce the theft of Nicholas's invention? She's on with a slickly handsome newscaster called the Promoter. He is probably an avatar while Helen only appears to be one.

If it weren't for the fact that I know she exists, I'd think it was the other way round - Helen the avatar and the Promoter a real person. She looks so improbably polished, splendidly sharp as if invented perfect by public acclaim. Too unblemished to be real. She has brightness around the edges, the shiny yellow glow found with avatars in virtual reality games.

Has Nicholas allowed her to do this? Why doesn't Reaching Out know? After all, we financed his research in Africa. How can I contact him? His wordfree is silent. On hold? Confiscated? What can I do? If only Nicholas were able to defend himself. It's impossible for me to arrange a prison visit; I'm not family. Martha should go. I'll call her. On hold. I'll lock her into a repeated call until I can speak to her.

What should I do first? At least Joe is safe at St. Thomas's – that was on the news. I've messaged Sister Julian but she's in the hospital in the old university and her messages are on hold. Later. Deal with the worldwide threat first. The rogue satellite. What can be done? Call a Reaching Out conference? I've ended my term as co-ordinator. I'll have to find someone to second my Reaching Out conference call. Who? Chang-fu would be interested, but she's heavy-going and will take some persuasion. That's it - Zuami! Esther may have involved him in the Genetic Wellbeing activities at Mybeki. Perfect. I'll try now.

*****

I've never known a conference to be assembled so quickly. So many others are putting in identical requests, it seems, all reacting to Helen on *worldaroundyounews*. Millions of hits on the Newsbank during the Mid Winter holiday. Most people, like me, can't be bothered to look inside. This time, sensing growing agitation, I did glance around it and found seething reactions on the feedback boards.

'How can the Planet Supervisors opt out of their responsibilities?' Holly is screaming frantically as the conference starts - her term for the USA is about to end. 'Those satellites belong to us all!'

'That Ross non-person is only leasing it,' Shilpa from Jaipur reminds us. 'Let's remain calm.'

'Right,' Zuami agrees from Africa. 'If Dom Ross Mackenzie is going to provide unlimited, clean, low cost energy, then I don't mind how he does it, as long as it benefits us all. It will be crucial for Africa.'

'But is it safe? What about people living near the energy receptors?' That's Telma from Rio. She must have accessed fears raised about the energy beams in the Newsbank, which I should have done too.

'Look,' Zuami was quick to voiceblock other responses. (We are all checked by a timing device: the first to respond holds the argument for up to three minutes, and others have to wait, making conference discussion an edgy experience.) 'Look, we'll come to that later. The crucial point is, do we support this initiative or not? Are we about to reject infinite, low cost energy on a technical issue? We should, of course, consult the inventor, Dr. Nicholas Middlethorpe. We must check the conditions Reaching Out stipulated before financing his sub-Saharan experiments. Why is Ross Mackenzie exploiting Dr. Middlethorpe's discovery? And why isn't he supervising the latest developments? '

'Or health and safety regulations?' three voices shout simultaneously, none gaining the right to speak, then Tony from Canada,

'Who is responsible for the safety of this electricity generating system?'

'I believe it's only a one-year trial satellite lease after all,' Keiko from Japan.

'But who is paying for it?' Mahmoud from the Middle East Alliance is always budget-cautious, 'money means influence'.

'Not always.' Ramon this time. I know he's near ending his tenure for Peru.

'We are informed -' Michel from Toulouse has a patient, slightly condescending voice and manner '- that the Goodwill World Parliament doesn't need money. Its statute decrees that all national entities contribute 2% of their gross domestic product. You all know about the GWP budget, don't you? 10% pays for our elected representatives, the Deputies of the Goodwill World Parliament or DWPs including the Planet Supervisors, and for worldwide initiatives like the Goodwill searches for missing people, peace-breakers and so on; 40% is redistributed to alleviate poverty and provide the citizens' benefit for leisuretimers as well as retirement pensions for all according to their status . The remaining 50% supports the social fabric – schools, hospitals and so on – in the Peace Zones and also provides aid for natural disasters in poorer parts of the world.'

'Like ours.' Jacques from Haiti is new, embarrassingly young and keen. He was orphaned by an earthquake. 'Indescribable suffering and lack of cohesion over the massive aid effort led, after long and pointless delays, to the building of sound social structures. They are lifting Haiti out of corruption and chaos. Otherwise aid comes, money pours in, attention passes and waste ensues.'

'That's one of the reasons why the Goodwill World Parliament was eventually founded after very long and fraught negotiations,' I comment.

'All right, all right, let's leave the money issue,' Keiko proposes, 'but who controls the spark that ignites the solar panels on the satellite? Whoever turns it on, can do the opposite.'

It's clear nobody knows the answer. I'm not alone in feeling the hand of doom grasping me. The inevitable motion is for each of us to bring pressure on our GWP deputies and Zone Government members to clarify the satellite leasing terms. Dom Ross Mackenzie must explain why an exception was made for him, why Dr. Middlethorpe and Reaching Out were side-lined and what is in place to avoid it happening again. All this must be clarified on the main *worldaroundyounews* board, with a declaration that they have followed the Goodwill World Parliament Foundation Charter and posted all their deliberations and decisions on the GWP Notice Board in the Newsbank.

It's some time since I felt such a shudder of dank, dark green fear.

* * * * *

So much out there is 'penned in ether', Eliza would say - deliberately, blissfully ignorant. Then we'd chase each other with comments and ideas. Funny person, Eliza.

I'm exhausted. I miss Nicholas, who should have been here for the conference. I've just tried to find a way to see him, but my request is blocked again. I am not a relative. His infinenergy laboratory near Mybeki was sponsored by our Reaching Out movement, not the Goodwill World Parliament. Facts are so soon forgotten. It was his invention. Does he know of this satellite business? I assumed that after the African experiments to check the beam's accuracy to a trillionth of a centimetre, he was ready to patent his discovery. Instead, Dom Ross seems to have done it. History repeats itself, though nobody realises this now history is considered irrelevant. Every new invention has a challenger. It seems inevitable. Wallace worked out Natural Selection about the same time as Darwin and Leibniz came up with Calculus when Descartes did. Parallel thinking? Nicholas has lost the philosopher's stone to a moneyed entrepreneur with a battery of scientists at his behest.

I'm slumped here on the sofa in a grey haze watching the last autumn leaves succumbing to winter and doing precisely nothing. I could go into my bedroom and fall asleep looking at Gaia's image. Or I could try to find out who prompted the viral slur about Nicholas and Joe, a plunge into the murky, troll infested waters of the internet. Or go to St. Thomas's to see how Joe is. Martha hasn't replied to my repeat message. I'll try her again. I only have to think and gaze at her identification number. All so quick and simple.

'Not simple enough for me,' Eliza would say. How did she manage to produce a scientific genius…?

'Hi, Magnus, I'm in a Zone conference. Can you call later? Thanks.' So much for Martha! Try Karen then. Just as easy.

'Magnus, you've caught me perched on the WC. Nicholas is still in custody. Martha has made an official protest. She's busy getting us family visit permits. This is not the place to talk. Can't you voice me another time?'

She doesn't seem particularly bothered, and she's his mother. What about those two scientists who were his collaborators? Esther is probably back in Africa and Raphael is some sort of scientific ambassador, Nicholas told me, for the Middle East Alliance. He could be anywhere.

Try. Nothing venture… I feel like ignoring my dark blue inner voice. Without the will or information to act, I am floating on a swirling yellow current to nowhere.

Esther's wordfree is security blocked with the message: 'user out of contact on confidential business'. She could be making love. Try Raphael's. His is blocked with the same message. Making love together? Hardly. That assumes they are close together. We're all closely linked on the wordfree, though we could be on the other side of the planet!

Roland Wrightson? He has just been elected our Planet Supervisor. Later maybe. He too is probably attending to zone business.

I could leave a message again for Eliza at the station hub. The signal is weak. Too close to the mountains, or is it because the outwebbers don't want it? Probably. So in a world of perfect communications, I can't contact anyone! I could retreat into my studio to dance, evoking sounds, rhythms and colours. I'll only get more disgruntled at my creaking joints and slow, unlovely movements. I should give up.

25

BREAKING NEWS

SCIENTIST DR. NICHOLAS MIDDLETHORPE HAS LEFT PRISON

The GWP delegates, at a special meeting, have highlighted the **Goodwill World Parliament Charter, statute 720** that decrees 'No world citizen can be accused on the basis of an anonymous declaration'. The renowned scientist has been cleared of the viral slur that he is a child abuser. His young protégé, Joe, has been traced through the **Goodwill World Safety Satellite's Missing Persons Centre**. He is now safely at **St. Thomas's refuge.**

worldaroundyounews.com

---

29 December

Nicholas *i-witnessNIC227.futurepast.com*

Free with nowhere to go. The shame of my family. I can't face them. I can't face anyone. Everyone knows about it in the Institute. If I see Joe the virus will propagate online in spite of the declaration of my innocence and I might be arrested again.

I'm bearing the burden of nothing I know I've done.

There's rawness in my guts racing up to my throat.

I should be happy. I'm free. But my invention is in jeopardy. The beam could cause immense collateral damage if they use inaccurate calculations. I'm powerless. Dom Ross's scientists don't have the final accurate calculations and nor do I!

I'm free. Not to look for Joe. Will the twittering mob ever pardon me for what I didn't do? I'm the victim of a viral slur. So is he. We are both forever linked, internetted. I'm officially cleared of an uncommitted misdeed; the condemnation is cyber-eternal - is the pardon? Tweets are still cheeping maliciously in my head and on the internet, virally breeding, uncontrollably, like an endless echo.

Joe is my curse, my affection, my distraction, my fixation. He fills a hole in my heart. He stopped me despairing about the lost datadrive. Then. Not now – it haunts me.

I might be *a brilliant scientist* but I wasn't well known, certainly not a celebrity. I am now, for the wrong reasons. Released from the white-tiled, eye-height windows of the Rehabilitation Centre, I should exculpate myself online - though I don't want anyone to hear me. That's why I'm thinking into my wordfree. Trying to tell it what was on that lost datadrive. Those calculations hanging round my neck. I've been interviewed twice on *worldaroundyounews.com*, not enough to be street-recognised. A relief, now especially. Helen said I was *quietly attractive.* To others I'm insignificant.

Not like Joe. Those brown eyes, wide open when he looks at me. Or creased in concentration when I explain my calculations or my experiments - my mental landscape. His body lithe and tense; his handstands, his physical grace.

Yes, I did love Joe. Do still. I ache for him, want him here now. To cuddle.

To hug a child. Is that lustful?

To find him beautiful - is that illegal?

To cherish him, think of him and want to do the best for him as a child, as a future adult, as a brilliantly intelligent being – is this a crime?

I'm wandering into the old town. Along narrow streets. Tall brick buildings where centuries of people have moved in and out of them.

Someone spied him in my bed, because there was nowhere for him to sleep, except the bare boards of my Institute rooms.

You fathers out there, have you ever slept in the same bed as your eleven-year-old son? Have you been imprisoned for it? Tell me.

No. Don't. I don't want to be seen or heard.

Rawness inside me. Tightness in my eyes and nose. I can't swallow.

Someone knew about me and Joe and the one bed. In my Institute rooms. Only Helen might have seen us there. Where else? Mid Winter, 25 December at mother's? Who from my family - Karen, Martha or her partner, Roland - our elected Planet Supervisor and a bit of a mystery – came into the loft at the cottage? Magnus slept there too. Any others?

I never want to return to my Institute rooms. I've scoured the bedroom for the crucial database. Not there. Lost. Did I message Raphael for the previous calculations? Sent to him on the datadrive Helen took back from Africa. They're not accurate enough. I could start again from them... back in Africa... Ross, of course, would love to provide the funding for his own purposes... I couldn't ask Reaching Out again...

No. I have no will to start all over again. None. None at all.

I must stop thinking about Ross Mackenzie. About Joe. And about Helen – stop thinking. If only...

Habit takes me on the usual way. Stop by St. Thomas's. Sister Julian?

I miss her. Never used to think about her. Just knew she was there. Understanding. Resourceful. Ready to help. A knowing look. A bowl of hot soup. A warm word.

She busy now at the old university setting up a medical centre somebody there tells me. I continue along the street to the city centre.

Joe's fatherless too - now. The Zueto tribe adopted him. A band of fathers – then. Wherever he is, I can't help him.

At least I can think my truth into an encrypted blog, a secret for fifty years. Then who would want to read it?

Lies spread like a virus in the veins of the internet. So easy, so false. So eagerly absorbed and believed. I'm free, but my imagined transgression is world property. It can never be deleted from cyberspace. Ever. Innocence leaves no online footprint. I'm starved. No love, no arms around me.

Here's the masterpiece museum of copies. Through the portico into the vestibule? Ceaseless publicity along the wall screens. The director has crammed the entrance hall with plaster copies: Apollo Belvedere, Venus de Milo, Laocoon, the Burghers of Calais... People stroke even hug them. This never happened when mother first took me to art shows. Blind people were helped to feel plaster casts. Others surreptitiously touched them. No hugging. No one notices what others are doing. Many are fondling ancient forms of beauty. No queues like the ones for Leonardo's painting. Plenty of people.

No buzz or excitement. There's a contentment that alienates me. The vestibule has mirrors that multiply the silent gropers. I'm there too, dazed and apart.

One in a crowd. Why bother about my invention, the lost calculations on the datadrive? I've forgotten the password. Bury all hope.

I'm sitting in the Main Square, head throbbing, mouth open to breathe, where it all started: someone scribbled a note and tossed it into the Mouth of Truth, soon copied into cyberfed gossip: 'Dr. Nicholas Middlethorpe has a young boy sleeping in his bed, so it must be sinful and illegal.' I'm putting my hand into the mouth and saying it's true but not sinful, hoping it will be bitten off if I'm lying. It isn't. I'm not.

I'm closing my eyes here in the Main Square, fingers in ears, to escape the vast encircling screens with incessant *worldaroundyounews*. I can't bear that voice, sharper than usual, but surely Helen's. She'd jettison anyone for celebrity status.

A thump… I open my eyes. People are walking past. Someone bumped into me. Nothing unusual. A side glance my way. They don't recognise me. Mild curiosity at most. Thump, thump, thump, thump, thump - faster, faster… Acid gashes my stomach. My heart is beating through my ribcage. It needs freedom too.

I can't believe it! Helen is announcing that Dom Ross Mackenzie is planting energy receptors worldwide to feed my infinenergy into existing networks! Stolen limitless, low cost energy will reinforce universal peace – she mouths it – how could she? He's the world's greatest benefactor. His satellite will bring the best for all. What's in it for him? Only 2% of all profits worldwide, just to maintain the satellite and pay for its lease from the Goodwill World Parliament… work it out on the wordfree - a huge sum. Could be trillions. We're talking of the whole world...

Helen is looking out right over us obviously reading from a teleprompter. She's unbelievably herself. Perhaps too like herself. I mustn't look any more. Can't stop my heart thumping. 'A reclusive scientist,' she says - me? 'Dom Ross Mackenzie… invented infinite energy…'

Lies, all lies. HE HAS STOLEN, STOLEN, STOLEN MY LIFE'S PURPOSE, MY INVENTION, MY DREAM…Stolen, stolen, stolen repeats in my mind with the relentless beat of a pulse.

How? How could she tell lies? Do this to me?

How many datadrives were there? Two in Africa? One with Ross Mackenzie's program? I left his in the bungalow so he couldn't have it back – it would have the imprint of my crucial calculations! What did I do with the other one? I think I gave it to Helen. For Esther? No, she was staying in Africa. For Raphael then? Yes. Another still was hanging round my neck with my conclusive theories. The one I've lost. Somewhere. And the lab break-in. Who? Why?

'…Mackenzie, a brilliant scientist with an unparalleled team, is tipped to be the next Nobel Prize winner for Physics -' For MY work '- for unparalleled benefits…to humanity…'

Ross Mackenzie needs nothing; he's wealthy beyond belief. I procrastinate. He has STOLEN my invention! From what? The datadrive Helen left in the lab for Raphael? No. He's messaged me that he has it. Could she have let Ross copy it? No. Impossible. Or has Ross Mackenzie somehow acquired the one with the last tested calculations that was hanging round my neck – how? I never took it off, but it's lost, lost, lost.

I can't stay here slumped on a bench, head between hands. People are staring. Some try to talk.

I don't want to know. I must get up. Go somewhere.

Hunched, hungry, head hanging, a miserable figure. Me.

Why bother? Who cares where I am, what I'm doing? My invention has been stolen. Helen casts me off for celebrity status. Mother fades into her outwebber world. Martha is always too busy. Karen is always away in China. I could voice Magnus. I'm trying. No contact. Left wrists glued to ear or heads bent over their implants, fingers tapping screens, people here in the Main Square are scurrying off.

I must get out! My inaccurate stuff is there on his satellite. Dom Ross has the answers. I'm stubborn. I resist anything I don't like. Bureaucracy. I procrastinate. I didn't have it patented – I can't face the forms to fill in, the pointless little questions and endless passwords. It's my gut inertia towards anything except problem solving.

Infinite energy. Solved and stolen. Just what I've always wanted to create. Lost. Mine.

Heart thumping. Head throbbing.

Get out. Away.

Look up. Someone's calling. Something about a hoverpod that's left.

Hoverpod? Why am I at the Central Station?

Someone's calling, 'A ride?' How did he know I've been taken on one? Deceived, cheated, cast off. If I'd trusted Dom Ross, would he have stolen my brainchild?

'A ride?'

Or if I had patented it first, before going to Africa... But how could I when it wasn't ready? Not then fully tested.

'Don't look so dejected.'

I look up at the speaker. He’s odd. Clad in a tight black and purple jacket and breeches, chunky boots and helmet with jagged yellow flashes on it, visor up, he’s a contemporary warrior doing battle with the hills, mountains and elements. Shape deceptive. Youthfully old? Heavy lids, raised veins on his hands. Here for the thrill? Perhaps, but - does anything matter? He doesn’t let me slip off the pillion or try to outstrip the hoverpod. People’s eyes peer out at us. Like everyone else, he leaves me.

The wind in my face is gathering speed, racing across the river plain to the mountains - fertile volcanic spaces of ages past.

Take the trodden path to mother’s cottage? They’ll look for me there. I can’t explain. She'll ask about Joe. The same weary explanations will be sighed over. Uselessly.

At least she won't know about it all: accusations, prison and the rest. So I don't have to tell her.

She’s in the kitchen area. The generator is low. There's a candle on top of the table. She’ll be playing the piano from memory. A few audible notes rise between gusts.

I'll knock at the door. Or just walk in. She'll stand up and open her arms to me like a good mother. She'll ask what is happening in a half-listening way. She didn't want me as I am - a son and a scientist. Worse, one whose invention has been stolen by the very people she distrusts. My infinite energy - limitless supply from cradle to grave for all hukind everywhere. It's my invention. Filched and furthered by the world benefactor, Dom Ross himself.

Will he be worshipped? Affordable charity is an easy way to secular sainthood.

The philosopher's stone. The future is here and who wants it?

I want to compose a declaration of the uselessness of existence.

Mine or everyone's?

Mine. I'm alone. I've been set free. I've escaped.

The lab is waiting for me to fill the empty new drives with my back-up material, wherever it is. I don't know or care. My rooms in the Institute are empty. The crucial datadrive lost there? Where? Waiting. For a child molester or a scientist?

I'll escape to the mountains, wind whistling thoughts away. What's the point of my life's work? Of inventing? Of thinking, feeling, caring, existing? My life's purpose is lost, like a child stolen. Now the thrill of it is off pitch and out of key.

What else to do with the endless future? I'm not yet thirty.

Helen keeps on floating into my mind. Bitter memories of laughing, living, loving burn through me. I can't scrape them out, discard them, stifle them, consign them to oblivion. They stab me.

Martha? She used to turn up at the Institute most weeks to talk about herself, her job, and her politics. Then she met Roland and didn't come any more.

Mum? She found me lank and unappealing. Not very boyish; not very anything. And mother? Parents don't tell children, even adult ones, why they part company.

Learn not to bother. In prison I tried to expel Joe from my thoughts. Not to care where he was; not to wonder why he came all that way to find me. Not to feel responsible for everything that has happened to him, and to me. He survived in Africa. He'll find his tribe here. I've deserted him, but he'll survive.

It's twilight. I can't see where the path is leading. Rainclouds hang over the lower slopes of the mountains. Below them, water thunders down the waterfall. The swirling, eddying, pounding... the fresh clouds of spray... down... down... oblivion.

BREAKING NEWS

AQUASTROPHE HITS FERTILE ESTUARY

The **Greystone River estuary** has been inundated by a freak downpour causing an avalanche. Despite warnings from the **Goodwill Meteorological Office**, shepherds were grazing their flocks of **sheerwool** sheep on the sparsely inhabited plateau below the **Sister Peak Waterfalls**. A spokesperson for the inhabitants who have gathered around the terminus of the **North Moorland Divergence Route** reminded the emergency services airlifted to the area that this is their only link to the web. The disaster squads were amazed when she told them that the inhabitants had had no warning of the aquastrophe. Sheep are floating past them in the **Greystone River**. News is breaking that the first casualty has been found in the estuary area.

Food, blankets, tents and hydraulic equipment are being airlifted in. **Roland Wrightson, the Planet Supervisor for the area**, is here to tell you what is happening and to talk to his constituents.

'As I speak, the **Sharp Start Contingency Disaster Aid** is already in the stricken area. Only one casualty, other than livestock, has been reported to date. The second wave of supplies is already being airlifted in. The aquastrophe has fortunately come before the sowing season and is washing rich volcanic soil from the mountainsides on to the plain. While this is undoubtedly a short-term disaster, it will, in the long term, provide us with an even richer agricultural terrain. I shall shortly reach the area. **Martha Middlethorpe, the local zone Member,** has a message for you. Over to you, Martha.'

'Thank you, Roland. The aquastrophe is not predicted to affect the densely populated city area above the Greystone estuary, but those of you living near the canal or the river must have your lifeboats ready for use with a water supply, engine fuel, wind-up torches, sealed food three-day supply packs, flares and water immersion suits. It is unlikely you will need them.'

'Good advice, Martha.'

Elsewhere…

worldaroundyounews.com

26

Magnus *i-witnessMAG931.futurepast.com*
29 December

Now that procrastination is treated as a mind-deforming condition, I must make sure that 'diversionism' isn't added to the lengthening list of clinical conditions. I'm passing St. Thomas's but NOT GOING IN. *Worldaroundyounews* announced that Joe is safe there. I would only get in the way. A young woman in yellow and grey is just entering a side door. She turns to look at me. I stop, resist the urge to follow her inside, and stride out towards our city museum. My drawings portfolio is heavier than I thought it would be and I'm willing myself to deposit it there. To create aquamarine waves. Do something positive. A real, autograph body of work by an unknown artist.

Maybe I don't want to be known.

I have always been fond of this ancient building full of sharp angles, however unsuited it may be for a modern museum. Pause as you enter, and look back through the portico columns to the street opposite of warm redbrick buildings, rectangular windows and panes glittering in the morning sunlight. I draw those shapes and colours into me to preserve these houses here in my portfolio before they are demolished and lost forever.

The museum vestibule is strewn with plaster casts of Greek and Roman statues long banished to the Art Cavern. I stroke them with others wandering through the thicket of classical sculpture. There's no space just to stand back to admire them, but… better than nothing? A sequence of

Claude's landscape paintings moves with me along the screens in the passage to the first gallery.

Here, portfolio in hand, I'm wondering where to find the director, and all I can see is a selection of world masterpieces emerging slowly on all the screens, enlarging, pausing and then diminishing to give way to the next. They reveal themselves to an accompaniment of in-depth commentaries uttered in short, sharp blue sentences backed by rainbow-hued music.

'A great spectacle, isn't it?' A voice projects over my shoulder. I turn to look down into the director's small sandy eyes, the colour of his suit. 'Try it. Interactive, you know.' He has the smug smile of someone saturated with his own success. 'My idea really, but others had to clamber on board and claim it for themselves. So we're in a crowded boat, bobbing unanimously towards a great future - the World Masterpieces Interactive Museum of the works in the Art Cavern, is based here. Try it!' A pink manicured hand grasps my arm, propelling me towards a disembodied, dark-lashed green eye to the left of a shiny bronze statue of Krishna dancing, legs and arms flailing towards me as the full screen image rotates to the nasal lament of an androgynous Indian voice.

'Speak to it. Say what you want and you'll have it.'

'The Sistine Chapel. Without commentary.'

'Impossible!' I can't help feeling irritated. Quite irrational. His enthusiasm for his virtual brainchild and his neatly pressed oatmeal suit irk me. Made of chaff compressed into fibrous cloth and fashioned into an environmentally positive garment, it reminds me of those yellowy boards they used to make out of compressed sawdust. To enliven it he’s wearing a pink-striped shirt, pink socks and a pink and white spotted bow tie.

'Impossible,’ he insists, ‘because the Art Cavern only contains moveable masterpieces. The unmoveable ones like the Caves of Lascaux, Tutankhamen’s Tomb or the Sistine Chapel are experienced near the originals through perfect replicas. Try again.'

Others busy accessing their chosen masterpiece through different eyes into the World Masterpieces Interactive Museum's virtual collection, turn in unison to look at me.

'I don't want to.' I suppose each of us has a different way of expressing shock, but I haven't ever seen an unremarkable face disintegrate so rapidly with eyes, nose, mouth and chin shifting their former relationship as the museum director exclaimed,

'Chose another, moveable work.’

'All right. Rosso Fiorentino's *Deposition* that used to be in a museum in Volterra, Italy.' I love its fiery reds against the cool blue sky. The eye icon blinks and the screen goes blank, before dissolving into glass green ocean breakers rising, cresting… and washing away beyond us in mottled foam.

'We can't have imaged it yet into the Interactive Museum,' the director whispers, his voice strained with a hint of desperation. He looks around furtively. The others are too engrossed to hear. Relieved, 'we haven't been able to image all the lesser works yet.' Then after a pause, 'it is a masterpiece, isn't it? We have nearly all the greatest works on virtual show, seen as never before in every minute detail'.

'They're not original. These are.' I'm tapping my portfolio, 'these are real but not great. Just drawings, authentic works on paper. Records of historical buildings in our city, some destroyed, others still in existence like this museum, but all under threat. Deemed no longer fit for future use.'

The Director is looking unsympathetically at the scuffed leather portfolio I hold out to him. 'Do you have an office?'

He does. The door is hidden behind one of the rectangular gold-rimmed mirrors in the vestibule. I step through it while he enthuses over his recent meeting with Roland Wrightson, the Goodwill Planet Supervisor for this zone, who agrees to back the next development of his World Masterpieces Interactive Museum and locate its core agency here. All over the world people will be able to access every moveable masterpiece in the safety of their homes. A visual, virtual, vibrant museum informed by Artipedia, with the latest on world art, updated by experts and the public alike. The whole concept will become a perfect medium to broadcast creative beauty, artistic invention and imagination, as long as hukind can invent and create, and so on and so forth. The Director, afloat on waves of enthusiasm, will sail his hangers-on into a future of virtually infinite options.

'We'll use the new Babel text: glyphics that all are familiar with, interlinguistically understood, for essential information: that is, briefly, date, provenance, like Mona Lisa, brush (depicted) 1506 (as is) Leonardo da Vinci, (as is) stork (depicted) 1452 Vinci, Italy (map), wreath (depicted) 1519, France (map), and so on. Think 'on' and you reach the next stage, in all existing languages, of course, like the *worldaroundyounews* tile. This is the greatest enterprise of hukind - after Dom Ross Mackenzie's infinite energy project, of course!'

So, like everyone else, he's proclaiming that lie. Poor, poor Nicholas. What can one do when it's promulgated all over the internet? A lie becomes universalised into cybertruth.

On and on the director goes, frantically digitising any available material from the past while waiting for the Goodwill World Parliament's permission to return to the Art Cavern with the same fifty licensed photographers to cover the second level of masterpieces, including Rosso Fiorentino, he adds. I leave through the looking-glass door.

Does he actually want my drawings? I'm not sure. I stressed they were 'real', but that didn't stop him proclaiming the worth of his project. However he did place my neat brown portfolio on one side of his desk and patted it as if to say, 'I'll look at you when I can snatch time from the Grand Scheme of Art for All'.

I'm out now under the museum portico and considering what to do. Turn left, to the town centre and a snack in the buzz of a gastrohub, or turn right to the solitary satisfaction of hunger at home. After that surfeit of directorial company, I head right towards a repast on my own.

It's sunny. I'm submitting, a bit guiltily, to diversion, and I shouldn't, but the knight and his lady that I sketched years ago are just by the side door into St. Thomas's, and I need to reacquaint myself. They are real and I can touch the stone, feel the chiselled hollow under her neck and… One of the refugees is there looking at me. It's the grey and yellow woman I saw entering earlier. I ought to explain my presence.

'Is Sister Julian here?' I have to say something.

'No. She's at the Old University. Do you know her?' This woman doesn't sound like a refugee.

'Yes. We're involved in…' Is she about to mention Reaching Out? We vow silence, unless we meet another member. She looks at me again, adding,

'I'm just leaving to help Sister Julian at the new hospital unit in the old university. Our zone government member, Martha Middlethorpe, has freed up funds to pay for the latest hospital capsules now inserted into the old laboratory area of the Commune. The money comes, appropriately, from the loan to China of the Leonardo painting found at St. Thomas's - all part of its exchange for the old university buildings. Refugees from St. Thomas are helping to run the hospital. Some are training as enablers – nurses in this case. It's a new direction for…' This time she is the one to trail off.

I must do something to stop me worrying uselessly about Nicholas. Joe may be all right, but Nicholas? She wouldn't know where he is.

'Can I come with you?' She nods slowly, staring at me. Almost like Gaia. This woman doesn't say much but she has purpose. She is smiling now,

'I think I know who you are,' she says. 'Nicholas mentioned you when we were in Africa talking about things back here. That is, if you are Magnus?'

She's intuitive. It's difficult to hide things from such a person, even if one had to. She has a glow about her, like Gaia, a quiet magnetic appeal. But Gaia was beautiful as well. She's walking briskly towards the web of old streets that cling to the main square, frowning anxiously at the vast greenish newstile screens there. The latest song contests are jostling for space interspersed with football matches and athletics on the sunny side of the globe. More about the aquastrophe that everyone is talking about. Have I missed something? From home to city centre, all public transport, shops and gastrohubs are screen-lined.

Hurry, hurry. This strange young woman walks busily along the part of the university untouched by the fire. We turn sharp right into Canal Street and take a side entrance. The roof on the other side of the main courtyard has collapsed leaving a skeleton of black beams.

'The scaffolding will go up this week.' She's following my eyes. 'Ten of our former prisoners have formed a co-operative and now hire that section on a peppercorn rent on condition they repair it. Martha Middlethorpe is helping us disentangle the red tape.'

Who is this woman? She must be a Reaching Out member, but that doesn't explain how she can step into Sister Julian's shoes and why I'm following her into a hospital. Even here screens line the vestibule and corridors. It's winter, but the moving wallpaper shows soothing scenes of swaying poppies and sunflowers that surge towards us to fade back in harmony with featureless, disembodied music. One's mind is supposed to become pleasantly vacant.

The ward capsules are small but not crowded rectangles. I'm following this woman to see what she is doing, but not to get involved. Definitely not. Just to know and stop me worrying uselessly about Nicholas. Then I'll go home for a meal. She is standing by one of the four beds. I feel I shouldn't be here. She's looking at me.

'He was half conscious earlier today and said something about a virus, persecution, untruths.'

It's Nicholas. She's stroking his hand, trying to connect him to an existence he doesn't seem to want.

'He floats in and out of consciousness. He tried to explain what happened. Only fragments.' She's reading my thoughts, just as Gaia did. Seeing my amazement she holds out her left wrist so I can read a wordfree bulletin on the *worldaroundyou news* tile:

'Eminent young scientist found after the aquastrophe, believed dead, washed up on a ledge near the perilous Sister Peak Waterfall. Imprisoned after anonymous accusations of paedophilia infected cyberspace, he was later released through the Goodwill World Parliament Charter, statute 720, forbidding punishment based on anonymous accusations. He has just been found by a shepherd grazing his flock who happened to look over the edge of the waterfall. Doctors have injected his shattered bones with the new plastioadhesive bone technique to bind in all splinters. It is hoped that this was carried out before the scattered splinters could puncture his arteries and lungs. The patient has not yet been declared out of danger…'

All this is blared out on every screen in the world creating more deep blue waves to drown the young man lying here unconscious. I turned my wordfree as low as allowed and looked away from all the screens I passed.

We wait, silently.

'Is he in danger?'

'Not sure.' She is cautious but firm. 'Be patient and pray for him.'

* * * * *

I left her in the main courtyard of the old university. She's called Celia and is going to the refugee commune there. I was not invited. Not that I need company. Hers, perhaps. Yes, but on her own.

Back in Newborough, hungry, I've turned on the heating, but it doesn't dispel the chill inside me. Can Nicholas, fragile at the best of times, survive his injuries as well as the virus racing through the limitless lurid veins of cyberspace? I keep thinking of my inadequacy. I didn't know what had happened to him when the world around me did.

My home spaces look the same but feel different. Strange. The screens are on standby, with pale blue tiles blinking their different logos to entice me to enlarge them over the Swiss mountain screenscene. I must have chosen it a while ago and haven't bothered to change. I'll find a veg dinner in the freezer to eat lying on the sofa and listen to some familiar dance music to cheer me up. Still an uneasy feel around here. Warning signs are throbbing on my wordfree and I can't dim them - or ideally, turn them off. They all highlight PERSONAL – ACCESS URGENTLY – WORLD REFERENDUM REQUEST.

27

NEWS BULLETIN

UNEASE OVER LEASE OF GOODWILL WORLD PARLIAMENT SATELLITE

Unease has been expressed by some **Goodwill World Parliament** deputies over the lease of a satellite to the magnate **Dom Ross Mackenzie**. A brilliant but reclusive scientist, entrepreneur and philanthropist, the owner of **Global Enterprises GWP,** has asked his PR to amplify his mission statement regarding universal low-cost energy-for-all that earned him the right to lease a satellite. This follows a heated debate at a special assembly today of the Goodwill World Parliament. Over to **Helen Runciman**.

'Welcome to Dom Ross Mackenzie's world-encompassing charitable foundation. It is backing the breathtakingly generous supply of unlimited low-cost energy for all, thanks to a technological breakthrough in **Quarry Hill laboratories** affecting the future of hukind.

'Dom Ross Mackenzie's satellite will transmit limitless energy from sunlight to the receptors established by his mineral resources conglomerate. These dual purpose dishes can function both as conventional solar panels and also as receptors for the potentially more powerful new solar technology to come. If this is a success, he intends to expand the network of receptors worldwide. Your future is here now.'

Back at the *worldaroundyou news* centre, (nominated yet again number one global newsblender) we must report that, as we speak, more dissenting voices are being heard in the **Goodwill World Parliament.** An emergency session has been convened. **Chinese deputies, seconded by Russian ones, are challenging the right of Dom Ross Mackenzie to lease a satellite owned by hukind** – that means you – to radiate the globe with energy while keeping his invention secret.

worldaroundyounews.com

Winter

Magnus *i-witnessMAG931.futurepast.com*

Inside my living room space is vibrating in rainbow colours, though it's not the usual rush hour of helousines returning to Quarry Hill. I've been to my bedside picture of Gaia so often to calm down, but I still shudder. I've danced my training routine and tried to invent other sequences, but can't. I don't know whether this trembling is just inside me or around me in this capsule, or in everyone's. Gaudy colours are tumbling about me.

My favourite virtual world website, i*ntoit.com*, has been chosen to host the coming referendum. It's flashing lights on the wraparound screen. ACCESS URGENTLY. I thinkopen its icon. An old man, who must be the avatar of the one I knew in Mybeki, raises his arm and unrolls a parchment scroll.

'This is the history of hukind that you are all writing. Now the time is come when every adult in our universal democracy must take part in our first peaceful contest in this new world of goodwill.' The crowd moves closer. 'As the oldest member of hukind, I am charged to proclaim that, after three debates, the Goodwill World Parliament has passed the proposal tabled by the Chinese President Chang, and seconded by Igor Durgenev, the Russian president. It recommends the first ever world referendum to decide the contested issue of whether the Goodwill World Parliament can lease one if its satellites to a private individual without a full and open explanation of its proposed use. World citizens are summoned to vote on the following:

'That the Goodwill World Parliament should immediately terminate the one-year trial lease of a satellite granted to Dom Ross Mackenzie of Global Enterprises GWP to provide a platform for his infinenergy invention, because Dom Ross Mackenzie infringes the democratic rights of hukind by refusing to divulge the full details of the scientific process that is about to provide infinite low-cost energy for all.

'All DNA registered world citizens having reached the age of eligibility, namely 16 years, will be issued with arrow or bullet votes to fire at the internet voting booth they wish to support. All viewpoints will be debated on the continuous *worldaroundyounews* bulletins over the seven-day campaign. The contest itself will last 48 hours.'

The old man's voice is almost drowned out by the crowd, until someone who is trying to reach the platform, arm raised above the bobbing faces, cries out.

'Remember, world citizens, that whatever this infinenergy is, it is stolen property. Dom Ross Mackenzie is not an inventor, he is a plagiarist. He has stolen the work of a brilliant scientist and patented it worldwide in his own name.'

'How do you know?' A handsome young man in retro denim.

'I know the true author of infinenergy. He is Nicholas Middlethorpe,' says the man who raised his arm.

'Ross Mackenzie's an imposter!' A wide mouth, angry eyes and a waving arm in the plaza crowd.

'Yes, an imposter!' Someone with dreadlocks from the far side.

'Why isn't he in a cyber debating room?' That handsome young man again.

'Because the ones for the referendum haven't been registered, stupid!' That comes from a willowy avatar with a flowing robe, not unlike an old style Roman toga. Her voice is low, her hair long, fair and wavy, and her hands wide and expressive. 'Give him a chance! Look at your screen icons! Debating rooms are being registered!'

Do I really know what is happening? It's all spilling into my living room and I'm being caught in the scene. The website *intoit.com* has been chosen for the referendum battlefield because it has, we are told, spare capacity. The first registrations are on screen and I am one of the artists bidding for the virtual booth designs. Reaching Out's debating room has just appeared. I'm thinking it open. It enlarges into a blank, so nothing has been posted, just its place in the debate. No ideas? No policy?

I'll thinkopen the conference section of the Reaching Out site instead. A conference has just been convened by Cheng-fu from North China. The current chairperson, Zuami from South Africa, is midscreen frantically collating responses and reminding all representatives of the crucial pre-referendum conference in five hours' time. That will be in the dark blue depths of the night here. I'll go and rest.

* * * * *

The insistent yellow beeps have woken me as they were meant to. I shouldn't be churlish – that's a word from my hazy past but I feel it now. No need to summon the room lights because the wraparound screens are pulsing out bright colours and the referendum debate icons are already competing for attention. Zuami's face zooms centre screen the moment I thinkopen the Reaching Out conference section.

'Because of the urgent need to proclaim our stance to our supporters worldwide in the hope they will follow us and target the booth we recommend in a week's time, we must decide what to put into our internet debating room, presently empty. Register now for your places in timed order below our icon.'

Hardly has Zuami faded back to a waiting image when an agitated Ana from Chile zooms in spilling her words over us – I'm amazed how the instantaneous translation catches her precise rhythm of speech.

'This invention may deplete the world's water supplies. They are already decreasing faster than we admit. Almost a quarter of the world's population has no sanitary system because of lack of water. The threat of disease lurks behind everything we do to improve the life expectancy of the poorest. We must know what lies behind Dom Ross Mackenzie's suspicious offer of low-cost energy – a free-for-all? Would any serious global corporation settle for so little? There's the cost of the satellite to start with.'

'Sounds suspicious,' Shilpa mouths gently as her image looms at us bringing spicy fragrance to dispel Ana's sharp ruby-tinted one. Shilpa's here, a wraith in front of me.

'We lack water. The snow line is receding even on the highest Himalayan peaks. Energy is needed by all, but at what cost? Environmentally, I mean. That's an old but still valid argument.'

'I'm a new representative,' this is thin, angular Mikhail from Petersburg, now appearing next to Shilpa and bringing the tang of northern snow with him. We haven't till now had much input from Russia. 'We're wasting time quibbling. We need to know why China, seconded by Russia, is delaying a universal benefit. World citizens need more energy.'

'China never acts without self-interest.' Carlos from Venezuela joins Mikhail in hinting that this is a subterfuge for China to curl its financial tentacles around the world's natural resources, with Russia keen to be there too.

I can see Beth's gold-edged image enlarging and her mouth opening before I can hear, the signal gap now cut to a nano, but still perceptible, second that will always be there, however hard scientists try. They can't abolish time and space, except in our minds, even if we dream of instantaneous communication. Ages ago there was the momentous breaking of the three minute mile record. Nobody remembers that now as no one can do it in two minutes, one minute or no minute. Challenges evaporate if there's no possible record to break, no chance of a nano-second celebrity.

I digress. I'm not listening to Beth as I should be. She's the large one who invades the space here, more than the rest. She's saying something about avoiding disaster.

'- the destruction of life and limb that gave birth to the Goodwill World Parliament. His invention –' It's Nicholas's, not Dom Ross's invention, '- provides a lifeline of energy for those damaged communities in Africa. We should support such positive moves, especially when they come without strings –'

'They don't!' Alabu's lean dark image is overlapping Beth's though she's not relinquishing her space to him. Zuami, from the chair, is dimming and diminishing them both by filling the screen himself and gliding into my room – and everyone else's.

'Alabu, go back to your place in line and only speak when it's your turn. Beth, you have one minute left.'

She's returning, but looking around as if for something to add. Lamely, 'we must support the peace initiatives embodied in the Goodwill World Parliament...' and she's fading out.

'I agree.' It's Tom of Calgary now, 'but that's what we're doing. The Goodwill World Parliament is deadlocked over the leased satellite. Secrecy – here by the person leasing the one-year satellite on behalf of hukind from the Goodwill World Parliament - cannot be justified. There's the whole question of space and the establishment of laws covering the right to exploit planets, asteroids and the rest. They belong to all hukind, so any mining or other activity must be licensed by the GWP, which will also take a percentage, still to be decided, of the profits. It is where we are now: a referendum to resolve disagreements through world democracy.'

'Thanks for the history lesson,' the unmistakeable voice and highland heather scent of disgruntled Lassie from Scotland. She must be next, as she is trying to fade Tom out with, 'let's stop regurgitating the past and go to the future instead. How should we in Reaching Out recommend the world to vote?'

'Or abstain.' Zuami, strictly speaking, should chair and not throw his ideas into the arena. He is now, as chairperson, permanently projected half life-size, into the room to the right of the main speaker who is enlarged and projecting as well. I hadn't really thought how closely linked sound and scent are to size. He's attractive, with endearingly irregular features, so he can screw up his face without making people look away.

'Have you finished, Tom?'

'Not really, because I suspect both China and Dom Ross Mackenzie – Russia too - of ulterior motives. I have no idea what those are, but think we should be neutral and wait and see.'

Lassie's image starts to flutter, but another, Abela from Uganda, races it to centre screen. Lassie mumbles but retreats to Reaching Out's grey-blue images of representatives waiting to speak. Abela starts up.

'All right, all right. We don't know what is behind all this. But China is asking the question for all of us surely? There should be no secrets about the way this satellite will energise the world, starting in Africa to compensate for the meteorstrophe, or whatever disaster it was that ravaged the Mybeki Peace Settlement Zone.'

I'm not concentrating enough, digressing into sketches for the Neutral Votes target booth. These arrows – or bullets - will travel along streetscapes from my resource book of ancient images, to – what can they target if they don't know?

Bad. Abela is fading and I haven't heard what she's been saying. It can be replayed if I think up her name and image, but Molly from Australia is on screen now.

'Australasia's internet debating room is up and running, loaded already with tweets, most in support of Dom Ross Mackenzie's philanthropic combination of entrepreneurship and aid for the world's chronic energy shortage.' Molly has a nice feel about her here almost beside me, though I can't touch her arm as I would like to do. 'Our zone government is undecided and unlikely to recommend support for his efforts.' I'm smiling at her. She has short curly fair hair and a dimpled chin. 'Look at Europe's internet debating room where Dom Ross Mackenzie's spokesperson, Helen, is explaining that this rare combination of successful inventor, entrepreneur and philanthropist is safeguarding a shy but brilliant scientist's invention of infinenergy so that it doesn't fall into unreliable hands.'

I try to protest but, hardly had Molly stopped speaking, and even allowing for the signal gap, a babble of protests from representatives vibrates their respective images on our Reaching Out strip, some heard shouting, 'can we trust Ross Mackenzie?' 'Who does he think he is?' 'Dictatorship by magnates, benevolent or not, is a threat to our freedom,' and so on, countered by, 'lack of trust delays progress,' 'learn to delegate, we're not gods!' repulsed by, 'nor is Ross Mackenzie, though he's trying to be...' - an unending cacophony that our chairperson seems unable to check. Zuami is struggling on my right with sound technology. He'll have to enlarge himself centre screen, maybe to giant size if that's on offer, to achieve a commanding volume and bring the conference under control.

I want to shift them all on to the Reaching Out internet debating room which may still be empty, and concentrate on the Neutral Votes booth design and colour scheme, but can't because, for my sins, as used to be said, I'm still an elected RO representative.

The internet never sleeps. I shouldn't have done so while its debating rooms for each world zone were filling up, by now overwhelmed with tweets, while maintainers sift the material and define trends. It seems that my colleagues on Reaching Out have surfed them all. I must concentrate and listen them out, whatever else I'd prefer to do.

Our first ever world referendum campaign is about to start. It's our chance to influence our planet. Now is the moment to enter those debating rooms.

NEWS BULLETIN

OVER 90% OF ALL DNA REGISTERED WORLD CITIZENS HAVE ALREADY CONFIRMED THEIR RIGHT TO VOTE

Overwhelming interest in the referendum has produced an unprecedented number of hits on all the **internet debating rooms**, except the one set up for the **Middle East Alliance** which contains little besides a brief statement concerning the problems posed by **intellectual property rights**. The spokesperson, Mustafa, points out that this should be urgently debated and ruled on by the **Goodwill World Parliament**. In the meantime, it advocates the inventor's right to control his or her intellectual property given the chaotic state of current laws in that field.

Africa's debating room fears that the most powerful blocks, echoing the **message of the world's magnates**, will bring pressure to bear on voters to allow these influential people to protect their own interests even when, like **Dom Ross Mackenzie,** they refuse to clarify what they are doing, only stating that it is for the benefit of hukind. Africa's spokesperson advises caution until more is known, supporting neither the right to a full explanation of Dom Ross Mackenzie's source of **infinenergy** nor the right to safeguard one's inventions. **South America** is concerned over its mineral rights and territorial integrity, so follows Africa in recommending neutrality. **Australasia,** undecided, criticises the Goodwill World Parliament's lack of debate about the need to balance an individual or nation's rights with those of the world community, and is issuing guidelines and laws in its territory to protect both. **President Igor Durgenev**, who seconded **China's proposal** that led to the current deadlock, appears on **Russia and the neighbouring Stan states' internet debating room** to express concern over historical countries' right to control their geographical territories' material resources. He and his team finally advise support for China and to vote for its proposal. **India,** in a visually alluring presentation, supports the right to clarification and, after much consideration, proposes that voters should support China's motion to the Goodwill World Parliament. The **European Federation**'s room currently provides the liveliest presentation with extraordinary visual pyrotechnics to illustrate both sides. **Hallelujah Helen**, Dom Ross Mackenzie's spokesperson, addresses a cross section of people from all the national zones. Individual viewers are invited to make up their own minds, but she stresses Dom Ross Mackenzie's right to retain his own invention and therefore seeks support for the line taken by **North America** against China's motion.

The future of your planet lies in your hands. Visit all the debating rooms to help decide how you will vote and to have your say. Make sure you have registered your DNA before the internet voting booths open. Remember that they are only open for 48 hours. Do not neglect your duty as a fully participating world citizen.

worldaroundyounews.com

28

NEWS BULLETIN

FIRST EVER WORLDWIDE REFERENDUM OR PEACEFUL GLOBAL CONTEST

Voting booths open internetwide on ***intoit.com*** when it appears on your screen. World citizens 16 years and older have 48 hours to decide how to vote. Register your DNA NOW, if you haven't already done so.

This world-challenging event allows every individual in even the remotest region to participate peacefully in a decision that might change their lives in ways as yet unknown.

The **three booths – YES, NO, NEUTRAL** – have each been designed by the winners of a global competition judged by the **Goodwill Planet Supervisors**. The winning artists followed the rules governing their position as volunteers in this competition by only taking expenses and the same honorarium whatever their status. These are paid out of the **Goodwill Fund** of voluntary contributions from nations, organisations or individuals, like Dom Ross Mackenzie of **Global Enterprises GWP**, Dom Alawana Magnawan of **Renewable Nutrition GWP**, Dom Sun Yan of **Maritime Resources GWP**, Dom Elena Rosparel of **Outsourcing International GWP**, Xiang Lu of **World Potential Company**, Dom Mikhail Olenski of **Arctic Discovery GWP** and Ramon Robles of **Forest Regeneration** who have guaranteed to donate 1% of their profits to the Goodwill Fund. It is overseen by the **Goodwill World Parliament**, founded to ensure universal disarmament and promote world peace and prosperity by brokering disagreements. The GWP is governed by the laws laid down in its **foundation charter**. To avoid corruption, its democratically elected deputies are paid at the highest producer level and consequently may not accept additional remuneration of any sort. Deputies chosen to become planet supervisors are only paid for genuine additional expenses. After much debate,

deputies agreed to these conditions, judged to lead to higher ethical standards.
The *intoit.com* icon is bursting into a firework display to Handel's Royal Fireworks Music, still a hallowed favourite centuries after its composition. It heralds the opening of the voting booths. ONE virtual projectile, either arrow or bullet, may be employed, each bearing equal weight in spite of potentially diverse destructive power in times past. No crossfire is allowed, as that, in any case, would disqualify a vote. The language of war is chosen to remind every one of us to guard the peace.

worldaroundyounews.com

---

1 January

intoit.com

I, an old man, open the Book of Hukind at the momentous page of now. From this instant and for 48 hours the world is deciding its future.

See the voting booths: YES on the left, supporting China's motion, seconded by Russia, that Dom Ross Mackenzie be obliged to divulge the full data and calculations for his infinenergy. In the interests of science and the future of us all, you may here, through your voteshot, command the Parliament to terminate the lease of the goodwill satellite to Dom Ross Mackenzie forthwith, unless he provides full access to his invention immediately after this referendum.

Here is your YES booth, designed by the winner of the YES design section of the contest – Reyhan from India. She is joining us now.

'Why, Reyhan, did you conceive the voting booth in the form of a serpent's mouth with wide pink lips, a curling tongue, yellow and green crazed skin and yellow bristles that are perpetually crushed and resprouting?'

'I started off with the dream everyone has of shooting something - arrow or bullet - into a mouth. It is the start of a journey of consequences from the past and developed along serpentine paths into the future.'

'Reyhan, place your signature here beneath the imprint of your design and the image of yourself, burnished and red lipped in your emerald green sari threaded with gold. They'll remain here for eternity in this Book of Hukind.'

NEUTRAL votes are to be directed to a bold and stately door with a shining brass flap where the letter box used to be in past times. The artist who won the NEUTRAL design section of the competition is Magnus. He has sent his avatar Gaia to represent him.

'Gaia, what is the meaning of the neutrality booth?'

'The artist has created it to show that neutrality is the only option viable in the present. The origin of the idea of infinite energy has not been verified, although the proposition is one that could be of immense benefit to all hukind. However, the whole operation expounded by the scientist entrepreneur Dom Ross Mackenzie has not yet been fully and safely tested. Indeed, it is not his invention at all.'

Murmurs from the crowd gathered in the plaza, heads swivelling this way and that.

'Gaia, place your signature under "Magnus in absence" here beneath the imprint of his design and the frame for Magnus's image to be forwarded to the Book of Hukind.'

Lastly, to the right of the two booths, comes the third, NO booth, a contraption like a huge cannon that ends in a globe, all shiny black. It was designed by Billy from North America who won the NO design section of the competition. Here joining us is Billy.

'You have, Billy, invented a warlike image for voting to resolve differences, reach a consensus and maintain world peace. May there be a reason for this?'

'It's to warn world voters of the danger of voting "yes" or "neutral" before their arrows or bullets, travelling to their chosen destination destroy individual freedom of invention.'

'Billy, place your signature here beneath the imprint of your design and the image of you, trim and tanned in vlason shirt and slacks with a wide-brimmed hat. Here for eternity.'

The images fade. All wait for the first projectiles from everyone anywhere in the world to select one of three possible journeys and determine everyone's future destiny.

To you – the WORLD.

The first votes are arrows whistling towards the red lips YES target. At a click we can enter it and travel along the serpent's body. Each YES voter has supported 'the right to know what infinenergy actually is', words that stream along the first dark curve. Then at the next bend, 'the democratic control of inventions that affect every living being could', to the next sinuous one, 'prevent unaccountable forces controlling the way you live.' Then, 'ensure a full and open debate on how this momentous new energy system will be maintained for all of us forever...' 'to avoid sabotage...' 'to ensure security...' and so on until the voter is giddy with the righteous conviction of being involved in a just and worthy cause.

Bullets and arrows are speeding towards all targets. There are fewer arrows now. NEUTRAL remains steady while YES gains – the bristles are standing up along the serpent's back – but NO falters.

Follow a bullet entering the barrel of the NO vote cannon. The dark interior is lit up by flashes forming words:

- Your brain is yours with ownership over its creations
- Dom Ross Mackenzie has just ownership over his own invention
- We cannot create a viable world order without trust and delegation

Shorter flashes of enlightenment ricochet round the globe at the tip of the cannon, echoing each other:

- Freedom to create
- Philanthropy without personal gain
- Give to others as they should give to you

And so they reverberate on.

The most conventional booth of all, the door with the letter box to aim at, NEUTRAL, is increasing its voting momentum. More arrows than bullets pass though.

Follow the arrow through the letter box into an alley, not the entrance hall of an old-fashioned house. The façades, shop fronts and inn signs are minutely drawn, conjured up from ancient times. A notice on a weathered brick wall advises caution. A sign above a bow-windowed shop proclaims, 'the true owner may not be inside; enter to find out'. Before the cobbled street tumbles downhill, a sign: 'Proceed cautiously and check both sides,' followed by another, 'what intentions lurk behind doors closed for hidden motives?' and so on.

I, an old man, foresee your votes fluctuating over forty-eight hours, destination indistinct. It is a portentous chance to vote for our future.

Which freedom does the world want?

The freedom for inventors like Dom Ross Mackenzie to retain the right to reveal as much or as little as they wish of their own inventions? Vote NO. Or the freedom for everyone to have a full explanation of inventions that may affect their lives? Vote YES. Or the freedom to remain neutral until the consequences of either YES or NO becomes clear? Vote NEUTRAL.

Consider the rival consequences of the **splitting of the atom** so long ago: atomic power stations producing energy and toxic waste as well as atomic bombs producing devastation.

NOW VOTE!

29

Magnus *i-witnessMAG931.futurepast.com*

Evening, 2 January

The lights outside are multiplying, pinpricks in the darkness. A beam sweeps across my sitting room and a low grey thudding penetrates the heavy insulation of my capsule. My wrist is vibrating; I think open my wordfree and a man is silhouetted outside my front door. As I feared, Dom Ross Mackenzie has landed his helousine in front of my house. His presence and powerful sense of urgency fill the entrance room.

'Can we speak?'

I motion him into the sitting-room, indicate the sofa, and sit down opposite to look at him straight on. He's smaller than me, lighter boned, trim and tight-lipped, as if about to say something against his will. He doesn't notice he has interrupted my evening meal. Shall I help him? 'Satellite problems?' That would be interesting to hear. He's looking around uneasily.

'Not exactly.'

I shan't ask any questions. That might shift his focus, though I'd like to know where he has left Helen. The orange lights from the helousine pinpoint us through the window. He's looking at right angles at me.

'Something wrong? Can I help?' He's surveying the room.

'Something may be missing from the whole infinenergy process.' He's now focusing on me, as if expecting a comment. I won't. I can't, anyway. So he has to explain.

'To put it simply, has Nicholas modified the crucial calculations? The precise angle of the beam that hits the receptors?'

'I've no idea.' Silence, so he has to fill it.

'I thought you might know. You are, I think, connected with the funding of his experiments in Africa, aren't you? I've set up the network, extended energy receptors worldwide and linked them to the existing electricity transmission systems where possible. Most are ready, but the full operation can't spark into action without his final calculations. My scientists tell me that the ones I have given them aren't precise enough. If the angle of the beam is incorrect, it might cause damage, miss the receptors and put lives in danger. Something has gone wrong and my scientists can't find out what it is.' He is looking at me steadily, as if I knew some secret. 'This system of infinenergy is for everyone all over the world. I shall only make a small profit - the satellite lease will be costly. Part of the profit will go straight to the charities I support and, of course, there's the GWP Peace Tax to pay.'

Sitting here at a right angle in front of me may be the greatest benefactor the world will ever know. He is promising unlimited solar energy for everyone, yet lacks some crucial calculations to set it all going. Might he still go ahead? My silence masks my amazement. How did Nicholas ever allow Dom Ross's scientists to develop the theory he was testing in Africa? Reaching Out was sponsoring it – I hope with my money.

'I'm asking for your help.' Why me? 'My scientists were working out a similar system so, in a spirit of co-operation, I lent Nicholas a special program before he left to test his theory in Africa. I thought that the datadrive returned to me from Africa would confirm or add to what my scientists were already working on, but parts were missing.' Dom Ross expects me to enlighten him. I remain silent. 'You are involved, I think, in Reaching Out? You could help me with the distribution of energy, bypassing corrupt governments who might want to exploit this new source of energy for their own ends.'

What can I say? Reaching Out doesn't work in the way he thinks. Nor is he supposed to know that I am in it. I smile. I may look foolish, but I'm not giving anything away that might undermine what I do. Or Nicholas's invention.

'You could let me have the means to access Nicholas's definitive calculations.'

Now I understand why he's here. Nicholas is unconscious - not, I hope, brain damaged from his fall – so he is unable to answer Ross Mackenzie's question now or, probably, for some time.

'I can't because I don't know them, but can I offer you half of my dinner?' He doesn't believe me.

After some inconsequential conversation, he moves behind my armchair and I feel a dark spasm of fear. I jump to my feet and raise my left arm to command my wordfree to open the door and then check the front door locks after him.

I'll finish my food and turn up Zaide's song to stop me thinking about what he's said. The tune must haunt me, not that man. Eliza says it's the most beautiful one ever written. The helousine drowns it out, hovering so close that it judders and vibrates me and every shape and colour inside here, before flying the philanthropic entrepreneur away to his mansion and laboratories on Quarry Hill.

I feel that strange bluey echoing pause before something important is about to happen to disrupt the flow of time. Breath held before the expected announcement; before the vivid outcome of the first ever world referendum – or peaceful global contest.

I seek Gaia's image in my bedroom and return with it to lie on the sofa, looking at her and letting the music mend the deep red gash in my heart till, on the dying note, I fear for Nicholas lying unconscious in hospital. What can I do?

The purple boom of a newsbreak is invading my capsule. I'm trying to think it quiet, but it increases in volume in spite of me. The *worldaroundyounews* icon is exploding into a scarlet volcano of staccato red notes. I'm focusing on the icon to open it on to a full screen and diminish the glowing sound to a pale green background murmur. This time it's Pedro, another immaculately groomed presenter with a condescending smile and the usual shiny outline. Helen has just appeared beside him in front of background images of Dom Ross Mackenzie talking to his scientists in labs stuffed with screens and every fabulous machine or robot you could imagine.

NEWS BULLETIN

RESULT OF THE FIRST WORLD REFERENDUM

The world awaits the outcome of the first ever world referendum to adjudicate whether the scientist, entrepreneur and philanthropist, **Dom Ross Mackenzie,** has the right to keep secret his invention to provide infinite energy for all hukind from a **Goodwill World Parliament** satellite. Helen, would you like to comment?

'Thank you, Pedro. There never was any cover-up, as has been hinted during the referendum campaign. It has always been abundantly clear that Dom Ross Mackenzie and his world-class scientific team have been able to harness and convert sunlight into eternally renewable energy through a beam directed on to energy receptors.'

'Exactly, Helen. The debate over freedom of information for hukind and individual freedom to own the total rights to one's personal invention could not be resolved by the Goodwill World Parliament. To decide whether an individual may lease a GWP satellite without a full explanation of the purpose of the lease which could have global consequences, Chinese deputies proposed a world referendum, seconded by Russian deputies. This proposal was passed unanimously. The Goodwill World Parliament decreed that there should be a **worldwide referendum** to choose between three options: yes, no or neutral - that is, undecided.

The votes from 87% of all DNA registered world citizens have been analysed as follows according to voter category:

Producers (brainworkers) Yes 22% No 61% Neutral 17%

Maintainers (technicians) Yes 74% No 22% Neutral 4%

Enablers (people workers) Yes 12% No 24% Neutral 64%

Leisuretimers (volunteers) Yes 6% No 12% Neutral 82%

The referendum result concerning the lease of a satellite to a world citizen confirms the Goodwill World Parliament's inconclusive vote in its last virtual Assembly debate. The Goodwill World Parliament is being convened to debate the result of the referendum.

Helen would like to end this news bulletin. Helen.

'Thanks, Pedro. On Dom Ross Mackenzie's behalf, I would like to repeat that he understands why many of you chose to vote neutrally, that is, to reserve your decision until various complex issues are resolved. He wants you to know that he will reconsider all the options open to him.

Consequently he will postpone the launch of his infinenergy satellite until they have been satisfactorily resolved.'

worldaroundyounews.com

Predictably woolly result on all sides. Pedro had a whiff of chilli about him - he must have eaten just before the broadcast. Helen, instead, came far too close with her clingy jasmine scent, almost as if sitting beside me instead of in front of the robots in Ross Mackenzie's lab publicity pictures. Not exactly unpleasant, but unwelcome. She looks different. Faded. Not as taut and tanned as expected. Rounder.

I must tell Nicholas what is happening before Dom Ross finds him. Warn him. Has he regained consciousness? Does he know what's going on?

* * * * *

3 January

I had Reaching Out assignments to finish, so it's afternoon before I can leave for the hospital. Roads are still slippery in oily rainbow colours from a light rainfall followed by frost. I mustn't do my fast walk; it's dangerous as on the third beat I glide into a sequence of steps. Mustn't rush. Stop heart pounding, feet flying. Next turn on the left towards the city centre. The Old University is a few minutes away. I'm almost there. Into the main quadrangle and the buildings the fire didn't reach. Along the passages to the hospital area with the soothing images. Poppies and sunflowers. Outside it's winter; inside it's early summer. Maybe that helps inmates move into a sunnier contemplation of their prospects. Ask where Nicholas is. I've forgotten his bed number, if I ever knew it. Ask. A desk, find a desk. Someone to ask. All the enablers are intent on their tasks and don't seem to notice me. Am I here in thought only? A desk. I must find someone behind a desk.

'Are you looking for someone?' A voice, not a person. It comes from a lightsoundsensor machine high above me. I twist my head up to answer.

'Yes. Nicholas Middlethorpe.' I pause. No response. 'I was told he is here.'

'I am scanning the records.' Pause. 'He is no longer here. Self-discharged early this morning. Anything else?'

'Yes. Is Sister Julian here?'

'No.'

'D'you know where she is?'

'No. Anything else?'

'No.'

'Then please leave before you enter the sterilised area. Thank you and good morning.'

Nicholas gone. This morning. Where was I then? In the midst of all the Reaching Out and referendum business. Where next? St. Thomas's. It's only ten minutes from here. Someone there may know about him. Maybe Sister Julian?

Stop. Pull back. Think. Who will I see at St. Thomas's? The woman, Celia, who accompanied me here? If she's not there – who? How do I find Nicholas? Who do I ask?

I'm shy, even when I have a good reason to go somewhere and a specific person to find. A recluse by choice. So here I am hovering at the main entrance to the 'Heritage Medieval Gothic Church of St. Thomas' as it says on the new notice board by my elbow.

Inside it's dark. I close my eyes, breathe deeply, lean on the recumbent tomb figures by the door and wait. Listen. Sounds at the end of this aisle by the ecumenical chapel. The one with the candle inside barbed wire, a cross, the name of Allah and the menorah. A familiar voice?

'We are **all** welcome here.' It can't be Sister Julian, but I know that voice.

'No, I will **not** have you near him. You upset people; this place too – everything!' A shrill voice, followed by others. Two women are standing by a pillar outside the chapel.

'Nobody upsets anyone here. Think of that candle. A candle is prayer. We are free, not caged in. Pray together silently, each in your own way.'

Silence. 'That's what this space is about,' the same voice continues. She's holding a candle and I can see she's too slight to be Sister Julian.

Two figures step out of the chapel. One is Helen, burnished as ever, hair shining glossy over her shoulders. Stouter with a heavier tread, she seems set on confronting the slender figure with a candle.

'What have you done to him?' echoes out.

'Nothing,' the other answers. They must have visited the hospital and know Nicholas has left. The chapel empties and the slight figure slips past me.

Helen follows, crying, 'you know where Nicholas is, and you're hiding him!' She closes in, grasps a shoulder and spins the woman round to face her, grabbing her coat lapels and shaking her.

No response,

'Lost your voice, huh?'

The other woman pulls herself away to cross the church towards the sacristy and I glimpse her face above the candle she is carrying. She is Celia.

NEWS BULLETIN

THE GOODWILL WORLD PARLIAMENT LISTENS TO REPRESENTATIVES FROM GLOBAL BUSINESS

Goodwill World Parliament deputies are postponing their next virtual session on the inconclusive result of the first world referendum so that they have time to consider a **crucial report on our planet's diminishing resources.** Several in the **global business community** are voicing their concerns.

Meanwhile, plans are being finalised for the gifted pianist, **Ezra Tenenbaum**, to return to the concert hall in the same city where thugs attacked him and severed his left arm below the elbow three months ago. Ezra Tenenbaum was found unconscious in a back street of the city where he was invited to give a solo performance. It is the first recorded attempt to steal a wordfree. After this devastating loss for a young pianist who studied at the renowned school for geniuses, it is a miracle that he can still play. He will perform the piano concerto for one hand by **Ravel** composed for **Paul Wittgenstein**, who lost his left hand in war long ago.

The distinguished scientist, **Nicholas Middlethorpe** has been the subject of a malicious story that went viral accusing him of molesting a young boy in his care. Coincidentally this boy, having shown unusual aptitude for mathematics, is sponsored by the philanthropist Dom Ross Mackenzie to study in same school for geniuses attended by Dr. Middlethorpe and Ezra Tenenbaum. The accusation against Nicholas Middlethorpe was subsequently quashed at an emergency court hearing, citing the **GWP Charter 721 that 'no citizen can be condemned on the basis of an anonymous accusation'**. However, his whereabouts are unknown after he unexpectedly left hospital where he was undergoing treatment.

Hukind owes much to these geniuses and is considering establishing W**orld Achievement Awards**, both current and posthumous, on a wider and more comprehensive scale than the long-established **Nobel prizes**.
We apologise that the independent World News Agency has been briefly unable to bring you the *worldaroundyounews* through lack of funds and energy. These problems have now been solved through the generosity of a conglomerate of global philanthroentrepreneurs.

worldaroundyounews.com

30

Helen *showspotHEL22.com*

3 January

Nicholas used to go on about Ross being power conscious but bored by people. It must be the energy business that keeps him conferencing in his screened study back here in Quarry Hilland talking, talking, talking to those sleekheads. Magnates and financiers of whatever sex all look alike to me. No style. No individuality. And in Ross's case, no energy for anything else. He doesn't seem to have any physical urges. I've never met a man like this before. Others just can't keep their hands off me. He is pleasant enough, but keeps his distance. Strange.

When I had to stay in South America on his orders – he'd say 'advice' – I couldn't get on with my fashion business. There, I thought, well away from people he knew, he would be, well, more physical. No. He wanted to get my agreement to a secret contract. Just him and me. I would have to sign a confidentiality agreement. As I have done. Now I'm back in Quarry Hill he can finance it. That's the sort of fun he likes. Why not? It gives me something to think about – if nothing else!

In Argentina I was the sad princess in a palace with the wrong prince, bewildered at the end of her fairy tale. I'm no happier here, getting plumper – all agreed, he repeats, and I know it's part of the plan. My face is thinner – pinched used to be the word. To be honest, in spite of the money, I sometime feel a stab of panic at the way my body is becoming lumpy. I knew it would happen, but I didn't realise it would change me quite so much. Still,

Nick won't mind. After all, he doesn't look anything special. What do I really mean? His body is in proportion thought not particularly co-ordinated. I miss him.

To be honest, in Argentina with nothing to do and nobody lusting after me, I didn't really care what I looked like. I paced through the marble palace or went outside. The sun was scorching the earth into dust and cracking still more lines in the mud where the ornamental lake should have been. Not that there was much talk there about landscape. It was all about business and people I never met. Ross gets on best with his virtual conference pals, magnates like him. They're producing wealth and scouring the globe in what they call a 'resource survey'.

Nick did worry about problems with our zone government. It infuriates him when he has to justify every bit of financial support for his lab. He said it's sort of inevitable. People need to feel their job matters. Ross doesn't bother about such things. He never mentions the zone government, or the Goodwill World Parliament for that matter, except for his irritation about the referendum. Every bit of him is concentrated on business and the inventions that are its lifeblood, like this energy affair. There seems to be some trouble with his scientists here at Quarry Hill.

I quickly confirmed my DNA, registered to vote in the referendum and survived the boring week of debate. Actually I ignored it and went out walking at sunset. The voting itself provided some amusement, at last, in the monotonous days I spent in Argentina. I realised I ought to vote for Dom Ross and his satellite, and I did, 'No', though I was secretly thinking of 'Yes', but then feared he could find out. DNA info might trace my arrow (more attractive than a bullet). Just in case, I played safe. 'No' to making him reveal his project. I then fooled around elsewhere on the web until Dom Ross invaded my screen in the library from the personalised one in his study – he could have come in person, couldn't he? – to fuss about what I should be doing in my current situation. He has no sense at all of other people's time and feelings.

Oh, help! I shouldn't be thinking this as my wordfree will register it all. Doesn't matter. Nobody will ever bother to access this.

I must get out of this place, his estate on Quarry Hill. To touch, to feel someone. More than Cara, my business partner, I need Nick. I know Dom Ross is looking for him. Nick isn't DNA registered. Officially he doesn't exist, except he does. He's behind all Ross's infinenergy, isn't he?

I'm in a muddle. Especially when Ross announced seconds after I'd finished my last news bulletin, 'You're no longer the hallelujah girl,' just like that. He may be unpredictable and inscrutable, but he should be more careful of what he says. Am I no longer the halle - or whatever - girl because I'm a bit plump as part of his project? Or because he is peeved since there was no clear victory in the referendum for him to keep his secret secret? Or something like that. And the satellite lease business. Whatever, he's not pleased and I'm no longer the visible part of his message.

It's early days, and I'm only a little rounder and a lot bit richer after he paid the first part of our secret contract.

I must see Nick. He stayed so long in Africa and didn't want me to remain there with him – incredibly boring it was – so I stopped refusing Ross's invitations. I didn't mean to get too involved, but offers of help with

Powerdress finance, plus a chance to live in luxury in Argentina and then, to culminate it all, a chance to feature on *worldaroundyounews.com*! Who could refuse? He has helped my career heaps. And tells me he is realising Nicholas's brilliant theories, though Nick has always said he doesn't want Ross's financial backing. Nick exaggerates. He doesn't understand. Ross is really generous. He wants to help 'people with talent' – his words.

Cara and the rest at Powerdress will tease me, but understand. I can't get out of Dom Ross's estate without his limousine or helousine or some means of transport. The gates are always locked and the code is automatically changed every twelve hours - high alert security, because of the lab secrets, and so on.

I've had an idea! I could take a ride on Ross's scooter – he keeps it by the side door, so I'll leave through the service area. I've only passed two people and they pretend not to notice me. They never ask questions. They can't read my thoughts – I hope! Ross has forbidden me to leave the estate. Too dangerous in my condition, he would say. I could thinktext his wordfree to ask his permission. He's quite good about answering, unless 'deep in invention' - which means he's with his scientists, in a conference or somewhere he doesn't want to be disturbed with all communication on stand-by. I can always try, but I won't.

If the red scooter is there, it means he isn't on it inspecting his property. That's what he calls recreation. Now I'm out of the side door and there it is, waiting for me! Purrh! It's fully charged and almost silent. I'll start off along the perimeter wall as if going to inspect the wall garden sheltering the experimental plants. They're out of sight of the mansion and labs. This path follows a ledge in the hillside. I can't see above the wall but imagine the view over the city to the coast. There used to be viewing points before I left for South America, but I can't find any now. They've been closed up, or perhaps I imagined them.

My heart's beating though I'm not moving fast, careful not to race the scooter. I mustn't rush. If he chances on me I can say I need air. I'm admiring his estate, or something. He did mention Sister J's prisoners-on-parole. Has she given her permission then? He doesn't really explain himself. These prisoners are about to be released or something, and they have, if I remember right, asked to clear his woods outside this perimeter wall. They cover the slopes of Quarry Hill. All he wants in payment is some firewood. He was complaining about it being chucked over the wall. If I find a pile and a prisoner, I might be able to persuade him to pass the scooter over it. That's my plan and all I can think about while bumping alongside the wall looking for the wood pile and a man for my purpose.

It hasn't taken long because someone is stacking logs where the wall curves back uphill. He uses the pile to step over the wall. Ideal. He can climb from one side to the other. There must be others there too. I can hear voices.

'Could you help me?' I hope this man doesn't ask me why I would like the scooter over the other side. He's looking curious. Before I got involved with Ross, I couldn't keep male hands off me. I sort of miss that. Though I fought them off in the past I'd now like to have their attention.

I'm not as surefooted as I was. Luckily they've handed the scooter, and then me, over the wall and steadied me down to the woodland side. Thanks, smiles, the reassuring usual comments. They don't behave like prisoners-on-parole or prisoners just released – whichever – but then how should they behave? They're all right. Even attractive, smelling of firewood and maleness.

I hope Ross doesn't access my wordfree. I can't turn it completely on to standby as he does. He said one has to pay for a special program to get one's standby isolated from interference. There are always more options and I never seem to have them.

It's bliss purring round the hairpin bends down the woodland road, wind whistling through my hair – whoosh! Like a child in a playground. I buzz through the Newborough suburb cautious not to break speed limits. I'm scanning the neatly spaced dream homes, identical but each with a visual quirk, like people. Beech Drive is further on in another older suburb, deserted like all these roads. Everyone's tidied into place: nursery, school, work or pastime activity. All producers, maintainers, enablers and leisuretimers busying away elsewhere. I like it. Everything is neat and predictable, unlike the old city I'm gliding into. I can feel the difference now: bumpier, untidier and unpredictable.

I must see Nick. He doesn't communicate much normally, and I haven't heard from him for ages. Maybe because of the Mid Winter festival, I thought. But it isn't. It's on the news. He's had an accident... is in hospital ... that's where I'm going ...the hospital in the Old University. Poppies and sunflowers are nodding as usual along corridor screens. A voice above my head asks what I want. Nicholas Middlethorpe has left. Not there. Help! Where is he?

The people at St. Thomas's might know I'm worried about leaving the scooter outside St. Thomas's. I'll wheel it inside and leave it by the knight. We met in this church, Nick and me. Nicholas, I mean. It's pleasurably upsetting. He was so young and raw and visibly entranced. I relished it. I'm stroking the stone outline of the knight, a warrior and genius in his way, like Nicholas, lying by the lady in the stiff ruff. Protecting her. But it's Dom Ross Mackenzie, not Nicholas, who is keeping me safe and protecting me in my present condition. It's part of our contract.

Voices. Flickering lights. People in the chapel at the end, down this side, or aisle of the church. Nicholas explained it to me: aisle, like wing in some other language. That must be Sister Julian holding a candle. No, too slight. There are other voices.

'Celia!' I'll call her name. I'm sure it's her half-turning, features candlelit. It is, and she's looking at me, surprised.

'Celia, where's Nick – Nicholas?' She pauses and goes on staring at me.

'Who are you to ask? You dumped him to fall into the arms of a rich industrialist.'

'Where is he?' Louder. I'm angry – with her and myself for shouting. The others inside the chapel turn round to stare at me, curious.

'Where IS he?' I aim again at Celia, who's looking around her like a frightened mouse. How could Nick take to her? Whatever she's wearing, it always looks faded, sloppy, like someone's discarded garment. Her hair's wispy, like an old woman's, though she can't be much older than me. 'What do we DO?' I'm surprised to hear myself so angry and shouting at that unremarkable woman.

'I wish I knew,' she half whispers, moving away to the far side of the main altar followed by prayer people. My wordfree is throbbing. I sit on one of those ancient pews, eyes glued to my wordfree. I'm following the latest news bulletin.

INTERNATIONAL PIANIST ATTACKED IN FIRST-EVER WORDFREE THEFT

The **Goodwill World Parliament** has just issued the following statement: 'We regretfully announce that the gifted concert pianist Ezra Tenenbaum is the first person ever to have his wordfree stolen. When taking a shortcut to his rehearsal studio three months ago, he was attacked by two masked men. They pushed him to the ground and severed his left arm below the elbow. He was speedily taken to the nearest hospital where he is recovering. Doctors report that he is already practising an adapted piano repertoire and may soon be able to leave hospital. This criminal attack, tantamount to stealing an individual's official identity, could not be reported at the time for security reasons. The Parliament is happy to report that there have been no further incidents of a similar nature. World citizens should therefore remain calm and go about their business.'

Worldaroundyounews.com

A first. Someone had his wrist with his wordfree cut off. Severed. In a back alley. This city, three months ago. A renowned pianist, Ezra

Tenenbaum. Why? This crime has never been committed before. A first, so kept off the news by the GWP and local zone government to avoid copycat incidents. This incident followed unexplained break-ins targeting scientific laboratories. Particularly those carrying out experiments with chemicals. GWP to debate whether to provide armed protection for such facilities. In spite of loss of his wrist this pianist – Ezra somebody - is coming - a concert in the Great Hall of the Old University.

What can I do? I'm sitting, mind empty. Like this church, except for Magnus and me. Candlelight and darkness. I must escape. Find the scooter. Where? By the knight. Out into the street. My wrist is aching. His – Ezra Tenenbaum's – wordfree was hacked off. Who wanted his wordfree? Stealing a wordfree by cutting off an arm? Horrific! Ezra's hand, wrist, wordfree – his mind's history! It could happen to anyone – to me!

31

Eliza's Journal

3 January

I'm writing this in charcoal. It has a nice, crumbly feel to it, friendlier than ink, or pens that simulate it. Anyway, I am out of pens. My store is finished and they have been discontinued for years. Everyone mouths words at screens now, or thinks into wordfrees. Martha says that often merely thinking is enough. Not for me. I need my thoughts to flow through me on to a surface. I still have a bundle of lead pencils which I am keeping for special occasions. Or in case I run out of everything else. After that, I do not know. I shall probably be extinct by then.

Once upon a time I used to thank my lucky stars that I am so ordinary that I can keep to myself and do what I want without anyone noticing. This is the proper sort of retirement, not the attention-seeking commitments that Karen seems to crave. But now I am not quite so sure.

Instead, I may be extra-ordinary. As are the other outwebbers. Only remote islands or mountain peaks, like the ones I can see from here, have no online or wordfree links. Few live there anyway, so why should they be connected? We outwebbers have chosen a simple, untrammelled existence without any need to conform to a new whim or design gimmick. So we are not ordinary at all. We're in the 1% of the world's population without any internet connection. We're far from the norm.

That might render us absurd. Sometimes, only occasionally, I regret my electronic isolation like now, when I want to find out if Nicholas has regained consciousness. I sat by him for some time in the hospital. Celia came to be with me. She was quietly confident he would recover. I wish I was. Something is wrong. As we used to say, I can feel it in my bones. I have gone down to the internet connection at the North Moorland Terminus, but there are no messages for me. Nicholas's wordfree, or whatever they call the device he has, is dead.

I shudder at mentioning it. I shouldn't use the word.

I am becoming superstitious.

Once upon a time I used to thank my lucky stars that I am so ordinary that I can keep to myself and

I shudder at mentioning it. I shouldn't use the word.

I am becoming superstitious.

*****

4 January – morning

I returned to the terminus and voiced the hospital. He has been discharged. I have sent messages to Martha and Karen. Where is he now?

I suppose, if I think things through as I try to do, the problem is that I am emotionally lost. Karen did come for Mid Winter. She only communicates sporadically, always by electronic means. She knows that I have to go to the terminus and cannot reply instantly, as is expected. She honestly admits this makes her less inclined to communicate with me. Now she usually sends news to Martha and me in a combined message, while more urgent or intimate matters are just sent to Martha who only comes here when she has something else to do in the Art Cavern. It somehow hurts, but I should not mind. Martha is no longer a child and I was the one to leave Beech Drive, though I felt Karen had left me long before that. Those stays in China became even longer, like now. Her blatant cultivation of her chance friend Chang Lin, who rapidly rose in political circles to become the Chinese President, now speaks volumes though not at the time. That was a physical desertion. It has become an emotional one now.

I can write this here in my journal that will never be read and will end with me. Why would anyone be interested in my stuff? At least I avoid what people write on internet social sites: no trite accounts of what I cultivate, eat and read, though I'm consuming my diminished reserve of books too rapidly. There is an outwebbers' book exchange, thank goodness, in one of the temporary shacks by the station.

I have even started speaking to myself – as well as Foxy! A terrible confession? Not really. It was to prevent myself thinking I was speaking to others, voices from the ghosts of my imagination: Nicholas, Karen, Martha, even Magnus, and always Sister Julian. I imagine her now, buzzing around at St. Thomas's or down in the old university hospital. Did she see Nicholas before he left? I went down to the North Moorland Terminus again and voiced her. No, she has not seen him.

To take my mind off all this I had to do something practical, so I charged my old electroVespavan and chugged off to collect logs and kindling wood. Foxy is becoming lazy and doesn't run behind anymore. He prefers to sit alert beside me, keeping me company.

4 January – evening.

What price peace and quiet? Beyond price. I only go down to the station on sufferance, sensing that even I ought to know what is happening. This morning Chris, my motorcyclist friend, tugged my arm. His face seemed youthful; for the first time I noted a network of wrinkles round his grey eyes and blond – or white? – eyelashes.

'Before coming here today I caught something on wordfree,' he was saying, 'There's been a terrible accident.' It was about the attack on Ezra. It happened some months ago but kept out of the news until now by the GWP Planet Supervisors like Roland to avoid copycat attacks. How can someone imagine, still less commit such evil? The whole point of the wordfree wrist inset is that it cannot be lost because it is part of one's body. I have lost my wordfree monitor – or it may still be at Beech Drive. I accept that it can be stolen. But Ezra's? His wrist cut off – I cannot bear to think of it. What greater harm could one inflict on a pianist? Dear, dear Ezra. So gentle, so sensitive. Nicholas's boon companion and so like him. How could anyone be so cruel? So pointedly cruel. Why him? All, I imagine, they would find on his wordfree would be a few thoughts, things to remember, musical ideas he would be humming, places where he had been invited to give a concert like our Old University, messages to friends like Nicholas, details of travel – All personal and vital to him alone. Oh Ezra!

Chris disappeared into the crowd and I was left standing next to a woman in a leisuretimer's outfit composed, as Helen once explained, mainly from vlason off cuts as that was all they could afford. Her trouser suit had been jollied up with old bits of flowered cotton patches providing pockets on her jacket and trousers. She must have come down from the Maternity and

Freetime Clinic under the Middle Sister Peak. It is now fully equipped and probably preparing for the influx of mountaineers when the skiers who followed the last expectant mothers have left. I am not sure whether they, like us, are unwebbed - through remoteness, that is, not out of choice. I wondered what this woman has been doing there under the Middle Peak? Food production, I imagined. This is what cooking is called. The capsules are all self-cleansing. Martha stressed this when her firm supplied them for the clinic before she won the election.

The July to December maternity clinics are run mostly by maintainers – the technicians – and enablers, largely nurses and physiotherapists – the ones who are responsible for what machines can't yet manage. I was an enabler myself, and have the corresponding pension. Karen says I should have challenged my status to have it changed from enabler to maintainer because I managed the haven homes. I did not want to bother with all those online forms to complete. My enabler pension is adequate. The newscaster was still speaking.

'Beside me is my friend, the illustrious Professor Karen Middlethorpe, who would like to talk to you.'

I was shocked. At least I now know where she is, unless she is only virtually in China. With this restless modern technology one never knows exactly where anyone treads the globe's surface. She is no professor, still less illustrious. What is this all about?

Karen spoke sweetly through slightly pouting lips. China will, it seems, relinquish its prized possession of the Leonardo painting of Leda – or 'the ancient Chinese maiden', according to Karen – so that it can be saved for hukind in the Art Cavern. Soon it will be available for viewing on the *virtualmasterpiecesmuseum.com* site, free for all. It contains age-old wisdom, according to her, as well as messages for the future that all can access. Surely the original has already been taken to the Art Cavern in the procession Magnus sketched at Christmas? I am confused, but that's probably how they want people to be. Sister Julian will sort this all out. She found the painting. Or a refugee did. I just don't understand what's going on. Enablers like me would side with the U S President Anya Lo Yin who says she wants openness, human values first and so on. She still seems to be Karen's friend. Amazing. Or perhaps not. Youthful friendships often last.

Back home and writing this in front of the log fire, I confess that I too asked for help to register my DNA and be able to vote, saddened by the realisation that Nicholas probably was unable to do so. A shiver – where is he? Martha came this morning, as worried as I am. She thought he might be here with me. He discharged himself. The man who accompanied him out told the nurse on duty that he was a relative, but did not leave his name. Nicholas has no relatives besides us. Martha immediately went to the Institute, but he has not been seen there. She has just left to hurry back and do more web-searching in the city. There seems to be nothing I can do. We were both crying. Nicholas fell into the Middle Sister Falls, lay unconscious in hospital with multiple fractures, and now has been wheeled out of the hospital by an unknown man. Why did the hospital allow this to happen?

What can I do? It has always been like this. I have my life: he has his. We have our choices to make. His tend to be startled reactions to everything outside his mental world, the one he has always preferred. Outside it, all seems to be oddly irrelevant to him. The Institute provides him with food and shelter. All he has to do is to solve problems, to invent ways of dealing with them, to try and improve the lot of hukind – his words. Helen and Joe may have changed him. Where are they? Out here I am losing touch.

This is what I must accept. An outwebber, cut off from others outside my geographical reality. Here I am under the Three Sister Peaks, in my little cottage overlooking the estuary. This is my choice. These are my limits. But now all I desperately want is to find out where Nicholas is so I can at least see him. I am sitting by the dying fire, head in my hands that Foxy is trying to lick.

32

Martha *i-witnessMAR727.futurepast.com*

3 January

I've never been edgy like this before. I shouldn't be. Surrounded by new technology, new horizons – just my scene. All I'm doing now is worrying about Nicholas in a place I suppose I'd call, but not feel, my updated childhood home. My wordfree is sound-prodding me. If I ignore it, the volume will increase and the beats morph from intermittent to continuous sound. That museum director is onscreen again. He looks as if he has just emerged from the Sahara, sand dusted, albino eyelashes, unsettlingly insubstantial. He has the current BIG IDEA; I can hear Roland repeat this in his dry, precise tone of voice.

'Remember, Martha, the museum director, like you, is average to quite visible to the online population.' That is, not counting the ill and the disconnected, like mum. Funny. Disconnected she may be, but at least I know where she is. My connected mother Karen, instead, is somewhere presenting bulletins from China in *worldaroundyounews.* The hugely popular Leda tour of China keeps her there, rarely here in the Beech Drive state-of-the-art home I designed for the two of them, where I am now and they never are.

No home for them or for Nicholas and me. How is he? Martha, Martha, Martha, you're inhabiting the online world, physically remote from the people who matter to you. You are literally encapsulated in the home you designed for your parents.

Stop thinking like this, you fool! Nicholas isn't DNA registered – trust Mum to forget to do this! Special places, like the school for geniuses he went to, slipped out of what is now the duty of every citizen. That is, to DNAregister every child at birth. Back when Nicholas and I were born, it was usually done in hospitals or schools, but some people missed out. Not now.

That sand dune man is still bothering me and sound beats are increasing in frequency and volume.

'Yes, yes. I'm voicing you, director. What can I do? You want a permit to enter the Art Cavern? For what purpose?'

'For the Virtual Masterpieces Museum, Deputy Middlethorpe.'

Personally I loathe that title. Let it pass.

'Why? Only trustees or accredited deputies of the Goodwill World Parliament are allowed into the Art Cavern, and only for specific reasons.'

'We need to start the second-level digitalising of masterpieces.' I remember now. He did mention this when he'd completed the first one.

I enlarge my engagement diary tile and scroll down to see if I'm scheduled to go to the Art Cavern. No. A pity.

'Just you, is it?'

'No. Fifty photographers.'

'Fifty? Why fifty?'

'Because I'm informed that I shall be confined to one hour's visiting time, so I'll need a photographer for each section.'

I'd better agree. I don't think other GWP deputies would want to be bothered about this. I can't spare any more time on it now.

'Right, director. I'll voice you later with a suitable date. Maybe two. Back soon.'

What a relief to think 'exit' without more ado. Some people do go on. I must, must, must find out how Nicholas is, but have to finish all my Goodwill World Parliament duties before the weekly session tomorrow. We're all supposed to be quick and efficient with the constant sharpening of electronic devices to speed up every imaginable function. That reminds me, I must claim for expenses. What expenses? Technological updates, mostly; new inventions; retuning screens and the rest. And a free pass for all transport when required on zone government business. That's rare. All is video conferencing now - video commissioning, persuading, virtual personal assistants and on and on. In short, screen gazing does 90% of it. But it still takes time. Now Nicholas...

My wordfree is sound-prodding again. Quick. I'll deal with it before it gears up to wail at me. It's only a business tile. Enlarge it. More orders for capsule homes like this one. So my design is a success. I must remember that when overwhelmed by competing tasks. I'm careful to show that I'm only concerned with my business on an unpaid basis since I became a GWP deputy and zone government member. My one definite success – a home capsule. What makes a home? I may well ask. I see that my assistants are sneaking in modifications. They haven't even asked me! I'll rapidly check the section responsible for interior decoration.

'We've only modified some trimmings, Martha, to update the interior living style.'

'Check with me first.'

'I will. Yes.' This pause seems significant. 'We did, but you were too busy to respond, so we went ahead. Sales have increased.' I pause, then -

'I authorise you to meet the current orders, but send me full details, financial and otherwise.' I wish I wasn't so vague. 'Come back to me before you take decisions on any future modifications. Or designs.' I may not be taking a salary, but it's still my business. That's all probably too abrupt, but I'm annoyed. Someone in my workplace is insinuating that my original home capsule design, this one here, is already retro. Luckily soon the whole office as well as the factory will be managed and worked by robots. They don't argue or become ill.

Enough of all this. Now to find out how Nicholas is. Beech Drive is deserted, as nearly always. Plenty of eyes peeping out of windows, I suspect, ready to message when I leave.

Sobeit. That's what we say for a consensus at the end of a Goodwill World Parliament virtual conference. Sobeit. It's become a sort of verbal seal.

I'm groggy with sleeplessness, glad there's no one in Beech Drive to follow me plodding towards the monorail pause. I hope I'm not too tired to jump inside the monopod in the time allowed, and also help up any unfortunate person, elderly or incapacitated, who can't cope with the average pause time. I must file a complaint to the Monorail management. The schedule should allow for pauses to be extended by at least thirty seconds to allow for slower passengers. They should cut the time taken cleaning the rolling stock in the robot managed washing tunnel to speed up the service. I've noted this on the 'to do' list – after I've seen Nicholas.

Only a few pauses before reaching the main square in the old city. People in the monopod are silent, nervously glancing at wordfrees. I've checked mine many times. It's an involuntary gesture; has been for years. Since it was implanted, to be precise.

Here in the main square the screens are showing some nature documentary projected in tech-enhanced three-dimension with lions, tigers, zebras and the rest like holograms prowling into our space to squeals of fearful delight from children and adults alike. Mindless funtime I call it. Everyone is the better for it. Out and about away from domestic wraparound screens.

'Relax in the open air. Satisfy your diversionist tendencies with no pressing tasks to fulfil. You need not fear procrastination as it's pure enjoyment time without any feeling of guilt...' so runs the mantra for today round the bottom of the huge public screens. I am guilty. I have been procrastinating. Why? No excuse. Lack of time? That's endemic with people like Roland and me, both GWP deputies and zone members. It's worrying about Nicholas. Not being sure what to do.

Fast walking along the old university walls, past the Mouth of Truth and –

Stop! People laugh at the drain cover in the form of some ancient god with a slit for the 'mouth of truth'. On holidays there's usually a tedious queue of tourists, but not today. Only a few stragglers from the crowd entertained by the jungle zoo virtually everywhere around us in smell and sound and, almost, touch. Now there are birds, huge cranes and suchlike, virtually flying over us. Amazing. Heavy bodied, like Leda's swan in

Leonardo's lost painting that Sister Julian found. Another version turned up in an auction, so I convinced our zone government to purchase it, just in case it was the original – one never knows! Mother was in China then, and started pestering me to send the painting on loan to the Chinese president. Amazingly she had discovered a similar Chinese legend. A huge sum was offered. What a wonderful chance to pay for the painting as well as fund our zone Centre of Genetic Wellbeing! It was easy to convince our zone members to invest money in a ground-breaking cause with infinite economic potential...

This monster's 'mouth of truth' is only a game. It's a funny feeling, though, however sceptical I am, really, about it all, but my palm slips easily through up to the wrist. Ouch! My hand has gone right in and the wordfree screen has caught in the mouth. Help!

Voices. Stay still. Turn your hand to the left. Don't force it or your hand will swell up. Gently does it! Aaaah! My hand's free.

'Deputy Middlethorpe, are you all right?' Anxious faces crowd around me. Some others further back are sniggering. I must escape.

'Excuse me.' Be dignified. 'I have crucial business to attend to.' I hope my face isn't red. It's burning. People are standing back, some smirking slightly, but I'm walking calmly away, face dressed in the faint smile of serene authority. Once inside the university walls I can hurry. No one is following me, I hope, but I mustn't look round.

Sister Julian convinced a rival firm manufacturing pre-conceived capsule units for institutions such as schools, hospitals, prisons and the like, not domestic spaces like mine, to donate some to her hospital in the Old

University buildings. I admit their capsules are good, though poppies and sunflowers are a bit tired as a corridor screen background. It's about the most popular wallpaper choice nowadays.

'Dr. Nicholas Middlethorpe, please.'

'I'm sorry, Deputy Middlethorpe. He has left.'

'Left? When?'

'This morning.'

'On his own?'

'No. A man – a relative – came for him.'

'Do you know where he was taken?'

'No.' The woman in Reception looks flustered. 'Now I must return to my duties. So sorry I cannot help you any further.'

'Please scroll back through the CCT images. I might recognise the person who came for him.'

'We don't have closed circuit television surveillance. Sister Julian doesn't like it. She calls a it a 'license to pry and spy'. Her words.'

Back despairing. Where is he? Past the poppies and sunflowers. Who is this man? We don't have any male relative. I'll message Roland and Magnus to find out if it was one of them. There's no one else. My wordfree is throbbing incessantly. A mountain of messages to climb. Hope, Martha, for a rare one from Nicholas, just to know how he is. Sit here in the quiet of the university courtyard and access them. Nowadays most can be symbol-answered. So much quicker. Voting on by-issues for the Goodwill World Parliament. 281 messages. Y, N, Y, N, N, N... Finished. Nothing from Nicholas. Wrapped in his mental bubble, he's always off on his own track.

Indulged. Message back from Roland. He hasn't seen Nicholas who must be better because he has left hospital. Wants us to go away somewhere such as Experience Dreamlands. YES! When? This evening. Time off. Wonderful idea! No. I can't go anywhere until I find Nicholas. Next – Celia. Meet her urgently. At St. Thomas's. She must have checked where I am. More message requests from constituents. I wish they'd come to old-fashioned surgeries as they used to, mother says. But that was long ago. Message from Magnus. No idea where Nicholas is. Oh dear - now delegates must have wordfree surgeries anywhere, any time.

If only I could occasionally switch this thing off! Totally off, not even on standby. Not now. It's the only way I can know if Nicholas has been found.

I'll avoid the jungle in the main square where three-dimensional creatures are still prowling or flying around. I can glimpse it on virtually every screen in outlets, and now on the one outside the museum. There's so much choice that most screens, the public ones anyway are on the same webchannel. How typical of hukind! Celia is waiting for me outside St. Thomas's.

'How is he?' She intuits I have been at the hospital.

'He discharged himself this morning.'

'He couldn't have done it!' She's almost crying. 'He was unconscious, sometimes semi-conscious at most when I saw him yesterday.' Does Celia know Nicholas is unDNAregistered?

'What can I do?' I'm almost shouting. 'Where can I look for him?'

'Who saw him last?'

‘In hospital?’ I said. ‘Probably me. Then someone, a man, came for him. He couldn’t leave on his own.’

‘Who was it?’ She stops in her tracks. ‘We have to find out.’

‘I’ll message Roland. Magnus too.’

‘Let’s start at the hospital.’

Yes, yes, yes. Though I doubt there will be any result. Roland and Magnus have messaged back. Neither has seen Nicholas. I’ll put my wordfree on standby and check those lists later.

I’m taller than Celia by a bit, and sturdier, though I’m hardly a heavy build. We’re hurrying back to the hospital the same way I came. That screen outside the museum is showcasing future developments in the Virtual Masterpieces Museum. Celia doesn’t seem to want to talk so I’ll message the director an access permit now from the GWP All Purposes Committee. I can also quick-reply some wordfree messages while trying not to trip over the cobbles that should be re-laid.

‘Wouldn’t they have registered Nicholas’s DNA when he was checked into the Old University Hospital?’

Celia’s right. That’s a worldwide legal imperative. ‘Have you tried finding him on the Geomap?’

‘Yes I have.’ She’s more techsavvy than I imagined. ‘No luck. They can’t have DNAregistered him.’ She looks surprised.

The main square has lost its jungle zoo and is screening a three-dimensional football match as we dodge the ball and predominantly male virtual players and I try to block out the crowd’s whoops. This is the sort of thing Joe would love, darting hither and thither in a mimic game. He was – is – so agile in wit and limb. Where is he?

'Pity about Joe,' Celia comments. 'I'm not sure whether he really fits in there.'

'Where?' Am I fated to hang on to the last tendril of the relevant grapevine?

'At Nicholas's former school. Didn't you know?'

I think I did. I'd heard it somewhere. Somebody might have told me. There's too much happening. Celia doesn't even glance at the Mouth of Truth as she fasteps past it to turn into the main entrance to the Old University courtyard.

She charges down the hospital corridor without noticing the poppies and sunflowers wallscreenpaper, though 'charging' is hardly the right word for someone so slight. I can hardly keep up with her.

'Good morning,' she smiles at the receptionist, not the one I saw earlier, 'I'm sorry to bother you, but could you tell me whether Dr. Nicholas Middlethorpe's DNA was registered when he was admitted?'

'We are not allowed to divulge confidential information.' What I suspected. My turn now.

'I am Deputy Middlethorpe and Dr. Middlethorpe's sister. Here's my identification and security card.'

She looks ruffled, turns away and stabs at the reception screen icon. It leaps up at her and she almost scowls at it. Her fingers dance in triplets in front of the keyboard.

'One moment, please.' She disappears into the back room. A few ripples of dialogue and she returns.

'I'm so sorry. I have only just started as a volunteer. I am told we assume that all admitted here are DNA registered.'

'90% of the world population is to date, but it should be 100%,' I inform her. Frankly I don't think the Goodwill World Parliament is doing enough to ensure universal DNA registration. Perhaps it's not fair to ask a new volunteer about this. We are afloat on a sea of volunteers – or leisuretimers - who have little buying power and less knowledge. Dom Ross Mackenzie and his confederates in the global business world secretly despise them as unproductive burdens on hukind, paid out of GWP funds.

'Why is this hospital so lax when it is just the place to check that citizens have their medical records decipherable through DNA registration?' I add quickly, 'Of course, with the individual's permission.'

She's floundering, with 'I imagine that unDNAregistered people are unlikely to exist here in the Greystone River zone,' while glancing anxiously at the door behind her.

'Can I see the hospital manager, please?' The volunteer disappears into the back room again. I turn to Celia who nods at me. Silence again. I return furtively to my wordfree to see if the All Purposes Committee has replied offering possible Art Cavern access times. One tomorrow. That might do. I don't know. I MUST FIND NICHOLAS before anything else. The Museum Director can wait. Everyone can wait.

'May I help you? In a navy-blue suit, crisp blouse and smile with hair pulled back into a bun, she appears efficient but not unattractive.

'Yes. It seems that this hospital did not register my brother, Dr. Nicholas Middlethorpe's DNA when he was checked in. I think it is required by law.' I pull out my Deputy Identification and security card.

'I, I'm not sure. We d-don't have the necessary d-DNA formatting codes.' She stutters and stares at the registration screen. 'We assume everyone who c-comes here for treatment is already d-DNA c-coded. Everyone except, it seems, d-Dr. Middlethorpe. Why didn't we c-check this? I, I d-don't know. He had emergency plasticadhesive b-bone surgery'.

She's looking at me and I'm staring straight back at her, desperate for a better explanation.

'Perhaps I should tell you as you are the d-Deputy for this area. Sister Julian, who f-founded this hospital, will be here l-later today.'

I frown. 'I can't wait till then.'

'Anyway,' she continues, 'Sister Julian is, how c-can one say, unconventional. A law unto herself; D-DNA checking d-doesn't c-come high in her priorities. She stresses instant h-help and c-care, and so on...' The hospital manager's voice is trailing off uncomfortably. We must find Nicholas, and this exchange isn't leading anywhere. Celia remains silent.

'The last time I saw my brother here he was semi-conscious. Why was he allowed to leave?' The hospital manager is almost scowling in thought.

'I must h-have been, no, I was off duty. When I returned he h-had already gone. Self d-discharged. He signed the d-discharge d-document onscreen' She's pattering her fingers over it to find the document to prove her case. 'He was wheeled off to a waiting v-vehicle. Someone f-fetched him. Here's the d-discharge form and h-his signature. That's all I know. V-

Virginia,' she calls out to the volunteer framed behind her in the back room door. I can sense that Celia is peering at the screen over my shoulder, scanning the discharge document for more clues. There's only a faint signature, but it's his.

'Virginia, were you h-here when d-Dr. Middlethorpe discharged himself?' She's shaking her head. 'Do you know w-who was?' Still shaking her head.

'Who fetched him?' I'm insisting, 'Who wheeled him out?'

'I could c-check the records, d-Deputy Middlethorpe, and let you know. May I have your wordfree c-code?'

'I need to know NOW.'

'All we can find is an o-onscreen note that a m-male relative came for him.'

'He doesn't have a male relative. Why didn't you ask for identification papers?'

'Dr. Middlethorpe signed the self-discharge papers. Here –' she swivels the screen round again to prove it.

I lean over the computer desk, trying not to be rude.

'Listen. We MUST know who this imposter – the so-called male relative - is. You have already failed in your duty to ask for identification. At least you can describe what he looked like.' A male, average height, she says, neatly dressed, light brown hair. It could be anyone. Dissatisfied, Celia and I sit and wait for more information. Our questions lead nowhere except to the electronic equivalent of shuffling papers.

'Yes, the man – Dr. Middlethorpe's relative - wheeled him to a waiting vehicle outside.'

'What did it look like?'

'I can't see the courtyard from here. We can only assume that Dr. Middlethorpe is with the relative who came for him.'

'Thank you.' I'm trying not to sound pompous. Lower your tone, Martha, I almost whisper to myself. 'Thank you so much for your help. I'm afraid we must leave.'

Celia is rushing ahead with me, rather ridiculously, striding after her.

'Wait, wait. What's our plan? The next step?' She has subsided on to a bench in the old university courtyard, head in hands.

'Celia, we must find out who took him away.

'We've tried everything suggested so far,' she says, looking up at me. 'I've checked he's not on any plane or train list. Could Eliza have sent an outwebber to fetch him?'

'I doubt it.'

Celia stands up with, 'We must find out. Follow every path...'

It's late. Celia wants to return to St. Thomas's so I'll take the monorail back to Beech Drive – what else can I do?

33

Helen *showspotHEL22.com*

3 January

The red scooter is chugging up the hill to the perimeter fence while my thoughts leap over it to Dom Ross Mackenzie. And what about poor Nicholas?

'He must know where Nicholas is!' That's me, shouting into the trees. I'm getting so heavy – Ross did warn me - and this scooter is puffing and slowing down. We're both running out of steam.

'Help!'

No one here. The trees are closing in, dropping evening shadows over me. Oh, I've forgotten! How do I get in? The prisoners- on- parole won't be there passing logs over the wall. Too late.

I'll have to ring at the entrance and explain to the gatekeeper. All that fuss.

The iron gates are so beautifully intricate that you can't see through them. Wrought, not cast iron, Ross always stresses, when in art-talking mood. The bell doesn't ring; it echoes. Probably because it's attached to some complex security set-up at the mansion.

'You want?' Where is this voice? I'm looking from side to side. No slit for a voice to come through, still less to see a face, and the gates are still firmly closed.

'Yes?' Why didn't I look up? There's a bald head poking out of the gatehouse window.

'I'm Helen. Helen Runciman. I've forgotten the evening password.' (I repeated it ten times before leaving, but have still forgotten it.) 'I live on the estate.' I'd better not say in the mansion itself. I know Ross doesn't like staff to live inside the walls. They all leave between five and six in the evening. He has changed the animal feeding times to fit into his daily routine. Only his cook, butler and gatekeeper live on site and they double up as security for house and grounds. Nicholas used to say Ross was either parsimonious or misanthropic (I'm glad I remember these words. I learnt them from him. Poor Nick...) He thinks Dom Ross is parsimonious, with a liking for solitude. Or his own company rather than anyone else's.

Nicholas. Where is he? I buzzed all over the place looking for him after wasting time with that Celia woman at the church. Martha wasn't at home or at Karen and Eliza's new house in Beech Drive. When did he leave the hospital? How long before I arrived? I should have asked. Things just don't occur to me at the right time.

'I can't reveal the password,' the gatekeeper growls.

I can never remember a word and number combination that's changed three times a day. How could anyone remember them all? Except the GREAT MAN himself, of course!

'Orders are orders. Gates only open with the right password.'

'Don't you remember me?' I stress the plea in my voice. 'Helen. I'm the Hallelujah girl.'

He almost falls out trying to look at me, and I preen automatically.

'Of course you are!' His gruff voice becomes almost tender. 'Come on in.'

Once out of his sight round the first curve in the drive, I can slow down a bit. I'll leave the scooter where I found it, by the side door. I always wear gloves when driving, so there won't be any fingerprints on it for Ross's scientists to check.

Now to the front door. You can't tell if there's a rare visitor because the limousine, helousine or whatever are left unseen in the park behind the lab wing. He doesn't like anything to obstruct the forecourt and his view of the estuary, or of others approaching his mansion. He's most particular, as poor Nicholas used to say. I wish I could forget how he deserted me in Africa, left me to drift. Oh, if only I could find him!

I'll try to sneak inside to my room without anyone noticing. Up the steps, across the entrance hall, then... There are voices in his study. Ross doesn't usually raise his.

'The man's drugged. Swims in and out of consciousness. His body is healing with all the miraculous plastioadhesive bone surgery he has had, but his mind wanders.' Murmurs. 'I've revealed enough about my energy program to satisfy the GWP and the satellite has just been launched. I must have his final calculation for beam accuracy, otherwise -' I can't hear any more. I'll pause and pretend to search for something in my bag, just in case someone comes out while I'm listening.

'Doesn't anyone else know the code and passwords?' Another voice, deeper, without Ross's soothing tone.

'This is a right mess. The satellite and all its promised benefits orbiting pointlessly around us. Not a shaft of energy.' Someone else, clearly baffled. Other voices, annoyed or furious.

'We have to be patient.' Ross, just controlling a slight tremor. 'At least I've sorted out the terms of the satellite lease without giving too much away.'

'You'll have to do better than this with my *worldaroundyounews* shares. I'm now thinking of selling my stake.' I can't make out what the others are saying. There's shouting.

'It doesn't seem very effective,' another comments, more calmly, followed by Ross in his reassuring way. 'We're attracting newsfinders and better newsblenders to present our input and interests more forcefully.'

Another, sharper voice, chips in, 'Let's concentrate on infinenergy. Now you have the scientist here, isolated, you should find a way to force the accurate calculations out of him, Ross.' Nicholas is here!

'He can't remember anything much when conscious. Let's leave it for now. The doctors are sure he'll improve. Give him time. He's safe here.'

Safe! I must find him. Is he in this building? I could ask Cook, but I've never trusted her or the butler. The gatekeeper? His attitude changed when he heard I'm the Hallelujah girl. Worth trying.

I must creep back to the entrance, down the steps without being seen from the study window – easier now as it's nearly dark - and run as fast as I can back to the gatehouse. Baldie comes out to meet me, smiling – I don't expect he has much to amuse him.

'Please, could you possibly tell me where the young man, Dr. Middlethorpe, has been taken? He came here with Dom Ross Mackenzie.'

He's scratching his bald patch. 'I don't see much from here if they use the helousine. The helipad is up the hill behind them chestnut trees. But I know that Cook has been going to the orangery.

‘Of course. Thanks a lot.’

It’s too dark now. I’ll go there first thing tomorrow morning.

* * * * *

4 January – morning

The orangery is just where I would have liked to stay. I even asked Ross if I could move over there; he looked at me strangely and said that it had other uses and why didn’t I like my en suite accommodation in the mansion. It’s awkward, as he keeps on asking me this and I have to invent reasons, excuses and remember to keep to the same ones as he never forgets anything. I can’t exactly say that I don’t like being close to his quarters. The orangery is on the other side of the walled garden and not far from the screened area with the cancer-retarding plants. Ross doesn’t like people going there, except the gardeners and scientists working on the project.

The orangery is perfect. A space with tall windows and heaters for the orange and lemon trees in winter. Behind the large storage space are two rooms, a bathroom and kitchen for a gardener, I suppose, but nobody lives there. It’s all on the ground floor so Nicholas could easily have been taken there in a wheelchair. I just hope Cook isn’t with him...

She isn’t. Nicholas is sleeping and breathing heavily. Almost snoring. He looks rested though.

Someone is coming, footsteps crunching the gravel.

‘Oh,’ says a kindly looking man, middle aged, middle size and quite uninquisitive. ‘You can keep an eye on him for a while. Cook asked me to do it from time to time when I'm working in the walled garden. She has to be in the house.' He's smiling as if he knows me and I do the same. I nod.

'Thanks.' He turns to leave, then hesitates before adding, 'They tell me to look out for a woman who's coming to see him. That's you, is it?'

I nod, not sure what to say. Someone else may be coming. I'll wait and see. There's only one bed with Nicholas on it, a side table, a lamp, a wardrobe and two chairs. I'll take one out where the plants are stored. The windows look over the walled garden and entrance to the experimental zone beyond. I'll lean back, close my eyes and listen to the latest versions of drong which I prefer to the betweeners' craze for Upstart Four. It will probably be chosen for the mix and match concerts someone has started in the Old University hall. It might even have been Sister Julian's idea after Mid Winter. I don't think Celia would have the ability to organise it. That pianist, whose hand was cut off by thugs, will be performing in a work for one hand. I must find out when.

Someone is coming out of the screened cancer-retarding plant area. Odd because he isn't wearing protective clothes. It's a woman! She must have lost her way and trespassed into the experimental zone. It has happened to me – once, only. I was beamed and boomed at by the security devices. I'll wave to her and show her the way out.

It's Celia – the last person I want to see!

'How did you get here?' She seems surprised. 'Are you looking for Dom Ross Mackenzie? He's in the mansion.'

'Why are you here for that matter, Helen? Haven't you got your own capsule home? One of Martha's?'

'Yes, but it's more comfortable staying here. Everything is done for me. I'm now embarking on a new, exciting and ambitious project. Top secret.' I shouldn't giggle, but I do.

How does she know Nicholas is here? Does Martha know? Why isn't she here? Ross must have told Celia that Nicholas is in the bedroom. Did he ask her to come? She slips in before I can stop her. He is still sleeping. She draws the chair closer to him on the side he's facing. I'll fetch mine from the Orangery and place it on the other side. She's holding his hand.

'No temperature,' she murmurs, as if to herself. No way is this miserable creature going to cut me out. Her actions presume she knows him better than I do. She's an ignorant little nobody.

'That's a positive sign,' she murmurs, 'after such serious plastioadhesive surgery.' She's a nurse, obviously. Do nurses stroke patients' hands? I suppose they might if they have time. There's plenty of it now, it seems, while we wait.

'Can you try to wake him up?' I don't want to seem impatient, but...

'Better to let it happen naturally. He's on the healing curve now. Better to coax it along its way, if possible a little faster...' She's talking to him now in familiar terms. Too familiar. We have made love. I'll tell her if she goes on like this. His hand on my side is under the sheet and coverlet. I'll feel underneath to find it.

'No, don't disturb him too much...' She would say that, wouldn't she? She has one hand, why shouldn't I hold the other? Who is she to say no?

'He must return naturally,' she stresses "naturally", 'into consciousness.' She's frowning. Seems to do a lot of it. Probably passes for deep thought. I'll shed a tear or two to show how deeply I care.

'No need to weep.' She misses nothing and has to advise me. A know-all. 'He could wake up at any moment. Look. He's turning over now. If he sees you in tears he'll fear the worst he can imagine. He may wake at any moment in pain as the medication isn't effective after such a length of time.' What's the worst?

'Isn't he out of danger?'

'Physically, yes. I'm not so sure about his mental state.'

She lets his hand go as he turns towards me and now I can stroke it. It's strange to see a left wrist without a wordfree. I've always admired his fingers: long and delicate.

'He always thought his hands were ideal to play the piano, but his genius was – is – for numbers, science and inventions.' I'm the one to talk now. She's said enough.

'He's a natural problem solver.' Celia always butts in like this. 'Like Joe. That's why Nicholas cares so much about the child. A sort of mutual fascination.'

Was that the only attraction? Someone launched the online suspicion it was more than that. Even I feared it was. It rapidly went viral. Everyone chattering in every online gossip forum there is. Nicholas was virtually executed.

Celia has gone outside. I'm alone with Nicholas. He's stirring, his eyes flickering. Outside Dom Ross is whispering something to her.

'I can't do that,' she's saying. 'I'm a friend and a trained nurse.' What's he asking her to do? I'm certain it's about Nicholas. I could move nearer, but don't want to lose physical contact with him. He has opened one eye, now both.

'Nicholas! 'He's looking at me. 'Nicholas! It's me, Helen!' His lips are moving.

'Helen, is he awake?' Ross is standing behind me looking at Nicholas. Celia waits in the doorway, observing us. I feel awkward under scrutiny. Nicholas, still silent, is watching us. Ross is propelling me towards the door, arm round my shoulder. 'Helen, can I see you later? There are plans I want to talk over with you. Tomorrow? Over lunch?' I don't want to leave.

Instead I'm neatly dismissed. He wants to keep me away from Nicholas. Why is Celia allowed to be there with them, and not me? So I'm to be kept ignorant of what's happening to him and she isn't. That won't be because Ross cares for her, but because he is involving her in another scheme of his. I'm furious, but what good does that do me?

I'm wandering along the edge of the walled garden wondering what to do.

The latest newstream on my wordfree has something about a concert in the Old University. Ross allows me to use the limousine if I contact him and the driver is free. He is. Now the gatekeeper is friendly, I don't have to remember the current password, but I'll try to. I may return late.

Ross has asked me to be careful about what I do, now we're nearer the start of our grand project. I think he wants me to stay in more. But I won't!

I must be at the lodge at seven this evening. Easy to get a quick bite from the general use fridge. Cook has orders to keep it snacked up for Dom Ross and his guests. There's a quick-heat oven next to it. I'm looking forward to this. I'll have a nap and put my wordfree on standby.

*****

As I roll through the main square in Ross's limousine, the streetscreens are brimming with scenes from a weary reality drama. Safe and mildly satisfying. In the past there would have been at least some reference to the event we're going to. Still, everyone seems to know about the concert as there are people heading towards the Old University entrance, though some still straggle round the Mouth of Truth. As a significant benefactor, Ross has his designated parking space inside. I'm swishing through the entrance gates like royalty! Whoosh, and the crowds part, though it's disconcerting having people pressing up close to the windows to peer in.

There's a crush of people, mostly betweeners in motley outfits. Fashion has deteriorated dramatically. They haven't a clue of how a basic colour garment with a strong cut can be brilliantly personalised with accessories. Cara thinks our Powerhouse business has become too upmarket. Too bad. I'm earning far more through the investment Ross is making with me and our grand new project.

Flyers are handed to us as we enter the building after my wordfree thought-payment. 'Mix and Match Concert Special: Ezra Tenenbaum, the world-famous pianist, will play the piano concerto for one hand by Ravel, revised for the right hand, after Upstart's latest 'raiser' to set the evening going. The show will end with an old-time drong miscellany.'

'I'm old hat now, aren't I?' I'm thinking as I follow the crowd up the wide flight of steps to the grand entrance hall where betweeners are mingling with over twenties among the ancients and even plus ancients. I admit that while climbing up those steps, I experienced a sudden age shift. Not quite to middle age status, but a distinct shift, nevertheless. It's that 'old-time drong miscellany' on the programme hand-out that did it. Twang! A few words and I feel years older than I saw myself just a few minutes ago. Drong, the music of my youth, is now forever lodged in the palace of old favourites. So Nicholas and I, with Roland, Martha and millions of others of the drong generation have aged into an 'old-time miscellany'.

'Thank goodness the fire didn't reach this part of the old university. It's where I took my degree,' a woman behind me is saying. She's looking almost affectionately at the stone walls, portrait paintings, coats of arms, busts – all that old stuff - and the raised platform where the grand piano shines behind the Four Upstarts arranging their instruments and microphone.

The only seat I can find is right at the back. Martha six rows from the front, and next to her are Eliza, Sister Julian and a dark-haired woman I don't recognise.

'Ladies and gentlemen, the programme is about to begin with an original work by the Upstarts!' The master of ceremonies looks like one of Sister Julian's refugees. Very precise diction.

Cheers from the back.

I know it's normal with the mix-and-match movement, but it is disturbing to hear the sound of soles swivelling behind me on the floor at the back where the betweeners, and others, are standing and later will dance to the boom, beat and riffs. This is the first time I'm experiencing the Upstarts off screen, and they're vibrant enough. I've never bothered about volume. Rhythm: good really. It invites foot tapping and the betweeners at the back are pounding the floor. Riffs: some inventive journeys with a lot of instrument and human antics to go with them, but not really good enough 'cos I'm sitting here thinking and not dancing them into my body. Magnus always did that when one was lucky enough to see him. His passion for dancing keeps him youthful, though he's definitely in the middle heading towards early ancient status. I long to join the betweeners, but not in my present state.

The rhythmic clapping fades when the dark-haired woman follows Ezra Tenenbaum on to the stage. Ripples of polite applause. Martha waves to him. He smiles back, sits and settles with the woman beside him, while the orchestra tunes up. Nicholas once said that these historical instruments aren't made any more. One of his dreams was to recreate violins in a 'Strad' or 'Stradivarius'– I think that's the name – workshop. Nicholas often talked about his schoolfriends, Ezra and Lizzy. Maybe the woman beside Ezra to turn the pages is Lizzy? She's the artist who creates works from nature in wild places, inspired by the Nazca Lines, whatever they are. Or, Nicholas said, sculpting with water – whatever that means - in a desert. There's so much going on here with everyone chatting, instruments tuning and sounds all mixed up around us. Silence. Ezra starts playing, crouched over one hand, his stump resting on a knee, eyes creased as if clenched. Notes climb and swing and dance around – the *arpeggios, allegro ma non troppo* and all the other strange words Eliza uses.

Applause. Shouts of 'encore!' People standing. Me too.

Some think that after what happened to Ezra, the wheel of fortune – or misfortune - has turned and passed us by. It's all superstition, Nick says, but who can tell the future? There will be an encore. The same refugee with the blurred way of speaking is announcing something.

'As a surprise encore, Ezra will play his own accompaniment for me, and I'll sing Mozart's aria for Zaïde.'

How curious. It's the song on Eliza's old CD that Nicholas told me she often played for him after she had tucked him in bed. She says it's the most beautiful song ever written. The voice rises. Some betweeners had started to get up during the ovation to stuff their cushions back into the storage benches at the sides of the hall and get ready to dance but, hushed by the opening notes, stand spellbound.

During the interval chairs are being stacked behind me so that everyone can listen and swing to the drong miscellany for the second half of the concert. Eliza and Sister Julian have left. Martha and Roland are following the grand piano as it is wheeled into a corner of the hall. I'm looking around, wondering who I can be with. Dance with. Alone?

Then Martha looks up, sees me standing alone and strides towards me.

'Now you're back from Argentina or wherever, I want some clear explanations from you.'

I hope I look puzzled.

'Why did you betray Nicholas?'

'Betray?'

'Yes. Flounce off with Ross Mackenzie. Give him Nicholas's invention, and –'

'I didn't.'

'You're lying.'

'I'm not.' She has come so close I think she might spit on me. I try to step back but she's pinning me against the wall.

'You left him in Africa and weaselled off to Ross Mackenzie. A blatant betrayal.'

Her eyes are on fire. I'm frightened.

'I only returned Ross's datadrive as promised. He offered to help Nicholas, to lend him some sort of maths checking program or something – I don't know. I've no idea of what they were doing, Martha.'

'Really? So you announce Nicholas's invention, HIS discovery, on *worldaroundyounews* as Ross Mackenzie's. You condone his THEFT, do you?' She's baring her teeth right close to my face. 'How's that for a betrayal? How could you do it, Helen?' She's shouting. Everyone has turned to look at their zone member mishandling me. She shouldn't behave like this.

'I didn't, Martha. Ross Mackenzie insists he was, is helping Nicholas!'

'Helen Runciman, you are guilty of making Nicholas attempt to take his own life and –'

'Martha,' Roland puts a hand on her shoulder, 'Martha, that's not true. It was Joe being –'

'Keep out of this, Roland! Keep out!' She turns to glare at him and then faces me, eyes flashing,

'And because of you, he's now in the grasp of the man who stole his life's work – and you, you –' she's trying to shake me. Roland's pulling her back. I duck under her arm and barge into the amazed onlookers, rush awkwardly down the staircase, shake the shoulder of the limousine driver who's dozing, scramble into the back seat, and urge him to speed back up Quarry Hill.

Lights are following us. Faster, faster...

The limousine glides too slowly round the bends up Quarry Hill. The midnight password? Baldie smiles. Home?

34

Magnus *i-witnessMAG931futurepast.com*

4 January, evening

There's no better place than in the cool grey stillness of the refectory at St. Thomas's to reflect on what's happening around us. Time seems to stop here in an instant of calm. The others are coming in: Martha and Roland, Ezra the pianist and the artist Lizzy – they must be staying here - and Celia, who was ordered to leave Quarry Hill. She's sitting next to Sister Julian at the head of the table. The full horror of the attack on Ezra struck us all when he rested the bandaged stump on the shiny brown refectory table, then hastily put it back on his knees underneath.

'I shouldn't have gone into the alleys behind the old university.' His voice was a whisper in the hush around him. 'I thought it was a short cut to the rehearsal. To the concert piano in the Great Hall.' The old story. A hit man – or men. Shadowy doorway.

We're all here this morning because Helen messaged Martha to report that, when she went to the orangery, Nicholas had disappeared. She has looked everywhere for him, in and outside the mansion. The gatekeeper, cook and butler - the only staff living on the estate -haven't seen either Nicholas or Ross Mackenzie today. She checked the parking area behind the science wing. Security lights went on automatically. The limousines were inside the garages, she thought, as all the doors were down, but the helousine was not on the helipad. Dom Ross is the only one who uses it.

'So who was the last to see Nicholas and Ross Mackenzie, separately or together?' Sister Julian voices what we must all be thinking.

'I may have been.' Celia looks odd, even more diminished than usual. 'It's hard to know where to begin. I had been looking for Nicholas, joining forces with Martha. All we knew was that a man had taken him away from the Old University Hospital. He told them he was a relative. Nicholas discharged himself. I was back here at St. Thomas's when an unexpected call came from Ross Mackenzie. Extraordinary. Just when I was thinking he must be the person who knows where Nicholas is, he messages me saying he wants to talk urgently. The upshot of that was a limousine sent here to drive me up to Quarry Hill. He took me to see Nicholas who lay asleep. Found at last! Helen was there.'

'What happened then?' Ezra asks, impatient at the pause.

'How was Nicholas?' Lizzy this time. They both studied at the Academy for Geniuses with Nicholas. Joe is there now.

Celia looks upset. She's finding it difficult to speak. 'He wasn't exactly in a coma. But he was sleeping, deeply.' She hesitates, not wanting to say what we're all thinking. 'Yes, drugged. But his eyes were flickering and half opened. The effects were wearing off.' She's pausing again. We wait. A fraught silence. 'Ross Mackenzie called me outside and said he would like to talk to me in the house. I didn't want to leave Nicholas. So he, Ross Mackenzie, returned to Nicholas's room behind the orangery and almost propelled Helen out of it and across the walled garden. I don't know what happened to her after that. She was clearly upset.'

'And you? What did he want?' I shouldn't be so blunt, perhaps, but we're all focussing on her. 'We've found Nicholas – and lost him again. Time is running out. Come on Celia.'

'Wait,' says Sister Julian, raising her hands as if in a blessing. 'Wait.' And she stands up to move behind Celia and put her hands on her shoulders. 'We'll find Nicholas.' Then, 'When you can, Celia, tell us what Mackenzie wanted'.

'It's nothing much really. He asked a lot of questions about Nicholas's work, which I couldn't answer. Something about datadrives. He seemed to think I was – or had been – Nicholas's assistant. That I was a scientist. Then he wanted to find out how I met Nicholas. When I said it was in Mybeki, he stepped away, hands in pockets, and started probing into what I had been doing in Mybeki. I then said I had to leave.' Again silence. We wait. Sister Julian is turning lights on. It's raining outside. She says that Celia has probably told us all that is relevant to Nicholas.

She hasn't. Celia is talking again, hesitantly. 'It's that he, Ross Mackenzie, also wanted to know everything about the Zueto community that I'd been working with and how Esther came to manage the new Mybeki branch of the Centre for Genetic Wellbeing, with money from somewhere. Where? He, Mackenzie, went on asking about her HIV resistant tribe. I know nothing about this. I'm no scientist. That's Esther's area. And Nicholas's.' Sister Julian is touching her arm. Celia is trembling. 'I think he wants to sabotage something. The source of Esther's funding, perhaps. Though he wants to get her support by any means, her people with it.'

'How did you get back here?' Martha asks.

'I walked. He didn't offer a limousine so I didn't ask. I tried to return to the orangery. I told him that I knew Nicholas well and that he wanted me to stay with him, but Ross Mackenzie ordered the butler to accompany me to the gatehouse. It was not an act of kindness, but at least he didn't threaten me. I had to walk all the way here.' She's almost sobbing. 'I felt useless.'

One of the former refugees starts to lay the refectory table. I break the silence with,

'We must decide what to do next.'

'It's urgent. We mustn't dither.' Martha this time.

'Who's dithering?' Lizzy says.

'Nobody's dithering.' Ezra is right. We're all tense. Afraid for Nicholas.

'Right.' It's Sister Julian again. 'We can plot Ross Mackenzie's movements on the Geomap, as he must be DNA registered.'

'We won't know whether Nicholas is with him as he isn't,' Martha reminds us.

'Try his wordfree.' Roland's idea.

'I have. No answer. It's on, though. He must have left it somewhere,' Martha says.

'Try again,' Sister Julian insists. I'm not going to say anything, but it's unwise to contact Nicholas. Ross Mackenzie will have checked his wordfree, if it came from the hospital with him, and will realise that we're trying to find him. At least a Geomap search won't alert him, though it can't tell us whether Nicholas is with Ross Mackenzie.

'Wait,' Ezra says, 'Nicholas is contacting me on his wordfree.'

'I hope Celia will receive this message.' The voice is faint, but he has been ill and, so Celia thinks, is still on medication. 'I'm fine and furthering my research. Don't worry or try to find me as I need to be left alone. Please tell everyone that I am well. That's all. I'll be turning this off, not to be disturbed.' A click. Then silence.

Where is he now?

'With Eliza? Where did she go after the concert?' Roland is right to be concerned.

'I took her to catch the last hoverpod,' Sister Julian this time. 'She was so distressed at seeing, well, what had happened to you, Ezra, and concerned that Nicholas had left the hospital. She saw him there. She was sorry not to talk to you, Ezra and Lizzy, after the concert. She remembers you both from your schooldays with Nicholas.'

'Let's concentrate on Ross Mackenzie.' I state the obvious. Roland is already doing it on his wordfree. 'But try to leave as little trace as possible of what we're doing on the internet.' Though I say it, I know that's impossible.

We're sitting in silence here in the dark rectangle of the refectory. Sister Julian says a prayer for Nicholas before offering soup and bread made by the new troop of prisoners-on-parole followed by cheese and fruit from others now working on a farm. The Old University is bustling with all the activities Sister Julian has hived off from St. Thomas's, as well as new initiatives, like the hospital.

Fed, satisfied physically but all still at a loss what to do. No plan of action. No one is leading. Martha is fiddling with her wordfree, like Roland, both trying to plot Ross Mackenzie's movements. Ezra is slumped over the table nursing the stump of his severed hand. He looks deeply upset, probably after what Sister Julian said about Eliza. As a pianist herself, Eliza may have found his interpretation of Ravel's concerto, rapidly transposed for the right hand, well below expectation. I wasn't there, but heard about the ovation. Sister Julian is comforting Celia. Lizzy is looking around, dazed, one hand on Ezra's maimed arm. I'm the only one disengaged. I'll have to do something.

'Where do we go from here? Do what Nicholas calls us to do. Give up the search?'

'I've had what he said analysed on speechcheck,' Roland announces. 'It's a fabrication, pasted together from bits of past messages from him. So it is his voice, but not him. It's very suspicious.' Nobody comments, so I repeat,

'What do we do? Leave him alone or try to find him?'

'How could you even hesitate?' Celia almost growls at me. 'I've told you. He was drugged. Ross Mackenzie has an agenda. I'm not even sure what he was trying to get out of me. Believe me, Nicholas is not safe. Look at what's happened to Ezra, and he's a musician, not a scientist.' She's shouting now, 'Did they think Ezra was Nicholas? Whoever did it all those weeks ago will have debriefed his wordfree and found out it didn't belong to a scientist. We must find him!'

'Right. Where do we go from here?' I don't want to dictate. 'Action. We don't know whether Nicholas is in danger -' Sister Julian has returned to the head of the refractory table '- so we must move. Quickly.'

'May I make a suggestion?' Sister Julian asks. Murmurs of consent. 'It may seem irrelevant, but I don't think it is. The three great monotheistic religions all study the Old Testament. All know the Book of Leviticus. It was probably written, or dictated, by Moses. In it we find for the first time in history the words: "Love thy neighbour as thyself," and "Do unto others as ye would they wouldst do unto thee." I say it in the ancient way, but it's perfectly understandable, isn't it?'

We're all looking at her, puzzled. She's closing her eyes, palms and fingers flat against one another, elbows resting on the worn table.

'As Jews, Christians and Muslims all meet in the Old Testament and know how to share these words, without shame or hesitation we can all think fraternally of Nicholas and pray for enlightenment. Where should we seek him? Let's be quiet for just two minutes...'

Some of us look up at the clock on the wall and then at one another. But not Sister Julian. We wait. This strange woman understands how to reach a decision by quietly unshackling the subconscious. Gaia used to talk about letting her mind float away and finding peace in a speck of sand.

Sister Julian breaks the silence.

'Where should we first start to look for Nicholas? Celia, what do you think?'

'Where Ross Mackenzie is.'

'Martha?'

'The same.'

'Roland?'

'He may have been moved somewhere else in the Quarry Hill property, even if Mackenzie isn't there and Helen can't find him.'

'Ezra?'

‘On his Argentinian estate.’

‘Lizzy?’

‘I agree with Ezra.’

I’m last. I hesitate, then,

‘Might Ross Mackenzie be in Africa and Nicholas with him?’

Martha again,

‘Maybe. But he usually goes to ground in one of his estates, here, in India or Argentina.’

‘Good,’ says Sister Julian. ‘We’re assuming he has Nicholas with him. Helen tells us that Mackenzie has left his Quarry Hill estate here.’

We all nod.

‘Right. Roland have you tracked him down?’

‘Yes, up to a point. Geomap lost him at our local airport. I’ve checked yesterday’s flight to South America and he wasn’t on the boarding list. He probably flew his helousine to the airport to catch it or another flight. He didn’t take this morning’s scheduled flight, either because it was fully booked. More likely, because he didn’t want to take a place in Nicholas’s name on either flight, thus leaving a trail for us.’

‘No further trace of Mackenzie?’ I ask anxiously.

‘No.’

‘He must have chartered a private plane,’ Martha says. ‘Geomap has some faint responses across the Atlantic, but there’s disturbance and the signal is poor. Chartered planes can, for security reasons, have a GWP licence allowing them to be screened from Geomap DNA detection.’

‘Any way of checking who has chartered a plane?’ I ask.

'It could be one belonging to a business associate,' Roland suggests, 'but it has to be at least 60% full according to GWP regulations. Who else might be on it? He could be flying to Africa, not South America. Or somewhere else. We could, with time, track it through the various files logged, but that's a job only done legally by the police to check criminal activities. We have no proof - yet.'

'Do we risk it, then, and send someone to South America?' I've never seen Sister Julian take over a meeting like this.

'I have an idea. 'Ezra is looking at her, fire in his eyes. 'I want to confront Ross Mackenzie. I need to see his reaction to my stump.' He stands up. 'I'll go there.'

* * * * *

6 January

And so he left. Ezra took the scheduled flight to South America the morning after our meeting in the refectory. Lizzy accompanied him. Martha had to go to Mybeki on business involving the offshoot Centre for Genetic Wellbeing. She would look for Nicholas there with Esther's help. I've set up a fund to cover expenses in the search for Nicholas. All of us have contributed some credits.

I now wonder whether Ezra and Lizzy should have gone. Sister Julian kept on looking at me and hinting that she and I are the only ones without emotional links to Nicholas or claims on Ross Mackenzie. I know what she means. Still, we have ties of friendship. His sister Martha and Roland are both GWP deputies and zone government members... Yes, I know what she wants me to do. Sister Julian could leave her domain to Celia and take off herself, except she is too conspicuous. She is gathering online followers worldwide, though she doesn't want to. Or so she says. She expected me to offer to go to South America, but I didn't. Should I have done?

Then Sister Julian spoke what I'd been thinking all along, but didn't say. 'Someone must co-ordinate Ezra and Lizzy's communications from Argentina and Martha's from Africa. They may need help. We must know what is happening and what we can do to help. A trusted person should gather their reports and transfer them to all of us. Magnus, could you do it? Agreed?'

What could I say?

* * * * *

At home in Newborough I have all the receptive areas in my cyber system on alert, but the only report I have received and circulated to the other investigators (as I shall call our group of seven), is from Lizzy. She voices that there is no record of any aircraft in the name of or associated with Ross Mackenzie or Nicholas at Buenos Aires airport. Nevertheless, she and Ezra are still trying to track Mackenzie's movements on Geomap and have touched down at Salta on an internal flight. This I can see is a remote northern region of dramatic mountain ranges with ragged rose-tipped outcrops and grey boulder-strewn riverbeds. The Geomap signals are bad and local people don't seem to know, or won't say, where Mackenzie's estate is located.

'We're no closer to Nicholas,' were her last words.

Here, while waiting, I have time to think. I've already called a Reaching Out conference. It'll be tonight. I've messaged that to Ezra and Lizzy.

'What about Helen?' Lizzy signals back. 'Ezra says somebody, he can't remember who, pointed out that she had stayed in Mackenzie's South American property. She must know where it is. We've tried messaging her but she isn't answering.'

Strange. Helen is usually prompt. I'll try her.

She is prompt. Hardly a minute later she tells me she can't recall the exact location because she was taken there in his local helousine. Has she taken stressless pills? She goes on and on about a kind of palace in the mountains, but that doesn't help them locate it in this vast region.

Here I am just sitting in a capsule surrounded by an array of technology that can't locate Nicholas, or even Mackenzie. I lean back on the sofa and, though I'm trying not to, doze off.

*****

I start and sit up.

My wordfree is throbbing. However tiny, Helen's image is unmistakable, though she has filled out a lot. Even if you can't make out features, her image glows with the auburn lights in her hair.

'Helen?'

'Magnus, I'm not well. I shouldn't see anyone because I'm part of a great experiment. Please, please let me know when you find Nicholas. I must, must see him. I love him...'

I used to confide in Gaia, and now people are confiding in me.

More throbbing, this time from Ezra.

'We have some leads to the mansion's location, but Geomap has not located Mackenzie in his Argentinian property. What should we do? I would like to stay in Salta until he is located, and then follow him. Lizzy wants to hire a 4 x 4 with a local driver to find the property. She thinks Nicholas might be there even if Mackenzie isn't. What shall we do?'

I'm right in the thick of decision making when all I offered to do was to co-ordinate communications and bring in Reaching Out, if relevant. This is getting out of hand. I voice back: 'Wait both of you for twenty minutes while I think and voice the other investigators. I'll forward Ezra's message verbatim and wait for responses.' Only a few seconds before they come:

Martha: I suspect Mackenzie has business in Africa. I have booked my flight there tomorrow.

Roland: Does Lizzy have news from Argentina?

Lizzy: Yes, I do. Argentinian mansion found. Shiny bright and empty. Searched every room followed by caretaker. Huge estate, much secrecy. Now back in Salta. Orders?'

Sister Julian: Eliminate all possibilities. Nicholas's life may be at risk. Try the mansion first.

Celia: Have you asked Esther if she has seen either of them in Mybeki?

Just like the World Referendum! 'Inconclusive' is the infuriating conclusion, precisely the enemy of action. It leaves me with the ultimate responsibility. So we're back as we were: unresolved, uncertain and with Nicholas, whereabouts unknown, at risk.

If he is still alive. I'm shivering and it isn't cold.

I've hived off into the Reserved Area of this blog all the latest Reaching Out conferences. There's much to be concerned about, not the least our loose structure. Safety from contamination, or so we hope. Three cells have been infiltrated and truncated. I fear mine might be next.

The Reaching Out conference button is flashing. I've posted, 'Find out if scientist Nicholas Middlethorpe is in Ross Mackenzie's property in South America.' There should be some response. Shilpa from India has taken over as chair from Zuami. She's looking out rather mournfully, her long face puckered in concern, unsettled fingers pulling and twisting her greying hair.

'Magnus, we've had an immediate response from Luisa in Argentina. I don't know if it helps. Luisa?'

'Here I am.' An olive face with oval eyes and long dark hair drawn under her chin. This must be Luisa. I haven't seen her before. 'Yes, Magnus, we have a cell up north, not far from Salta, and they've been watching Dom Ross Mackenzie. He has a vast estate there with an energy receptor in the grounds. There's also some sort of genetic-botanical activity inside the walled areas. Most of it is run by robots, but a caretaker lives there. Some specialist workers have access for a few hours every day. Is this any help?'

'Yes, yes it certainly is. Any sign of Ross Mackenzie and is there someone with him? A young scientist, Nicholas Middlethorpe?'

'They don't know. The helousine that belongs to the owner has flown in and out a number of times.'

'This is a huge help. I'll have to leave the conference. Please excuse me, Shilpa, and everyone for having called it. I must follow this up urgently. Thanks, Luisa, Shilpa, all of you.'

I fade them out. Too bad. I urgently voice Ezra and Lizzy with the crucial information Luisa has flashed out to me: the caretaker's DNA registration and the location co-ordinates for the magnate's palace, as they call it.

Ezra soon messages me that they are in the 4 x 4 heading north towards Peru, and I've forwarded all this to the investigators. Celia voices me. She can't understand why we haven't located Ross Mackenzie as he is DNA registered. Can Nicholas be with him? Who knows; we don't. I repeat that Nicholas is unDNAregistered. Celia's convinced Ross Mackenzie is going to Africa but is unwilling to trail him there, probably because of tension between them after she was called to his Quarry Hill property, and then ejected.

'Martha is about to leave for Africa, Celia. Nicholas had a lab there. It's where he carried out the crucial tests, as you know.'

I feel as if I'm in a tunnel and at the end, the opening, a voice is calling me to leave. I must follow it. Go. Now. It may never call again.

'Can you, Celia, co-ordinate all messages from Lizzy and Ezra, and soon me? Good, I'll relay that to the two in Argentina now. Reception will worsen when they reach the mountains.'

'Reception must be good in and around his mansion, Magnus, otherwise he would hardly have sited it there.'

'Correct.' It's obvious. I'm not practical like Celia.

I'll book my Mybeki flight now. Packing – just a change of clothes. The same as always – before the meteorstrophe. Before leaving I check everywhere for something missing. There it is – Gaia's stone.

BREAKING NEWS

UNTENANTED SATELLITE CAUSES CONCERN

The satellite leased from the Goodwill World Parliament, amid much concern expressed by some Goodwill World Parliament deputies, has been orbiting purposelessly now for some time because of the inconclusive result of the first ever **World Referendum**. It was called to decide whether the renowned global philanthroentrepreneur, **Dom Ross Mackenzie**, should relinquish his lease unless he agrees to publish in its entirety the core theory of his enterprise to supply the world with infinite energy at practically no cost. There has been a partial response from the magnate, offering world citizens a summarised description of his invention.

Reports from the latest session of GWP deputies reveal distress at the waste of this valuable satellite, to which the only reply from the **Office of Infinenergy** is:

'Dom Ross Mackenzie has already paid the GWP for his lease of the satellite, so he will keep control of it for the stated period.'

Dom Ross Mackenzie is en route, destination undeclared, and declines any further comment. His PR, **Helen Runciman**, is also unavailable.

Please send your comments to me, **Karen Middlethorpe**, at:

worldaroundyounews.com

35

Martha *i-witnessMAR727.futurepast.com*

7 January

Little often happens when much is expected but, in retrospect, that can be worthwhile. I'm thinking about it here on the Mybeki airjuggernaut. I'm safe with what I think into my wordfree as it's encrypted. No one can discover my thoughts for fifty years. That's a relief as I'm so upset, not knowing what has happened to Nicholas and where he is. In shock too about being here, horribly early in the morning, on this one destination juggernaut with Dom Ross Mackenzie. Normally he travels in his private aircraft, but he may have used all his current GWP airfuel allowance. Those men sitting inconspicuously obvious are bodyguards and the ones he's talking to must be fellow global entrepreneurs. One wonders what they are pursuing 'to benefit hukind', as Dom Ross would add by default. It may be the next marketable world asset - water? - of such crucial importance to us all. They must be watched.

I'll thoughtmessage this to Roland, Magnus and the others. They'll tell me to ask Ross where Nicholas is, but I can't confront him here on the airjuggernaut. In front of the others he'll only deny he knows anything. I'll have to get him alone, somehow, in Mybeki. If only Roland were with me, I'd get him to do it. Alone with Ross Mackenzie. Man to man.

'I'm worried too about Nicholas, and about Dom Ross retaining a monopoly over infinenergy after the inconclusive referendum result,' Roland said, stretched out last night on the bed. He looked tired, older than his years, his jaws slightly sagging and pockets under his eyes. He's middle-aging suddenly, I thought, and so am I, perhaps. I glanced at myself in the long mirror on the closet door; the woman in it looked insecure and faintly absurd. I'm only twenty-seven!

He's worried about Japan joining Australasia as a neutral country backing neither China nor North America and is concerned about the consequences. In the meantime, Dom Ross retains a monopoly over infinite energy for the world.

'What about Nicholas's share?'

Roland puts his hands over his face. 'I don't know. This could give Ross Mackenzie the power to blackmail. China and Russia are correct to say that all should have the right to know how infinenergy is created with full details of the projected revenue, cost and profit or loss. That will be difficult without Ross Mackenzie's co-operation. Nicholas would be caught in the web. Perhaps it's better for him that he's gone missing – temporarily.'

'No, Roland. I must, must find him.' I can't stop sobbing. 'Who is Dom Ross responsible to?'

'No one,' Roland said, 'as far as I can see. He's registered as a world citizen, has three residences that I know of and probably is taxed on those, while still avoiding any national domicile and consequently any taxation of his other accumulated wealth. Global businesspeople are all following suit to control vast swathes of the world economy with little or no accountability. Mackenzie puts 2% of his net profits into the GWP charitable fund, giving him the right to put GWP after his conglomerate, Global Enterprises. He estimates that, and his own charitable fund, will gag any protests.'

Roland is right. I see now why he was the unanimous choice to be the Goodwill Planet Supervisor for our zone, though I was, frankly, annoyed at being passed over, female discrimination and all that. He was still talking.

'Dom Ross protested that he had patented infinenergy, but I could find no evidence.'

'Is that because he has stolen it from Nicholas and we can't prove it?'

Nicholas seems to slip through this network of interests, financially and physically. I swallowed a stressless pill without him noticing. I had to do something to salvage these rare moments together. It worked. It wasn't the best of shared time, but good enough to think back on, warmly. And we did plan when we'll meet again. Our time in Experience Dreamland may have been disappointing, but it made me realise that I needed him.

We are landing. I hope Ross Mackenzie hasn't noticed me. I'll hang back. That won't be difficult as the plane is full. I could put on a sunhat and keep my head down. No, a hat always attracts attention.

Esther is behind the barrier waving at me. She's not the only one there, but all are turning to see who she's waiting to welcome. Out of the corner of my eye I note Dom Ross speaking to a sharply-dressed man beside him who also glances in my direction. Others turn their heads, enough to make me into a minor celebrity, so people ahead step aside to have a look and clear a way for me. Just my ill luck! Esther and I embrace before an audience of hundreds.

'Why has Dom Ross Mackenzie come?' I whisper. She hurries me away. 'Don't talk here.'

I have to ask Esther. 'Do you know what's happened to Nicholas? Where he is?'

'What's happened?' Esther stops to stare at me. 'How is he recovering from his fall? Is he still in hospital?'

It's complicated. I try to reassure her. 'I'll explain later, after we've finished our tour of the Centre for Genetic Wellbeing.'

Esther fills me in on the train to Mybeki. 'Rapid advances are being made towards the total eradication of AIDS, not just in Africa, arguably the worst hit continent, but worldwide -' this is some way from what she was funded to research in Nicholas's lab, but no matter, '– the unique factor being my people's immunity to AIDS. Maybe some forms of cancer too. This has led...' Anything to do with disease gets priority funding. I'm impressed, I admit, by what's being accomplished, but can't pretend I'm not still upset, even angry, at the way she lured some key research away from my zone to hers in Africa. All because of her tribe.

We're in white overalls now and touring the various labs, more than I can remember back home. I mustn't complain. They have received a massive donation. I should be happy for them. I also need to find out the role of the so-called 'Main Office' of the original Centre for Genetic Wellbeing in my zone. It's all becoming so complex.

As far as she knows, Nicholas hasn't returned to Africa. She's concerned about the fate of his lab in the Zuetoland near Mybeki. Ross Mackenzie must have removed him from the hospital with a made-up assertion - being Nicholas's relative or guardian. But now Dom Ross is here and there's no sign of my brother. Helen has messaged me to say he isn't at

Quarry Hill. Has Nicholas returned to check his calculations for the beam's angle which, he said, is crucial for safety reasons. Esther is speaking to me.

'Didn't she tell you, Martha, that she's coming here?'

'Who?'

'Your mother. Karen.'

I'm annoyed. Angry even. Have I missed her on my wordfree? I triple task through the text, voice and thought messages. Nothing. Why doesn't she tell me what she's doing and where she is?

'Let's go and eat somewhere so we can catch up with everything,' Esther says, taking my arm. 'You must be tired and hungry.' I feel too sick to eat, too exhausted to protest.

She's reassuringly normal. As we walk through the streets I note they've changed from the detailed description Nicholas gave me. There is now a cocktail of skin tones. So many have come from all over to work, study or trade, not just because of the GWP peace settlement after the devastating tribal wars, but also because of the unique medical research being carried out here. I miss the thrill of meeting street traders, their chatter, chants and curses; their colourful local costumes and the humdrum variety of a different culture. To be honest, I expected more glances in my direction, though I still get some because I'm quite tall with naturally blond hair.

'Where are the street traders, Esther? Nicholas talked a lot about them. He was fascinated by them.'

'They're in the new covered market. I'll take you there after lunch, if we have time. It was built recently so that the main street could be cleared and paved for sanitary reasons. Only domestic animals are allowed. Even animals and poultry have their hygienically designated area.'

No cows, donkeys or mules in a colourful street mayhem, nor the occasional prized horse. What would Nicholas's admired Zueto chief Walanka look like in shirt and trousers? Fine, I imagine, if that's his choice. Deep in muddled thought, I sit through lunch in a cafe-hub half mesmerised by Esther telling me all about her family, her tribe's great gift to medicine, and so on, and so on... It seems it's because hukind first emerged in this part of Africa.

'Is anything left of Nicholas's laboratory?' Esther orders food for both of us before answering. 'It may have been incorporated into the Mybeki Centre for Genetic Wellbeing, but to be honest, I'm not sure. It's becoming difficult to know what's happening with this contemporary capsule architecture. It's so easy to incorporate new capsules into another structure. I thought you were involved in all that?' She's looking at me suspiciously.

I need rest after an early morning flight; time to gather my thoughts. I was so worried about Nicholas that I forgot to ask Jan to find me somewhere to sleep, assuming it would be easy in Mybeki to step into a simple lodging house for a couple of nights. Now I'm not so sure.

Esther hasn't mentioned what Raphael is doing in the Middle East Alliance, though they worked together for at least two years in Nicholas's lab. Still, she does have a huge project to manage here, not just the new research centre but, it seems, she has taken on the whole of Mybeki and its future in the Peace Zone. Predictably, she's on the local council, or Mybeki Community Action Group as they prefer to call it, and so is Chief Walanka.

'Stay with me,' Esther says without hesitation. I shouldn't have asked her to recommend a hotel. 'There's always room. We just double up.' I feel even more tired at the thought of sharing a room, let alone a bed. Other insomniacs will understand me. I need to be able to roam at night, find a light to read, a place to try and settle my thoughts.

*****

I'm lying gratefully on a low rug-covered bed in a small room with hardly enough space for me and my travel bag. The walls are of bark and twigs twisted into an attractive pattern. They block sight, not sound, but I always travel with earplugs. Esther has a partner who is trilingual – there are two tribal languages here – and does something to do with agriculture ... ploughing, or something ...lots of nephews and nieces, all friendly and curious ...no doors, but curtains instead which they hitch up... over their necks ... look in and giggle...

Awake, I'm staring at a woman sitting in the half light at the end of my bed. Who is she? She's not from these parts. Looks vaguely oriental.

'Martha, are you awake?' I know that voice. 'What are you doing here?'

'Why are **you** here, mother, is the question.'

'You never told me you were leaving for Africa, Martha. The last I heard was of some conference, an update on sales of capsules and that Nicholas was convalescing at Quarry Hill.'

I'm completely awake now. I was too upset about Nicholas to explain my sudden flight to Africa. She's right. There's no excuse, as there is with Eliza, not to be in touch with my mother who is fully enwebbed. However, she's the one who has changed since I let her go to China with the Leonardo painting. More guarded. Less forthright. Not outwardly hostile, but...

'Why are you here, Mother?'

She's moving a bit uneasily. 'Have you rested enough? I'd prefer to talk in the open.'

It's strange to find a mother one hardly recognises. She was always tall like a column, just the opposite of Eliza's rounded figure, now more padded in spite of her fixation with the vegetable patch. But mother's face has changed. To take out the sags, her eyes have become narrower and her cheekbones more prominent. She doesn't look like herself, younger, but like a nondescript, vaguely Chinese woman of uncertain age. It all amounts to sad self-delusion.

* * * * *

'Is there sympathetic business penetration in Mybeki?' Mother says. 'Seeing Ross Mackenzie with the others makes me cautious.'

'Why?'

'Because I'm with a Chinese delegation looking at the minerals deep in the meteorstrophe crater. We're also here in connection with the Mybeki Centre for Genetic Wellbeing.'

We've both rested, she in her hotel, me with Esther. She's explaining all this but I'm only half listening as we're walking across the plateau. It's calm, beautiful in a stark way, wild and unfertile. The crater is marked by the jagged rocks thrown up on the edge nearest us. An avalanche of pebbles reaches into the depths untouched by the sun.

'It's mysterious,' mother is saying, 'full of possibilities.'

We pause at a mound of stones with a faded photo near the top. Nicholas – he must be somewhere here? - told me about this. This person was killed in the disaster. A woman connected with Magnus, I think, and with Celia. Others have been here and rearranged the stones in a star-like shape at the base. Celia asked me to bring two stones from the cairn back with me without explaining why. I choose two distinctive examples - one, blue veined and egg shaped, the other round and brown with pink streaks - careful not to disturb the star pattern.

'We must return before dark,' I remind mother, surprised that she hasn't really told me anything. Dusk gallops down from the mountains edging the plain, Esther warned me. There's already a tremor in the afternoon breeze.

'Yes,' she says, 'but I have to tell you about Leda.'

'The painting?'

'No, the story.' Of Leda herself?

'Go on,' I say. We're both adults now. I can be impatient with her.

'You know that I found an ancient Chinese legend that predates the Graeco-Roman one?'

There's a grating edge to her voice that I haven't noticed before.

'Yes'

'I told you this, remember? I obtained a vast sum from China for our zone government in exchange for the loan of Leonardo's Leda and the Swan. I accompanied the painting to Beijing to save the zone government transport and security costs. You assured me it was Leonardo's original work, the one Sister Julian exchanged for the old university buildings.'

We are now striding back, evening unrolling behind us and the last rays striking the high walls of the Mybeki Centre and lightly brushing the roofs of the town's single storey buildings around it. I can't make out her expression.

'Yes, that's what happened.'

She's coming closer now, her eyes like searchlights. I guess what she's up to but won't play along with her anymore.

'Is that all you have to say?'

'Yes,' I say. She'd better hurry if she wants to vent more of her repressed anger as we'll be in Mybeki soon.

'You sent me to China with a copy. You lied. I could report you for obtaining money through fraudulent means. You...' and on she goes, releasing all her fury. That will clear the air all right. I should have seen this coming. When she pauses, I'll explain it all.

'You could say it's a studio work,' I start off. 'One can't tell the difference even right up close. You see, nobody in China noticed anything.'

'That's not the point. It was subsequently announced on *worldaroundyounews* that the original had been deposited in the Art Cavern. I'm not going to be tricked by my daughter – '

'I'm not tricking you. Mum must have told you that painters can have two patrons wanting the same work. This happened with Leonardo's Virgin of the Rocks. One used to be in London, probably painted later with studio help, so experts say; the other was in Paris. Both contain Leonardo's brushstrokes. So?'

'So Leonardo did two versions of Leda and the Swan?'

'Yes. In fact, yes...his studio helped.'

'With the one I took to Chine? The painting that turned up in an obscure collection somewhere? So it's not the one found at St. Thomas's, the one that was taken to the Art Cavern?'

I had better remind her of what happened because she seems to have forgotten the circumstances.

'Yes, if not actually the first version, it is identical. Experts agree that Leonardo painted Leda's head, and probably her hands, while his assistants completed it.'

We're in the outskirts of Mybeki now. She's shouting. So much for her desire for secrecy.

'A fraud. A con-trick carried out on your own mother. It's as bad as matricide...'

'Mother, calm down. You know that our Universal Legal System requires every original work to be placed in the Art Cavern, so it's inevitable that compromises have to be made.'

'Maybe. But the amount paid by the Chinese government was for the original. Got it?' She's almost spitting now.

'I'm certain I told you how it was at the time. It is a great success in China, so it is fulfilling its purpose.'

'But they've been told it was the original.' She's going on and on. 'They were admiring, on trust, Leonardo's own handiwork. They could imagine him there creating it while they looked and experienced it - I don't know how else to put it.' She's uneasy, trying to explain all that stuff about the artist's aura not being in a studio version.

'Think of pilgrims in the past, Mother. Think of them going to the place where a revered person has lived or a world-shaking event has taken place. If they believe and honestly feel there is spiritual or intellectual fulfilment, or better, both, does it matter whether the relics are there or not, or are even fakes? Does it really matter when the pilgrims' emotions are sincere?'

'I'm not going to argue this.' She's backing away. 'You're too obstinate.' It's my fault, as usual. 'You must return the money gained through false pretences, and I'll return the copy.'

'Sorry Mother.' I'm walking rapidly towards Esther's house and she's following me. 'It's not a copy; it's a studio work. As I said, most think Leonardo painted the head and hands. Deal done, case closed.'

I fear it isn't from the way she's edging right up to me.

'Why's the painting so important to you, mother?' There must be a subtext. We stand silent outside Esther's house listening to her shouting into her wordfree.

'All right! All right! I'll come. It's inconvenient but I'll come. I do have family commitments, you know, and friends staying...' Esther bursts into the street almost bumping into us.

'Oh Martha, I didn't know you were back! Please come with me. Ross Mackenzie is available at long last. I've been trying to see him since he arrived. It's urgent. He's here, I hope, because I've been messaging him to come.'

She's off down the street, still speaking. I follow her and mother follows me. I don't know why Esther wants me to accompany her, but I'm curious. We're to meet Ross Mackenzie at the Centre for Genetic Wellbeing, though it must be closed by now, after sunset. Odd. We could go to one of the new hotels, perhaps the one Ross Mackenzie is using. Now's my chance to ask him about Nicholas.

The Centre is still open. As we enter the lobby, Dom Ross and five others leap to their feet and approach us, hands out. Esther ignores the greeting.

'You arrived early this morning and haven't even bothered to make an appointment to see me.'

'Dear Madam, I am now completely at your disposal, with five of my colleagues.' Dom Ross's silky voice exuding calm reassurance stops her in her tracks. He's smiling, offering his hand again, so she can't really avoid shaking it, and so do we.

'What about –?' I stop. Esther had better ask her questions first.

'There are too many of you. We can't talk in my office.'

'What's wrong with this lobby?' Dom Ross asks amiably. Everything, I think. Easy to overhear what we say. There are security cameras so probably internet probes as well. After all, this is a world centre for high-powered medical research, independent but closely watched by pharmaceutical companies worldwide. I suspect some of his colleagues represent their interests. Esther must know this.

The receptionist and porters have gone home, so Esther and I fetch chairs to circle the low table in front of three armchairs. Infuriating how the men – and mother – stand and wait. Esther is waved towards the armchair in the centre. She sits and looks around unsmilingly at the gathered company.

I'd like to edge away, become more peripheral, but she points me towards a chair, completely ignoring mother.

'I suppose I had better begin.' Esther pauses to select her words, her approach. 'You, Dom Ross, informed me to say that you had invented a way to solve the energy shortage in this area. Correct?'

He smiles and nods affably. I bristle – using Nicholas's invention?

'Yes, and we have already established an energy receptor here for the whole area, as promised.' Esther laughs, impolitely.

'Indeed. But it doesn't work. Is this really your invention? I've been working with Dr. Middlethorpe and wondering whether your receptor is connected to his infinenergy.'

'Well, I'm partly financing it. These are only temporary problems. Beam direction. Easily resolved. Almost inevitable with such an ingenious solution to the worldwide energy shortage. My scientists are coming soon to incorporate the lab that Dr. Middlethorpe used into our exciting new buildings here. But I have something else, an offer from all here with me to – '

As I look at Esther I can't help thinking of the legendary basilisk, emitting fire from its mouth. I feel precisely the same. Nicholas's lab is to be handed over, just like that!

'Oh yes!' Esther says, 'and we are left relying on our back-up generators. You know full well what will happen to our laboratories if the electric current falters. Not just blackout, but numerous trials will be aborted. We must have a constant electricity supply. We moved here to be close to our trial area for the AIDS vaccine, but only on your assurance –'she's thumping the arm of her chair '- that the energy supply would be forthcoming. Now look what's happening! Already two important experiments have been destroyed. They'll have to be restarted from scratch.' She pauses. 'And Dr. Middlethorpe's lab is my responsibility. Where is he?'

The other entrepreneurs are looking at Dom Ross, who is unperturbed and will, I expect, resolve this problem in his usual way: throwing money at it. If only I could do the same!

'We are already diverting funds to tide you over this immediate setback. In addition, we have another unbeatable offer to make for this centre, Esther – may I call you Esther?'

'Whatever, Ross, but we have all we need, thank you.'

A slight frown. A crack in his composure. Few refuse an offer without strings attached, or so it seems. Dom Ross isn't used to it. I don't know why mother is thinking her reactions into her wordfree. The battle of words continues between Esther and Ross without a resolution. Maybe it's because something has gone wrong with the whole infinenergy satellite project after the referendum. Does Nicholas know about this? Or is it a question of ownership? Our zone government too has lost its way over the status of this offshoot research centre.

Mother is standing up to excuse herself. She has to leave; it's already late. Esther and Dom Ross are still trying to work out a compromise. She asks him again about Nicholas. Dom Ross just repeats that he has no idea where he is. His colleagues are stirring uneasily. Mention is made of some new development in water technology which seems beside the point. As I get up to follow mother, Dom Ross raises his reassuring tone a few notches to say,

'Deputy Middlethorpe, I have something to suggest that may interest you.' Now's my chance -

'Dom Ross,' I'm almost shouting, 'If Nicholas is no longer at Quarry Hill, where is he?'

Mother stares at him, opening her mouth, but he has already turned to join the other magnates and leave with them. She hurries after them saying over her shoulder, 'Martha, I'll be in touch. Voice me immediately you hear anything about Nicholas and I'll do the same.' The door swings her out after them into the dusk leaving Esther and me looking silently at each other.

NEWS BULLETIN

ASTOUNDING NEW ENTERPRISE IN AFRICA

Worldaroundyounews returns with a new format linked to the website ***intoit*** which was chosen to organise and support the first ever world referendum. We continue with 90% of the former team.
I'm **Karen Middlethorpe**, from our global reporting team. Today we feature a new world-class enterprise in Africa. Let **Chang Lin, China's president**, update you.
'Hi, world friends! I am Chang Lin, President of China and a driving force behind efforts to save life and conquer disease. We are putting money into a **world-beating enterprise in Africa to eliminate AIDS** and to test and create medicines that will cure or alleviate the great killers of hukind,

beginning with cancer. You will be hearing more from **Esther**, who heads the new **Mybeki Centre for Genetic Wellbeing**, to be renamed the **Leda and the Swan Foundation for World Health**. May I introduce Esther? Here she is.'

'Thank you, President, for –'

'Please call me Lin.'

'Yes, Lin. Thank you for funding the expansion of the unique research we are carrying on here in my –'

'Africa.'

'Yes, Africa, for the conquest of disease –'

'Thank you Esther. I must leave you all to follow my crowded schedule. Citizens of the World, the future is yours!'

worldaroundyounews.com

36

Magnus *i-witnessMAG931futurepast.com*

8 January

'There's water down there.'

I thought I was alone; I wanted to be alone with Gaia; by her cairn looking down into the gash in the earth's skin where she lies buried. Alone, but with her. To write a poem to her in deep red across the sunset, words dodging between bats darting out and over the chasm.

'There's water down there,' came that voice again, too close behind my shoulders. 'It's not dry like the scorched land around us.'

I wasn't frightened. I recognised the voice. Ominous. I turned, deliberately slowly, saying,

'And what, by chance, brings you here, Dom Ross?' though he did nothing by chance. It may be because I wanted his words to reveal cracks in his suave demeanour that I noted the dust on his neatly pressed safari suit – never shorts; trousers are more dignified. They hide knobbly knees. More lines forming round his lips curled his habitual smile almost into a grimace. Five out of ten for trying hard, I thought, but not good enough.

'Business, I'm afraid. This is not the sort of place one would choose for pleasure.'

'Hardly.' Would he be tempted to fill the silence? To say something about Nicholas? He continued looking down into the gully, tossing stones experimentally, I supposed, in every direction. I winced when he hit the cairn, though he didn't seem to notice it. There was a touch of violence in his movements. Or even anger?

'Something amiss?' Not wrong. Things don't go wrong for Dom Ross Mackenzie. There would only be some minor difficulty, soon to be resolved by throwing brains and money at it. Time no problem.

Except for his satellite.

'I'm fine.' I would tease what it is out of him. He'd reveal something about Nicholas without realising it. Silence, so I continued,

'Strange, this gully.' He nodded. 'So many geologists, scientists of all sorts, palaeontologists and all the "ists" imaginable have come here, and still they disagree over what the meteorstrophe has revealed.' I paused. 'Is your receptor ready for the energy beam trial?' No response. 'I hope not. If the beam misses the receptor, it could devastate even a sparsely-populated area like this.' A slight repeat of the nodding. 'I'm only an artist by training -' no reaction from him, '- and a dancer, but surely analysis of the rocks should have already revealed what there is of value?'

'Not when there's an ownership dispute. Or something more sinister.'

'Well, yes.' I hoped he would say more, but he was turning away. Now. Ask now.

'What's happened to Nicholas? Where is he?'

'Why should I know? I helped him convalesce and then left him to his own devices. He may have wanted to return to his lab here. I'm going back to Mybeki.' And he strode off. Two figures that had been standing apart discreetly followed him.

* * * * *

I'm staying in the same bungalow. The Zueto people are in a new village that Gaia never saw. Celia did. They both told me that the tribe moves on about every two years after exhausting the land and water. Chief Walanka appears less imposing in his new multipocket jacket and trousers that zip on and off below the knee. He looks efficient but ordinary. For the first time I find him seated on a white plastic chair, offering another to me. I had been scouted. He is expecting me.

But there is no Gaia, of course, nor Celia. Martha group-messaged us yesterday to say that Ross Mackenzie was on the same airjuggernaut, but no sign of Nicholas. My knowledge of the Babel language is limited to a smattering of the glyphics, not the spoken words, and the chief's command of English is, well, limited. He knows less Babel than I do.

'Man here,' he begins.

That must be Mackenzie. 'One or two?' Is Nicholas with him?

He frowns and looks around him.

'Man calls,' and he beckons two of the villagers standing in a wide arc observing us. A young man and woman come and bow to me before returning to their places in the audience. The rest of his words are in their language, his words echoed by the crowd, increasingly excited. Here I am, isolated on my linguistic island in just the situation that should not exist, in theory. The Goodwill World Parliament has decreed that Babel is to be taught to everyone as the world's spoken and written glyphic language belonging to all, monopolised by none.

* * * * *

So with sign gestures and, 'Please come to Mybeki,' Chief Walanka agreed to meet Esther, who can understand us both, at the Leda and the Swan Foundation. Though I thought-messaged her to say we're coming, he and I are left sitting here silently watching the to-ing and fro-ing in the lobby of the former Mybeki branch of Martha's Centre for Genetic Wellbeing. Some world briefing is taking place and Esther's in the midst of it all. In spite of being harassed, she never looks anxious, as Celia does. Her rounded contours and short wiry hair maintain an appearance of cool without even a hint of a smile, just a firm expression of concern.

She comes over to welcome us and bows to the Chief, saying a few words in his language before beckoning us to follow her outside. No listening apparatus here, just empty parked vehicles, people hurrying in and out of the main doors and the three of us standing apart. The Chief speaks and gesticulates, while Esther shakes her head and tries to break the flow of words.

'Magnus, is your wordfree on stand-by?'

'Yes.' It has been all along.

'Mine is too. None of what I tell you must enter your spoken or thought record. Right?'

'Yes.' What I think into my blog is encrypted so no one can access it for at least fifty years.

The Chief grasps Esther's arm, throwing words at her. She gasps. Ross Mackenzie is trying to buy two members of his people, a young man and woman.

'Buy?' I snap out.

'The wrong word.' Esther wipes her forehead and looks round for some shade.

'To pay for them to study, the Chief says. That would be at a school or in the Greystone University Language School near the Xiang Lu Institute, wherever, but only on condition that they agree to provide blood and other unspecified samples for Ross Mackenzie's scientists.'

Now I understand why Chief Walanka refused, although the two young people singled out clearly wanted to take up this offer of free education. They were, if not angry, displeased.

Esther pauses to look anxiously around the parking lot where nothing is happening.

'Listen, Magnus,' she says with urgency. 'Too much is changing here in the Foundation. Martha came, sent by the principal Centre for Genetic Wellbeing to find out what is happening to its offshoot. Without any warning, deliberately I think, Ross Mackenzie returned with other magnates and barged into my office this morning with a fantastic offer to buy out the Centre – sorry, the Leda and the Swan Foundation! Coming so soon after the Chinese takeover, and that was tough enough with Martha and our zone government here initially opposing it, I was worn down to muttering, "No, not now," fearful that the Chinese government might create legal mayhem. There are no secrets now. Eavesdropping is normal. Then, while Dom Ross was in my office – you won't believe this – Nicholas opened the door as if on cue. He looked odd, didn't even greet me – not the way he used to behave – and asked what had happened to his lab. Ross Mackenzie must have known he was here as he didn't acknowledge him or show any surprise. At some point Dom Ross pointed out that he was paying for Joe's studies at the Academy for Geniuses, or something like that.'

'"At least he's safe there! You can't use him for your experiments," Nicholas almost growled at Dom Ross, adding, "don't you dare touch Joe!" and walked out of my office.'

'Where did he go, Esther?'

'Ross Mackenzie jumped up to follow him, but Nicholas knows where the fire escape is and flitted round the parked cars into the web of alleys off the main street. He lay in wait for me when I left the office and begged me to lend him some money. I did, asking, "What d'you want it for?" "To disappear," he said, "after I've checked my lab." I showed him where his capsule is and he searched the computers. His lab capsule is now part of this Foundation so it can benefit from our security and, such as it is, the electricity supply. Things might improve when Dom Ross directs the satellite beam on to his receptor here in the desert. Nicholas seems terrified of this happening, and that makes me think that Ross Mackenzie's version of infinenergy may be incomplete and possibly dangerous. I don't think Nicholas found what he was looking for. I offered him a bed for the night, a meal, and to get his ticket for wherever. All he took was the money. I feared Ross might be paying someone to follow him. No one emerged from the shadows when he slipped into a side street and vanished. To the airport, I expect.'

Back here in Mybeki for the first time since the meteorstrophe, in this bungalow without Gaia, I'm trying to straighten out my thoughts, deal with my consternation and organise a brief message to the others: 'Esther has met

Nicholas in Mybeki but he has disappeared again. Ross Mackenzie still in Mybeki. So is Martha. Magnus.'

NEWS BULLETIN

BRAVE NEW DISCOVERIES ENHANCE HUKIND'S HAPPINESS

Before describing this life-enhancing scientific discovery, I must stress that in theory it was well known in Antiquity, not only through the **Greek story of Leda, wife of Tyndareus, King of Sparta**, but in an ancient **Chinese legend** that must have travelled to Greece along the trade routes from Asia to the West. In common to both legends **Zeus,** or the most powerful god in whichever pantheon, took the form of a swan to seduce **Leda**. She gave birth to – laid – two eggs, each with twins: **Helen and Clytemnestra**, epitomising strife, and **Castor and Pollex**, who, though male, came to symbolise concord. There are variants, but this dominant theme was depicted in paintings by **Michelangelo** and **Leonardo**, both lost until the recent discovery of Leonardo's studio version, now touring China to great acclaim.

So what is this new discovery made at the **Leda and the Swan Foundation for World Health in Africa**? Following closely on the recent announcement of a forthcoming pill to prevent some forms of cancer from research using a group of people who are genetically resistant, comes the creation of human stem cells by 3-D printers and the exploration of stem cells from different birds and animals to benefit hukind. An end result will be a vital store of spare organs for any of ours damaged by accident or disease.

Foretold in Antiquity, only now, through prodigious leaps forward in biochemistry, the neurosciences and genetic research on different species do we have the future in our hands, and it is smiling at us.

I, **Karen Middlethorpe**, am proud to have found the Chinese legend of the Lady, or Leda, and the swan that gave the Greeks their legend and to us all the premonition of this health-and-happiness creating discovery. All is now possible.

worldaroundyounews.com

BREAKING NEWS

POTENTIAL CANCER CURE

The director of the new Leda and the Swan Foundation for World Health would like to speak to us from Africa. Esther, please tell us what is happening.

'Thank you, Karen. As you have heard, my name is Esther and I was born in the Zue-, in an African community, but have had a worldwide education culminating in a fellowship to work in a famous laboratory at the **Xiang Lu Research Institute, Greystone University**. Here in the **Leda and the Swan Foundation, a world leader in immunology, cancer research and organ creation and replacement surgery**, we are about to announce a way to prevent the formation of cancerous cells, in particular for those who have a genetic predisposition.'

Esther, this is great news. We look forward to the official announcement. Now to another fantastic piece of scientific news. Laboratories near **Jerusalem, the capital of the Middle East Alliance**, have been experimenting with ways to store energy and to convey it over continents to provide a worldwide supply network. Ongoing experiments are furnishing exciting results. Here too we await outcomes.

Artistically, much is happening. In spite of complaints on the website *www.moanersandgroaners.com,* the **World Virtual Masterpieces Museum** and **Artipedia** are proving so popular that the system is at risk of collapse through overload. The Director, however, is upbeat. Let him explain:

'The Virtual Masterpieces Museum that I founded only a few months ago, proves that there is a demand worldwide for art to be thoughtavailable to all. Gone are the days when individuals or groups travelled to contemplate these masterpieces in museums or the places where they were created. That was a luxury for the few. The Virtual Masterpieces Museum is a right for all. The masterpieces that must still remain perilously *in situ*, such as the **Sistine Chapel**, **Caves of Lascaux** or the decorated **Etruscan tomb chambers**, are being reproduced so that visitors can have an identical experience near the originals which are sealed and preserved forever.

'Similarly, Artipedia is now available to all, translated into every language recognised by the **Goodwill World Parliament**, though in twenty years' time it will be only available in the **universal language of Babel glyphics**. That is when it is estimated Babel will be read, if not spoken, by every member of hukind, saving space, time and money.

All great works of art that can be transported are now preserved forever in the **Repository of the Originals in the Art Cavern**. Art Now exhibitions of contemporary art are being mounted in museums worldwide. They can be seen without any barriers, and in the case of sculpture, handled to provide physical delight, all with Babel glyphic subtitles and explanations. Look at this show in my museum. Here are, for example, original works on paper donated by a local artist, Magnus, who recorded our historic city before demolition started to make way for modernisation. Online, all can experience the new installation that the artist known as **Lizzybizzy** is creating in the **Sinai Desert**, inspired by the mysterious **South American Nazca Lines** to –'

Thank you, director. I am **Karen Middlethorpe** and will return with our next news bulletin in two hours' time. Enjoy your afternoon.

worldaroundyounews.com

37

– 1 –

Nicholas i-*witnessNIC227futurepast.com*

January 8

I can calm down now. Think quietly. Work out what to do.

I bought a stand-by ticket for the first airjuggernaut to leave Mybeki. Destination Jerusalem. To find Raphael. We're in flight and I'm thinking into my wordfree. Once mum said something like, 'There's a divinity that shapes our ends, rough hew them how we will.' Or quoted it. And we discussed the idea. Fate or providence or a divine power, as Sister Julian says, has destined me to escape to Jerusalem.

Escape. Yes, that's the right word. Deep down, I'm fearful. Ross sent me to Mybeki with the promise to pay for a re-run of my final calculations on the lost datadrive. He even transferred my lab capsule to the Mybeki Centre for Genetic Wellbeing, just before it was taken over by China and renamed the Leda and the Swan Foundation for World Health. He now wants to buy the Foundation. Why did I let him persuade me to return to Mybeki? The calculations had to be re-run. The GWP satellite with my payload is still in orbit and I know how to access it – I think. But that power-crazed fool, who is supposed to be a scientist, had my lab linked to the research labs in Mybeki to save energy! Absurd – and potentially dangerous. I'm terrified. Ross will load infinenergy on to the GWP satellite he has leased. He now thinks his scientists' calculations based on what they have found out about mine, are accurate! They are not. Lives could be lost if my calculations are a trillionth of a centimetre out and the beam misses the receptor.

Why no sound from Raphael? He was supposed to be funding research into batteries. Storage for excess energy created, to use when needed. Wherever. I've passed him all my research on energy storage. What's happening? We were working together on it at the Institute.

My memory is returning. Fits and starts. The thunder of water. Falling. I'm shuddering. No help for what I need to remember – useless fragments that don't fit. Helen's hair spilling over her shoulders. Small enclosed rooms. People fussing round me. Someone stroking my hand. Stumbling away somewhere. A helousine. The meteorstrophe's crater.

My name is on the last available passenger list, so if Mackenzie is searching for me now, at this very moment, will he find it? That megalomaniac might imagine I'm fleeing to Jerusalem, the nerve-centre of the Middle East Alliance. That's where Raphael lives and works. He described it to Esther and me when we were together in my lab at the Institute. It seems so long ago. His Energy Research Centre is in a science and technology park. It fuses talent from Israel, Palestine, Lebanon, Jordan and Syria – all of them. It's just outside the open city of Jerusalem straddling the area where there was once a partition wall. Occasionally, he said, one met Arab pensioners who recounted stories from the bad old days when the wall separated them from their fields. Now all has changed. Irrigation is transforming agriculture. Only the desert or rocky areas can be built over.

Raphael. He might help me remember those passwords. The key to my final calculations.

*****

I think I dozed off. We've landed in Jerusalem. I must find the science and technology park. Information. Easy. The North-East circular coach times flicker across the airport infostrip. Second stop. It's near the airport. All seems to be an industrial area, well sited for communications. Hills lie grey on the horizon.

Stops flicker across the screen above the driver's head. Here it is: Science and Technology Park.

It should be easy to find Raphael as he's... what did he tell us he was setting up? An institute. Linked to our joint research. A, yes, Solar Research Unit. Or centre. Or was it 'Energy Research' something-or-other? And what's his surname? Did I ever know it? I must have done.

I'll ask someone who got off with me. 'Sir, d'you –? 'He points at the information kiosk. Need I have worried? There's a wall screen with lists of institutions, maps and buttons.

*****

It didn't take long to find Raphael's lab. Or to catch up with everything. I couldn't remember enough, but he understood most of what had happened. Esther must have kept in touch. The familiar Raphael is here. At this crucial moment.

'Have you brought it, Nicholas?'

'What?'

'Your final calculations? The accurate angle of the energy beam. The ones you were working on. You were going to send them to me on an updated datadrive.' Oh, yes. No, I've lost the datadrive. Can't find it. Nobody can. Lost.

'You mean the latest datadrive, the final calculations? Not the one sent back from Africa for you, Raphael?'

He sighs. I must be infuriating. I would be to myself, if I had the energy.

'Yes. Precisely that one. You said you would let me have the latest version after your crucial tests in Africa. Before that, Helen left a database for me in the Institute lab. I still have it.' He's repeating everything while looking at me reproachfully. 'Nicholas, you messaged to say that you had revised the precise angle of the beam and would let me have the accurate calculations. They never came.'

Those warm brown eyes. He seems older than me though I thought we were about the same age. He may be older. Esther is. I am living in a state of confusion.

'You were worried that someone,' Raphael moves his chair closer, 'someone might be trying to steal your idea, patent it before you did. So I tried to find it online, to see if you had stored it away somewhere. You know how it is, nothing is secret. I messaged you but your wordfree didn't respond. Your African lab had moved to Mybeki. I was trying to protect your, our, great project from theft and supervise this research centre here in Jerusalem at the same time.'

He's looking at me strangely. Worried. Why?

'I know you don't have a wrist wordfree, Nicholas, but you could perhaps have stored those calculations on your wordfree monitor. Did you?'

'I just don't know. Can't remember. I don't think I did. Too dangerous.'

'Nicholas, you look distraught. Grey-faced - no, I mean tired...'

Am I distraught?

'We'll go out for a meal now. There's a small restaurant near my home. I'll message Ellie that you're coming, but it'll be a bit too noisy near bedtime for you to eat at home. She'll get the mini-guest-capsule ready for you. It's well insulated so you won't hear the children. We can start probing your wordfree tomorrow. If the calculations aren't there, we'll try the Institute's datasafe and the Goodwill World Parliament's cyberstore to see if your final calculations were put into a cybersafe. Don't worry.'

Say 'don't worry' and I become more agitated than ever. I should be doing something other than eating and sleeping. My life's work is lost. The final result is on the datadrive I had round my neck. It has disappeared. I didn't copy it on to my wordfree or the hard drive in my lab. Someone tried to steal it. And I've lost it! Gone forever. My mind's in shreds. There's a dark hole. Something missing. Someone too. Someone I care about - I can't recall who.

– 2 –

Magnus *i-witnessMAG931futurepast.com*

Newborough, 10 January

I'm contemplating the stone left here on the table in front of the settee. Still dazed in rainbow-coloured angles after my return from Africa. Why is it here? One from Gaia's cairn is by her picture beside my bed. Perhaps this one should be there as well? Somehow it doesn't make sense. Is this stone for Nicholas? Or for Joe? No, for Joe. I remember now. Martha brought it back from Mybeki and left it here for him. Why should she think I was seeing Joe?

I'm even more muddled by the Reaching Out conference call to start about now. I posted a question, then forgot I had done so. Ana from Chile is the current chair.

Ana: 'Can you tell us what the issue is, Magnus? Are we all ready?'

I still find it unnerving to watch my own image shoot out from so many others and zoom into the full slot while Ana fades back into a small clip, hardly larger than an icon.

Magnus: 'I am concerned about the donation made anonymously to Reaching Out many years ago which subsequently paid for a state-of-the-science lab custom-built for Dr. Nicholas Middlethorpe in Africa to test his keynote research at Greystone University. The lab was transferred, without the scientist's permission, to the Mybeki Centre for Genetic Wellbeing. Now that this Centre has been sold to the Chinese and renamed the Leda and the Swan Foundation for World Health, has the lab donation been returned to Reaching Out?'

Ana: 'Does anyone know?'

Beth: 'Obvious. Ask for the latest statement from the Reaching Out Bank. We all have access. It isn't shrouded in secrecy, you know.'

Ana: 'Have you any idea, Magnus, where the anonymous donor would like any unused money to be transferred?'

Magnus: 'To the Reaching Out interfaith project, perhaps the one involving Islam, Christianity and other religions in joint enterprises. Much has already been accomplished in the Middle East Peace Zone, especially with children – including girls – at school. Ahmed in Aleppo has been telling us about rebuilding communities around churches and mosques, especially the churches there and in Raqqa. They were torched and then deliberately used as military command centres during past sectarian conflict. Our sources say that weapons may still be hidden there, so Reaching Out must investigate whether the arms amnesty needs reinforcing in these areas.'

Ana: 'Ahmed, please set this in motion through the GWP Peace Protection Service and reconvene shortly to report back to us. The anonymous donor must be asked. Can you do that, Magnus? Next is Tom. You have tabled your query.'

So I see myself shrinking back to a tiny place among other images.

Tom: 'The Goodwill World Parliament has already voiced its concern over the control and marketing of natural resources. We've participated in the first world referendum on the hiring of a satellite based on the promise of infinite energy by a global conglomerate. Philanthroentrepreneurs like Dom Ross Mackenzie seem able to do what they want. His scientists say they now have the correct calculations for the energy beam to transmit constant solar energy and have set out fully what these are online for all the world to see. So now he can lease a satellite and install his energy beam or whatever, on it. Only the –'

Ana: 'Come to the point, Tom.'

Tom: 'Stop monitoring me. What I'm saying isn't a simple soundbite. Well, if you do want one, here it is: will powerful global corporations control every aspect of our lives even, for who knows, charging us to breathe clean air? Already a consortium of astro-entrepreneurs is preparing to mine asteroids. Can they be weaponised? If so, who is responsible for what such people do? Have we, the world's population, any legal protection? For instance, how can we be sure that Ross Mackenzie's Global Enterprises' energy beam is safe?'

The icons, nearly two hundred of them, are vibrating with rapid responses too fast for the automatic translation program to function. Ana is waving her arms in a vain attempt to restore order while Tom looks on, quietly amused, as the representatives' icons respond around him.

Ana: 'Thank you Tom. I see from the responses that this requires a new agenda. Please submit your responses to Tom and they will be circulated a week from now for discussion at the next conference in two weeks' time. I now declare this conference closed. Minutes will be circulated.'

The screen is clouding over. I check the password for the Reaching Out banking statement. There is the money, no more or less than was paid in anonymously. So the Chinese have returned the exact amount Reaching Out invested in Nicholas's Mybeki lab.

I'd always assumed that Esther, Celia and Sister Julian somehow supported Reaching Out. At grass roots level RO is divided into cells, almost like terrorist ones, to prevent infiltration. I don't believe they are in any of these cells though they have some idea of what's being discussed and carried out, never mentioning anything directly related. When Sister Julian and I are alone, which isn't often, the conversation usually turns to some project she's developing that needs an 'infusion of money', as she would say.

Sister Julian senses how to find one's weakest spot all right. The fire in the old university was, she said, arson. The aim was to destroy the historic buildings so that restoration would be too expensive, or structurally impossible. She knows I have drawn all the buildings so at least people in the future could see what they looked like before demolition to ensure 'a better environment for all'. However much goodwill those enthusiasts for the future may have, they should leave some visual continuity for people like me who grew up here. They should build elsewhere, like the technological zone in the Middle East Alliance where Raphael's Energy Research Centre spreads over stony, uncultivated land. Those destroy-the-past, welcome-the-future sorts of people can rarely be stopped. They have their new Greystone University, and they still covet the site of the historic one.

So Sister Julian knows what I want. She's canny. About what Gaia means to me. About my obsessive drawings of the historic buildings. About my dancing. About – do you know what she said the last time I saw her?

'Secrecy,' she was talking about Nicholas's lab and his experiments there, 'breeds suspicion, not always of the right kind. That's why, regretfully, the GWP Peace Protection Service has to inspect, and even break into places tipped to be producing weapons from chemicals or whatever.' She paused to look at me. We were both thinking of Nicholas's labs at Greystone University and in Mybeki.

'The Middle East Alliance, Magnus, is the hinge of the future; Jerusalem, its capital is the heart that beats out the rhythm of three great religions. It lies between East and West. That's precisely why there have been so many conflicts in the Mediterranean where the ancient trade routes travel east along North Africa and Asia to Mesopotamia, the land between the Tigris and Euphrates rivers, and north-west along the Danube to central Europe.'

I wish I could obliterate the screens and leave for a mountain or desert to scan infinite zones of uselessness. Then return, and do what I could still do for Eliza at the Mid-Winter – Christmas – dance into oblivion possessed by a daemon. As I did...

I'll dance the rainbow rhythm on the floor: 3 beats, then 3 more to square the number into 9. Dance it again and clap twice: 9 x 2 = 18. 8 + 1 = 9. Swirl rainbows of colour and add them, back to 9. Faster, 3 x 3 = 9 and clap 3 times, makes 27; add and we're back to 9 again. Weave words into colour and rhythm and beats of the body – pulse, claps, twirls. 3 x 3 = 9 beats, times 7, makes 63, and they add up back to deep blue 9! Rhythms, beats, stamps and calls entwine in my dance and song, reliving Gaia.

– 3 –

Martha *i-witnessMAR727futurepast.com*

On Jerusalem airjuggernaut – 10 January

Screeches in my head. Out of breath without running. Heavings inside me – is this what panic means? Helen's screams are incised in my memory and on this infernal wordfree. Even though it is at its lowest volume, it's still recording all my thoughts and I can't turn it off or stop my pulse recharging it. Mercifully this thought-blog is encrypted and no one will ever read it. At least, not for ages.

We all supposed Helen was just putting on weight. She didn't want to leave Ross Mackenzie's estate on Quarry Hill. Then out of the blue came a voice message calling for me. Urgently. I didn't want to help her after what she did to Nicholas, but I couldn't ignore her plea. I found her in the throes of a difficult birth. I've never fainted in an airjuggernaut but am going to, as I did then. It all happened in the birth capsule I had clasped on to our zone's new Centre for Genetic Wellbeing. Ross Mackenzie was pacing outside. He paid for the birth capsule, but I, or the company where I was a director, manufactured it, fitting it out with cutting-edge medical equipment and robots.

Cutting. In every sense. The baby was whisked away for tests to see if he was free of the pancreatic cancer-sensitive genes that Ross Mackenzie inherited. It's all part of an important experiment, so Helen says. It's something about genes and cancer prevention. She agreed to artificial insemination because Ross Mackenzie has invested in her Powerdress label and saved her business. She hasn't seen her son since his birth. No wonder she's bemused and distressed. As I am, with Nicholas found in Mybeki, now in Jerusalem, and with Helen distraught, not knowing what to do with herself. 'It's for the good of all hukind,' Ross Mackenzie insists.

Celia and Joe are sitting side by side across the aisle from me, both dozing with seats tilted back to the sleeping position. I've seen Eliza. She isn't surprised when we just turn up and keeps a reserve store of food for us. The hoverpods are so frequent in daytime that I didn't have to wait. Motorcyclists still race alongside but, as you don't see their faces under the helmets, you can't tell whether they are the same as before. A new generation, perhaps, letting off steam. Anyway, I didn't have much time to think, not that yesterday's thoughts are worth recording. They are there on blogfile, mental mumblings, all inconsequential.

Eliza was at the piano, so I walked in and listened. She didn't jump, but just turned to smile.

'Do you remember this?' I didn't.

'I used to play it when you and Nicholas went to bed. When I tucked him in he asked me for it, and I put on one of the CDs we had in those days. It's Zaïde's song. The most beautiful ever written. Mozart's music. Listen: "Rest gently, my sweet life, sleep until your happiness awakes," ' and she stopped, her voice tremulous. I recall one of Sister Julian's refugees singing it at the old university concert and Ezra accompanying her with one hand. 'I don't know German,' she continued, 'but this translation gives an idea of what she is singing, and that's enough for me. The music really says it all. Nicholas asked me to give him this song on a pellet for his birthday, so I did. That's why I associate it with him.' That's why she was playing it, to summon him back, at least in her memory. Is it a coincidence, then, that she's thinking of Nicholas precisely when I walk in to make sure she knows he is safe?

'Thank you, Martha, thank you for coming here to let me know he has been found. That he is in Jerusalem with Raphael. I often go down to the North Moorland Terminus hoping to find news of you both and Karen. I try to be patient, Martha.'

'Come with us, then, to be with him in Jerusalem.' She looked frightened.

'No, Martha, I'll wait for him here. Thank you, but – no, sorry.'

Out there living in nowhere, Eliza has learnt the resignation she never had in her working life. It was all problem-solving then, hammering away at obstacles until she demolished them. She made me tea, toasted bread on the old toasting fork asking if I preferred jam or a boiled egg, and busied around in the kitchen living room just as if I was a child again.

'I hope,' she said, 'he's out of Dom Ross's grasp.'

I wasn't sure.

While on the hoverpod returning to town, Raphael messaged me to say that Nicholas needs to see Celia, Joe, me, Eliza and Karen. Magnus too. That's why I'm on this airjuggernaut bound for Jerusalem. Just after that I thoughtmessaged mother – no idea where she is. She's still an anchor on *worldaroundyounews,* without much to do, she says. Material is gathered for her and she can present the news wherever she happens to be as long as it is against a neutral background and she can read the cues enlarged on her wordfree. Roland buzzed my wordfree and we talked happily for five minutes or so. It should have been longer, but I'd arrived at the terminus in the Main Square and my wordfree was vibrating with more messages. Celia will fetch Joe from the Academy. Mustafa, a voice from my election campaign, urged me to travel on the same airjuggernaut to Jerusalem as Celia and Joe. He has ended up as the publicity manager of Raphael's new Centre. Is Magnus still in Mybeki yearning over Gaia's cairn? The jigsaw is almost complete but, airborne, I sit wondering if it's about to crack apart again.

A message from Mustafa, this time asking me to confirm that I'm with Celia and Joe and giving me the co-ordinates for Raphael's centre. I confirm I am and note the info.

Still more messages are buzzing in. Ezra and Lizzy have left Argentina. Ezra has been invited to play Ravel's Wittgenstein piano concerto in Jerusalem. He still doesn't know why his wrist was severed. Neither the zone nor the GWP investigations have found any leads. Nothing. The world is moving on and his wrist tragedy seems marooned in the near past. A message from Lizzy. She must complete her sculpture in the Sinai desert for its inauguration. It has been entered for some international competition 'Utility and the Arts'.

I'm used to dealing with an avalanche of messages, delegating them to Jan my PR to answer, but most are now marked 'confidential'. Before leaving for the airport there was just enough time to call in at St. Thomas's. The side door is always open; the knight and his wife still there. I passed them, moving down the aisle to voices in the last chapel.

'Think of what we all have in common,' a voice, Sister Julian's, was saying. 'Love thy neighbour as thyself,' she's quoting again from the New Testament, 'think of that here, in this little ecumenical chapel - a place of peace.' I can hear her words now, as if she's beside me whispering, 'think, wonder, pray, act.'

I've swung my seat to the sleeping position copying Celia and Joe across the aisle, but thoughts still flood in and linger. Childhood memories. Then what mum had said about Zaïde's song, and Mozart, and the masterpieces in the Art Canyon.

Art, great art, reaches out across time and space. Her words.

I can't bear it! I'm trying to sleep like the others but Helen's distress, in spite of my anger about what she did to Nicholas, troubles me; the difficult birth while the dark shadow of Mackenzie was hovering outside. I held her hand to calm her, but it wasn't enough.

Sister Julian's forgiveness. Always. In that chapel with the lit candle and a barbed wire curled round it. She's appealing again for money, this time to create a hospice, using my firm's capsules, in the burnt part of the old university. I'll see what I can do on my return from Jerusalem.

I almost forgot! Roland reminds me that the new generation of wordfrees are to be launched next month; they will monitor our emotions and feelings and link them to our personal record on the Goodwill World Parliament Health and Hygiene Register. Already the most hacked website, it analyses and disseminates physical and mental health data. We all use these records and even rely on them without thinking about where our health issues or the contents of our minds will end up. Or the consequences. But I'm involved on too many fronts to tackle all that now.

Another task. I must find out what's become of the young man and woman from Esther's people who have arrived, sponsored by Ross Mackenzie, to study at Greystone University. How could they have the entrance qualifications? The thought-correction icon is flashing at me – I usually ignore it. It informs me that they are not at the University as such, but at a specialised language institute in the vicinity. It's one of a world network set up to prepare for the switch to Babel. It is also, curiously, preserving with the latest technology as many languages and dialects as can be found in the world before they are lost forever. They can do this through the massive capacity of cloud computing. All we think and create flies up into the 'cloud cuckoo land' as I imagine it. Amazing, all those flights of thought in myriad tongues stored in infinite cloud warehouses, readily available for any use forever, subject to the compacting and encoding requirements. Who is responsible for it all, I wonder? Does anyone know?

BREAKING NEWS

BIRTH OF PANCREATIC CANCER-IMMUNE BABY – A WORLD FIRST

The **Greystone estuary** is not only reckoned to be the most fertile area in the world, but it is also the birthplace of the first pancreatic cancer-immune person. This baby has been genetically modified to prevent him inheriting a predisposition for this type of cancer from his father. This earth-shaking event took place ten days ago in a world-beating clinic-capsule recently manufactured in the nearby engineering enterprise area and clipped on to the new **Centre for Genetic Wellbeing**, a public private partnership.

The mother, **Helen Runciman**, former Hallelujah girl and anchor on this channel, was chosen for her outstanding looks, her physique and resilience. These all came into play during a protracted delivery which did not, however, require a caesarean section.

Both the mother and the male baby are doing well. No images are available and the spokesperson for the Centre has requested the crowd of reporters and photographers to disperse.

The astonished world is waiting to discover the outcome of this unprecedented event. Meanwhile, the website for the Centre for Genetic Wellbeing is overwhelmed with messages, not all congratulatory, some even offensive. The same spokesperson has requested everyone not to mob the online site and to wait for the next communiqué.

I, **Karen Middlethorpe,** will be reporting next from **Jerusalem, the capital of the Middle East Alliance**, where important events are about to take place.

worldaroundyounews.com

– 4 –

Nicholas *i-witnessNIC227futurepast.com*

Jerusalem 12 January

I'm trying to remember exactly what happened after I found Raphael in Jerusalem. He and I were concentrating on the infinenergy computer database from Africa that Helen had left for him in my lab back home. I was called to the entrance lobby. A dream come true! Celia, Joe and Martha were there. I could hardly believe it! Celia hugged me and Joe was incoherent with joy. Martha observed us smiling, before giving me a huge hug. Nobody told me that Dom Ross had sent Joe to the Academy where I met Ezra and Lizzy. Joe said he loved the maths and science but was struggling with the language side. Above all, he missed me. For his safety, he said, he was not allowed to leave the school or grounds or to see anyone outside, except Dom Ross, of course, who is paying for him. I don't like that.

He looks well, taller and handsome, though I shouldn't be thinking that. A dream? He was tugging my arm impatiently. Wait, Joe. Leave me a moment with Celia. She stepped back smiling and Joe thrust his closed hand towards me, opened it and there – how? Why? When? – There was the datadrive I brought back from Africa with the final, accurate calculations. The one I had hanging round my neck. The one I had lost!

The other scientists, the older ones, turned to look at us as they criss-crossed the lobby. 'Raphael!' I cried out, 'Raphael, Raphael! Here it is!'

'Go to him?' Joe asked.

'We'll find him,' Celia took my hand. 'Show me the way.' And I led them to Raphael in his lab, now ours. He looked up, surprised when I held out the datadrive.

'Here it is, Raphael. It's what you wanted. The answer to everything we've been doing. The final, accurate calculations.'

'The grain of gold in the desert,' he said looking at it, mesmerised.

'Joe, we searched everywhere for it. Where did you find it?' Martha asked.

'Under bed,' he said, frowning to try and explain. 'A light. Little shine,' and he held out the gold chain that Helen had given me. 'Between bits of wood.'

We looked at one another, puzzled.

'I know!' Martha said. It must have slipped between the planks of the old floor to the foundation below them without pulling all the chain behind it.'

I sank on to a lab stool, sighing in relief. Silence. Everyone looking at me.

'Try it.'

We had started from the rather obvious question – how to obtain enough constant energy from the sun. We went through layer after layer of painstaking research and experiments. We voyaged through the complexities of scientific discourse and experimentation; through trials and disappointments to sparks of expectation and discovery. It was like building a pyramid to pierce the clouds in the hope that the apex might be the solution to it all.

Now silence draws us together, scarcely broken by my voice commands. The screens respond. On and on, structure after structure, further, almost there to the peak of the pyramid. A child and four adults staring entranced at the illuminated lab screens surrounding us studded with numbers and symbols swinging, turning, surging, and retreating. We're just like the group in the digital copy of the orrery experiment painted long ago by Wright of Derby that watched over my youth.

A wave of darkness sweeps over me like the steel blue rivulets when I tumbled into the waterfall. Out of reach, the summit of my intellect, the purpose of my research. Out there, beyond my grasp, are the passwords. I must remember them to open the key calculations locked inside the datadrive, found at last. Or is everything lost again? I'm trying to recall the crucial passwords. I've forgotten them. I'm panicking. No other way to access the datadrive. Joe is pulling my arm.

There, framed in the doorway of Raphael's lab is the predator. Standing. Surveying us.

'Amazing lab!' Dom Ross Mackenzie smiles and looks around, holding out his hand, 'You must be Raphael? I'm here to help. May I come in?' He looks quickly at the screens. 'Just amazing!'

No one speaks.

The screens falter. Go blank. Mustafa may have done this deliberately. I just want Ross out. Of here. Of my invention. Of my life. Just out - as mum used to say,

'Dom Ross, we are busy. We can't be disturbed.'

'But Nicholas –'

'Dr. Middlethorpe.'

'Dr. Middlethorpe, I didn't see you here.' Lying again.

Raphael refuses his hand and I do the same. How could Dom Ross, the thief who patented my discovery, know I am here? His solar beam equations are inaccurate and dangerous and that's why he can't leave me alone. He has chased and cajoled me, and has somehow tracked me down here, just when the calculations are displayed over the lab screen for all to see. But not the final ones on the datadrive that Joe found. Those two passwords for the last equation - I still can't remember them.

'Who gave you permission to enter this building?' Raphael confronts him. No one else moves.

'The director who controls your labs, Raphael, and all the other enterprises in this high level research centre. He's a personal friend. I have made a considerable investment –'

'Out!' Raphael shouts. 'Out. This is my lab. Out you go!' Slight, athletic Raphael is advancing towards Ross Mackenzie, arm raised to push the predator into the passage.

'Not so fast, young man.' Dom Ross, almost smiling, grasps his shoulder. 'I have been granted permission to enter your lab and to have a full explanation of your research as well as to witness precisely what you're doing now. You only have to continue what you have already started with Nicholas. I won't disturb you. I can record all you say and your screen calculations without bothering you. Just carry on.'

'No we will not.' I'd like to throttle him!

'But Nicholas, I've invested vast sums in your brilliant project. It's about to be realised on a scale which you haven't the means, contacts or capacity to do yourself. The satellite is in orbit; the eternal beam of limitless energy is ready. All we need to know is the final angle. The receptors are ready and waiting.'

I'm at the door, holding it open. Between gritted teeth, I say,

'Please leave.' This is the first time I've ever stared straight into his snake-like eyes. They flicker, then turn away.' Dom Ross, we are very busy. Please leave now.'

'But the director, my friend, who –' With an unexpected thrust, I push Ross out, slam the door, lock it and lean on it to breathe out in relief.

'Quick. The password, Nicholas, before he tries to contact my boss.'

'Raphael, I still can't remember it.' I'd hoped the argument would jolt my memory. No, nothing... I despair.

Unexpectedly Joe begins dancing. Rhythm of 3s, like Magnus, only with hand and finger movements linking them. 9 sequences of 3, 27, add 7 finger movements to 2 with nods, and back to 9 the square of 3. 3x3 foot beats to 9, repeated 5 times with different eye, face, knee and elbow movements, to 45, 9 again. 5 fingers grasp 4, with the little one bent back, and so back to 9. Joe, this mysterious child found by the railway track at Mybeki, dances looking at me, his eyes staring entranced. Did he watch Magnus dance at my mother's cottage for the Mid Winter – Christmas - and memorise his movements? Or did Magnus teach him? No. Just before the final experiment, there in Africa with Joe helping me. I remember now. Just to amuse him, I explained Magnus's dance of numbers and colours...

The pyramid is etched in my mind against thunderclouds. A pain in my head like jagged lightning shatters the peak. Ah! Here's the clue! I bend close to the screens with Raphael behind catching his breath. I am thinking in Magnus's number sequence. It ... it might be working? It is!

I can sense something strange. Is there always someone spying? A presence troubling our concentration. Can Ross Mackenzie's scientists hack into our lab here? All my thoughts, ideas, emotions, aims in life are intertwined in this discovery - unlimited energy for all without damaging any eco or other system! Free from any taint. It's mine, the tip of that pyramid, set firm on centuries of invention.

Banging on the lab door. 'We're almost there!' cries a voice outside, 'all but those final calculations.' We? 'The energy beam will soon be released from my satellite. You, Nicholas, will be acknowledged...' The door rattles. 'I'd prefer not to alert the director. It would be bad for you, Raphael. I'm willing to forget you assaulted me, but I have his permission to enter.' More thumps.

Raphael is looking at me, frightened. Joe is clutching Celia.

'I have it!' Joe has given me the sequence. I key it in. Yes. It works. My calculations dance out of the lost database. Now the last bit. The crucial one.

'The last password, Nicholas. Be calm. Sit on that stool. Just think.'

More rattling.

We must stop Ross Mackenzie and his scientists seeing the calculations on screen here and following the equations, numbers and symbols, and applying them. NOW! Stop them directing the inaccurate energy beam from the satellite on to receptors. Worldwide. He's trying to creep all over my invention, to control it, the power and the profit.

'That password was to access the final calculations. Now you need the second one for the accurate beam angle,' Raphael whispers. He is waiting for me to fill in the flashing section onscreen. I'm pausing. In the panic I'd forgotten there was another password. Silence.

From outside Ross Mackenzie intones a voice message on everyone's wordfree:

'You can let me have those precise calculations now, Nicholas Middlethorpe. The GWP has allowed the lease on my satellite. I have posted the full theory of infinenergy online for all to see. Following from the result of the world referendum, I can now authorise the constant energy beam to be directed on to receptors worldwide from the calculations on the datadrive you duly returned to me, refined by my scientists. The satellite is in orbit. You will be fully acknowledged when you demonstrate the final beam angle. I can speed matters up by getting my scientists to double-check them for you.'

Did Ross Mackenzie see Joe's dance? He can't have followed the calculations. Everyone waits. Martha, Celia and Joe are standing behind me. Like Raphael, they are focusing on me. Silence.

'I can't... I can't remember the final password for the angle of the beam.'

I'm trying. Thinking so hard. Concentrating on the datadrive in my palm. Pausing... my mind collapses into a flurry of equations, symbols, numbers, chunks of light and dark. Then, nothing. A total blank.

* * * * *

We did just have time to eat before the concert. Not much. A quick stop at a snackhub on the way there. *Worldaroundyounewsflashes* were all over the street screens shrieking about Ross Mackenzie's satellite in orbit with the solution to the world's energy problems. I could feel him as if he were still by me, spreading a sombre atmosphere, saying nothing. Just hovering, uninvited. We entered the concert hall.

He was there. After going up to the dress circle to check our seats, I returned to the balcony and leaned over to watch people coming into the lobby. Ross Mackenzie stood apart, looking around him. Then he moved quickly, stopping just behind Ezra who was welcoming friends. I leapt down the stairs two at a time, to stop Ross accosting my friend. Too late. He touched Ezra's shoulder from behind, and I overheard,

'Nicholas, you must be reasonable –' Ezra turned round sharply, 'because we have – Oh! I thought you were Nicholas.'

'I'm not.'

'My apologies, Dr. Tenenbaum. Of course, I have come to hear you.'

'Mmm,' and Ezra thrust his stump under Ross Mackenzie's chin. 'What d'you know about this?' Ross stepped back, pulling his chin in and clutching his dinner jacket.

'I really don't understand. What a tragic accident!'

'Yes. Someone is using money as power? Someone aware of the dubious private medical clinics that perform illegal operations? Someone –' Ezra lets his damaged arm fall, '- who wants to destroy a career.'

'You have the wrong person, Dr. Tenenbaum – Ezra?' Immaculately calm, the philanthroentrepreneur continues, 'I have nothing but admiration for you and your inestimable talent – genius rather – and I am also a founder member of the GWP Musicians' Benevolent Fund which...' Bells were ringing for the concert.

'Ezra! Quick!' Lizzy appears, swings her arm over his shoulder and propels him away.

I glance back as I climb the stairs to the dress circle. Ross stands stranded in the almost empty foyer. The concert is already sold out.

Ezra plays superbly. Ironically, the loss of his hand has transformed a fine pianist into a famous musician overnight. At school, he found out that when I needed peace, a snatch of beauty, a still moment, I used to listen to a song on an ancient CD that I loved. Ezra is playing it now for me at the concert, tucked unannounced between other works. A tall soprano with tousled hair and effortless voice is singing while he accompanies her with one hand. Why doesn't he let the orchestra do it, true to Mozart's score? Ah, he wants the song to sing its way back into my memory. To remind me of a special moment, just us, back at school.

The last password? Zaïde!

*****

Our wordfrees have been buzzing with congratulations, and now a worldmessage from Dom Ross Mackenzie states that, since the global energy shortage will soon be solved through the infinenergy beam on his satellite payload, he and his associates will now be concentrating on developing and marketing asteroid mining with robot scientists.

Raphael can't calm me down. Ross Mackenzie has inaccurate calculations. The beam could miss the receptors causing irreparable damage and loss of life.

What is happening?

What can I do?

Call a world alert?

Where to begin?

Ross M is voice messaging me. People are crowding around me. Where am I? Raphael's lab? Or a bigger space, a lobby? The screens are flooded with images and figures, not symbols and equations... What's happening?

WORLD EMERGENCY BULLETIN

The philanthroentrepreneur and scientist, Dom Ross Mackenzie, is about to use his satellite payload to project the infinenergy beam on to receptors without being in possession of the accurate angle. These nano equations have only recently been calculated and tested by the inventor of **infinenergy**, Dr. Nicholas Middlethorpe.
The presidents of the USA and China have jointly decided to request the Goodwill World Parliament Global Energy Safety Committee to intervene with the utmost urgency. They are both leaving important duties to inform world citizens through *worldaroundyounews* about this dangerous development. If it goes ahead with inaccurate calculations it could cause loss of life. Dr. Middlethorpe and Dom Ross Mackenzie have also been summoned to appear at this crucial meeting in one hour's time. All world citizens are requested to witness it.

I'm summoned to appear on the news. I don't want to go. Raphael puts his arm around my shoulders and says it will be easy. Others are crowding into the entrance foyer of the laboratory building where we are. Mother, now as the *worldaroundyounews* presenter, is there organising everyone. Ross Mackenzie too. I'll keep well away. His face is redder than I've ever seen it, his hands clutch his jacket. Nobody wants to talk to him.

The newscasting equipment is ready and she is positioning him on one side of the adjudicator from the Goodwill World Parliament and me on the other, well spaced out. At the appointed time the two presidents are videoed in and seemingly placed on either side of the group. I'm next to the U.S. President Anya Lo Yin who is smiling at me while the Chinese one, Lina Chang Yun, is motionless beside Ross Mackenzie who looks sulky.

It's awkward to smile back at an image. At least we're not asked to shake a handful of air.

WORLDAROUNDYOUNEWS CRISIS DELIBERATION ON THE IMPENDING LAUNCH OF THE INFINENERGY SATELLITE

Citizens of the World, wherever you are, please follow very carefully what these leading world figures have to tell you about a possibly harmful way of producing infinenergy to solve the world's energy needs.

The inventor of the infinenergy beam, Dr Nicholas Middlethorpe on my right, has highlighted the inaccuracy of the beam's angle and the potential damage that could ensue to lives and property if used. However, the philanthroentrepreneur, Dom Ross Mackenzie on my left, asserts that his team of scientists has thoroughly tested the satellite and beam. Dom Ross has personally supervised the setting up of receptors in areas most affected by energy shortages, having allegedly invested heavily in accuracy and related safety measures. Populations worldwide are desperately awaiting this source of infinite, unpolluting, low cost energy. In some areas it will save lives.

Adjudicator - President Anya Lo Yin, is it legal for Dom Ross Mackenzie to go ahead with his plan to create infinite energy from a satellite?

Anya Lo Yin - 'No, not if the beam's angle is incorrect and there's a risk of collateral damage to life.'

Adjudicator - Dom Ross Mackenzie, please respond.

Dom Ross Mackenzie - 'My scientists assure me that the beam is as accurate as can be calculated with the data they have. However, if Dr. Middlethorpe makes available the results of his final tests, then the slight risk of collateral damage would be removed.'

Adjudicator - Dr. Middlethorpe, why will you not divulge the results of your final experiments?

Dr Middlethorpe - 'Because I am not in partnership with Dom Ross Mackenzie and his associates who have illegally patented my discovery of infinenergy.'

The presidents are looking at each other in amazement.

Anya Lo Yin - 'A stolen patent? This is intolerable.'

Lina Chang Yun - 'The whole enterprise must be stopped. Calculations are incorrect, the patent stolen, so the whole enterprise is illegal.'

Anya Lo Yin looks at Lina Chang Yun who nods.

Silence.

Ross Mackenzie - 'My scientists assure me that the beam is accurate and that the receptors are in remote areas where collateral damage is unlikely. The world should know that 2% of any profit made in this enterprise will be put into a charitable foundation and used to perfect future developments in this crucial field.'
Lina Chang Yun - 'Charitable foundations are not the way to avoid responsibility for possibly dangerous situations caused by this infinenergy beam, however excellent it may be in generating low-cost energy and however efficient the receptors and the distribution. More testing is required.'
Ross Mackenzie - 'The testing has already been done. I, Dom Ross Mackenzie, have the patent and it has been approved.'

My heart's in my throat. I'm trembling. Where can I look? At the unblinking eyes of the imaging machines?

Adjudicator – 'Dr. Middlethorpe. You created infinenergy. Should this unique, inexpensive and unpolluting method of generating energy go ahead, even if there are possible dangers, including loss of life?
Dr. Middlethorpe - 'No. Because Dom Ross Mackenzie is using the incorrect angle of the beam. He took it from a faulty database, one he lent me to check the mathematical calculations which I didn't want to return to him, but somehow he got hold of it. What his scientists extracted from it was incomplete, inaccurate and dangerous.'
Ross Mackenzie - 'Why don't you let me have those final, accurate calculations? I'll make you a partner, Dr. Middlethorpe. Make you rich. My scientists can carry out all the tedious, practical realisation of infinenergy so you could just get on with...well...your inventions.'
I won't speak to him ever again.
Anya Lo Yin - 'I, President Anya Lo Yin, will refer you, Ross Mackenzie, to the GWP Court of World Justice for having illegally registered a patent and stolen Dr. Middlethorpe's intellectual property.'
Lina Chang Yun - 'I, President Lina Chang Yun, require the Goodwill World Parliament to rescind Dom Ross Mackenzie's right to use a satellite for the infinenergy beam until it can be legally and safely employed with the correct calculation for the angle of the beam as directed by Dr. Middlethorpe.'
Anya Lo Yin – 'I, President Anya Lo Yin, propose forthwith that the Goodwill World Parliament remove Ross Mackenzie's title of 'Dom' at its coming assembly.'

Lina Chang Yun - 'I, President Lina Chang Yun, second that.'

Dom Ross - Ross Mackenzie is looking round like a hunted beast. I can't believe what I'm hearing.

Anya Lo Yin - 'I, President Anya Lo Yin, propose that the infinenergy patent is re-registered in Dr. Middlethorpe's name and that the GWP World Energy Initiative grant Dr. Middlethorpe the funds to continue his infinenergy experiments at the Greystone University Institute and to develop its practical application with an organisation approved by the GWP. Any future contribution of Ross Mackenzie and his scientists regarding the creation and supply of energy must be under the auspices of Dr Middlethorpe and his team.'

Ross Mackenzie - 'This is unlawful! You are obstructing me, an eminent philanthroentrepreneur, from developing my legal business interests –'

Adjudicator - 'You are about to be impeached for acting in a way that could endanger human life on an epic scale.'

Ross Mackenzie - 'How dare you? How dare you? I'll say no more.'

worldaroundyounews.com

Ross Mackenzie glares at the unseen world judging him, and strides off. The bulletin concludes with the adjudicator thanking the presidents and me, all smiling, and then handing over to the newscaster – Mother. She and I are left watching Ross Mackenzie's helousine through the foyer windows as it flies him off to the airport. Shamed, but untamed?

* * * * *

Lizzy has just messaged us in Jerusalem to say she has a helousine ready for us to see her waterfall aqueduct from above. L-shaped stone channels convey seawater over rocks down to a reservoir excavated below sea level. The water flows over desalination filters developed by a team of scientists from the Middle East Alliance. It gathers speed and volume to race first into a shell-shaped reservoir. Just below, it flows into an oasis with a shallow play pool and then fills the points of a star-of-David swimming lagoon. Further away, palm groves shade watering troughs for cattle.

It has won the Utility and the Arts award for 'the most environmentally sensitive and practically innovative as well as visually life-enhancing landscape sculpture'. It is already becoming a popular tourist area for water sports, children's aquatic games and helousine flights to decipher from the air the shape and multi-meanings of this prize-winning work of art. It is a playground of beauty and joy that also helps to assuage the world's thirst.

'You can see the colours and shapes from above, but not the textures,' Lizzy explained. 'There are symbols locked inside those shapes, which the different cultures here understand and explore in their oral histories. They are being recorded.' I looked down as the helousine hovered and let her creation speak to me, without thinking. That's how the next phase of my life will come, from unlocking the subconscious to explore everything accumulated there. Studying and learning, experimenting and discovering.

Another chapter of my life is opening. It concerns water purification and supply, starting with the River Jordan and then the Tigris and Euphrates. I shall tackle the world water shortage next.

BREAKING NEWS

THE CONTROVERSIAL SATELLITE TO BE RECHARGED: INFINENERGY PROJECT RESTARTED

The **Energy Research Centre in Jerusalem**, the capital of the **Middle East Alliance**, is collaborating with the renowned scientist and inventor, **Nicholas Middlethorpe.**

The **Goodwill World Parliament's satellite, originally leased to Ross Mackenzie,** is now leased to the **Energy Research Centre in Jerusalem**. This transfer was uncontested. Deputies are waiting to hear how **infinenergy** translates into minimal cost energy for all hukind.

Ross Mackenzie has released the following statement:

'The only reliable, durable and perpetual guarantor of independence in the world today is profit. Nothing comes free. Profit promotes experiment and discovery, such as the inestimable resources from asteroid mining which I am about to explore in a consortium with other astro entrepreneurs. Our robot scientists will investigate and extract specimens. Profit delivers services of inestimable value, such as genetic solutions to suffering and the replacement of severed, damaged or diseased limbs and organs, as well as the prevention of diseases such as cancer.'

Where else will such breath-taking ambition lead this entrepreneur who is, however, under investigation for the theft of intellectual property. The case is pending and he is forbidden to carry on any business or industrial activity until it is resolved.

Ross Mackenzie has been questioned about the paternity issue regarding **Helen Runciman's cancer immune child**. He refused to answer directly whether he would assume moral responsibility, repeating that his organisation would take full financial responsibility for the mother and her offspring.

Centres worldwide for nuclear fusion are pooling resources and collaborating to speed up the research for clean energy avoiding the accumulation of radioactive waste. They are about to announce a crucial breakthrough, backed by a consortium of international entrepreneurs. They are noting the new and diverse ways of creating power, like the **infinenergy satellite,** and the innovative creation of the first **Utility and the Arts award.** The winning work of art is a visually exciting sport-and-entertainment creation. The water not only desalinates for industrial and domestic use, but also powers turbines that provide all the surrounding zone's energy needs. This is an environmentally-sensitive artistic creation which speaks to the globe's fast-approaching power and water crisis.

The artist known as Lizzybizzy has been commissioned to create another work of beauty and meaning by the **Dead Sea**, rendering the water useable for irrigation and washing, and eventually for drinking.

'It's a challenge,' she said, 'that I'll meet head on to create a work of living art with seawater, sand and sun as my main creative elements.'

Here is a landscape artist to watch.

Bulletin from **Karen Middlethorpe**, Jerusalem.

worldaroundyounews.com

Eliza's Journal

Through a glass, darkly

I find myself down at the station hub quite often now, though I prefer to let my visitors describe what is happening in the city below. The human voice and touch. Presences that linger as I remember them.

I need time and space to absorb all that they tell me, not the ever churning cauldron of the worldwide web. I want to live out my life with people and the print they leave behind in this room. Ezra's touch on my piano. Lizzy's pattern of stones edging the path to the gate. Magnus dancing, as he did yesterday with Joe. He has allowed me to set his Gaia poems to music. Sometimes I sing them as he dances. He is working on a new sequence called 'The Peace Conflict', recreating the sound of the heart beating as the *basso continuo.*

Sister Julian, on a visit to her living shrine, asked him to sing and dance for the crowd gathered there. I dusted my recorder and took it down to accompany him. I have started baking bread and pastries for everyone who gathers there when she comes. The outwebbers and pilgrims mingle round the Moorland station hub message board and the shrine. Hordes of young people have joined my motorcycle friends there. Sister Julian still rides pillion with one of them, her red cloak like a sail. She is collecting funds for the hospice that her new cohort of prisoners-on-parole is constructing, inserting Martha's capsules into former lecture rooms in the old university. She is never without a project and is already planning the next.

The past visits you in confusing ways. When his tours bring him to the city, Ezra always comes to see me, sometimes to stay over. Of course I love to see him. I remember him at Nicholas's school, already a sparkling pianist, but with fun in his eyes and joy in his hands. Now, with his severed wrist, he carries with him that unresolved tragedy. Nicholas tells me that Dom Ross Mackenzie echoes online the web-wide chorus of disgust and regret whenever the subject crops up. I refuse to give Ross Mackenzie space in my thoughts, but when Ezra comes, I can't help thinking of him.

Not very long ago, Martha asked me to go and see Helen just after her child was born. She was in her specially designed home capsule near the Centre for Genetic Wellbeing. The shadow of the person she used to be, she was hemmed in by every up-to-the-second technological invention and frequently checked by clinic staff. She flung herself into my arms.

'How are you Helen?' No crib, no evidence of her child.

'Still sore. Lots of stitches.'

'That is often the case.' I tried to sound reassuring.

'This wasn't normal,' she worried. 'It was all over the news bulletins.' Not having seen them, I paused.

'Was it difficult? The birth, I mean.'

'I was given a total anaesthetic. Unusual, I think, but they don't tell me anything, except that I'm a pioneer. At the frontiers of science, a heroine.'

She looked around warily.

'They don't let me see my child. I want to care for him. They express my milk and deal with the feeding themselves.' Another long pause. 'I can't say what I want to happen. They repeat that the child isn't mine; I just gave birth to it. It's an experiment. That's written all over the contract.'

I wanted to do something but felt helpless.

*****

The buildings for routine maternity and freetime use on the plateau below the Three Sister Peaks are being extended. There is talk among outwebbers of compulsory purchase. We restored abandoned shepherd's huts and crofters' cottages on non-agricultural land thinking we would be safe. Never assume anything. Subsequently new zone laws were passed to prioritise our land for 'outreach development'. I have asked Martha what that means and how she can help to protect the rights of our outwebber community. She says she will try, but to be honest, I do not think her heart is in it. She is all for the 'common weal' – a term recently recycled from the past – even if it wounds a number of lives.

Since then I have not spoken to her about it. She seems not to notice how worried I am, though she drops in for tea and cake while on some errand for what I call a 'secret society', but she refers to as 'The Company of World Art Trustees'. They are responsible for the Art Cavern and, probably, for the Book Cavern as well. Recently she has been coming with the Museum Director, now the advisor on cultural matters to the Goodwill World

Parliament. I even began to suspect they were lovers, but I don't think that's his inclination.

I am in touch with Karen to try and work out, through Martha's mediation, what should be done about 12 Beech Drive. I think Martha wants to move in permanently, with or without Roland, and let Karen live in her smaller capsule. Karen is still undecided.

*****

Joe and Magnus are working on a world dance together. They usually come with Nicholas and Celia so we can all spend a weekend together. Joe is a slender, olive-skinned young man now. His eyelashes were – still are – long and curled up at the tip. No wonder this foundling was cherished by Chief Walanka and the Zueto people. He had to run away because they would never have allowed him to leave. Joe is doing brilliantly at Nicholas's old school – or academy - and there is talk of him being given a global studentship for three top universities, two years at each. It is the hot idea for gifted children, I am told. This handsome young man is adding eye and hand movements to the foot ones for the dance he is creating with Magnus. He has probably hooked into the world wide web to find Indian dances. Being unhooked, I wonder at his movements that seem inborn and lead me to other thought paths.

Joe still shadows Nicholas who is now his legal guardian. Celia is very protective of them, of Nicholas in particular, from any slurs about him and Joe. She is sweet and gentle but can be intrusive. She looks at you firmly with her green grey eyes. No great beauty like Helen, she is attractive in a fragile sort of way. So, nicely, quietly, she gradually draws me out. She needs to know who Nicholas' father was, and will not take 'a donor' as an answer. She is also a donor baby, like Nicholas. Her mother wanted a child before she was too old.

'We have the right to know, don't we? It's one half of our genetic inheritance.'

Well, sometimes. But I would prefer all that to be left buried in the past, so why must she dig it up? Karen and I were careful to choose the same donor – one who had opted to remain anonymous - so that our children would be half-siblings and untroubled by paternity issues. We brought them up lovingly as brother and sister. Why all this bother?

Celia says it's because she and Nicholas asked the Goodwill World Population Ministry to suspend her wordfree contraceptive so they could have a child. She is pregnant. Nicholas is happy but withdrawn most of the time outside his lab, just like when he was working out his infinenergy solution.

'My mind's working overtime,' he says, looking on in a contented way with a smile on his face. He has been spending periods in the Sinai desert with Lizzy and her water sculpture. He is also looking at the water situation in the upper reaches of the Jordan River to prevent the Sea of Galilee drying up, and finding ways to protect agriculture in the region. Martha says that the Goodwill World Parliament is sending a delegation to try out his new way to monitor water use and reuse. The thriving regeneration of Aleppo and the northern area of Syria too may be threatened by water shortages. His lab team is also probing the potential of 'space harvesting' as they call it.

Asteroids, it seems, may provide water and minerals 'with potential', as they say. Strange and wondrous.

I am outside these young people's linked-up mode of living and just echo what they say. They sort of pity me, I can feel it. I miss out on what is happening in the world; I am thin on fact and fat on imagination, a relic left over from history. However, I sometimes remind them that they enjoy spending weekends with me. They do not come only out of duty, I hope, but because they need the calm here and a respite from infinite world chatter in unconnected peace. Strange as it may seem, they even admit there is a sort of beauty in an off-screen world of seasons and changing views of the mountain peaks, the city below and the estuary.

When they are not here and I am not in the garden or on a long walk away from the encroaching Maternity and Freetime buildings, I often follow the causeway to the Art Cavern as that has the best mountain views. I imagine the paintings and sculpture I treasured as a young woman in galleries and museums. When I ask, Martha says she will try to take me back to the Cavern, but she never does. I have even drawn up a list of the works of artists I yearn to see again, like visiting old friends from my youth. I tinker around with it to amuse myself while waiting and hoping.

* * * * *

Who will read all this? No one. Martha wants to, but I say, 'Not yet' meaning 'never'. Karen as well. She arrived yesterday to fret over her future. I don't ask and she doesn't mention Lina Chang Yun, now in her second term as President of China. I suspect they are not as close as they were when I left Beech Drive to settle here.

My enabler's pension is enough for me. Guaranteed to my sort worldwide, it is more than the leisuretimers are allocated, most of whom have contributed little to the GWP pension plan through their volunteering. Karen is trying not to show it, but she is furious at being, she thinks, downgraded to maintainer level rather than belonging to the top category of producer, like Nicholas and Martha. Poor Celia will be down at my pension level when she retires. Karen sees her past as unofficial researcher and adviser to the Chinese president, with particular reference to China's covert influence in Africa, as meriting the highest producer pension. The trouble is that it was all unofficial. Her role as anchor in the *worldaroundyounews.com* is only a second level maintainer's task, a conveyer of information, selected and honed by others.

Who am I to judge? Martha, re-elected both zone member and deputy to the Goodwill World Parliament, could be her mother's powerful advocate, but it does not seem to be working out that way. Karen is writing a book on the Leda legend and its authentic origins in Chinese mythology. Or so she says. Leda's sons, Castor and Pollux – their European names – epitomise the Confucian principles of persuasion and patience, even if events do not at first serve China's aims and objectives. Leda and the swan, or deity in disguise, have a second set of twins, though they are not as prominent as in the western tradition. No war, like the Trojan one, is mentioned. Karen explains that this is because the female twins, Clytemnestra and Helen, prefigure the western way of extending influence and showing one's might through challenge and conflict, her shorthand for outright wars. Not very Confucian. I hope I have understood her thesis, at least in its current form.

She is entangled in all this Leda business. I was taught that Helen, because of her beauty, was the innocent cause of the Trojan Wars, a pawn in the power struggle, a victim. Karen argues the contrary. All those visits to China have changed her. She is actively promoting 'peaceful conflict', whatever that means. She surprised me yesterday by saying she would like me back with her in Beech Drive. It never felt like home as Acacia Avenue did. Strange. I thought she had moved on, as I have, to living independently.

Long ago I picked up hints that Magnus is involved in a network of cells working to improve the lot of people worldwide who fall outside the four designated GWP categories. I am not supposed to know anything, but I suspect that Sister Julian has something to do with this enterprise. Whenever I see her with Magnus there seems to be something conspiratorial about what they say, something outside the reach of the Goodwill World Parliament. Roland refuses to admit the network exists because it would upset his plans, though Martha must wonder, like me, how far their organisation reaches and what exactly it does.

If she is not part of it as well?

Once Magnus did vaguely approach me, but a quick glance around my cottage and he slid away from the subject. No internet connection.

I suppose they are trying, in this organisation or whatever it is, to escape what Nicholas called the 'pyramid structure'. Last time I saw him he was describing how fragile he felt with his infinenergy theory at the apex of, so he hopes, a lasting way to ensure sufficient, unpolluting energy. He is crucially perched at the top of an increasing army of producers and maintainers who supervise the energy beam satellite. I do not fathom all this though I can sense its complexity. 'One wrong foothold from an assistant, technician or whoever in the complex process,' he explained, 'could wreck everything.' He paused before adding, 'And then there's the finance.' Precisely. The backers talk about 'enabling great discoveries' and so on, but their funding comes with conditions. Ross Mackenzie has been found guilty on numerous counts and is forbidden to carry on any form of business in his lifetime. However, people like him are quietly ubiquitous: the undesirable guests at the banquet of discovery.

'Self-interest isn't necessarily negative,' Sister Julian commented when I was trying to unload my anxieties about Ezra and the mystery of his amputated hand. I need to know who did it and why. Others seem to accept this injustice will remain unresolved. Why did it happen? Sister Julian calms me down though she does not always provide solutions. I suspect she does not even want to think of a possible case of mistaken identity and whose wrist was meant to be severed.

'As long as self-interest respects that others as well have their own agenda, it isn't necessarily wrong.' She smiled mischievously. 'I have my agenda and am open about what I would like from the latest group of prisoners-on-parole and also about the next step at the hospital.' She tightened her eyes in concentration, her face more wrinkled every time I see her, adding, 'and I don't worry away at insoluble problems like you, Eliza. I accept I won't find out who was behind the arson. I suspect it was someone in the local zone government who wanted to sell off the old university. But the exchange with the Leda and the Swan painting was fair, if not entirely in the zone's favour. That is if you want to wade into the deep waters of the monetary value of works of art. I shall only talk about their spiritual value. But you know all that anyway.'

It was unusual for her to talk for so long. 'I am as upset as you are about Ezra's hand.' She shook her head sadly saying that all we could do was to give him support if he needed it. And pray.

Celia cares more than I do about what is going on around her and also out there in the world, probably because she is literally tuned into the news. We outwebbers are used to getting snippets without much context from our visitors. Recently we have returned to former times and started our own fortnightly outwebber *Gazette*. It was launched two months ago by Ben, a retired journalist on a maintainer's pension like Karen. He managed to salvage an old printing press when they were chucked out. We have all contributed to pay for the construction of a printing shack powered by a possibly illegal link to the station hub and a supply of ink and paper. Ben has organised other volunteers to select local, regional or world news from the station online hub. He hopes eventually to find other volunteers to become 'specialists' to report on the various power blocks like China and the Middle East Alliance. I hear about the latter from Nicholas through his collaboration with Raphael and Lizzy. Esther visits from time to time and updates us on the amazing development of schools, industry and agriculture in Africa where once rebels kidnapped schoolchildren and tortured victims, and on the Chinese presence in Mybeki.

Anyone reading this journal might think that my mind and memory are storehouses for others' opinions and biases. Maybe. But I look forward to the return of that pleasure some of us used to have of sitting down by a window or, in summertime, in the garden with a mug of tea or coffee, perhaps even a biscuit or two, and the reassuring feel of a newspaper or book in our hands. A time to imagine.

Well, what did I read this morning in our *Gazette*? I usually scan our local city news speedily to see if there is anything about Nicholas's lab or Martha's activities, or Roland's, but this morning I stopped sharp at the headline: 'Outwebbers threatened by imminent development of the cluster of Maternity and Freetime Community Clinics under the Three Peak Mountains. It seems that they are too isolated, and rather than extend the North Moorland Divergence Route, they are about to develop an area around the station hub primarily for the maternity clinics. The present buildings, set some distance away because we outwebbers had come first and claimed the right to our zone around the station hub, will be reserved for skiing and as a mountain resort.

The proposed newbuild will involve compulsory demolition of our homes, especially those within sight of the station, like mine. Writing this down calms me a little. I panicked when I read about it this morning and have fretted with a headache all day. Ben has found out we have no legal right to this wasteland. We are considered to be squatters in once abandoned huts. Consigning thoughts to paper strangely seems to help me.

I must contact Martha again about this. It seems that the zone government has started it all, and that means Martha, Roland and company. How could they?

* * * * *

The issue of expulsion from our cottages for the redevelopment has been sidelined for the present. Martha and Roland were sympathetic but unspecific when I asked them to address an informal meeting of outwebbers. Ben our editor fillets *worldaroundyounews* because of time and space. Strange, though, that there is nothing in our Gazette on what has happened to Helen's cancer-immune baby, born in our city's Centre for Genetic Wellbeing. Either it is all secret or our local correspondent does not want to know. I asked Ben who said he had not seen anything about it. He added that he leaves his collaborators free to select what interests them from the unremitting buzz of our station hub info-online. He mustn't dictate, only facilitate – they are all volunteers after all.

I want to know: I do not want to know. If it is not in our paper, then I want it to be there. I need to know what is happening to Helen's child. She is never mentioned on the news we see at the station hub, or elsewhere online, it seems. My only way of finding out is through Sister Julian. She was praying with a crowd down by the shrine last week and included the child in her prayers. She told me she saw Helen recently at St. Thomas's.

'How is she?' I enquired anxiously.

'Bright and wanting to find out something from one of my former refugees who runs our children's home.'

'Bright?' I thought of how I saw her last, down and dowdy after childbirth. 'What was she wearing? How did she look?'

Sister Julian screwed up her eyes. 'I never notice people's clothes. Her soul was singing. She is on to something about helping ill people, especially children. I think that's why she came to see us.'

Will he be a normal child if he is genetically modified or isolated for scientific experiments? Like Martha, aged about four, running across a field towards us uttering a sequence of 'ums' like links in a chain, to hold us entranced, all waiting for what she wanted to say? By the time she had reached us, still umming, she had forgotten it! There she stood, smiling, sunshine dancing over her curls, in complete command of us adults.

Esther seems to be liaising with the research centre down in the city from the one in Mybeki bought by the Chinese. When she starts to tell me what is happening to the Zueto cancer research student volunteers at our Centre for Genetic Wellbeing, I back away and do not want to hear any more. Instead I consider what I would like to see in the Art Cavern when Martha arranges my visit.

I asked her, on one of her brief visits here to inspect to the Art Cavern, about Ezra and where his attack took place. She was brusque and said I would have to go into the city with her if I really wanted to know. She would show me online 'back home'. So I had to return to Beech Drive.

I had almost forgotten what it was like to be surrounded by differently animated wraparound screens. When Karen and I were removed to that house through Martha's planning, I thought, or hoped, there would be space on the walls for my pictures. Martha then suggested displaying them on easels in the main living areas. Now she considers some should go on display in the museum.

'I'll talk to the Director,' she said, pulling her hair back from her face and twisting it into a bun. 'He'll certainly have a look at your oeuvre –'I like her unmerited choice of that word, '- and we'll see what he can do.'

It is years since I trembled, thrilled at the prospect of exhibiting a painting or two. We shall see what actually happens.

'Now look at the screens.' She fixed on an icon shaped like an old gramophone loudspeaker.

'It's a thought monitor,' she turned carefully to tell me face to face, 'to take my thought orders.' Back facing the icon, she must have thought, 'Mybeki wise old man'. There was an almost imperceptible shudder around the screen walls. 'All screens,' she added, smiling over her shoulder at my perplexed expression on hearing some strange burbling, 'use Babel language. Everyone has to learn it now. It's quite easy. There are lots of quickstart Babel programs online'.

The screens were changing, tipping us into a new landscape.

'Martha, where are we?'

'Africa. Moving on the Geomap into Mybeki.'

'What do you mean?'

'Look at the main square. I want to see who's there. I don't yet recognise anyone.'

'There's quite a crowd. What's this all about?'

'Be patient. I want to see who is there today.'

Martha left me sitting utterly bemused in my old chair from Acacia Avenue. People are milling around seemingly in our sitting room now part of the Mybeki square, as if expecting something to happen. I could hardly hear what was being said in the crowdbabble. Something about an important announcement. A sudden silence. There on the steps of what looked like a public building, a gaunt figure dressed in one of those popular inter-gender tops and trousers the colour of sand, was speaking, holding open a large book.

'Listen to a message from the Goodwill World Parliament. In order to pursue an inquiry into the maiming of the renowned pianist, Ezra Tenenbaum, all who have met or seen him are required to register with the GWP Universal Legal System so that the preliminary inquiry may start.' Now sitting, this figure continued. 'As some of you may know, as well as relaying important information from the outside world, I am the custodian of the Book of Hukind.' He picked up a pen up from the steps saying, 'here begins a new chapter and you are writing it'.

*****

Back home, I went down to the press shack for my copy of our outwebbers' *Gazette* and offered Ben my services as occasional art and music journalist for the *Gazette*, just so we can imagine what is going on elsewhere. And to keep in touch with Ezra and Lizzy. I was annoyed that he was not more enthusiastic.

'I thought you would offer to do it, Eliza,' an almost casual response, probably because I shall have to learn how to surf the online waves of information at the station hub and voyage around all that is happening in art and music worldwide. A daunting prospect.

*****

Writing for the *Gazette* is consuming my days. I've had to stop baking and there's little time for me to gather my thoughts in this journal. It is just what an outwebber was supposed to reject. All this scuttling around online creates anxiety. I'm expected to write a major report about how and why

Ezra was maimed. At the time of the accident everyone was asking but all he could remember was that, returning to his rooms from a rehearsal, someone ran up behind him and hit his head. He woke up in hospital surrounded by police and without a hand. This is the first time a wrist wordfree has been stolen. There was an online rumour that he must have been some sort of spy for there to be such a radical need to access his wordfree. Sometime later he came to the conclusion it was a case of mistaken identity.

All right, a case of mistaken identity, but who actually did it? Is it possible that Ezra was mistaken for Nicholas? They are the same age and height. If Nicholas did have a wrist inset, it would contain valuable information for scientists. Surely whoever carried out this horrible attack would have known he had a wristfree monitor – easier to steal. Or perhaps it was assumed, by perpetrator and accomplices – that he would have a wrist wordfree like everyone else. Ezra may have saved my son's left hand. Without his wrist, Nicholas could still have carried on his scientific career, but Ezra, in spite of his world renown as a pianist, can only play Ravel's famous piece of music transposed for his right hand and a few works that other musicians have composed for him.. Whoever did it missed out by stealing the genius of a musician, not a scientist. A futile tragedy.

One of my recent articles was on Ezra and his latest series. He often appears with the former refugee who sang Zaïde's aria at the concert in the old university. Lizzy accompanies him everywhere. I've asked Ben how to contact them.

'That's not our job at the *Gazette*,' he said. 'We relay information. As you know, outwebbers have disabled their wrist wordfrees. Except here at the station hub, there's no internet connection. The people in the GWP Universal Legal System will track them down.'

So I'm waiting to write a report on the Inquiry into the attack on Ezra. It is endlessly delayed by unnamed clients instructing their lawyers to challenge the GWP Universal Legal System's authority to proceed with the Inquiry.

Ben reported in the last issue of the Gazette that the outwebbers' appeal against the forced eviction from our cottages is making slow progress, the outcome still distant.

*****

Karen is spending more time in the city. 'There's always space for you.' On whose terms? Has she swopped 12 Beech Drive for Martha's minute capsule? *Worldaroundyounews*, bought by the Chinese Government, has a number of competing world news rivals, encouraged recently by the Goodwill World Parliament in the name of choice. She has now been replaced by a young male newscaster, in spite of her appeals to the Chinese president, Lina Chang Yun. She's trying for one of the other news outlets and tells me that Helen too is attempting a comeback.

*****

You either proact or react. I want to regress – that's why I became an outwebber – but now I'm proactive and neglecting my journal. Too many hours spent at the hub and in the press shack and not enough at home. A vertical line in my forehead is deepening from all the frowned concentration. The screen down at the station hub has been replaced by a larger one; even so, the space is crowded with too many of us looking at it. This is the transcript of the most recent news bulletin that Ben advised me to watch for my contribution to the *Gazette* about Ezra.

BREAKING NEWS

METAL DETECTOR FINDS GREAT PIANIST'S WORDFREE FROM SEVERED WRIST

The renowned pianist, **Ezra Tenenbaum**, has been reunited with his wordfree, formerly embedded in his severed wrist. It was found by a leisuretimer using a metal detector in a refuse zone on the periphery of **Rio de Janeiro**. The pianist shrugged off the discovery, saying that the contents were unimportant and out-of-date. However, the **Inquiry instigated by the GWP Universal Legal System** has asked for it to be deposited at its headquarters in **The Hague**.

Worldwide protest over the disgraced former entrepreneur **Ross Mackenzie's statement** approving cancer-retarding plants and related diet is increasing because of suspected links with his now illegal Quarry Hill research establishment. Follow this newssite for exclusive reports about further developments.

The **Goodwill World Parliament** has just published for online discussion the proposed law to limit the number of children any sperm donor can have. Some have provided semen resulting in over 1000 births. Half-sibling unions are becoming statistically more likely. **Inbreeding,** as once found among isolated communities in pre-motorised times, could become a global problem.

May I introduce myself? I am **Helen Runciman**, the special correspondent for the *newtimesnews.com,* mother of the **first cancer-immune member of hukind** and chair of the **Cancer Research Unit** at the **Centre for Genetic Wellbeing in the Greystone River zone.**

newtimesnews.com

Notes for my journal.

An interminable meeting at the station hub about the new maternity buildings in our outwebber area. No clear idea where we can live. Disturbing.

Ben asks for another article on the Art Cavern. Told him I need to interview Martha about it. When will she come? Yearning for old telephone system. Keeping this journal in note form, to write up later.

Two meetings about the maternity buildings. Told to think about future generations and so on, and on. When times are hard, attitudes shift and the unconventional are cleared away to the perimeter of pressing concerns. It was ever thus. Still no sign of Martha.

Celia has started to write occasional notes that I pick up at the station hub. Nice that she bothers. She is well. Her mother is coming for the birth. Protocol. I would like to be there. Probably Karen as well. A surfeit of mothers and absence of fathers.

Why has Ben asked me to pen an article about the new law to limit the number of each male sperm donor's children and remove the current anonymity option for sperm or egg donors? It is now being fast-tracked by the Goodwill World Parliament. Tried to refuse, but he turned away before I finished protesting. Should I link it with our struggles over the maternity buildings and our homes? Issues crash into one another.

I managed, with help from another outwebber, semi-journalist like me, to send a message to Martha. Had hardly finished before she replied. No time as usual to ponder over my journal.

She came with Roland, in a hurry as usual. I asked her how she would vote on the proposed sperm donor limitation law. Roland said he supported it, though I did not ask him. Martha mumbled something about Roland having a father and mother, therefore their child would have at least one grandfather. I didn't even know she was expecting. 'That's why we asked Karen – and you - to swap Beech Drive for my capsule.' What about Nicholas and Celia? I thought but remained silent. They seem to be happy enough with the extra rooms they have rented in the old Institute building. Joe has his own room, Nicholas is close to his lab and Celia can walk or take the monorail, now that she is pregnant, to St. Thomas's and the Old University Hospital.

I wonder where I can live after my cottage is demolished. They now say it will be rebuilt, but where? And when? Where do I go in between? Beech Drive would have been the obvious answer, but Martha and Roland, and the baby will fill it. Martha's old capsule is for single occupation and Karen lives there.

I expect some arrangement will be made. Still, I would like to know.

I haven't been writing anything because I'm too upset to think. I have resigned from the Gazette. It is no consolation that Ben is furious at me for 'letting him down'.

In theory there is now time to write up all my notes and continue my journal. I do not see any point in doing it.

Days, weeks even may have passed in uncertainty. I happen to be sitting outside, now that it is warmer. I am looking down over the city and the estuary with the sadness of it soon being for the last time, and there striding up the path towards me comes Nicholas. I have never seen him stepping out like that. But Joe is almost outpacing him. He is growing up so fast.

'The child is born!' they call out, almost in unison. 'A girl.'

'Lucy.' Joe adds, 'Light.'

My heart begins to sing beyond any expression of joy. For them. For me. For us.

'Pack. Come and see her and stay a while with us.'

This is the moment when the old man opens the Book of Hukind and, in thick ink with a scratchy pen, starts a new chapter about our lives to come.

I shall continue this part of my journal when I return.

EPILOGUE

Impact report: site clearance, North Moorland Divergence route terminus.

The last of the insalubrious huts and cottages of the few remaining inhabitants, or 'outwebbers' as they call themselves, have been cleared to make way for the expansion of the Maternity and Freetime Centre on non-agricultural land.

There is a pile of stones with slab seats circling it and a cross on top by the North Moorland Divergence Route terminus. It is never without flowers or garlands. Sometimes an old woman in a red cloak over a black undergarment with a round, puckered face and darting eyes stands there. There are always visitors around her. She is like an ancient saint who should be removed to the Freetime Centre for her own health and safety. She harangues her followers about art works being God's vision mediated through hukind, and that the results are the gifts he gives for all to treasure and enjoy. She repeats that they should not be locked away in the nearby Art Cavern for no one ever to see them.

She refuses to move away from a cottage on the hillside near the Art Cavern to the south-west of the Middle Sister Falls after I authorised its demolition.

I am messaging head office for advice on this dilemma.

Archaeologists are sifting through the site and have come up with a journal found in a metal chest in the above-mentioned cottage. This is a rare and valuable discovery for historians overwhelmed by the volume of internet material of scarce interest. Nobody writes in long hand anymore, let alone keeps a handwritten journal. Some of them describe the thrill of holding an original source at the place where it came into existence. The journal is a tangible link with the writer, Eliza Middlethorpe, and is now placed for safety in the Historical Documents section of the Book Cavern. It is currently being scanned and will shortly be on the Book Cavern website for all to read.

Amy Bright – zone planning advisor

Notes for a possible research paper or publication

The Eliza Middlethorpe journal has led to much detective work on my part. No problems about the author who seems to have been somewhat of a recluse. It is what she refers to, often obliquely, mainly about her son, a scientist and inventor, and his circle that intrigues me. She was an outsider, looking in on his group of reformers and inventors connected in some way with the Goodwill World Parliament and the local zone government as well as organisations such as Reaching Out and the Leda and the Swan Foundation. It is a once-in-a-lifetime discovery. I could hardly believe my luck, and there was more to come.

Inputting the names she mentioned, I found reports from Helen Runciman and Karen Middlethorpe, both newscasters on the now discontinued *worldaroundyounews.com*, and an open access blog from Helen Runciman. They give a fascinating but incomplete picture of events concerning Eliza Middlethorpe's son, Nicholas the inventor, and her daughter, Martha the politician, as well as, less frequently, an acquaintance referred to as Magnus. I found the three of them on *i-witnessfuturepast.com* but all three blogs were encrypted. I tried for months to find the passwords to access them, but in the end gave up. There was no point in continuing.

This all changed unexpectedly one dark winter evening when I went to Eliza's cottage. It had been left as part of a shrine to some holy woman. Arranged along one side, I found ancient CDs, an antique CD player, sheet music that I can't read and old-fashioned paintings of people and places that nobody does nowadays. These were all displayed as part of the shrine. I asked the caretaker if I could listen to some of the old CDs on the player as part of my research on Eliza Middlethorpe. No problem.

On that rare occasion when one has nothing to do but doesn't feel like surfing on one's wordfree, I picked a CD haphazardly from the pile I had taken and tried it out on Eliza's old machine. It was a song and someone, a woman, was singing it. I had never heard it before. It was undeniably moving. Beautiful even. I can't find the right words. Anyway, I looked to see what it was called, and there it was: Zaïde.

Serendipity. Zaïde was the obscure password for Nicholas's blog. From his accounts I soon worked out that his sister Martha's was an obvious one, her partner's name, Roland, and the same for Magnus, his mysterious love, Gaia.

The rest is in what you have been reading.

Hilary Stoneborough - researcher for the Goodwill World Parliament Hukind History module.

About the author

VR Thornhill lives in Yorkshire where she founded and teaches in an adult education organisation. It offers lectures, day schools and visits at home and abroad on art, architecture and garden history. Valerie enjoys travel, designing gardens and lecturing worldwide. Above all, she loves writing. Her publications include a collection of short stories, *The Children of Kumbhalgarh* and a novel, *In Restoration,* that won the 2012 People's Book Prize for fiction. Valerie is currently working on a partly biographical work of historical fiction based on family associations with India and the industrial revolution.

Also by VR Thornhill

1955 The Summer When…

In Restoration

The Children of Kumbhalgarh and other stories

The Tycoon's Tale

Cynthia Loves Her Fiat 500

Acknowledgements

John and Stephen Wilton-Ely, Susan Cockcroft and Erica Wilkinson for their unfailing patience and help, and for the advice generously given by James Wilton-Ely, Annalisa Izzo, and Robert Cockcroft.

My thanks to Ben Gardiner for help with the layout and publishing.

Printed in Poland
by Amazon Fulfillment
Poland Sp. z o.o., Wrocław

63422998R00275